M000012996

TITLE: Twins of Orion: The Book of Keys

SERIES: Book 1

AUTHOR: J. Rose

PUBLICATION DATE: October 18, 2017

HARDBACK ISBN: 978-0-9966025-0-1

PRICE: $17.99 U.S.

PAPERBACK ISBN: 978-0-9966025-1-8

PAPERBACK PRICE: $9.99 U.S.

EBOOK ISBN: 978-0-9966025-7-0

PAGES: 402

AGES: 8 and up

Please send any review or mention of this book to:
Pleadine Books Publicity Department
3330 S. Broadway #55, Englewood, CO 80113

publicity@jrosebooks.com

TWINS of ORION

THE BOOK OF KEYS

J. ROSE

To Stephanie,
Thank you for Everything.
May all your wishes come true.

J. Rose

PLEADINE
BOOKS

Publisher's Cataloging-in-Publication Data
provided by Five Rainbows Cataloging Services

Names: Rose, J., 1981-
Title: Twins of Orion : the book of keys / J. Rose.
Other titles: Book of keys.
Description: Englewood, CO : Pleadine Books, 2017. | Series: Twins of
    Orion, bk. 1. | Summary: Twins must learn how to harness their powers
    in order to be reunited again and stop the worst evil from escaping. |
    Grades 4-8.
Identifiers: LCCN 2017909775 | ISBN 978-0-9966025-0-1 (hardcover) |
    ISBN 978-0-9966025-1-8 (pbk.) | ISBN 978-0-9966025-7-0 (ebook)
Subjects: CYAC: Twins--Fiction. | Separation (Psychology)--Fiction. |
    Courage--Fiction. | Magic--Fiction. | Child abuse--Fiction. | Fantasy. |
    BISAC: JUVENILE FICTION / Fantasy & Magic. | JUVENILE
    FICTION / Family / Siblings. | JUVENILE FICTION / Social Themes /
    Physical & Emotional Abuse.
Classification: LCC PZ7.1.R6694 Tw 2017 (print) | LCC PZ7.1.R6694
    (ebook) | DDC [Fic]--dc23.

Printed in the U.S.A.

First Edition, October, 2017

TABLE OF CONTENTS

For Lynn,
Who supported the twins' story from the beginning

CHAPTER

— I —

PETER'S STRANGE VISITOR

When Peter looked out his attic window he didn't expect to see a magical bird on his lawn, but there it was. The light emanating from its feathers brightened the dark corners of his attic room.

Peter's mind spun with memory—and a warmth filled him. In his dream, the phoenix-like bird had led him to his twin sister Rory. He hadn't seen her in seven years, and an ache of longing filled his chest.

But this couldn't be real. In his recurring dream, the bird had shown him a magical house. And magic wasn't real.

The blue and gold bird stopped preening its long tail-feathers and looked up at him.

Peter stepped back from the window, stumbling over his desk chair with a loud clatter. He froze, afraid his adoptive father, Judge Talbert, had heard the noise.

No sounds came from below.

Peter quietly put the chair upright and turned off the old box computer. He was shaking far too much to finish his paper this morning.

He looked around his bedroom to center himself in reality. The dirt under his fingernails was real. His favorite book, *Adventures of Arthur the Great*, was real.

Birds appearing from dreams were not.

The elegant bird stared up at him. It cocked its peacock-like head, much like a dog asking its master to follow him.

Should he dare?

No. He couldn't do it. Talbert would catch him, and he'd be beaten like last time he tried to run away.

But the bird wouldn't give up. Suddenly it appeared in his room, perching on the pile of boxes in the corner. Peter scrambled back, knocking over his alarm clock.

How had it gotten in here? His circular window didn't open, and his door was still closed. He shooed the creature.

Judge Talbert would surely come up from breakfast and whip him for the commotion. Nothing was supposed to disturb their perfect neighborhood. Strange glowing birds and music *definitely* did not fit. He silently begged the unearthly bird to go away.

Instead, the bird glowed even brighter, and a sweet melody played in Peter's head. It was as if the song vibrated within him, urging Peter to follow.

He was *definitely* seeing things again. Had he interpreted it right? Did the bird really want him to follow it?

Don't be ridiculous. You're not going after an imaginary bird.

"Stop," Peter whispered.

The bird looked up at him with an expression of sad disappointment. Then, in a poof of golden air, it disappeared.

Peter spun around. Where had it gone?

He plopped on his cot, feeling empty without the bird's warm presence.

Talbert's voice boomed from downstairs, "Peter!"

Peter shook his head free of his crazy thoughts of flying away on a magical bird, and sighed at his dingy existence. It had been a few years since the judge had relegated him to the attic. It was punishment for standing up to Talbert when he'd beaten the new kid for breaking an artifact. Apparently Peter was a bad influence on the other adopted boys.

Over time he'd come to enjoy being alone. Who would want to share a room with five other boys? Peter was more than happy to have Talbert keep thinking it was a punishment.

"Get down here this instant!" Talbert roared.

Peter's mind raced through all the things Judge Talbert could be mad about. Had he made a mistake in his assigned tunnel? Every day the older boys were given a tunnel to dig, and the younger boys were assigned a tunnel or pile to sift through. Even though he was thirteen, Talbert had relegated Peter to the younger group because of his knack for finding things.

Peter took a deep breath behind the door at the bottom of the stairs, squishing the thick carpet between his toes. He gave himself a silent pep talk. *Just face him, take any punishment, then go back to your room. Get it over with.*

Even as Peter told himself that, his hand shook as he pushed open the door to the second-floor landing. He'd just healed from the last whipping. He wasn't ready for another one.

Judge Talbert stood in the foyer with his arms crossed, wearing his usual expensive brown suit. It matched his toupee, which looked like an overgrown caterpillar. Who did Talbert think he was fooling?

The judge didn't hesitate. "How could you do this?"

Peter forced himself down the carpeted stairs in silence. He knew better than to answer the judge's questions.

"Don't you know how important it is?" Talbert stared at him underneath his high-arched eyebrows, as if he could burn a hole right through him.

Peter still felt lost. He had finished his tunnel duties yesterday, catalogued his finds, and taken out the trash. What else was there?

"Why have you not been completing your homework, boy?"

That was what Talbert was mad about? Peter knew exactly what the answer was. But if he spoke his mind, the repercussions would be worse than not finishing his homework.

Peter looked at his five adopted brothers sitting frozen in the living room, all dressed up and ready for church. He stared coldly at the judge and said nothing.

Talbert waved his cell phone in the air. "This email says we have to come to a parent-teacher conference about you not turning in your homework. Explain yourself."

All the fibers in his body wanted to say something, but he knew he shouldn't.

"Don't you know how bad this makes me look? You not doing your studies?"

Peter gulped, seeing the short leather whip stuffed in Judge Talbert's belt. He couldn't stop himself, and blurted out, "How bad it makes *you* look? What about me? I'm the one who ends up looking stupid when I don't have my homework done."

Talbert grinned, obviously pleased with himself. "Then why don't you get it done if it's that important to you?"

"I'd get it done if I had time." Before the judge could say anything, Peter added, "And I'd have more time if I didn't have to spend it searching for Orion's stupid lost artifact for you!"

Peter's eyes widened. He'd actually said it. A brief feeling of satisfaction washed over him.

Judge Talbert slapped Peter on the jaw. Hard.

Peter crumpled to the floor, face red and throbbing. His breath caught in his chest.

Judge Talbert looked like he was going to boil over. "How dare you disrespect my father's work. The forgotten Gods left behind items of great power—and I intend to find them."

Peter got to his feet, and fought back the automatic swelling of tears. Hate burrowed through his eyes. He wished he had more power to stand up against his so-called parent.

Talbert let loose on Peter. "Who do you think you are, speaking to me like that? I give you a home when no one else wants you, and this is how you repay me? All I ask is that you give a little in return for my generosity, and you can't even do that."

Peter hated that the judge thought working them to the bone, and creating false criminal records that forced them under his care, was generosity. Did Talbert even know the meaning of the word? But Peter remained frozen to the ground. He was getting off easy with only a slap.

Judge Talbert leaned over him, spraying spit all over Peter's face. "You are nothing, and you will never become anything worthwhile to anyone." The judge stood up, straightened his suit, and declared to the room, "As punishment, you will lose your privilege to go to church today. And you will start clearing the cobwebs and searching the secret tunnel Jeremy found yesterday. I'm sure this one will lead to Orion's separate temple."

Peter avoided Jeremy's eyes. Peter knew the boy would be fuming right now—what if Peter found Orion's treasure of power instead of Jeremy? And Peter got Talbert's reward instead?

A sly smirk crossed the judge's face. A grand idea had obviously crossed his mind. "Actually, come to think of it, your talents are better suited for dirty work than God's work. From now on, you will stay home on Sundays and do all your homework. And when finished, you will head straight to the tunnels and complete two shifts."

Peter didn't move. Two shifts on a Sunday? How was that going to help him get his homework done? And now he wouldn't be able to go out on his one non-school outing of the week. Since Talbert was on the school board for Peter's all-boys school, he barely had a break from his adoptive father.

His brothers in the living room seemed shocked too, but they said nothing. Peter couldn't fault them for that—he would have done the same if he were in their position.

Judge Talbert's wife, Melina, came down the stairs in a flowery Sunday dress. She'd been standing on the landing the whole time. She spun at the bottom, her skirt flaring out around her, before she slid over to the judge and planted a kiss on his cheek.

"Good idea, Richard," she said in her sweet, high voice. "Personally, I think you should have done it long ago. There will never be a God for this boy. Even our magnanimous God couldn't help poor little Peter."

Peter held back rolling his eyes. He hated her perfume. Did she purposefully put enough on to make people gag? It made any interaction with her that much worse.

She squished Peter's chin with her hand. "You are lucky to have us, and don't you ever forget that." And with that remark, she spun back around to face her husband. "Shall we go?"

"One more thing." Talbert tapped the whip at his side. "My office. Now."

Peter closed his eyes, attempting to quell the rising nausea. It happened so frequently, he should be used to it by now. But he could never get used to that little leather whip.

He resigned himself to obeying Talbert when the front doorbell rang. Peter halted. Who could it be? Talbert *never* had unplanned visitors. Even solicitors had learned to avoid this house. The judge had a habit of making sales people cry.

Talbert grabbed Peter's arm, and dragged him into the office, pushing him onto the leather couch. Talbert leaned over him. "Say a word, and I will destroy you. Remember, no one will believe a little runt like you—especially with all you have on your record."

The moment Talbert left, Peter rose from the hated couch. He picked up the gold-plated gavel from the desk to throw it at the painting of Talbert seated in his throne-like chair. Realizing his fury had almost gotten the best of him, he gingerly set the gavel back on the desk.

"Can I help you?" Melina said in her cutesy voice.

Peter slipped the brown curtain aside and peeked through the glass-paneled door. Talbert's back was to him. He was likely giving the stink-eye to the tall man in the doorway.

There was something intriguing about the stranger. He was dressed in a slick pin-stripe suit, complete with buttoned-vest, his long black hair tucked neatly behind his ears. He was pale, as if he never went outside—how Peter knew he looked, too.

"Good morning, kind lady. My name is Kyros, and I'm here to speak to Richard Talbert about a boy, Peter Kyros."

Peter's eyes widened. Someone was looking for *him*! *Peter Kyros—was that his real last name?*

Talbert approached the door, taking Melina's position. "I'm Judge Richard Talbert," he said, emphasizing his title of power. "What has he done wrong now? You won't get a penny from me."

"May I come in and speak to you?" Kyros asked in a deep and gentle voice.

"No. State your business here," Talbert said. "You're making us late for church."

Kyros cleared his throat. "Yes, well, I've recently learned you have my boy. And I've come to take him home."

Peter's body tensed around him. Had he heard right?

Talbert gave a deep belly laugh. "That's a good one, sir. Peter must have set you up to this. His parents are dead."

The man's long face hardened. "I do not find it funny, sir, that I have been kept from my son for thirteen years. And now you stand before me claiming I am dead? Where is the boy? I would like to see him."

All joviality left the judge. "This is not funny. He has been mine for seven years. The day you abandoned him is the day you lost your rights."

"I am Peter's father, and I have come to collect him."

"I am not just some simple-minded lay person you can trick. In case you didn't notice, I am a judge, and you will have to go through the court to get to Peter, which means you will have to go through *me*."

To that, the man just grinned. "I think you will find I have other ways of getting what is rightfully mine."

"Ha! And I think *you* will find there is no way for you to win against me. Now leave my property, or I will call the police."

"I will be back."

Talbert slammed the door.

Peter leapt back onto the couch, his heart pounding, hoping Talbert hadn't noticed him peeking. The image of the tall man's eagerness burned an image in his memory. He closed his eyes, savoring the moment before Judge Talbert exploded through the office door, the curtains swinging wildly.

"What did you hear?" Talbert yelled.

"N-Nothing." Peter shook his head wildly.

"What is it with people thinking me a fool today?" Talbert grabbed Peter's arm with a fierce grip. "Pay no attention to what you heard. They are all lies. You would do well to forget the whole situation. And if you see that man again, run."

A strong desire to burst out the front door overcame him. He could chase after that man, and be with him forever. Anyone would be better than Talbert.

"You set this up." Talbert sneered, and grabbed his longer whip from behind his desk. "You have to learn you can never escape from me."

Peter slid off the couch, and kneeled on the floor with his backside facing Talbert.

Closing his eyes, Peter prepared to count.

"I think we'll do your back instead of your legs today, what do you think?"

Peter knew better than to answer that. Talbert would routinely switch up his whipping from his butt to the back of his thighs, but his back was always Talbert's favorite.

The whip came down on Peter's back. Harder than normal. If Talbert did his normal ten at this rate, Peter would miss school. He inhaled sharply to help keep his mind off the intense stinging.

Talbert struck again on the other side of his spine.

Melina called from the foyer, "Come on honey, I can't be late for church today. I have to set-up for my book club."

Her voice had never sounded so sweet. Silently, Peter prayed Talbert would listen to her.

Talbert straightened, and wiped the whip down with his handkerchief as he always did.

"You heard my woman," Talbert said, as Melina slipped into the office. "You're in luck today. When I return, we'll continue with your shirt off."

Was Talbert trying to trick him?

"Well boy, what are you still sitting there for? Don't you have some homework to do?" He laughed at his own joke, putting his arm around Melina's slender shoulders.

Peter didn't push it. He'd gotten out of a whipping session, and he was alright with that. He half-crawled, half walked through the office door, and up the stairs. Holding onto the railing, he took the stairs one at a time, afraid he'd fall down them again.

Once in his attic room, he fell on his cot, exhausted. Why had his father shown up now after all this time? And how was he going to get all his homework done *and* complete two shifts today?

Peter wanted to cry, but he felt only cold emptiness.

It was almost the thirteen-year anniversary of him and Rory being found. Nobody had any clue who his parents were, or where they had gone. All he knew was neighbors had reported crying babies to social services, and they had come to rescue him and his sister.

Other than the twins' names engraved on their cribs, no one had any idea who they were. His social worker had even let Peter in on a secret that there weren't any birth records for them, and the house they'd been found in had disappeared.

Thinking of his sister made him nostalgic. He pulled out a heavily taped shoebox that was wedged between his cot and the slanting wall.

Peter wiped his hair out of his eyes, and opened the box, which contained an old house key, a few buttons, *Grimm's Fairytales*, and his baby shirt. Peter smiled at the birthday card Rory had made from construction paper that read, "Happy Birthday to us!" with a big heart. It wasn't much, but his few possessions meant everything to him.

His hand lingered on the baby shirt, the blue fabric worn from so much handling. It felt important to him—his mother had surely touched this shirt. There was a splotch of blood on the bear's face. As usual, he couldn't help but wonder where it came from.

Inhaling deeply, he imagined the items smelled of his old life, even though that was only wishful thinking. The smells had long since died away.

Peter had done everything humanly possible to keep his sole possessions while moving around through the different foster homes.

A thought percolated in his mind, and he tried to catch it. Maybe his father's visit was the key. If he could find him, then he wouldn't have to live with the Talberts anymore! But would he be able to find his father without Talbert knowing about it? There was no chance the man could get past the judge. He was too powerful and had too many connections.

His father had shown up without a woman, so did that mean his mother was really dead? Was that whose blood was on his shirt?

Delicately closing the lid containing his precious items, he curled around the box, and smiled, thinking of what it would be like to live with a real family that loved him. Deep in visions of playing with his long-lost parents and twin sister, an idea jolted him.

He needed to get out of here. He couldn't take it one more day.

Peter leapt up to look out the window. The bird from his dream was still there.

And he was going to follow it.

CHAPTER

— 2 —

PETER'S MIDNIGHT RIDE

Peter hoped the bird would still be outside after he'd ignored it all day. He'd wanted to leave that morning, but Talbert had come home early from church—just to watch over him.

Homework done, he did a quick CTRL+S to save his paper, and stretched his aching arms. He'd sifted through more dirt that afternoon than he ever had before.

Peter looked up at the first bright star he saw—he knew it was a planet, but he made his nightly wish anyway. "I wish I could be with my sister again."

The star gave a bright flash, as if answering his wish.

Peter looked up at the stars—would she still love him? After all, it was his fault they were separated. He'd only been six when Judge Talbert had made him choose between going with him, or neither of them ever having a home. After being in so many foster homes, he couldn't do that to Rory.

It was the worst choice of his life. He remembered looking over at his sister with her big, blue eyes. She'd looked so eager to come along. Rory had hit her tiny fists on Talbert's large belly. "I want to go too!" Rory had begged. "I'll sleep on the floor."

Peter had almost made the right choice when he'd moved away from the overbearing man to stand beside Rory. He'd grabbed her little hand and proclaimed he'd stay with his twin sister forever.

But then Talbert had leaned over his small frame, and whispered, "I guess you don't care about your sister if you don't want her to ever have a home."

In Peter's shock, he had loosened his grip on Rory's hand. Talbert grabbed Peter and carried him out of the Rutherford Adoption Center. He'd only been six, and his life had changed forever.

Peter stared up at the stars. In his heart, he knew finding Rory wouldn't help him escape Talbert. But being with her would make everything right.

The magnificent blue and gold bird glowing on his lawn pulled Peter back to the present. It was not time to linger on old memories, it was time to find out what the bird wanted. Hopefully it would be a quick trip, and he'd return before Talbert noticed him missing.

Peter pulled his winter coat over his plaid pajamas and crept downstairs. He listened carefully—everyone was sleeping.

Since the front door was locked from the inside, Peter snuck into the garage and grabbed Melina Talbert's spare key from her wheel well. The judge always warned her not to use the little magnetic box, but Melina put it back every time her husband took it. Peter slid the box open, and pulled out the house key. Luckily, Talbert didn't know he knew about the hidden key.

Once outside, Peter tiptoed across the dead grass. The October night air smelled like the salty sea—a storm was coming.

Come home. Follow me. A melodic voice sang in his head. Peter looked around for any sign of Talbert or the other boys. If he were caught, that meant a whipping—with his shirt off. He'd surely miss a week of school like the last time he'd run away.

The bird looked at him so earnestly. Peter shook his head. *I must be going crazy.*

"Fine then," Peter whispered. "Just hurry."

As he approached the bird, it grew three times its size. *Jump on,* the voice sounded.

Peter tentatively touched its soft wing, and a jolt of energy surged through his spine. A warmth filled him that he'd never known before. He imagined this was what it felt like to be held by his mother. To be unconditionally loved.

The bird nuzzled Peter's hand, like a dog showing affection for its master.

Well, I've come this far. Peter climbed on its back, almost falling off before re-centering himself. The bird took off, and Peter risked a glance over his shoulder at his white-paneled house with the black shutters, and two pillars marking the entrance.

The full moon cast an eerie glow over the sleeping houses.

Wind blew through his long hair. He shivered—not from the cold, but from the sheer excitement of flying. In a manner of minutes, the bird had carried Peter to an old, dilapidated Victorian house— the very one from his recurring dream.

The pink paint was faded and peeling away, and a crumbling stone tower jutted out from the side. An eerie mist surrounded the odd structure. The mist didn't simply hang around the house, it permeated Peter's skin and made it prickle.

The bird nodded at him to go through the iron gate.

And Peter couldn't argue. His core ached to be inside the house. There was something in there for him, he could feel it. The last line of the dream he'd had every night for a month echoed in his mind, *"Thirteen years is long enough. It is time. Time to come home."*

His heart leapt with a grand idea. This was the perfect place to run away to. No one would expect him to be hiding out in a long-forgotten house.

But first, he'd have to make a proper plan.

"Can you take me back to Talbert's?" Peter asked.

The bird nodded its head towards the house.

Peter shook his head. "No, I need a plan."

The bird looked at Peter with a knowing gaze, before kneeling down to let Peter on its back.

As the bird took off, Peter raced to think of all the things he'd need to do to successfully run away. If he was going to hide out in this place, there could be no mistakes. Peter would need food, clothes, and his box of possessions.

A twinge in his gut urged him to do the right thing—to help his adopted brothers escape too. But what if that allowed Talbert to catch him? Images of the cuts and bruises he'd received the last time he'd run away flashed in his mind. He had to do what it took to survive. Once he was safe, then maybe he could devise a plan to save them. Peter swallowed, feeling completely awful, even though he knew he had to protect himself.

Now *when* could he escape? He needed a time Talbert couldn't easily catch a lone boy walking the streets. Instantly it hit him—Talbert had the Mayor's Ball in a few days. It was on the most haunting day of the year, the perfect time to escape—Halloween night.

Instead of turning back towards Peter's neighborhood on the cliffs overlooking the ocean, the bird flew the opposite direction, towards an area bordering downtown.

The bird stopped at a yellow two-story house, hovering right outside a second story window. The bird increased its bright glow.

"Oh no, stop it!" Peter whispered. He pulled at the bird's neck, trying to get it to turn around. It was going to wake everyone inside and get him in trouble!

The bird nodded its head towards the window.

Peter looked inside the room. A girl with long brown hair was ferociously practicing the same kick over and over. A shimmering blue locket bounced around her neck.

The bird sang a lovely melody. It filled Peter with a warmth he'd forgotten. This was . . . no, it couldn't be. It was the song he and Rory used to sing together to help each other sleep in their old foster homes.

"Is that really her?"

Peter's breath caught in his chest.

Time seemed to slow.

The bird nodded its head slowly, and the creases around its eyes spread out in joy, as if it were smiling.

Peter leaned forward to get a better look. He was now inches from the window. The girl seemed to have a second sense, and looked outside. Their eyes met and Peter knew. It was his twin sister.

Rory's mouth dropped, and she blinked several times in rapid succession. Tentatively, she approached the window. She leaned over her desk, opening the window.

"Peter?" Rory asked, her voice barely audible. "Is that really you?"

He nodded back, heart swelling with joy.

"Wait—are you flying on a bird?"

All he could do was nod, his voice suddenly dry.

"It's like the bird that's been following me around, except mine is red and gold," Rory said, a perplexed expression on her face. "Come inside—it's cold out there."

A voice came from inside the house. "Rory, who are you talking to? You know it's quiet time."

"Oh no, my foster parents are coming," Rory said. "Hurry inside."

Peter shook his head. If her foster parents caught him, they'd drive him straight back to Talbert—and to a severe punishment for leaving the house. He'd have to meet her somewhere else. But where?

He gasped as the incredible idea hit him. "I need help—meet me at the Victorian house on 5th and Elm on Halloween night."

"Wait. What?"

"Oh, and bring food."

She looked at him like he was crazy.

Rory's parents knocked on her door.

"Don't let them see me," Peter begged. "Please."

Rory called over her shoulder, "Just a minute."

She leaned out the window. Peter reached forward. Their fingers met, and a little jolt coursed up his arm and to his heart. From Rory's dazed expression, Peter could tell she felt the same. The connection—it was still there.

Rory climbed off her desk and pulled the curtains shut.

His heart raced, and he couldn't think. As the bird flew off, Peter looked over his shoulder and caught Rory peeking through her curtain—she gave him a thumbs up.

She was coming.

Peter hugged the bird, and the bird did a loop in the air, as if it felt the same joy as he did.

Once back in his room, Peter had to hold himself back from dancing around his attic—and waking Talbert. The excitement was overwhelming—he would surely be reunited with his sister soon—for more than just a fleeting moment. He couldn't remember the last time he'd felt this much joy.

In only a few days, he would see Rory—if she came. He pulled out a spiral-bound notebook and started writing a plan for escape. This time he would succeed. This time, he would not get caught.

His eyes blinked with sleep, and his cot called to him. He knew he needed enough energy to get through tomorrow's tunneling duties, but he found it far more fun staring through his little window at the vast expanse of stars and dreaming of other worlds—ones that included his sister, and *not* Judge Talbert.

*   *   *

Peter jolted awake, his covers damp with sweat. It was that haunting dream again. Every time it was the same thing—the power of the house drew him in, but he could never get past the impenetrable red door with its fiery dragon door knocker.

He hoped when he went there in person, the bird would help him inside. If he didn't have a place to hide out, his plan would fail.

Too jittery to sleep, but too early to get up, he read one of his favorite books, *Famous Dragons of the Ages*. Probably not the best choice after having a nightmare with a booming dragon voice, but it always comforted him. The dragons in the book were his friends.

When his attic room brightened, he stepped to his desk to work on his escape plan. Even though Halloween night was perfect, he still wasn't sure how he was going to pull it off.

Telling wouldn't work. Last time Peter told a teacher, social services had visited to find a beautiful house with well-fed children. Talbert had even rearranged the hidden excavation workshop to look like a playroom. Alerts to authorities got swept under the rug as false claims from a psychologically-damaged child. So, he couldn't try that route again.

A pang of guilt twinged in his gut for leaving his brothers behind. But he couldn't think of a way to sneak out with so many people.

Peter looked out his small window and enjoyed the sun on his face. Then he caught sight of the bird on his lawn. The previous night had been so freeing, he hoped it hadn't been just a dream. Getting away from Talbert and being reunited with Rory—it was almost too much for someone like him to wish for.

Once he was safe in the Victorian house with Rory, then he could look into finding their father. But why after thirteen years had his father finally shown up? Where had he been? And why did Peter suddenly matter to him?

CHAPTER
— 3 —

RORY'S UNEXPECTED GUEST

Rory paced her bedroom while chatting with her best friend, Sun-hi, on her cell phone. "What's going to happen when I see my twin brother tonight?" Her heart raced with anticipation.

"Stop being so nervous," Sun-hi said.

"I don't know . . . maybe I should've told the Gallaghers that Peter needs help." When Rory had told Sun-hi about her brother's visit, she'd left out the part about Peter showing up on the back of a magical bird. Even her best friend would find that crazy.

She also didn't understand where Peter wanted her to meet. He'd said to meet at the Victorian house on 5th and Elm, but that intersection was near Sun-hi's house. And she lived in a neighborhood of McMansions. If he lived in such a nice neighborhood, how could he possibly need food? That man who'd come to adopt him must be an awful person to not feed Peter.

Beatrix scratched at her door. Rory let the black lab in and petted her soft coat.

Rory knelt at her suitcase with all her belongings. Beatrix waddled over and licked her face. "Move, Beatrix," Rory said, wiping the saliva on her red and white baseball shirt sleeve. The dog was supposed to be her foster sister's, but ever since Rory had moved in six months ago, Beatrix had stayed by her side.

The dog jumped on her bed with the colorful cherry blossom comforter Sun-hi had given her.

Rory dug through her clothes and other possessions to find the little wire elephant her brother had made her in their last group home. She clutched the animal tightly—it was the only thing she had left of her brother. She smiled at the memory of how she used to call Peter, 'My little elephant.'

She'd always assumed that one day they'd be reunited— but not like this. His request for help had made him sound really afraid.

"What's going to happen is you'll finally meet the brother I've heard you talk about incessantly," Sun-hi said. "Then you'll come over to my Halloween party where I'll beat you in my costume contest."

Worries bubbled in Rory's mind, pushing thoughts of Peter to the side.

"Rory? Are you there?"

"Yeah," Rory said, clearing her throat. "What?"

"You went silent for a bit—everything okay?"

"I don't know . . ."

"Just tell me."

Rory took a deep breath. If she couldn't share her darkest thoughts with the only person she really trusted, then who could she tell? "It's just that I failed my Tae Kwon Do black belt test over the weekend. Everyone will know."

"Did you post it on social media?"

"Of course not!"

"Then no one will know," Sun-hi said.

"But I will know."

"Master Kuma said you could have the chance to test again in three months," Sun-hi said. "That should give you plenty of time to work on your focus—you know you've got the technique down."

Rory thought for a moment. "You know, I'll just bring Peter back here after I find out what he needs help with." Rory secretly hoped her friend would offer to help.

"Why don't I come with you?" Sun-hi asked.

A great warmth filled Rory's chest. But she didn't want to let it show, so she replied in her coolest voice, "Yeah, that would be great—I could use a ride."

Wanting to avert her overwhelming emotions, Rory asked, "So what costume did you finally decide on?"

"Mulan. Mom's put the final touches on the *hanfu* dress."

"That's perfect. You look just like her."

"Say that again and I'll whack you. You know I was born in South Korea, not China, doofus. Consider yourself digitally slapped."

They giggled, and Rory laid out the last pieces of her costume beside Beatrix.

"So I'll see you in an hour?" Sun-hi said. "Mom's ready to put the pins in my hair. You know how my parents hate waiting."

"I'll be ready."

"Hope you're ready to lose," Sun-hi said, giggling.

"Just wait till you see my Night Fury costume. It'll cream yours in the costume contest," Rory said, ending the call.

Anxiety buzzing through her system, Rory looked in the mirror and attempted to apply the mascara her foster mother had let her borrow for this party. This was her third attempt after watching several how-to videos online, and if she didn't get it right this time, she was going to give up. She opened her eyes wide, involuntarily opening her mouth—and gently rolled the wand over her dark eyelashes. Success!

She looked in the mirror, examining her slick superhero costume. The red mini-dress hung over a spandex body suit that consisted of wide black and red streaks, and was topped off with a black eye mask. Almost perfect.

Rory pulled her favorite piece of the costume out of the box: a deep red cape.

She slipped twelve rubber bands out from under the tight costume sleeve—there was one for each foster home she'd been in since she'd been separated from Peter.

As she finished packing to meet Peter, the image of the red and gold bird nagged at her. She couldn't focus until she looked out the window to see if it was still there. It was. She'd thought she'd been hallucinating at first—until she'd seen Peter hover outside her window on the back of a blue and gold bird. That meant the red and gold bird following her *had* to be real.

Why would the bird trail her when it could fly free? If she had wings, she'd fly to her brother and go far, far away from here. She'd fly to a place where a real family loved her, and not just temporary foster parents.

The Gallagher's weren't really all that bad. They gave her good food, which was much better than the Chapinsons who only fed her ramen. And their house was more fun than the Pulitos who made all their foster kids clean the house constantly. But there was almost *too* much goodness—it left her feeling like everything would crumble around her at any moment.

And she knew the truth. They were only caring for her while it suited their needs. It wouldn't be long until they found some excuse to send her back into the system. That's what always happened.

A knock at the door below interrupted her thoughts. Who could that be? She hadn't heard a car, and it would be awhile before Sun-hi could get here. And trick-or-treaters would come to the front door, not the side-door.

Beatrix's ears perked up from the bed. A low growl eliminated from her throat.

Rory heard Linette and Alan Gallagher greet the guest. It wasn't long before they were arguing with him. The man spoke so softly, it was hard to hear what he said. She could hear her loud foster mother Linette though. "You don't belong here. You have to go through proper channels to see Rory."

She stuffed the wire elephant into her bag and turned to the door.

Beatrix blocked her path. "I wouldn't go downstairs if I were you."

"Excuse me?" She blinked. Now she was hearing things.

"I don't like his smell," Beatrix said with a drawl. Her voice was nasally and deep, unlike the cartoons with cutesy kids voices for animals.

She edged around Beatrix, then went through the door. She had to get her head straight. If she was hearing animals, she was under more stress than she thought.

The Gallaghers had said her new social worker would be stopping by this week, so maybe it was him. Rory pulled on the black boots she'd made from duct tape to go check it out.

She leaned over the railing at the top of the stairs, wanting to get a look before walking into a potential 'tell Rory how she is wrong' danger-zone.

But the guest wasn't a social worker. With his crisp pinstripe suit, he looked way too rich to be one of them. Were they being robbed by the mafia? Cause that would make this family a lot more exciting.

"You can't show up uninvited like this," Linette yelled in that definitive tone of hers.

It sounded like her foster mother needed help.

As Rory walked down the stairs, she wasn't sure what to make of the scene before her. Alan and Linette stood around the kitchen table, and their daughter Michelle sat in front of a lemon cake—Rory's favorite. Smells of rich coconut milk wafted from the stove. Alan had been cooking Thai curry.

A tall man with slicked-back black hair stood in the middle of their kitchen. The Gallaghers' dazed expressions mixed with the superior expression of the man-made Rory feel something wasn't right. She felt queasy looking at him.

Linette Gallagher stood with her pudgy arms set firmly at her hips. At least the disapproval wasn't directed at Rory this time. "Like we said, if you give us your number, we can call you. Please leave."

Alan Gallagher's wide face normally held a calm and jovial expression, but not this time. Standing beside Linette, he scrunched his mouth back and forth like a mouse—a sure sign he was even more uncomfortable than usual.

Except her foster sister didn't seem to notice anything strange—she was texting wildly at the kitchen table. Michelle was twelve, but acted like she was the older sister. Probably came from her being their real daughter.

"Be assured, I will return—I'll come back when she's here," the man said with an air of arrogance.

"Then count on the cops coming right behind you," Linette said, walking the tall man out the door.

A few paces from the door, he halted as if he sensed Rory's presence, which was crazy of course. No one could do that. He turned to look up at her pressed against the stairwell.

A small grin crept up his pale cheeks. If vampires were real, Rory was sure this is exactly what they'd look like.

He stepped inside the kitchen, bringing the cool breeze in with him. "Rory!" he said with a kind of sly excitement. "I can't believe I'm finally meeting you."

She didn't know him, so how did he know her? "Who are you?"

As the guest looked her over, his grin turned into a wide smile. "Do you still have your mother's locket?"

No one had ever mentioned knowing her mother before. Rory's mouth dropped. She brought her hand to her chest, where the locket lay hidden beneath layers of the costume.

Raised over a bed of blue crystals, several interlocking gold circles formed the front of the locket. It opened to show a picture of her mother, which Rory cherished above all else. The back had a symbol engraved on it—three stars in a shape of an isosceles triangle.

It was all she had of her mother.

"Mr. Kyros," Linette said, annunciating each syllable as if it were a reprimand. "You are not allowed to be here—"

The man placed one hand gently on Mrs. Gallagher's shoulder. His outstretched arm revealed a glowing bracelet encrusted with silver gems that appeared fluid. There was something unnatural about it.

When he pulled his hand back, Linette's mouth continued to move wildly, but no sound came out.

"Now, that's better," he said.

"What did you do to her?" Rory asked.

The man waved his hand dismissively. "Just a little trick I hope to show you some day."

"Undo it," Rory said. "What gives you the right—"

"I've travelled a long way to find you," he continued, completely ignoring her protests. "Come, let's chat outside in private."

Rory noticed his black and silver boots didn't match his slick suit. There was something off about this guy. Although, after seeing the phoenix-like bird, and hearing a talking dog, she didn't quite trust her own senses.

"Who do you think you are that you can order me around?" To prove her point, Rory marched up the wooden stairs. She turned to see what type of reaction she'd caused.

Not the reaction she usually got. If he was frustrated, Rory couldn't tell. His long features remained unreadable.

"Now, how do I put this?" He looked off to the distance like he was thinking of something sweet. "I am your father. I've come to take you home."

All her senses heightened. The smell of the sweet lemon cake mixed with the autumn scent of crushed leaves. The TV blared on about police finding an elderly woman's corpse in her house after it had been rotting for seven years. Linette stood by the oven with her arms crossed, urging Rory to make the right choice with only her eyes, while Alan ever-so-slightly shook his head, and her foster sister held a fork with cake mid-bite.

Rory's chest constricted with shock, like she had been plunged deep into the ocean. "Wait. What?"

"I'm sorry your mother and I left you two. It was hard times." He moved farther into the kitchen. "However, I'm here now—and I want us to be together again. I live in a beautiful place called Inara—it's far from here, but I think you'll like it."

Rory, never at a loss for words, didn't know what to say. She had both dreamed of finding her parents so they could be a family again, and of discovering their location just so she could get back at them for abandoning her and her brother.

Moving through all those foster homes and group homes, she had hoped her parents would show up and take her away from this mess, but she never actually expected it to happen.

So what was her father doing showing up here at the same time Peter had?

Emotions battled for top position. Hate won, and flooded out all the excitement, including all the questions she'd stocked up for years. Rory strode into the kitchen to punch him, then stopped—she'd get kicked out of Tae Kwon Do— and lose everything she'd worked so hard for.

But she couldn't get in trouble for words. Rory looked into his grey eyes and gave him the sharpest glare she could muster. "Seriously? After thirteen years, you think you can just show up here and take me away? Shove off."

Mr. Kyros inhaled sharply through his nose, then smiled. "Of course, I completely understand. I left you. I mean me and your mother—we made a terrible mistake."

"I don't want to talk to you—I don't even know you," Rory said.

"Your honesty is refreshing." Mr. Kyros ran his hand along the rim of the kitchen table. "Your mother's going to be disappointed—she is so eager to see you."

Rory scowled, then softened. Her mother. "Why don't you come back another time? You can answer my questions before I go to this Inara place. I don't know where it is, but I know it's not in Rutherford."

"If you come with me now, you will be able to see your mother," he said.

Here he was trying to reach out to her, and she was turning him away. She stuffed the guilt aside. No. He was the one who abandoned her. He could come back when she was ready.

Wait. What was she doing? She and Sun-hi had spent countless hours daydreaming what it would be like to actually meet their birth parents. But this was nothing like what Rory had expected. "Go away."

"I admit I am disappointed to hear that," her father said in a restrained voice. "If I could just have one thing before I go?"

Rory leaned back and glared at him. She wanted to yell, 'you don't have the right to ask me anything,' but held back.

He continued, "Your mother, she is not well. I want to bring her a small bit of joy in lieu of bringing you to her. Now, perhaps you would allow me to return her precious locket?"

Rory felt the man's desire under his carefully selected words. She didn't want to give up her locket. It was all she had of her mother. And there was no way she could trust him. If Rory could see her mother, she wanted to be the one to hand it to her, to see the joy in her mother's eyes. "I'd like to give it to her myself."

"I see," her father said tersely. "I didn't expect to come all this way just to be turned down."

Mr. Kyros reached out to grab Rory. She instinctively stepped out of the way, and punched him in the side. He bent over, a look of shock on his cold face.

Stunned at her actions, she wasn't sure what to do next. Her mind was drawing a blank, as blood rushed to her extremities, ready for another attack. She'd never had to defend herself in real life before. It was always practice kicks in class.

Her father made a move to grab at her again, and she knew he was serious about taking her with him. In one motion, Rory ducked and jumped back.

Her father had just attacked her.

Even worse, she had attacked him back.

CHAPTER

— 4 —

RORY ON THE RUN

I n a rush, Rory's mind cleared. "We have to get out of here!"
She yelled at the Gallaghers, who stood, mouths gaping.
She turned and sprinted up the stairs.

Alan had his cell phone to his ear, and was speaking rapidly.

Her father regained his regal composure. He twisted his
wrist in a ridiculous fashion, like he was conducting an orchestra,
while mumbling jargon words.

With a strange squishing noise, Linette dropped to the
ground—frozen in the exact position she'd been standing in.
She blinked rapidly, though her expression remained solid like
a doll's. Michelle sat frozen in her chair, thumb hovering
above her phone, mid-text.

He turned and made eye contact with Rory. She could see
the intense desire in his eyes.

A shiver ran up her spine.

Rory's heart thudded violently. She slammed her eyes shut.
This could not be real. *I am not seeing things. I am not seeing
things.* She took a deep breath, then opened her eyes. Linette
was still frozen in an awkward position on the checkered floor.

Rory had to go help her. She started back down the stairs.

Her father stepped over Linette's lifeless body and towards Rory.

"What? You didn't—" Alan yelled, dropping the phone. "You can't go up there!"

Rory had never heard her meek foster father speak so loudly.

Her father raised his arm.

Alan rose into the air like he was being pulled by puppet strings. His body crystallized with frost before dropping to the ground. Her kind foster father lay sprawled on the kitchen tiles, unmoving. He didn't deserve this.

Fear coursed through Rory. She had to get out of the house. But he was blocking the exit.

And then her father, with his piercing dark eyes, paused at the bottom of the stairs. "Hello, Rory," he said with an eerie calmness.

"What was that for?" Rory yelled.

"Will you come down here, or shall I come up there?" He spoke as if he were asking her down for tea.

"I will never go with you," Rory said.

"You don't have a choice. I was just attempting politeness. How did I do?" he said, speaking softly.

"You killed my foster parents!"

Her father looked down the stairs as if admiring his handiwork. "Not dead, just frozen." He continued stoically up the stairs.

Rory jumped in her room, slamming the door behind her. She leaned back on her door, suddenly aware she was trapped. Nothing in her Tae Kwon Do lessons had prepared her for this.

She desperately searched the room for options. She'd watched enough T.V. to know he could easily kick open her bedroom door. And she couldn't fight him—he could freeze people!

Beatrix barked at the door.

Rory heard his steady steps up the stairs. He wasn't hurrying. Just a few steps to go. She had to find something to block the door.

She lunged towards the dresser, and slid it across the room. Jewelry and glass animals flew everywhere. Not as hard as she expected. Must be the adrenaline.

Something tapped on the window.

She jumped.

It was the bird.

It cocked its head and narrowed its face, silently communicating with her. Could it be possible that she could fly on the bird like Peter had?

Rory grabbed her bags atop her desk, crawled on top of it, and opened the window where the bird was hovering.

Cold air pooled in. Rory crawled into the window frame. She reached out to touch the bird. The feathers were soft and real. She wasn't just imagining things. Under her palm the bird grew five times its original size. She wasn't sure how, but this bird was as real as her Bruce Lee poster.

The glowing bird sang a wordless melody that vibrated within her—a call to get on.

The door exploded open. Her father stepped through the cloud of debris into her room.

Beatrix leapt to attack.

He waved his wrist and the dog froze like her foster parents.

As Rory climbed on the bird, her heart twisted, seeing her beloved dog hurt.

She wrapped her arms tightly around the bird's red neck, and it bolted from the window. *This is not real. This is not real.* The bird dropped, and Rory's belly flipped like in her favorite amusement park rides. *Okay, it's real.*

Her father lunged for them, but they were out of reach. He shot a bolt of silver light at them. The bird swerved sharply to the side. He attacked again and the bird climbed higher in the night sky.

"I know the truth now, little Zenmage," her father yelled from the window.

What in the world was he talking about?

Rory leaned against the back of the bird, clutching its neck tightly. The golden head feathers tickled her nose.

After flying for a few minutes, Rory felt comfortable enough to open her eyes and look down. She was flying—really flying!

She risked sitting up, still clutching the bird tightly in her hands. The wind blew through her long hair and her red cape flew behind her. She almost felt like a superhero.

Looking down, she marveled at how tiny everything seemed. She'd never flown in an airplane, but imagined this was how it looked.

A grid of streetlights, houselights, and stadium lights stood in contrast to the dark of night. The ocean's white waves rolled in to crash against the cliffs. Everything was bathed in moonlight.

Rory sighed, her breath catching in her throat. She had made it out alive. She hugged the bird, grateful it had taken her away from that monster. She choked back tears.

As they soared a little lower over Rutherford, away from her deranged father, she wondered where this strange bird was taking her.

When she saw her father running inhumanly fast after her, she almost lost her grip.

And even worse—the bird started dropping in elevation. "No! Stay up here!"

Rory squinted at the neighborhood they were descending into. There was Sun-hi's house! It was taking her to the party. "No, don't go that way!" Rory didn't want anyone else to get hurt. What if he attacked her friends?

Instead, the bird landed a few houses down, in front of a strangely familiar dilapidated Victorian house. Rory gasped—it was the house from her dreams—and most definitely the house Peter had mentioned.

There was the odd stone tower that didn't belong. The peeling pink panels, and the long porch—all there. The bushes surrounding the house had long since died, and the large oak in front was barely clinging to life. It was a pitiful sight. So how come she'd never seen it before? And why would Peter be in such a frightening house?

Rory clutched the bird's feathers, half wanting to race in and see Peter, and half wanting to fly away. The bird shrunk back to its normal size, forcing Rory off. She fell to the ground, instantly scrambling to her feet.

As Rory stepped in front of the massive iron gate, the bird took one giant leap over the fence, its long tail feathers fluttering over a familiar emblem. It was the same as on Rory's pendant—three stars in the shape of a triangle.

As the bird flew low to the porch, Rory was sure of one thing—it was leading her inside. Should she? It hadn't led her wrong so far. So what was in this house that was so important for her to see?

Rory looked over her shoulder. She could make out her father's form, his tan trench coat trailing behind him.

She yanked the gate only to find a rusted padlock and chain wrapped around the fence.

There was only one way to fix this. She took a step back, dropped into a low fighting stance, and tucking her front leg, spun quickly to kick the lock with all the power she could muster. The lock smashed to the ground.

The black gate creaked loudly as it opened. Rory looked around, sure that someone must've seen her. Maybe someone would stop, rescue her, and bring her somewhere safe.

And then it struck her—is that what Peter meant? He needed someone to rescue him from this house?

Rory swallowed, and gathering all of her courage, took one step onto the first stepping stone. She stood awkwardly for a moment, half in the yard and half on the sidewalk. When none of the overgrown weeds reached out to grab her, she put her other foot in and bolted towards the door.

The bird was still looking up at her from the porch.

There she was struck by another problem—no door handle. A brass dragon head stared out from the center, with a snake ring in its mouth. Framing the red door were evenly spaced metal studs, as if trying to make the door appear even more impenetrable.

Not sure what to do, Rory clasped her hand around the metal snake and pounded the ring against the door twice. The sound echoed ominously inside. She pushed the door.

Nothing.

Rory ran her hands along the door, looking for a hidden door handle. The door seemed to warm to her touch, which stood out because the cold wind was blowing hard on her neck. Gears twisted and clanked as the wood vibrated beneath her hands.

Suddenly, the door swung open. Caught off guard, she barely caught her balance.

Rory stood on the threshold and peered inside. It seemed darker inside than outside, as if the light of the full moon couldn't penetrate its windows.

Frantic, she tried to think of something, anything, that would save her. Miss Kuma always said being brave wasn't the absence of fear, it was taking action even though you were afraid. Sounded so much better in theory than in practice.

The iron gate creaked open behind her.

Rory took a deep breath and stepped into the house. The floorboard creaked. The door slammed shut behind her with a jolt that seemed to shake the entire house. She was plunged into complete darkness.

Rory caught a flicker of light pooling in from somewhere upstairs.

"Okay, bird, if you're really here to help, now would be a great time for some assistance," Rory whispered.

No sooner had she spoken than she felt the soft breeze of the bird flying past her. The bird exhaled small bits of flame, lighting several candles along the walls. The fire illuminated the wax drips that lined the floor underneath the massive candles.

Wow. This place really is old. Doesn't even have electricity.

The bird brought with it a sweet scent, like lilies—her favorite flowers. "Thanks, bird."

Her heart skipped a beat as she looked up at giant glowing eyes over the staircase. She let out a nervous laugh when she realized it was only a wall-sized tapestry full of fantastic creatures all battling under dual moons: dragons, human-sized angels, gargantuan giants, and monks in white robes.

Strange. It didn't match any of the designs she had studied in art history. It was almost as if an ancient Japanese artist was crossed with a painter from the Renaissance.

Rory shivered, trying to shake off the cold from the biting wind outside. She wrapped her red cape around her.

A loud pounding on the door startled her.

"Rory! Come outside right now!"

Her father was here.

And she was trapped.

CHAPTER
— 5 —

PETER'S HALLOWEEN ESCAPE

Today's the day! Peter was giddy with excitement as he finished his sifting for the day.

He raced through the dark tunnels till he got to the excavation workshop below the house. A few of the boys were washing off the artifacts they'd found that day—a couple arrow heads, bone fragments, and some gold flakes.

His heart raced at the thought of his radical escape plan. Ever since he'd snuck out and followed that bird, he'd thought of nothing else.

Halloween. The perfect night to wander the streets as a kid, and not be caught.

Best of all—he'd come up with a plan to free his brothers too—assuming all went well. They deserved a real family, and it wasn't right for him to leave without them.

Peter hung up his helmet, headlamp, trowel, gloves, and tool bag. He took extra time going up the stairs, trying push his fear down. His finger shook as he pressed the buzzer, silently praying Judge Talbert wouldn't suspect anything.

Of course he did.

Talbert raised one furry eyebrow. "You're done early."

It was true. He had skipped his last class so he could start his shift sooner. He needed time to prepare. For his plan to work, the boys needed to be beneath the house. Working.

Peter's timing had been good—the judge was in his tuxedo, his toupee neatly combed. Mrs. Talbert's hairdryer buzzed upstairs. They'd be leaving soon. And anyone left in the basement while Talbert was away would have to stay there till he returned.

"Guess I was just lucky," Peter said with a practiced straight-face. His stomach churned with nervous energy as he waited in the doorway for Talbert to let him pass.

"Did you find anything useful today?"

Peter shook his head. "I continued unearthing that strange human-like skeleton with the wings."

"A waste of time." Talbert loomed over him. "But I suppose we'll need to get past it to find Orion's lost treasure."

The large man stepped aside from the bookcase door and let him pass. Peter knew the judge would inspect his work later, and would provide five lashings if his work wasn't complete, but this time he wouldn't be there to receive them.

Peter climbed up to his little attic room. As he slipped on his favorite green-striped shirt over a long-sleeved white shirt, he tried to clear his mind. He didn't need to get caught and have Talbert put an even tighter leash on him. Peter imagined Talbert pulling him out of school, which would be dreadful.

Out his window, the setting sun cast an orange and red hue across the sky. Streetlights flickered to life as kids trick-or-treated with their parents or older siblings in tow. The Blue Acres neighborhood drew kids to get the good candies everyone handed out—except at the Talbert's.

With relief, Peter noted the blue and gold bird was still there. Waiting for him. It had even shown up at his all-boys school. No one else had noticed the glorious bird with ornate feathers perched on the bench outside his classroom window—somehow only he could see it.

The bird shifted and called up to him in an impatient song, *follow me.*

Melina's hairdryer stopped humming. It was time to complete the pirate costume with the hot pink cape his school librarian had helped him get. His hands shook so hard he fumbled trying to tie the string around his neck. He clenched his jaw silently in frustration.

Visions of police lights from the last time he'd been caught flashed through his mind. He couldn't repeat that experience. This time, Peter's plan was really quite simple. He was honestly surprised he'd never thought of it before. It was due to the bird he even had an escape option. Now he had a solid place to hide until he could find his father.

Peter folded the old bandana into a triangle, and tied it around his head like a pirate. He pressed his ear firmly against the attic door, waiting, listening. It felt like they would never leave. Melina kept running back up the stairs to change her necklace.

Peter's heart thudded like it wanted to leap ahead of him and right down the stairs.

Finally, the garage door hummed and clicked closed below. He wanted to race down the stairs and out the backdoor as fast as possible, but instead forced himself to pause and double-check his checklist. Flashlight? Check. Water bottle? Check. Warm clothes? Toilet paper? Matches? Check. Talbert's favorite Swiss Army knife? Double-check.

His stomach growled at the thought of the week's worth of peanut butter sandwiches in his pack.

Even though he remembered everything he read, Peter looked through his books, deciding which one to bring. Ever since he was little, the words stuck to his brain like images. But there was still something satisfying about re-reading his favorite stories.

He selected his favorite book, *Adventures of Arthur the Great*. He felt slightly braver having it with him.

Peter took one last look around his attic room, hoping never to see it again. The only thing he'd miss was stargazing out the circular window.

He had all his belongings in his backpack, and now the only thing holding him back was fear. He stuck his head out of the door at the bottom of his stairs. No one was in view.

Slinking down the carpeted stairs, Peter's ears picked up each sound. Children laughing outside. The clicking of the hall clock. He checked—still early enough for the other kids to be working in the basement. He had just enough time. There could be no delays.

Peter raced towards the phone in the living room, his hot pink cape trailing behind him. He had never been allowed to use the phone, but had learned how to dial 9-1-1 at school. Holding the cordless phone tightly, he made the call.

"9-1-1, what is your emergency?" A kind female operator asked in a clear voice.

Peter didn't even have to act afraid, his voice came out as a croak. "There's a house fire. 4115 Osman Drive."

He held his breath, almost sure the woman on the other end would call him out for lying. But she didn't.

"Is the fire at your house, and are you inside the house or outside on a cell phone?"

"Mine. Inside."

"Are you in a safe location?"

"Yes." Peter tapped his foot anxiously.

"What is your name?"

"Peter," he said automatically. He cringed. He shouldn't have said that.

"How old are you?"

"Thirteen. Please hurry." Why was she asking so many questions? He wanted to get out of there, but had to be sure they would come.

"I need you to tell me a little more about the nature of the blaze. Do you know how the fire started?"

In his head he answered, *Me, but only if I have to.*

"Peter, are you still there? Is anyone injured?"

This was it. He closed his eyes. "There are kids trapped in a basement system of tunnels behind a bookcase on the main level. You have to get them out. Pull out the big blue book on the third shelf to open the secret door. Then in the basement, slide the metal shelf over."

Silence hung on the line for a brief moment. "I'm dispatching the fire department. How many children are trapped? Can you help them out?"

He was about to answer when he heard the familiar sound of Talbert's BMW pull up to the driveway. Peter barely heard the woman's question.

His mind a pressurized blur, he spurted out, "Five. No, I can't. I need help." He dropped the cordless phone. It bounced on the beige living room carpet. The woman's voice garbled through the phone.

Peter raced towards the backdoor, which he had previously unlocked. How could Talbert be back from the Mayor's Ball so soon? Peter closed the screen door as quietly as he could, and shivered in the chill night air. He leaned against the house, trying to calm his wild heartbeat so he could think straight.

"How could you forget the gift for the Mayor?" Talbert scolded his wife from the foyer.

"I'll just be a minute. I should change this necklace too—and wear the one your uncle gave me," Melina said, running up the stairs as she spoke.

What was he going to do? This was not part of his plan. If the Talberts were home, the firefighters might not come in, and the boys wouldn't be freed.

Peter pulled the handmade cardboard eye patch down over one eye, and pulled the orange newspaper bag for candy out of his pocket.

Hearing Talbert still arguing with Melina, Peter raced along the tall, wooden fence to the front of the house. He prayed the 9-1-1 operator wouldn't think it was a prank.

Backpack hidden under his hot pink cape, he felt stupid. But successfully executing his plan was more important than his embarrassing piecemeal costume. The bird waited on the meticulous lawn, almost grinning at him. Peter stared blankly back at it, willing the bird to help him somehow. He knew he'd need some sort of miracle to escape getting caught by Talbert.

Stars and storm clouds speckled the sky. Candle-filled paper bags lined the lawns, which added a warmth to this otherwise cold and dreary neighborhood. At the end of the block, a zombie-themed party raged, music blaring. The first two-story house to the right looked the most cheerful, with jack-o-lanterns lining the walkway. He'd go to that one.

First, he'd have to blend in with the other kids. Making sure Talbert wasn't looking, Peter put on a fake smile, and slipped in line behind a group of kids. Peter looked up at his neighbor's grey-paneled house with its white shutters and a front porch, which had a similar rectangular-design as most of the houses in this neighborhood.

Talbert exerted too much control over the boys and would never expect Peter to leave the house. Peter braced himself against the biting wind.

Peter suddenly realized he'd made a cardinal sin of sneaking and *not* getting caught—he hadn't put the phone back on the receiver. And he'd still been on the line with 9-1-1. If Talbert had seen it, Peter's carefully laid plan would fall apart.

Peter followed the small group to his neighbor's house, where a middle-aged woman dressed in a Mary Poppins costume opened the door. She wore a tailored blue jacket with a ruffled blouse, long skirt, and a black brimmed boater hat adorned with daisies.

"Trick-or-treat!" a boy in a detailed Green Goblin costume said, grabbing a handful of candy from the woman's bowl.

"Hey! One piece!" the woman said.

The boy ran down the steps, and looked at Peter hovering there. "Haha! Dumb costume."

Somehow, the stinging words hurt more than when Talbert said cruel things.

The boy took Peter's hot pink cape and flipped it over his head. Laughing, the boy and his friends walked down the street.

Peter flipped the cape back over his backpack and walked up the steps. *My first time trick-or-treating!* He wasn't sure what the appeal was supposed to be.

His neighbor stood in the doorframe, smiling widely. "Trick or Treat!"

Fear gave him a narrow focus on the woman's overstuffed orange bowl.

It wasn't why he was here, but the candy would be good extra food. Talbert never allowed them to have sweets. Peter was about to grab one when he saw Talbert's silver BMW pull out of the driveway. Peter looked down and away.

"Are you going to take one or not?"

The car passed and he closed his eyes, breathing a sigh of relief. He chose one mini chocolate bar. "Thank you."

She smiled back. "So polite."

It was now or never. It was starting to look like his 9-1-1 plan was going to fail, so he had to tell someone else. He could only pray the adult would listen for once. The words poured out of his mouth, almost as if someone else were saying them, "You have to listen to me. Next door, Judge Talbert uses us to dig tunnels to find lost artifacts of the forgotten Gods. There are five kids stuck in the basement. You have to rescue them."

The woman scowled. "That's not a nice trick, boy. And you already got your treat."

"It's true," Peter insisted. "I promise you. I could show you." That had not been in his original plan, but he was desperate.

But a line of kids had showed up behind him, ready for candy. The woman clutched the bowl in one hand and pointed away. "You go along and finish your trick-or-treating, and stop playing games on people. Richard is a good person. It's not nice to spread rumors. Besides, we all know there is only one God."

Stupid woman. No one ever listened. Crestfallen, Peter slinked through the kids walking up the steps and crept to the side of his house.

Peter fidgeted in the bushes beside his garage. Maybe he should just leave now for the Victorian house. He'd at least made an effort to free the other boys.

The bird joined Peter and he petted its soft head. It nuzzled back, like it was an old friend. The bird comforted him, and he felt a deep sense of peace and knowing. "You're right. I have to wait here. We'll leave after I'm sure 9-1-1 believed me, and my brothers are freed."

The bird nodded back, its three small head-feathers shaking along.

Peter considered slipping into the house to check on the phone, but didn't want to miss the emergency teams arriving. And what if Talbert had tricked him and was waiting for him inside?

Peter fingered the matchbook in his pocket, ready to execute his last back-up plan.

Only a couple minutes later, sirens wailed. The operator really had called them right away. The rest of the questions must have been to help keep him calm. He covered his ears. He silently prayed they wouldn't need to actually see smoke to enter the house.

Judge Talbert's shiny BMW pulled up in front of the house.

No. It can't be.

Peter clenched his fists. He'd been so careful developing his plan, and nothing was going right.

He smacked his forehead. Dispatch must have called Talbert somehow!

"What's going on here?" Judge Talbert roared at the two firefighters jumping out of the red fire engine. Melina stayed in the car, out of the wind.

"We received word of a fire. Please step out of the way." The fireman held up his hand.

A firewoman hooked up a hose to the fire hydrant.

"I am not letting you into my house. There is no fire. This is a prank. Now get off my property!"

"We have to inspect the property. You can either do this the hard way or the easy way. Let us in."

"Never. My son . . ." he cringed at the word and added in his calm, manipulative voice, "is trying to get back at me for not letting him go trick-or-treating. I promise you this is all just a big misunderstanding."

Talbert *had* seen the fallen phone. He must have been circling the block trying to find him.

The silent fuming was the worst—Peter could sense Talbert imagining a horrific punishment for him.

Peter barely breathed, for fear if he let go, they wouldn't find his brothers. What was he going to do if the firefighters believed Talbert, and didn't search the house?

Peter's body forced a sharp inhale.

"Get out of our way," the firewoman said. "We received a report there are kids trapped in a basement tunnel."

"Stop! There is no one else here but me," Talbert said.

Peter couldn't believe Talbert would've let all those kids die to protect his reputation.

A voice shrieked in Peter's head, '*He's getting away. He's getting away again! You have to do it!*'

Peter sprinted behind the house. He lit a thin match from a folding matchbook he'd swiped at a gas station, and held it out over the row of bushes that lined the back of the house. Should he really do it? The match fizzled out, pinching his finger with heat. He dropped it into the bark chip mulch.

He sighed, and whispered, "please," before lighting a second match, and tossed it into the bush.

Expecting a small fire to kindle slowly, just enough to create smoke, he lit a third match. Instead the match he'd used immediately engulfed the shrub. Flames leapt onto the white vinyl siding.

Peter jumped back at the unexpected blaze and stumbled, falling on his butt. The match he'd been holding dropped and fizzled out in the grass. He raised his arm to protect his face from the intense heat of the fire.

"This is ridiculous!" Talbert roared from the front yard.

Peter scrambled to his feet, ready to run into the house to save his brothers, if necessary. But it wasn't.

The firefighters must have smelled the smoke. Instantly, their tones shifted. Peter couldn't make out what they were saying over the roar of the fire.

Peter wanted to stay and watch, but the heat radiating from the back of the house made him gag. His face was hot. If he didn't leave, he would faint . . . and be caught in Talbert's clutches forever.

As Peter ran to the back of the yard, he tore off his backpack. He dove at the fence, pulling up the panel he had previously weakened, and stuffed his backpack through. Peter slipped under the panel, the loose board sliding shut behind him. The bird flew over the fence—sure would've been nice if he could've flown too.

He had to see—had to make sure Talbert was taken away for good. Hoisting his backpack onto his shoulders, Peter sprinted all the way around the block. He hid behind a large maple tree across the street a couple houses down, and watched as the firefighters entered the house.

The fire was truly massive now. Dark smoke billowed into the sky. Peter knew he should go, but he had to make sure his brothers were rescued. He hadn't expected the fire to become so disastrous. It was just supposed to be a little flame.

Peter held his breath, waiting to see if the firefighters would find them. "Please. Please," he whispered over and over again.

Lightning flashed overhead.

All trick-or-treating halted. Kids and their parents stood in scattered groups, looking up at the burning two-story house. A dozen teens in zombie costumes stared up at the fire, looking truly brain-dead. Someone had turned off the party music, and the silence mixed with the hustle of the firefighters and the roaring crackling of the blaze was eerie.

Rain fell from the blackened sky, helping to douse the fire.

As the firefighters were engrossed in their work, and the cops pushed onlookers back, Talbert slinked away from the house. One of the teenagers pointed at Talbert and laughed— Talbert's toupee had shifted and he hadn't even noticed.

Peter pulled himself tighter to the rough bark of the tree, not quite ready to leave the area. Several excruciating moments later, a firewoman emerged with a small boy in her arms. It was Isaac, the new kid! Peter breathed a sigh of relief.

He wanted to leave, but first he had to make sure they were *all* out. A second fire engine and two more police cars arrived.

Excited for the moment Talbert would finally be arrested, Peter studied the crowd and gasped—Talbert and his BMW were nowhere in sight. Peter spun around, frantically looking for any sign of Talbert.

"Let's get them out of there!" the firewoman shouted before plunging back into the burning house. A second firefighter dropped his hose and ran into the house after her. Saving lives was their top priority. One firefighter stayed holding the hose, water arching over the back of the house where the flames were most powerful.

His attic room over the garage was now engulfed by flames. Peter stared, entranced. So much time he'd spent in that room, and now it was gone in an instant. In all the excitement, a stream of loss coursed through him. He couldn't truly relax and enjoy his triumph until he was safe in the Victorian house.

One fireman aimed a massive, bulging hose at the roof, dousing the fire. Another carried the last two kids out.

It was over. Judge Talbert couldn't hurt his brothers anymore.

An intense warmth, not from the fire, filled Peter's chest. He choked back the rushing emotion. Despite his fear, a wide grin grew. Judge Talbert could never hurt another child again. His risk had been worth it. The boys were free.

He was free.

But he wouldn't be if he stood here forever. Now was the time to get away, not linger.

For a moment, Peter almost joined the group of rescued kids. He would be safe from the judge now. But then the bird pulled on his sleeve, reminding him to stick to his plan. As Peter let the glowing creature pull him away, he reveled in how everything had turned out better than he could've imagined.

There was only one flaw—where was Talbert?

CHAPTER

— 6 —

PETER'S REUNION

Goosebumps prickled Peter's skin. He took one last look over his shoulder.

That was a mistake.

Judge Talbert's BMW turned the corner. Before Peter could run, Talbert caught Peter's gaze. A deep scowl of pure hatred crossed Talbert's face. He pointed at Peter, mouthing a threat.

Peter slipped behind the maple tree.

The crowd dispersed from gawking at the receding house fire. A miniature ghost, a vampire, and a werewolf holding an umbrella walked past him, blocking Talbert's view.

Now was his chance.

Peter slipped beside the furry werewolf and walked off with them. The bird followed. Once they turned the corner, Peter broke into a run, grateful it had stopped raining.

Starting an all-consuming fire hadn't really been part of his plan. He couldn't even figure how it'd happened. The leaves had barely ignited before jumping to the house, as if the white siding was covered in gasoline.

Peter kept glancing over his shoulder as he ran, expecting Talbert to catch up with him at any moment. Instead of following the strange bird directly, as it wanted, Peter went three blocks in the opposite direction to keep from being caught.

It didn't work.

He was almost out of his community when a dark figure stepped out from the shadows.

Peter stumbled backward, tripping over a crack in the sidewalk. The man rushed forward and caught Peter by the arm before he could land. It was so fast, he wasn't sure how he'd done it.

Dim yellow light from the lamp post shone over the man's sharp pin-stripe suit. Peter blinked. It was the man who'd come to collect him!

This could not be happening. Was he really standing alone in front of his father without Talbert looking over his shoulder? For a moment the judge's harsh words that this man was an imposter flitted through his mind, but he shook the unwanted thoughts away.

Peter cocked his head up at the man who towered over him, not sure what to say. He'd never been one for many words, and awkward situations only made it worse. He didn't want to say anything that would make his father reject him.

"Hello, Peter," the man said in a kind and gentle voice.

Peter felt he could sink into the kindness of his tone. "Hi."

"I've been searching for you for many years. I can't believe I'm finally saying this."

Peter took in every word.

"I'm sorry it has taken so long. I am your father, and I've come to take you home." He spoke clearly and crisply, obviously putting much care into his words.

Peter fiddled with the end of his pink cape, and swallowed before whispering, "Father?" The word caught in his throat and he had to repeat it. It felt so weird saying that to someone.

"Yes?" his father replied, his grey eyes sparkling in the light. His smile was warm and inviting. He gently lifted Peter's eye patch, resting it on top of his bandana. "There, I don't think you'll be needing that anymore."

Peter didn't mean to cringe at his soft touch. He smiled to make up for his reaction, then explored his father's long features, taking in every detail. He had a high forehead, the same dark hair, and a sharp nose much like his own.

His father bent down, holding out his long arms, and Peter stepped into them. Every nerve in his body tingled with energy. The embrace made the stinging of his back wash away like it wasn't even there.

His father loosened his grip, and Peter squeezed tighter. He couldn't remember the last time he'd had a hug. Eventually, Peter stepped back and his father held him at arm's length.

So many questions swirled in his mind. "I'm supposed to go meet Rory, but Talbert is chasing me."

"I see." His father sighed and closed his eyes. "Well, I don't think that meeting is going to happen. She's in my enemy's clutches."

Peter gasped. "Can we rescue her?"

"That is my plan—in fact it is something I'd like your help with."

"And what about Mom?" Peter asked, tentatively hopeful.

His father's expression wilted. "Oh my dear boy, I'm so sorry—your mother's been missing for thirteen years now. No one has any clue where she is."

"Oh," Peter said, disappointment taking over. All the highs of the evening came crashing down.

His father switched tunes quickly. "Look, let's go home now. After we get you safe from that awful guardian of yours, then we can look for Rory, okay?"

"Right!" Peter said, almost forgetting about Talbert's hunt for him.

His father took Peter's hand and walked the opposite direction. The bird flew low beside Peter, pulling his hot pink cape. He shooed the bird away.

"What is it?" his father asked.

Peter looked from the bird and back to his father. *The man couldn't see it!* Not wanting to appear psychologically disturbed, Peter shook his head. "Nothing. Just an itch."

The magnificent bird scowled at him and flew off. Peter was almost insulted it had abandoned him, then realized he didn't need the bird anymore. He had a *real* home to go to now—not some creepy, abandoned house.

Headlights flashed behind them. Peter would've halted in his tracks, but his father grabbed his arm and pulled him behind a tall fence. When they reached the shadows between the house and the fence, Peter looked over his shoulder to see Talbert's BMW glide by.

They waited for the car to pass, then ran the opposite direction down the sidewalk. They'd lost Talbert . . . for now.

As they ran, Peter kept looking over his shoulder. Every few minutes, the BMW surfaced, and his father led them in a new direction, zigzagging through the neighborhood. There was only one road connecting Blue Acres to the rest of Rutherford—how were they going to get out?

He was so overjoyed to finally be with his father, his surroundings became a blur. When they finally stopped, Peter was surprised to find himself at the gate to the temple ruins.

His heart fell, brow furrowing. This was a cruel trick. This was not a house.

His father easily pried open the gate, but Peter held back, not daring to take another step. The man turned to face him. "What is it?"

Peter scoffed. "This is home? I'm not stupid. No one lives in the ancient temples. I can't believe I followed you. Who are you really?"

His father squatted in front of Peter and looked him in the eyes. "Sometimes it's hard for adults to explain things that are commonly familiar to them. What I am going to say will sound bizarre to you. I want you to listen carefully. Can you do that?"

Peter nodded, but he was still skeptical.

"You are not from this world. I am not from this world. We are from a different planet. And the only way home is through Orion's old temple."

Peter laughed. "That's the dumbest thing I've ever heard."

"Listen—"

Peter barreled on. "I'm not some stupid kid you can kidnap. I have to get out of here—Talbert knows I called the authorities. Now that his house has burnt down, I'm sure he'll stop at nothing to catch me."

His father only grinned, his eyes lighting up.

Peter didn't think that was anything to smile about.

"I think we both know who started that fire," he said.

"Who?" He pretended, twisting his foot in the dirt.

"You," he said matter-of-factly. "You come from a line of powerful mages, including those with the power of fire."

Peter raised an eyebrow. This was just stupid. He had to find a way out of here.

"Think about it. That became a massive house fire in a short amount of time."

"I-uh." That much was true.

"Don't think I wasn't watching. I was merely waiting for Talbert to leave for a sufficient period of time, so I could come visit you."

He didn't know what to do. He liked what this man was saying, but isn't that what all kidnappers did to lure kids in?

"I see you still don't believe me, but we have to go now. Look." His father pointed.

Peter turned to see Talbert headlights barreling up the hill. He'd be here in a few minutes.

"You have to make a choice now. Come with me, your father who loves you, or stay with your wicked guardian."

It was an easy choice. Of course going with his crazy father was better than staying here, where he'd never be free of Talbert.

Peter sprinted through the open gate so fast his father had to run after him. Peter paused in the middle of the eleven temples, not sure where to go. There was no space ship, or anything remotely science fiction looking up here, just sand and the crumbling stone ruins.

The symmetrical temples sat in a circle around a stone pedestal, perched on the edge of the cliff. One of the temples had already fallen into the ocean. A second, covered with vines, was precariously close to dropping hundreds of feet below. Each of the temples was designed to represent the personality of their God.

Made of volcanic rock, they were in various stages of decay. Only a couple still had their pyramid-like layered roofs. The once intricate carvings of animals or earth symbols were washed away by thousands of years of ocean winds and storms.

A few retained their rectangular doorways, portions of stairs, and columns carved into the walls.

From the pamphlets he'd read, he knew they were built long before the Egyptian pyramids. No one knew what happened to the people who'd lived here so long ago, or why only one of the temples had been blackened from fire.

He'd been here plenty of times to help Talbert in his mission to find the forgotten Gods' lost artifacts. Peter looked over to the line of evergreen trees where their secret tunnel opened up to.

His father ran straight for Orion's temple. Peter followed, but paused on the threshold, looking inside. It was dark and the light from the moon illuminated the pedestal in the center. The elevated throne area had completely crumbled.

Orion's temple was in surprisingly good shape—it had all four of its walls and a partial roof. Over the doorway, a faded symbol had been crossed out and was replaced with a carving of intertwining dragons.

Peter looked up at the twinkling stars and wished on the first star he saw. *I wish to be free of Talbert and be with Rory again.* Then he silently thanked the heavens for granting half of his wish.

"Hurry on in here," his father said.

Peter's breath quickened. "How are we going to travel to another planet if you don't have a spaceship?"

"We don't need one." His father studied him for a moment. "You appear to be a smart boy, so I will tell you the truth. When the Pleadines moved the two disgraced Archangels, and the people they had gifted magic to, from Earth to Inara, they created five portals. Me and my, uh . . . colleague learned how to open them. Very complex magic."

Peter wanted to believe it with his whole being, but a nagging sensation told him to be leery. "Is Kyros even your real name?"

A slight look of contemplation passed the man's eyes before he said, "My colleagues usually refer to me as The Researcher."

Peter couldn't help smiling. Now he knew where he got his knack for researching from. His father was one too! He ran his new name over his tongue a few times. "Peter Kyros." He liked the sound of it. Anything would've been better than 'Peter Talbert,' even 'Peter Twinkletoes.'

He stepped into the temple. The thing was, once he was inside, it felt familiar somehow. His father beamed, and put his arm around Peter's shoulders. "Do keep in mind people will think you a heretic if you express belief in the story I've told you. But I could not have my boy be one of the ignorant masses—we must take it upon ourselves to learn the truths of the universe. Now, let's get going, shall we?

The faint noise of a car door slamming echoed up the hill.

Hearing that was all he needed. It didn't matter if his father was a loony. If he could at least protect him from Talbert, that was good enough for him. Peter nodded quickly in the cool, misty sea air.

The Researcher pulled a dark wand out of his suit jacket pocket, and transformed it into a magnificent black and silver staff. At its tip were four metal bars in the shape of a diamond, encompassing a glowing silver gem.

Peter's stepped back, his mouth slack. *That* was not normal.

"See? I wasn't lying. Hard to believe though. Now, I need to focus, unless you wish to get caught."

The gate rattled at the bottom of the hill.

Talbert was coming.

Peter stepped closer to his father. It felt like he was standing in a haunted temple–almost as if the absent Gods would jump out to attack them at any moment, reclaiming their homeland.

Talbert's footsteps drew closer. Peter looked over his shoulder, expecting Talbert to burst through at any moment.

The Researcher raised his staff above his head, and chanted in a language Peter had never heard. It wasn't even Latin–he had to listen to the church choir sing it every week.

Talbert's silhouette blocked the light of the moon. "You're mine!"

In one quick motion, his father slammed his staff on the ground and took him by the hand. Peter instinctively pulled back. But The Researcher pulled harder and spit out one final word.

Talbert lunged and grabbed Peter.

In that moment, Peter's world changed forever.

A spiral of white light appeared above them, and he was sucked through the air with his father and Talbert desperately grasping his arm. In the black void, stars and galaxies sped past. He thought of the millions of wishes he could make on each of them. The first one would be that Talbert would disappear through the stars, never to be seen again.

With only his father's firm grasp to ground him, the weightlessness and lightness of being felt limitless. He yearned to explore the vast sea of stars, but an unseen force pulled them, closer and closer, to a light on the other side.

Even with Talbert grasping his wrist, Peter found himself filled with an unexpected feeling of pure joy. He soaked in the feeling. He could stay in here forever, floating free—no fears— just pure life.

His father pulled him through the light and Peter thudded on a mattress-sized pillow on the ground. He blinked several times in the darkness. The fall had broken Talbert's grip.

His father immediately stood to light a candle on the stone wall. It tilted over and lit the line of candles on both walls, like a row of dominoes.

More magic.

Instead of the open temple, they were in an underground room lined with several shelves of neatly organized artifacts that appeared to be from Earth. There was a whole shelf dedicated to the chronology of computers. Another shelf contained every musical device Peter could imagine, including a gramophone. There were items so old, someone must have been traveling to and from Earth for over a hundred years.

Talbert lunged at Peter and clasped him in a bear hug. Talbert whispered in Peter's ear, "You're never getting away from me now."

Feeling Talbert's hot, sweaty arms clasped around him, Peter gagged. He writhed and kicked to free himself from Talbert's crushing grasp. It was no use. Peter fell limp so Talbert would relax his grip.

His father whirled around with surprise at Talbert's presence and raised his staff. "Let go of my boy, and I won't hurt you."

Talbert scoffed. "I don't know who you think you are, but I am a judge, and—"

"Look around," his father waved his wrist. "You're not on Earth anymore."

Peter could feel Talbert's forced breathing though his back, sending a tingling sensation up his spine. He felt he was going to puke and squirmed even harder.

His father pointed his staff at Talbert and chanted a string of words.

Talbert let go of Peter and dropped to his knees, clasping his hands around his neck. Peter scurried back and ran behind his father. Talbert was growing pale, and the blue veins in his neck popped out.

"You are now in *my* realm." His father chanted a few words in that same strange language, and Talbert's wrists flew behind him into magical handcuffs. He fell over face first into the oversized pillow.

His father wrapped his arm around Peter's shoulder. "See, I told you I would protect you."

"Please let me go," Talbert begged from the floor. "Don't send me back—I can be useful to you."

"And why would I need help from a little worm like you?" His father sneered.

Peter almost whooped hearing Talbert put in his place. "Send him back," Peter said, trying to sound brave.

"In the morning. It takes a significant amount of magical energy to open the portal, and I need to refill my reserves."

Peter looked up at his father, who really did look awful. His grey face was sweaty with fever.

"Are you okay?" Surely he hadn't finally found his father only to have him die on him.

"Just tired from all the magic use. I'll get my medicine, and I'll be fine." His father grabbed Talbert by the tux's collar and dragged him out of the room.

Talbert begged and squirmed all the way. "Please. I'll do anything. You have such great power. How do you do it?"

His father ignored Talbert.

Peter scurried after them. Relief washed over Peter when his father threw Talbert in a laboratory-looking room with medical tables and strange equipment. Peter finally felt comfortable asking what had been nagging at him. "How did you light the candles?"

"Simple magic. I can't wait to show you all I know." His father leaned across the wall, breathing heavily.

"Magic? I thought that was a joke—something to get me to go with you," Peter said.

"Did you think coming through a portal across space to another planet was a joke?" He obviously didn't find it funny at all.

Peter tried to recover his dignity. "No, but I thought it would be more scientific, like a wormhole or something."

The Researcher shook his head. "I'm so glad to have you back. I've thought about you every day," his father said.

It felt good to hear him say it, but he couldn't help himself. "Then why did you leave us?"

"That is a longer story than I have time for right now. But I can tell you it was an accident. Your mother and I love you two very much."

My mother. He wanted to find out everything about her. But obviously now was not the time, so he settled on an easy question. "Where are we?" He removed his hot pink cape, which seemed especially silly now.

The Researcher leaned over him and looked at him sharply, with bloodshot eyes. "This is your home. You are in the capital city of Nadezhda, on the continent Tilla, on the planet Inara." He coughed, blood specks splattering the back of his hand.

Peter gasped at the blood. "We need to get you to a doctor."

"Don't you worry about me," his father said, putting his hand on his shoulder. "Now, let's get you up to bed so I can still have enough energy to make my cure."

Peter followed his limping father down a dark hallway lined with several doors. His father paused to catch his breath before they turned down a narrow stone corridor. "Before I take you to your room, you must know there are many dangers here you do not yet understand. Tell no one where you came from—they won't believe you anyway. If anyone asks, your mother died and you came to live with your father, The Researcher. They will know of whom you speak. Do you understand?"

Peter gulped and nodded. "Tell no one."

"That's a good boy," his father said, patting his shoulder. He muttered a spell that dried their clothes.

They stopped at a dead end where his father leaned against the wall, hand on a candleholder beside him.

"Now listen. This area with the portal is our little secret. You and I are the only ones still alive who know about it. If anyone finds out about my space, it could prevent us from getting Rory back. And you wouldn't want that, would you?"

Peter shook his head. He didn't know what to say. He had spent years dreaming of finding his family and what it would be like, but never once dreamt of anything like this.

CHAPTER

— 7 —

RORY AND THE HAUNTED HOUSE

Rory stood in the entryway, letting her eyes adjust to the dim candle light. The foyer was huge, with several doorways and a wide staircase off to the side. Her father banged on the door.

She let the food bag fall off her shoulder, its contents spilling across the floor. An orange rolled to the foot of the stairs.

"Peter, are you here?"

A snicker came from the other side of the door. "Oh little girl, Peter's not in Rutherford anymore. Your brother got himself into a little trouble setting a house fire."

What did he mean by that?

Her father performed a melodic chant outside, using words she didn't understand. Whatever he was doing, it wasn't having any effect.

Rory stepped back.

He stopped his chanting and spoke to her in a sweet voice, "Dear Rory, I know you can hear me. I can feel your presence on the other side of that door. It calls to me."

Rory shivered. She felt slimy all over just listening to him.

"I think you and I got off on the wrong foot," her father said. "Open up and I can help you. I can reunite you with Peter and your mother."

Did he have Peter? Is that why he wasn't here?

"That's what you want, right? But I can't free your mother without you."

Rory had a feeling he would say anything to get to her. Really *do* anything, since he had just ruthlessly attacked her foster parents for no reason at all.

"No. I will never come with you. I hate you," Rory yelled. "They were good people. How could you do that to them?"

"They'll be fine," he said tersely. "Probably already moving around now."

"I don't believe you." Rory looked around the foyer for any possible means of escape.

"Now Rory, you have to trust me," her father said in his deliberate manner. "You are my daughter and they wanted to keep you from me." Her father paused, as if expecting a response.

She had none.

"Can you possibly imagine how it feels to finally find your children and be kept from them?" her father spoke in a deep and gentle voice.

She didn't know what it felt like as a parent, but she sure knew what it felt like being separated from her parents all her life. Rory's shoulders relaxed. "I'm sorry, I don't know what to say."

"I hear you've been living without your brother for the past seven years." His tone softened. "How could a twin live without her other half?"

Rory felt that gaping hole in her chest she felt whenever she thought of her brother. "Peter? Is he okay?"

"He is well. Come out, and I can take you to him."

It all seemed so reasonable.

"Now, touch the front door—it will open for you. This house is magical—that's why only you and I can see it."

He was being ridiculous again. "Wait. What?"

"My dear, how do you think I got past your guardians? Magic. And as my daughter, you must have it in you too."

So she really wasn't hallucinating? The unearthly bird was just magic? Her concept of reality shattered. If she'd been mistaken about magic, was she wrong to distrust her father too?

When she didn't answer, he added, "Only the greatest of wizards—a Zenmage—can call on their Zamsara bird. And I saw you fly off on yours."

She felt her heart swell with pride—she was a special kind of wizard. Which seemed ridiculous, since only a second ago she didn't believe in magic. Rory held her hand out to the door. Should she?

The Zamsara bird swooped in front of her, making her step back. Rory shook her head. The bird was right. What was she doing? Father was obviously a liar, talking about magic and all. If she *did* have magic, how come she'd never seen it before?

She blinked. But she *had* seen it. This bird standing in front of her was obviously made of pure magic.

And it didn't change the fact that her father had attacked the Gallaghers, and it was the bird who'd saved her. "Bring Peter and my mother here. Then I'll come out."

"I'm sorry to tell you that is not possible. Peter will be returning home with me—don't you want to come too? If you don't come with me right now, you will never see them again. Is that what you want?"

So that's why Peter wasn't here to meet her?

Rory pulled at the rubber bands on her wrists. Was she putting Peter in danger by not going with her father? But she couldn't—every nerve in her body held her back from letting him in. And the bird was glaring up at her with the sharp focus of a parent telling her, 'No.'

"I'll never trust you," Rory said.

"I understand you not wanting to trust me after I left you and your brother. Really, my sweet, sweet girl. I do need your locket. Your mother needs it to get well."

The bird gave Rory a harsh glare and Rory felt this strange sense of knowing—like the bird was a part of her and she a part of the bird. The words hurt, but she said them anyway, "I'll never go with you."

"Stupid, stupid girl. I will hunt you down and find you. There is no planet you can escape to where I cannot get you. You are *mine*."

"Go away," Rory yelled. *Planet?* Had she heard him right? Rory shook her head, refusing to inherit his craziness.

Her father gave one final slam that had such force, Rory was surprised it didn't break down the door. Rory shuddered, grateful for the protection of a magical door.

She cocked her head, listening intently for what he was doing on the other side. He chanted again in some language she didn't recognize. He did this for several minutes before he spit out a slew of swearwords.

She heard slow, deliberate footsteps descending the creaky porch. Rory peeked out the foyer window.

Her father was leaving.

She figured he'd probably wait for her to leave so he could ambush her. She had to find a way out. Now.

Rory turned to see the Zamsara bird light the candles on the second floor, then perch on the railing. The bird cocked its head towards the first room, as if it had been waiting for her to go up there all along.

Testing the first stair, she carefully put her foot on the step. When it held her weight, she gingerly continued, cringing with each creak. Though the second floor was lined with rooms overlooking the foyer, the bird only had eyes for one particularly damaged door.

Now standing in front of the cobweb-covered door, Rory took a deep breath, wondering what she would find when she stepped inside. She pushed it open with just the tips of her fingers.

Upon seeing a nursery with skeletons and dried blood splatter, she immediately slammed her eyes shut. She turned and ran back down the stairs and stopped at the front door. She leaned over, hands on her knees, to steady her breath.

Decayed skeletons were not part of her reality.

The bird flew over the balcony straight down at her. The light of the candles lit its red feathers, making it appear as if it were on fire and diving in to attack. Rory raised her hands to protect her face.

Instead of attacking her, the bird landed softly in front of her and pecked gently at her boots. Rory backed up against the front door when the bird surprised her even more by rubbing its cheek against her black and red costume tights.

Her heart softened, the fear melting right off her like ice cream in the summer sun. She would go check out the room again and see why the bird had led her here.

As if on cue, the bird flew back into the nursery. Rory trudged up the steps, pausing just outside the room. *You can do this.* She took a deep breath, pushed open the door, and stepped inside.

The full moon shining through two long windows cast an eerie glow across the horrific scene. The bloodied stuffed animals. The broken rocking chair in the corner. A skeleton in a faded dress lay between two cribs covered in dust and crusted blood splatter. And yet another skeleton was against the far wall in once-white robes. A mouse nibbled at a red rope around its waist.

Any smell of rotting flesh had long since faded. What was left was a mix of mildew and mouse droppings.

She bent to inspect a long cut across the discolored dress, decayed atop the yellowed-skeleton. The cloth fell to dust under her fingers. There had been a fight in here. A mouse crawled out from under the skeleton. She shrieked and scrambled to her feet.

Her heart racing, she was overcome with a feeling of knowing. Her instincts were telling her it was something far too awful to allow into her mind.

Rory pulled at one of the rubber bands on her wrist so hard it snapped. She winced at the sudden sting.

The bird perched atop a rocking chair in the back corner. It cocked its head, looking at her curiously. Unwanted thoughts of a mother rocking her baby in that chair filled her mind.

Rory picked up the faded green leather book off the chair and blew the dust off, careful to blow away from the bird. On the book was the same three-star emblem from the back of her locket. *Too weird.*

If the book was her mother's, then was that her mother on the ground between the cribs? An overwhelming feeling of lost hope overcame her.

She tried to open the book, but the metal clasp would not budge—it was locked. She stuffed it in her shoulder bag.

Exasperated, Rory was about to leave the awful nursery, when a crash of thunder boomed. She shrieked, almost jumping out of her skin. She was lucky it was glued to her body, or she might have actually left her body in that moment.

Lightning flashed outside, filling the room with an eerie white light. It illuminated something she hadn't noticed before. Two faded words engraved on the cribs: Peter and Rory.

She had to get out of here. She could barely breathe. This was the place they had found her and her brother thirteen years ago. But why had they just left her mother's body there?

She had to do something. Had to tell the authorities. Her mother deserved a proper burial. And Rory wanted to know who had killed her.

A soft pitter-patter on the roof told her it was raining outside.

Thud.

All her senses heightened at the loud noise from below. Her heart pounded louder. The dark corners seemed to hide even more secrets.

Was someone inside the house? She held her breath and listened intently. Had her father found a way in? She ducked behind the back crib, which held the second skeleton. A thin rapier-like sword lay beside it.

Thud.

The bird flew around her and out of the room. *Great, just when I need it, the bird leaves me.* "Come back," she whispered. "Please."

The bird squawked, urging her to follow it.

Thud.

This was not good.

Rory crouched and looked out the doorway. She didn't see anyone. She half expected to spy a ghost ambling towards her.

She crept down the stairs without running into anyone . . . or any *thing.*

At the bottom of the stairs, Rory looked around in the candlelight. The bird cocked its head to the half-sized door beside the stairs. It seemed the book and that awful room were just part of this Zamsara bird's intentions. What other awful things did it have to show her?

Rory glanced at the wide front door. Maybe she could jump on the bird again, fly past her father and get Miss Kuma to help.

Lightning filled the great entry hall again, instantly making up her mind for her. She would explore whatever was under these stairs. Perhaps the bird was leading her to a secret way out.

The bird flew ahead of her, lighting the tight spiral staircase as it flew. As Rory descended the stone steps, the steady thuds grew louder and louder.

The moment she stepped into the damp basement, the scent of mildew overwhelmed her senses. She got a better view of the long room once the bird lit the candles lining the stone walls.

The culprit of the awful racket was a simple bucket! Water was dripping into a metal bucket.

She let out a nervous laugh. She had been scared by a drip. It was like a new version of Chinese water torture.

She sighed, her breath coming back to her in gasps. She was okay. No one was here. She was still alone, besides the bird, which was both lonely and comforting at the same time. She wished Sun-hi were here.

Rory looked around, trying to figure out why the bird had led her to this grimy place. The room stretched the length of the house and had two tunnels leading in opposite directions. A way out!

No one had been here for ages. A punching bag lay on the floor, covered in thick mold. Beside it stood a table, broken in half.

Weapons lined one wall of the room: spears, axes, staves, spiked ball and chains, and various sizes of swords. She wondered if they belonged to her mother or father. She knew that her father had a violent side, but what kind of person was her mother to have so many deadly weapons in their house?

The bird flew straight to a small pipe organ in the corner, by the tunnel. The dozen vertical pipes sticking out of the console were painted green with hundreds of symbols she didn't recognize. They almost seemed to move when she looked at them out of the corner of her eye. *So cool.*

The bird nodded her over from the oak bench, its long red and gold tail feathers hanging over the edge. It felt good to sit, even if it made her costume filthy.

Her old piano teacher was also a pipe organist at a church. He always said playing one was like having an orchestra at his fingertips. The Gallaghers had signed her up for piano lessons on their rampage to get her to try new things other than Tae Kwon Do.

Lightning flashed, filling the room with an eerie glow. The storm raged on outside.

The bird looked up at her expectantly. Rory looked around mischievously. She kind of wanted to play it while she had the chance.

The bird nodded to notes painted on the music stand. *They must have really loved that piece.*

Rory pressed a large 'on' button, and the organ hummed to life. A few wooden stops, which made the organ play different sounds, automatically pulled themselves out. *Weird.*

Her right fingers pressed the keys to *Twinkle Twinkle Little Star* on the top keyboard. A sweet flute sound mixed with round bass poured out of the pipes. The melody seemed a little too cheerful for the moment, but it was the only piece she'd learned.

In spite of herself, she smiled.

Halfway through the song, the pipe organ started playing on its own. She pulled her hands off the keys. The notes painted on the stand lit up as different keys on both keyboards played.

A humming melody emanated from the console. The tune repeated, pulling all the stops. A large, bombastic sound emanated from the pipes. The keys compressed up and down feverishly, like a master musician was at the console. Rory covered her ears, the sound vibrating her core.

"Make it stop," Rory called to the bird.

The entire organ glowed a bright white, the jumbled symbols dancing wildly across the pipes. A spiraling darkness appeared in the air beside her and the bird slipped into it.

Before Rory could think of anything else, she found herself being sucked through the black space and into the unknown.

CHAPTER
— 8 —

PETER THE ADVENTURER

The sound of silence. So sweet. Peter stretched out in the middle of a warm cloud of down blankets.

The events of the night before came rushing back, and he pulled the comforter up to his chin and curled up. All nuzzled in—Peter felt this is what it must be like to be tucked in by a loving mother.

He loved the soft blue nightshirt his father had given him the night before. On top of it, he found himself in a luxurious bedroom that was four times larger than his cramped attic room. Even the thick coating of dust on the wooden furniture and the spider webs in the corners couldn't dampen his mood.

Beautiful lilies painted on the ceiling were now chipped, and the soothing teal paint was faded and dull. The best part was the slender bookcase beside his bed.

He was in a new place—with a new life!

After his father returned Talbert to Earth, Peter would never have to dig for ancient treasures or see Talbert's whip ever again.

Exuberance taking over, Peter kicked off the covers. He stood to get off the four-poster bed and found the mattress springy. He attempted a jump and rose a few inches. He tested the springs again and bounced even higher.

I'm freeeeeeee!

It was only when his stomach grumbled that he stopped, and jumped off the bed.

In fun, Peter opened the armoire, put on one of the brown leather vests, and a big leather belt. He danced around the room with a brown cloak that was much too big. He poked the dying fireplace, pulled books off the shelf—before promptly putting them neatly back—and threw the floor-to-ceiling curtains open.

White sunlight filled the room. Except for Rory, he had everything he needed to start a new life.

Seeing his backpack on the small desk, he raced over to inspect its contents. Relief washed over him. *All there.* He would be able to ask his father about the contents of his memory box soon, but now was time for food.

Beside his backpack sat a silver platter. He lifted the lid and a thin golden light ran along the bottom, as if he were breaking a seal.

The steaming plate of food smelled scrumptious. He dug into a bowl of star-shaped grains mixed with red and blue berries. A sweet cream-filled apricot pastry and sausage finished the meal. The food was more delicious than anything he'd ever had. Sure, Talbert fed them, but only well enough to keep the school from noticing anything was wrong. And Melina's food was always boring and bland.

Feeling full, Peter realized it was the first night in a month he hadn't had that eerie dream. So where was the bird that had started all this?

Peter stood contemplating what he should do next as he sipped the last of his sweet drink. The reddish-brown liquid tasted like a cross between sweet coffee and cinnamon.

He opened the top desk drawer to find a neatly organized, albeit dusty, set of writing supplies: Blank scrolls, a ball of string, a dried ink bottle, calligraphy pens, black wax, and a seal. He turned the heavy stamp over. Fancy DVB letters were imprinted above two intertwined dragons.

It wouldn't hurt anything if he tried to make a stamp, right? Peter pulled out one of the scrolls, which read, *Orders from the desk of Lord Disangelo Van Brutus*, at the top in a calligraphy script. Guess this was his room—so what had happened to him?

Drat. He didn't have a way to melt the wax. He'd have to find something else to do. His father had explicitly told Peter he was not allowed to leave his room. But how could he stay cooped up in this one room, no matter how large it was, when he had a whole new world to explore?

Peter opened the oversized door a crack. No one outside. He would just look around the halls surrounding his room—a little exploration couldn't hurt, right? He had so many questions to ask, and all his father could say last night was 'no time,' and 'in the morning,' and, 'stay in your room.'

Peter had only gone several feet when he heard footsteps. Afraid it was his father, Peter raced back inside. He leapt onto the ornate wooden chair as if he were just finishing up his breakfast.

The door opened.

His father stepped inside. Even without his pinstripe suit, his father still dressed sharply in a fitted black jacket that went down to his ankles.

Peter smiled, trying to hide the fact that he was out of breath.

"Good morning, son."

"You got rid of him, right?"

"Who?"

"Talbert—you took him back to Earth?"

"Of course—first thing this morning after I felt recharged. You have nothing to worry about." It was surprising how much better his father looked after only one night. Color had returned to his cheeks, and he looked refreshed with energy. That must have been some potent medicine he'd had.

Peter rose out of his chair to hug his father. "Thank you."

His father patted him on the back. "You have nothing to fear. You really should work on that—fear is a weakness. And I won't have my son being weak."

Peter stepped back and nodded, "Yes, sir."

His father raised his eyebrows and looked him up and down. "What's this strange outfit you're wearing?"

Peter looked down sheepishly. "Nothing. Just playing. I'm sorry."

His father chuckled. "Why don't you put Disangelo's old things back."

Peter ran to the armoire and hung up the leather clothes. Those were fun, but he wanted a sharp outfit like his father's. The silver symbols that lined his hood and wrists appeared magical.

"Now, I have some things to take care of today, so I borrowed a beginning magic book for you from the library," his father said.

"There's a library here?"

"Of course. We have to keep all our books and historical documents somewhere," his father said, placing the book on the desk. "You really should learn to make your bed in the morning. Good habits create a good life."

Not wanting to get punished, Peter raced to his bed and pulled the covers over the pillows.

"Nice and quick. I bet you'll have no problem reading the first few chapters of this book by tomorrow."

"I love to read." Peter flipped open the book, *Magicology* by Grandmaster Adhara Telos. It was a beautiful, blue leather-bound book with worn metal engravings bordering the cover.

"Now, do not leave this room. I'll come check on you later."

His father seemed surprised when Peter wrapped his arms around him before he could leave. "Please let me come with you."

"I'm going somewhere dangerous. It's not safe yet. Once you've studied more, then maybe."

Peter swore to himself he would study so hard his father would be forced to take him along. "Okay."

"Why don't you get dressed with the clothes I brought you—it's unsightly to stay in your pajamas all day," his father said before leaving.

The clothes were laid out on an old-fashioned armchair facing the window. It had carved arms and luxurious fabric. It looked like someone had spent many hours looking out over the garden. Peter slipped on the black pants and green pullover shirt, which were surprisingly warm.

Why should he read at the desk like he used to, when he had a comfortable bed to study on? He grabbed *Magicology* and jumped on the bed, making a mess of the covers. He'd show his father how smart he was and finish the whole book.

Peter settled down under his comforters, cozy with *Magicology* in his lap. He flipped to the first page and enjoyed reading the introductions until he got to one passage. He reread the line—spells required a channeling device, whether that be the standard wand or staff, or other magic imbued items, such as a sword or gauntlets.

Peter looked up from the text. He didn't have any of those items. He'd have to ask his father for one. The book was broken up into sections by level: Beginner, Novice, Apprentice, Adept, Expert, Master, and Grandmaster. Though it said most never reached the level of Grandmaster even if they studied their entire life.

By lunch he'd finished the book. He didn't completely understand it, but at least he'd read the material.

He got up to stretch just as an albino servant entered with his lunch. Ignoring all of Peter's attempts at communication, the boy silently placed a tray on his desk and left. After eating a delicious lunch of root soup, hot bread, and chocolate cream pie, Peter decided to look around.

The bookshelf immediately caught his eye—maybe there'd be something good there. The hardback books were covered in such a thick layer of dust, it looked like no one had read them in several years.

His hopes fell when he realized most of the books were on war and fighting strategy. There were even two copies of: *Strategies of War*, by Disangelo Van Brutus. The two non-fighting books were: *My Life with Levicus*, by Lady Adara, which was signed, and the *Fall of the Shadow Titans*, by Blane Skorpin. The last one seemed interesting enough, and he pulled it off the shelf.

After finishing the small book about how the Shadow Titans wrecked havoc on the lands before Levicus locked them away, he craved a new adventure. He'd just go to the library, grab some more interesting books, and come back.

Luckily, he remembered passing the library on his way up to his room. The castle had surprisingly good signage.

Peter paused in the entryway, staring at the old, dark room. When the blonde librarian gave him a curious expression, Peter stepped inside like he knew what he was doing.

He ignored the people studying at the tables in the lower area and went straight for the rows of tall bookshelves with ladders attached. In the corner he found a separate room with what appeared to be the oldest books in the library. Everything was lit by hanging orbs of glowing light—must have been magic so torches wouldn't accidentally burn it down.

He was about to step into this room, when he felt a tingling sensation. It felt like the bird's presence, but when he turned around it wasn't there. The feeling led him towards the middle row. He followed the strange sensation until he felt compelled to reach out to one of the books.

That was weird. He flipped over the thin book in his hands. *My First Zenmage Spells* by Quidner Asdorn.

After checking out the little book and a couple more to hide what he'd found in case it got him in trouble, Peter found several more neat places: a bathhouse, the throne room, a chapel, and a large training arena—but no sign of his father.

When he got back to his room, he leaned against the door, relieved he hadn't been caught. He read in the chair overlooking the window until it was dark.

He heard loud music and shouting coming from outside. He tiptoed across the hallway to the stone railing that overlooked the castle's main courtyard.

Below, under the light of Inara's dual moons, people were throwing square cards into a massive bonfire. He heard something about Festival of the Dead. It was quite solemn, and he felt he was intruding by watching, but he stood transfixed by the fire. The heat. The way it danced.

A warmth filled Peter's chest. He wasn't sure what home felt like, but figured this must be it. Was it possible he'd never felt at home at Talbert's—not just because of how awful the judge was, but because Peter was really an alien?

Peter wanted to join the festivities, but didn't want to get in trouble. There was so much going on: People huddled together in quiet contemplation, musicians playing their instruments, sending soaring tunes both melancholy and uplifting into the air, and merchants selling various goods out of their caravans.

To top it off, a real live king sat on a throne at the top of the steps overlooking the courtyard. He wore elegant black velvet robes with gold trim.

He couldn't believe it. This was like a story out of one of his favorite books. He dared not hope the castle would come with knights and best of all—dragons.

After watching for hours, Peter's eyelids drooped, and he feared falling asleep in the hallway and getting caught. Looking up at the unfamiliar stars, he made a wish. "I hope my father hasn't brought me all this way just to abandon me."

Except for the different sky, Peter was surprised how much Inara was like Earth—if he hadn't known otherwise, he would've thought he was in a castle in England.

He crawled into bed hoping his father would visit with news of his sister in the morning.

✳   ✳   ✳

Peter was reading on his bed when his father stepped in the room—without knocking first.

Quickly, Peter draped the comforter over the books he wasn't supposed to have. But he stood too quick, and catching his foot in the comforter, pulled the books off the bed. Peter cringed with each thud as they tumbled to the ground.

His father approached him, using his pointy staff as if it were a walking stick. He picked up one book at a time before slowly turning each over, studying the spines.

Peter stood still, his hand clasped behind his back.

"Curious. I thought I brought you one book, and yet you have three on your bed, which I know aren't from this room," his father said. "Now tell me—you left your room, didn't you?"

Seven years with Talbert had taught Peter to remain silent. He clamped his mouth shut.

His father raised his voice, "Now be honest with me—you went to the library."

Peter shook his head. *Don't say a word.*

"What are you, mute?"

"I'm sorry." Peter sank to the floor, and mumbled, "I finished the book and wanted something else to read."

His father lifted an eyebrow and glanced around, as if not sure what to make of him. "Are you lying to me? I won't have my son be a liar."

"No, no, it's true. I've always read quickly."

"Look, I want you to stay in your room. It's a very important day for me. I don't have time to spend it worrying about you." His father dropped the book he'd brought on Peter's pile. "I guess I didn't need to spend time getting you this then."

Peter remained silent, afraid to say anything that might earn him a real punishment.

"I'll come back later for our first magic lesson. Now I want you to stay in your room and study all the spells in the first chapter."

Peter sighed as he watched his father walk down the corridor. Rereading books wasn't fun because he remembered everything he read. He saw the pages in his mind like images.

Looking down at *Magicology*, Peter wished he had a wand to try out some of the spells. Maybe he could find one in this room.

He looked through the desk again and found nothing new. In the armoire, he found several brown leather garments and pieces of armor, a few broadswords, and a heavy cloak. Peter pulled out a box of toys, but no wands.

He picked up a small rubbery ball from the box, then looked around, feeling silly for what he was about to do. He dropped the ball and it bounced more than he expected on the carpet. He tried to catch it when it came in the air, but missed.

He knocked it under the bed. Lunging under it, he coughed from all the dust. Instead of the ball, his hands clasped around a wooden box.

Ignoring the toy, Peter pulled the box out. The dust was so thick that even after he blew the dust off, the patterned carving was still coated with a thick layer of grime. He sneezed. Sitting on the floor beside the bed, he opened the box.

Inside was a wand with two slender Eastern dragons curling up its intertwining dual-wood base. Wow. It was so beautiful—why had someone hidden it away? The inside of the lid was engraved, *Happy thirteenth, my sweet boy–Love Mom.*

This 'sweet boy' was his same age. With all the fighting literature, Peter didn't think he had turned out so sweet.

A little card was tucked into the corner, and he unfolded it. "I had this specially made from the juniper tree you like to sit under. The wandmaker said it would accentuate your gift. Your father doesn't know—it will be our little secret."

Peter fingered the spiraling cinnamon brown Juniper wood with the fine-grained Maple—such good craftsmanship.

After sliding the box under the bed, he carried the wand back to his desk and opened *Magicology*. If he learned the first spell, he could make his father proud. He would choose a simple spell—one that couldn't turn into accidental destruction like at Talbert's house.

The beginner level spells were all from the realm of earth-based magic. So first he'd learn how to do transformational, moving, and household spells. A footnote said he could do the dark spells that were frowned upon when he reached Expert level—but it would be decades before he could get there.

The first spell moved an object. It did *not* move living creatures—that was dark magic.

Carefully, Peter balanced the wand in his hand like the book had described, readjusting a few times to get it right. He cradled the base gently in his two center fingers with his pointer finger outstretched on the wand. He adjusted his thumb so it would have a solid connection to the wand. Apparently most of his power was channeled through his thumb and forefinger. It was so awkward, he thought he must be holding it wrong.

Gripping it a little tighter, he swished it in a neat up and down motion, like a conductor. Feeling he'd practiced enough, Peter said the spell for moving the book across the desk, "*Ma'Lazuz.*"

It didn't move. He recalled what the book said, "You have to trust in yourself in order to properly tap into the magical energies of Inara."

He sighed. The second time, his spell gave the book a little shake.

He would just have to keep trying. He imagined where he wanted the closed book to go and swished his wand down. The book flew across the desk and smashed through the window.

Oops.

Peter ran to the window, stepping on the broken shards of glass in his brown leather shoes. *Magicology* had fallen on a rose bush in the garden below.

He was *so* in trouble.

CHAPTER

— 9 —

RORY LOSES HER CAPE

Rory held her eyes tightly closed. No light seeped in. Her body moved swiftly, air rushing around her. She had to be floating—nothing was touching her. There was an absence of any kind of scent, but it was stifling to breathe, like thin air at the top of a mountain.

Her heart raced to match the speed of her flight. What would she see if she opened her eyes? The ground hundreds of feet below? She had to peek, had to figure out where this invisible force was taking her.

When she forced her eyelids open, it felt like she hadn't really opened them at all. Darkness surrounded her. Little flecks of light shot past her on all sides. Everything moved so fast, she couldn't catch her bearings. It appeared she was in a tunnel in space, but how could that be?

Rory scrambled to hold onto something, anything. But there was nothing. The feeling of moving at the speed of light and in slow motion all at the same time made her nauseous.

And where was the bird?

Suddenly, a dark energy clutched at her chest. All sense of safety dissipated.

"Why hello little one," a deep, raspy voice said. "I see you've come to let me out."

She squinted, trying to see who, or what, had spoken. A deep fear, like one she'd never felt before, took hold.

"You won't see me." The voice sounded as if it hadn't had water in ages. "I have no body in here. But you do. You have exactly what I need."

Her mind raced. What in the world was she supposed to say to that? She had to get out of here, away from this creature. *Please, please,* she silently pleaded.

"I see I was right all along." The creature coughed violently.

Rory looked up to see a solid black figure. It was like someone had cut out a human shape from the stars, and left behind only blackness.

The creature moved slowly, inching towards her as if treading through rolling waves. Rory willed herself to move faster. "Go away!" she screamed.

It had no effect.

Rory writhed, willing herself to escape this void. The creature was so close, she could feel its stale breath.

"Help!" she screamed, but only the creature could hear.

It crawled on her back, pressing itself against her cape and wrapping its dark hold around her neck.

Rory gagged at the pressure against her throat.

No.

She would not give in. She didn't want to die in here. She closed her eyes, thinking of her self-defense lessons. She brought her hand up and hung her weight across the creature's arm. It felt of cold nothingness. She brought her other arm straight up and twisted in a circle. There was no ground to take the creature down to, so she kept circling her arms, like a crazy arm tornado.

The creature broke off—just long enough for the space tunnel to pull her farther away. A black circle appeared at the end of the star tunnel. Was she being sucked into a black hole?

It rushed back at her and latched on to her cape with a tight grip. Somehow it could move freely in this void, where she couldn't.

Rory struggled to untie her cape.

Out of nowhere, a new energy surrounded her—a warmth like the heat of the summer sun.

It scared the creature off.

The warmth was immediately replaced by a jolt of electricity that coursed up her spine. She felt a connection—to what she did not know—but she felt solid and whole for the briefest of moments.

When the energy dissipated, the black cut-out creature returned. Rory writhed every inch of her body with the new power she felt coursing through her veins.

She could just barely reach the circle devoid of light. It was only an arm-span away.

The creature clasped her red cape. It choked her, pulling her back violently. She pulled the loop around her neck to open her airway.

Her fingers clasped the red bow string of her cape, and tugged hard. As if suctioned away, the creature flew back with the cape in hand.

The warm energy returned. The creature clamored back. It seemed to be held in check by the warm energy.

The creature reached for her neck.

Rory touched the empty space at the end of the tunnel. It sucked her through.

She fell onto a bed, immediately jumping to her feet, fists raised. But no one was in sight.

She ran her hands over her chest and arms, as if to wash the creature off. She couldn't sense its dark presence anymore.

What? She'd been sucked through a space tunnel just to enter someone's bedroom? It looked like a normal rustic room with a wooden dresser, rocking chair, slender bookcase, bassinet, and a full-body oval mirror. But it had no windows.

Through the open double-doorway she could see the front door. It was so close—just on the other side of the living room.

The moment she jumped off the bed, two inhuman guards materialized. They thrust their pointed spears at her. Rory stepped backwards. Okay, so she couldn't go that way.

On second look, there was something odd about them— she could see slightly through their blue forms, like looking through water. They appeared to be made of hundreds of tiny symbols, all moving. It was like the dancing symbols on the pipe organ—magic.

But why were they attacking her, and how was she going to get past them when she didn't even have a weapon? She investigated the room for something useful, but no use. She had to run. A small door across from the bed was her way out.

Rory walked backwards towards the door, hands raised in a protective, yet open gesture. She took a breath and flung open the door.

Her heart sank. It was just a tiny bathroom with no window. Not a way out. Standing outside the bathroom, she could make out the kitchen at the end of the cottage, and see out the large bay window to the country beyond. The evergreen trees off in the distance swayed in the wind.

How was she going to get out of this strangely rustic cottage and find a way back? She went around the room, banging on the log walls, looking for any kind of weakness. It was useless. The walls were thick, solid. A framed photograph fell to the floor, glass shattering.

She picked it up, and blew off the dust to reveal a portrait of a couple holding two infants. Rory gasped. It was the same woman as the picture in her locket—her mother. But what was this doing here? And who was the man in the photo with his arm around her mother? He was a muscular man, not like the slender person who'd come to her house.

She dragged herself back on the bed. Had she escaped her father only to be trapped again? And where was that Zamsara bird? Did it really lead her all this way just to abandon her?

She hated to admit she needed help. Master Kuma—she'd know what to do. Rory pulled her phone out of her bag and brought up her Tae Kwon Do teacher's contact. Miss Kuma's kind expression, with her rich brown skin and proud expression stared back at her. It was Rory's favorite picture— Miss Kuma had her arm around Rory's shoulder, just after she'd earned the right to test for her black belt.

But as Rory pressed the call icon, an error message popped up, '*No Service.*' Rory tried all her tricks to get it to work— including restarting it. Nothing. She stuffed it in her bag, feeling so alone.

"Hello? Is anyone out there?"

The only sound was the creaking of the cottage, and the wind swirling around it.

As she stared past the guards an idea struck her. If she could sneak past them, she could sprint for the front door. There was just enough space on the right side of the guards, she might be able to slip through.

With the tip of her duct-tape boot, Rory pretended to inspect the lines of a painted symbol spilling out from under the carpet, then bolted towards the open space.

Whack!

A strong force repelled her. She fell on her butt. A bizarre tingling sensation ran up her arm where she'd hit the invisible field.

The guards angled their spears down to attack, but snickered at her instead.

She touched the space in the wide doorframe behind the guards, and struck something that felt like hot Jell-O. A prickling sensation ran up her arm. She poked again. And again in another spot in the air. There was some sort of invisible wall behind the guards.

The two guards aimed their spears at her.

Rory leapt to the side and kicked the first guard's knee. She was surprised to find it solid. It lost its balance only slightly, then whipped around.

Rory clambered onto the bed and kicked both her feet. The guard stumbled back into the barrier. A fizzle rippled through the substance like electricity. Quickly righting itself, both guards lunged at Rory.

The spears stopped inches from her throat. Rory was pressed up against the bed with nowhere to go. If she moved to get on the bed, they could spear her. If she ducked, they'd spear her instantly.

The front door opened and an old couple entered. The woman dropped her basket of squash.

In unison, the old couple both planted their left feet forward, and made a large circle with their left wrists, stopping sharply with their palms facing the guards. "Stop!" A power resonated from their combined voices.

Instantly, the guards pulled back to attention.

Rory didn't breathe until she'd slid across the bed and ducked behind it.

"Stand down," they ordered.

The two guards resumed their post at the barrier, spears held out in front of them.

Although the old couple had just controlled the magical guards, they didn't appear to be dangerous—they looked like plain farmers. The man was dressed in brown slacks and a grey tunic, with a wide leather belt around his muscular waist. The woman wore a long peach-colored dress with a flowery apron. They looked as if they might have been strong warriors in their youth, but now their faces were wrinkly and spotted.

"That was close." The tall old woman slammed the door shut behind her.

Burt nodded. "Somethin' isn't right."

Rory held her shaking hands. No matter what, she wouldn't let them know she was afraid.

"Do you think they finally made it home, Burt?" the woman said in a gravelly voice. "Or has—" She gulped. "*He* broken through?"

"Couldn't tell ya, Maggie," Burt replied. "We gonna' have to test her and anyone else that might have escaped through the portal."

Rory half expected the bird to peek around from behind the man's knee-length boots. But no.

Burt pressed his palm on a wooden panel behind the front door. A hidden cabinet flipped around, revealing a weapon rack. He pulled out a spear, threw it to Maggie who easily caught it, and pulled off a sword for himself.

The couple approached the edge of the enclosure. "Who goes there?" Burt cried out in a scruffy voice. "If it is you,

Levicus, you shall never escape. The room has been heavily fortified by all twelve Zenmages."

A what? Rory's father had mentioned that word.

Leaning against the bed, she called upon her courage. If she kept hiding, she'd never get out of this room. She stood quickly. "Obviously, I'm just a girl, not this *levi-something*."

"Declare yourself then—and anyone else who's with you." Maggie poked her spear forward. It couldn't penetrate the invisible barrier.

Not sure what they meant, she offered her name. "It's only me—Rory Collins. Let me go!" She held her fists tightly at her sides to stop the shaking. Suddenly, the invisible field flashed a bright red color.

"You're lying girl," Burt accused. "Tell the truth."

"How could I be lying? That's my name." Then she remembered. That was the family name the hospital had given her. She didn't know her biological name. "Um, Rory Gallagher?"

"What game are you playing at girl, offering us two names?" Burt said. "What are you?"

"I don't know what you want me to tell you, I was abandoned." Rory said. "Be fair—who are you? And why are you keeping me in here?"

"You won't trick us that easily," Burt said.

"Why's there only one?" Maggie whispered to Burt, "We'll get in trouble."

One of what? "What are you talking about? Where am I?"

Maggie grabbed Burt's arm. "You know, I think it's really Rory. Her magical force wasn't strong enough to be Levicus."

"Don't be fooled," Burt said. "The barrier is doing its job—it's supposed to hide the magical energy tracings of the teleport location behind it." Even so, Burt stepped close, studying Rory closely. "I don't know—it could be Levicus doing his shapeshifting trick."

Maggie shook her head. "No. Levicus has never met her in this form, so he couldn't shift into this shape. He'd have to shift into an infant."

Burt stroked his square chin.

"My dear, can't you see?" Maggie said, a wide smile forming. "She looks like a miniature Katrine—she has the same soft features and mischievous blue eyes."

Katrine. So that's what her mother's name was. "How do you know my mother?"

They ignored her.

Burt's face lit up. "You're right!" Suddenly, Burt had a slew of questions. "Where's Peter? Did Asdorn's pipe organ in the house work? Why did you come home now? Let's get you out of there."

Rory stared, stunned.

Maggie grabbed Burt's arm. "No, I think we should keep her in there till T. Veckler arrives. She looks like she'll run off. Keeping her in the room is better than tying her to a chair out here."

Burt sighed. "You're right, my love."

"We better send T. Veckler an Xpress letter right away," Maggie said. "He'll be so excited she's returned."

"T. Veckler excited? Have you met him?" Burt said.

Maggie chuckled. "Yeah, you're right."

The old couple turned away from the barrier.

"Wait! Why are you keeping me here?" Rory climbed across the bed, stepping carefully in front of the guards. They eyed her suspiciously, but made no move. "Let me out!"

Maggie faced Rory and clasped her hands in front of her face. "I'm overjoyed you've come home. We've spent the last thirteen years guarding this location, and waiting for your return. Will Peter be coming too?"

Startled, all Rory could do was shake her head.

"I can tell you're a runner—just like I was when I was a young girl. I'm going to have to keep you in there until someone from the resistance arrives tomorrow," Maggie said. "He'll take you somewhere safe."

"I'm ready to send the Xpress," Burt said. He stood at a narrow desk under a square contraption on the wall beside the front door. It was made out of sparkling, black material. Burt pulled a small wooden tablet from a slot on the side, and leaned over the desk to inscribe a message on it.

"You know what?" Maggie said with glee. "I'm going to make you a special dinner with squash and greens I just pulled from my garden. Maybe even a sweet pie."

Rory salivated, thinking of how hungry she was.

"What if we escorted Rory to Turopia ourselves?" Maggie twisted her hands together. "Could you imagine the honor we'd receive?"

"You know we can't do that—it is our duty to protect this location." Burt added in a kinder tone. "We can't be too careful or times could go back to the way they used to be. And I know ya' don't want that, Maggie."

"You are right, my love, but why did you have to call *him*." Maggie shuddered, grey hair falling into her kind face. "That man creeps me out."

"We both know he's not like that anymore. And we aren't either. We have to trust him. Besides, those were our instructions since Darius disappeared."

Burt dropped the tablet into the slot. It popped back up a few seconds later, completely void of any message.

"Now we wait." Burt took Maggie's wrinkly hand and the couple walked out of sight.

Whatever they were guarding—it couldn't be that important if they stationed an elderly couple here. "I just want to go home. Tell me where my brother is!"

A few minutes later, pots clanging told Rory they were making dinner.

Rory took a step forward. "Wait. Please—" The two half-visible guards angled their spears towards her. She held up her arms in surrender. "Fine."

Even if the old couple was excited to see her, she was still trapped. She'd have to get this T. Veckler person to take her home, and convince him this was just some big mistake.

Rory plopped on the quilted bed. Out of habit, she picked up her cell phone. Still no signal. The adrenaline rush gone, she found herself longing to be home. Not the home she'd had with the Gallagher's for the last six months, but the one she'd built for herself at Red Bear Tae Kwon Do. Master Kuma was right—she had to make her own life—and for the first time in awhile she felt a longing to do just that.

Rory sat up with her back against the headboard, arms around her knees. All the emotion she'd held back all night through the escape came flooding in. It was like she was plunging over Niagara Falls without a barrel. Nothing to hold onto. Absolutely nothing. She cried uncontrollably, in a way that left her aching.

CHAPTER
— 10 —

PETER'S FIRST MISTAKE

P eter looked around the corner to make sure his father didn't catch him outside of his room. A few court ladies, clothed in fine Renaissance dresses, giggled as they walked down the wide corridor. He tiptoed behind them on his way to the side courtyard. He just had to get *Magicology* and make it back to his room before his father noticed him gone.

Peter slunk around the large stone archway into the garden. A couple walked arm in arm through the roses that lined the middle of the garden. Luckily it was a big space—he might not be seen.

He looked up, seeing the broken window, and followed the trail of glass to a smashed rose bush. The book lay on the grass below the red roses. When the couple turned to the back of the garden, Peter raced and grabbed the book.

Ow! Blood pooled on his thumb.

He cringed as he pulled the glass out. Must have been stuck in the metal grating on the front cover. He shook *Magicology* to make sure no more glass remained.

Three teens walking a black lizard the size of a dog entered the courtyard. They were dressed in beautiful Renaissance-like clothing—the larger red-haired girl in front sported a long green dress with thick borders that flared out at her elbows. Her black and gold cloak made Peter wish he'd brought his own for warmth.

All three wore thick double-wrapped belts holding small swords. They didn't even notice him—something he was quite used to.

The olive-skinned girl turned to her friend with the red braid and said, "Don't be like that, Miss Red—I know you avoid the Festival of the Dead, but I thought you would've gone this time."

"It doesn't matter, Lila," Red said. "Nothing can bring her back. She was such a powerful wizard—I don't know how anyone could've drained all her blood."

"It's so gross." Lila wore a simple pink dress much like Red, but made of rougher material. "We'll surely find someone else to help you with your magic lessons."

Red's round face was covered with twice as many freckles as Rory.

The large black lizard tugged at its leash. Red put her hand softly on the blond-haired boy's arm. "Come on Holdon, let him off his leash already."

The slightly older boy with the black-rimmed glasses leaned down and unhooked the leash from the collar. It waddled straight towards the exotic flowers in the back.

Distracted by their arrival and their strange pet, Peter stood there staring at them before he realized what he was doing.

Holdon, donning a much nicer grey tunic than his own, approached him. "Who are you? I haven't seen you around the castle before."

Peter wasn't sure what to say, so he shrugged.

"What are you doing here?" Red asked, looking down at him. "You don't belong in the royal courtyard."

Peter's mind raced. How was he going to get out of this without getting in trouble? He clutched the book tighter to his chest.

"Perhaps the young one's mute," Lila said, tucking her long black hair behind her ear.

Peter scowled. He wasn't *that* young. Must be the stupid bowl cut Talbert had all the kids wear. Peter made a mental note to make his father get him a haircut—maybe like the short cut the blond boy had.

Holdon sauntered over with the two girls. "What—your parents not teach you how to speak?"

Ignoring was definitely not working like it usually did. Time for a new tactic. "Hi," he croaked out. "I'm Peter. I just moved here. Do you want to be my friend?"

Holden laughed.

"You don't know who I am, do you?" Red grinned at her two friends.

Peter shook his head, feeling stupid from his failed attempt.

"Must be one of the new arrivals," Holdon said, putting his hand on the sword at his waist. "Sanctuary city's too full, and they're sending their refugee garbage here."

Peter's heart dropped. He'd hoped they'd want to be friends, but they obviously didn't have any desire to be his. Peter turned and walked towards the stone archway. He didn't want to be friends with someone so mean anyway.

"I think you're forgetting something," Red said in a teasing voice.

Holden stepped in front of Peter, blocking his path. "And where do you think you're going?"

Peter ignored them. He just wanted them to leave him alone so he could get back to his room before he got into real trouble.

"You should bow to your princess when you enter and leave her presence." Holden grabbed Peter's back and forced him to bend over.

Peter winced—his wounds still sore from his last whipping.

The moment Holden let him loose, Peter bolted through the stone archway. Why had they been so mean? He hadn't done anything to them. Maybe his father was right about not leaving his room. He raced through the castle, hoping his father hadn't found his room empty.

Back in his oversized room, his eyes immediately went to the hole in the window. He pulled the curtains shut, plopped in the chair, and opened *Magicology* just as a knock came at the door.

Peter pretended to read a passage he'd already memorized about animating inanimate objects. The door opened.

His father's eyes widened. "That's my boy, studying away."

Peter pushed away the guilt that he wasn't really studying at all.

"Come here, I have something for you." His father patted the bed beside him.

Peter put the book on the armchair and went to the bed. He couldn't get his mind off those kids. Making friends was so much harder than it looked. His father extended his arm to embrace him. Peter instinctively cringed.

"I'm not going to hurt you." His father cocked his head. "I'm your father, not your cruel old guardian. You're safe here."

Peter sighed and allowed his father to hug him. He pushed the thoughts of Princess Red and Holden to the back of his mind. They were royalty so he wouldn't have to interact with them much anyway.

"I brought a surprise for you," his father held out a silver wand.

The simple, solid metal channeling device was magnificent, but the dragon wand he'd found was far more beautiful. Peter held back the desire to tell his father all about his find. A nagging thought at the back of his mind told him not to tell him about it. What if his father took it, and he ended up needing it for protection? That made him wonder about the previous owner of his wand. "Am I going to get in trouble when the person who lives here comes back?"

"He won't," his father said with a sneer. "He's dead."

His father didn't seem to want to talk about it, so Peter dropped the subject. If he was dead, then why did they keep all his stuff in the room?

"This silver wand is the only wand I have. They can be a little challenging to learn magic with, but I'm sure you can handle it—until we can get one made specifically for you. Let's go to the garden and you can put some of those spells you've been learning into practice."

Peter's eyes widened, but not in excitement. What if those teens were still down there? He wasn't ready to see them again.

His father looked at him, as if to figure him out. "You don't want to learn magic?"

"I do, it's just . . . do we have to go to the courtyard?"

"It's not safe to practice the magic I want to show you inside. You wouldn't want to burn the castle down, now would you?"

Peter shook his head. He had to try another method so he wouldn't let his father down. "I want to, but I have a stomach ache."

"That's not a good enough reason. I'll stop by the healing center and pick you up a draught."

Peter couldn't think of another excuse. He smiled up at his father, who stood. Maybe it would be okay with his father there—they wouldn't make fun of him then. His father looked so formidable in his black and silver outfit with the pointed staff. He must be someone important in this world.

Resigned to make the best of it, Peter grabbed two magic books, and let his father lead him to the side courtyard surrounded by three high castle walls. The ivy-plagued walls gave the large garden a homey feel. He averted his eyes from the damaged rose bush, hoping his father wouldn't notice the broken window. He needed to learn a spell to fix the glass.

"I'll go get that draught. Stay here." His father strode off through the archway laden with spiraling vines.

Peter immediately looked around for any sign of those teens. His heart dropped when he saw them huddled in the back. Luckily, they hadn't seen him yet.

He flipped through the small hand-written book, *My First Zenmage Spells*. It would be fun to try one out. Then he'd be able to impress his father when he returned.

Peter set the book on the grass and read through part of the introduction, and through the first spell.

The book said Zenmages would find themselves primarily drawn to one of the five elements: Air, Water, Fire, Earth— and very rarely, the spirit element. A new Zenmage was supposed to test out the beginner spells of each and see which one they had an inclination towards.

The first one he tried was the air element—manipulating the air to spin around an object.

He rolled the spell over in his mouth to make the foreign words feel more natural. The language felt soft and warm on his tongue. He pointed his silver wand at a row of flowers. "*Chal'Aviyr.*"

Nothing happened.

As he tried the second time, the three teens with their large lizard came to the front of the courtyard. Distracted by their appearance, Peter only managed to create a tiny wisp of air in the grass, like from a sizzling match.

Wanting to get on their good side, Peter gave a quick bow, bending at the waist. He'd never really had to bow before, so wasn't sure how it was supposed to be done.

Red nodded back to him.

Holden laughed at him. "What was that?"

Attempting to ignore them, Peter tried the spell again. It came out a little less smoky, and blew a blade of grass around.

"That was pathetic," Red said. "It doesn't look like you have much magic in your blood."

"That wasn't nice. Leave me alone," Peter said, speaking braver than he felt.

"How dare you speak to the princess that way," Holden said. "Someday she will be your queen."

Peter cowered and looked around, hoping his father would return quickly. He didn't want to run away and have his father find the courtyard empty. Then he'd think his son was a coward.

Using the tip of her leather boot, Red kicked the cover of his book closed. "No wonder you're having trouble—these are spells for Zenmages, of which you are surely not."

Peter's blood boiled. It wasn't his fault he didn't know about the magical ways of this world—he'd only been here a day. But his father had forbidden him from telling anyone he was from Earth.

Why wouldn't they leave him alone? He couldn't best them physically, so he stuck to his ignoring technique. He'd try the spell again, show them he wasn't stupid. A bigger swirl of air spun on the ground.

"Ooo, you can spin a wisp of air," Holdon said, "Look what real wizards can do."

Holdon spun around in a full circle and sharply pointed his wand at Peter. "*Me'albatz Bol'Gadiym.*"

Peters pants dropped down to his ankles and his shirt lifted over his head.

Embarrassed and aching with fury, he shoved his green tunic back down and pulled up his pants. Fear and rage battled for dominance. The panic was winning. Anxiety welled in his belly, making him nauseous. He had to make the fear go away before he vomited.

"Was that really necessary?" Red slipped her arm through Holdon's.

Holdon yanked his arm back. "He has no respect."

Peter's mind raced to think of something to calm him down, when a line from the Zenmage book popped into his head.

Start by being willing to face my fear. He stood up straighter, his face still red.

"Ooo, the baby's angry. What are you going to do, air-us to death?" Holdon laughed and stepped nose-to-nose with Peter.

Peter clenched his fists at his sides and stepped back. Fury was in control. Images of the page showing the starter fire spell, and Talbert's flaming house burned in his mind. Before Peter knew what he was doing, he spoke the words of power and sent it towards the boy.

It was only supposed to be a small wisp of flame, like the dancing circle of air. Just enough to scare him away. Show him he wasn't a weakling. Peter watched in horror as the flames circling Holden's feet spiraled up around the boy like a coiling snake.

Holdon screamed. He danced around to break free, but the fire clung to him.

Red aimed her dagger-wand and shouted several spells. They had no effect.

Peter leapt back. He hadn't read the water section of the Zenmage book yet. What was he supposed to do?

"Make it stop!" Red shouted.

CHAPTER

— 11 —

PETER LEARNS OF THE AYEVEN

Peter's mind raced through the books he'd read. He flicked the wand imagining the fire going away and the flames squeezed tighter around the larger boy. Magic wasn't working. He'd have to try something else.

Remembering what he'd been taught in school about 'Stop, Drop, and Roll,' Peter charged into the fire pillar. He tackled Holdon to the ground and rolled on the grass till the flames disintegrated.

Covered with soot, but not hurt, Holdon coughed and got to his feet. "I'm going to kill you."

Peter stood, dusting the ash and dead grass off his clothes. Holdon pushed him back down. Peter crawled away.

Princess Red loomed over Peter as he stood again. "What are you playing at?"

"I'm s-sorry." Peter looked around for a way out. Perhaps he could outrun them. He hadn't meant to hurt anyone.

Red stared at Peter, a gleam in her hazel eyes. "How did you do that? You *have* to show me."

Peter blinked, not sure what to say. *Definitely* not the response he was expecting.

"Are you serious, Red?" Holdon said, wiping ash off his face with his blackened sleeve. It only served to spread the filth around further.

Red switched to a tone of fury as quick as if she were flicking a switch. "I'm getting my father. He'll know what to do with you."

Okay, *that* was more like what he expected. Peter glared back at her. But inside he couldn't help think that it *worked*. It actually worked. Did that mean he was this Zenmage thing?

Then she added in a lower tone, "And when you're in the dungeon, you can tell me all about how you did that fire magic."

"That's it?" Holdon asked. "I guess I'll have to deal with him myself." He drew his sword.

Peter took a step backwards and tripped over a dip in the grass. From the ground, he looked up at the older boy, the sword pointed over his chest.

Red put her hand on Holdon's shoulder. "Come on, you can't kill him."

"He's a runt," Holdon said, still pointing the sword down. "No one will miss him."

Peter's heart raced. He tried to think of a spell to get out of it, but for all the memorized pages, his mind was a complete blank. He tried to remember the anti-fear quote that had helped earlier, but that was a blank too. "I'm—I-m—" Peter started when a tall figure walked into the courtyard.

"I believe I will miss him," his father said with a scowl. "Any problem with my son is a problem with me."

'Son.' He called me, 'son.' Peter beamed.

"The Researcher," Holdon said, bowing slightly. "I was just—"

"Just leaving," his father finished.

For how bold Holdon was a moment ago, Peter couldn't believe how quick the boy sheathed his sword. Holdon scowled down at Peter. "Don't think you'll get off that easily."

The Researcher turned to watch the three leave with their oversized lizard. Peter picked up the Zenmage book and *Magicology*.

Although Peter wanted to learn more about Zenmages, he was afraid of being in the courtyard when they returned.

"Smells smoky," Father said. He handed Peter the draught.

He was so queasy now, he actually needed it. He drank the minty liquid.

He had to get out of here before Red returned with her father. If she was the princess, that meant her father was the *king*.

"We should go," Peter said, even as relief from the medicine filled his belly.

"What's wrong? I thought you wanted to learn magic."

"I do."

"So?"

Peter decided on a partial truth. "Those mean kids who you scared away—they forced me to do some magic. It didn't go well. They're going to come back. I just want to leave."

"No. You need to learn to have courage and stand up for yourself. Do you see me worrying about being like everybody else? No. Do you think Levicus would have wanted me as his second in-command if I was like everyone else? No. You have skills other boys don't—so stop being a weakling and step into your power."

His father walked over to a perfect circle of grass bordered by a stone path that branched out into four directions.

Peter stayed rooted to his spot. Being himself never worked.

His father turned and looked Peter in the eye for several moments, making him uncomfortable.

"What are you doing over there still?" His father asked. "I see we need to have a talk—this fear issue of yours is turning out to be a problem. You need to learn to control your emotions, or you're never going to be able to control your magic. You understand, don't you?"

Peter nodded, even though he didn't really get it. He'd lived with fear as long as he could remember—could life even be possible without it?

"Come. Knowing magic will help you gain some confidence."

Peter walked over beside his father.

"This is where you will direct all of your spells." The Researcher placed a bronze bowl on the ground before him. "It's a magic deadening device. It contains your magic when you practice."

Peter placed his fingers on the wand, as he'd seen in the book, tapered end forward.

His father adjusted his pinky. "I see you've been studying—that's my boy."

Peter felt pride well within him.

"Now, I'm not fond of wands, but they are the best tool to begin with, before you can graduate to using staves."

"One like yours?"

"Someday, maybe even one as powerful as mine," his father said, spinning his staff around. "Now, you seem to have a knack for fire magic, so instead of starting with the boring moving spell, let's do a true test of your fire magic abilities. If you are willing to play along with my little experiment, I'd like to try the basic fire spell from that Zenmage book I see you borrowed from the library."

"Can I light candles with it like you did before?" Peter asked.

"Yes, with some training and control—though what I used was a regular magic spell, not the elemental Zenmage kind."

Peter smiled. He *did* want to learn that!

"Imagine flame filling the bowl as you point the wand at it and say the word, *Chal'Esh*."

Barely able to handle the idea he was doing proper magic, Peter raised the wand above his head and brought it down as he said, "*Kallesh*."

The bowl spun around, but produced no flame.

"You pronounced it wrong," Father said, making the sound a few times. "Place it in the back of your throat."

Peter sighed and tried again. "*Chal'Esh*." A flame the size of a match lit in the bowl. How come it had been so easy before?

"Did you imagine the flame?"

Peter shook his head. "I forgot."

"The power is in the intention," Father said.

Why couldn't he get it right? He was usually so quick to learn things, it was frustrating to keep failing. Peter pursed his lips, and thinking of a flame, waved his wand again. "*Chal'Esh*."

A small flame appeared in the bowl. He'd done it!

"I wouldn't be so excited if I were you—it's just a small flame. Honestly, I thought you would've learned more from all the books you claim to have read."

Peter scowled. He *had* read them. Adults never believed anything. He considered trying to prove himself by telling his father he memorized everything he read, but he'd never told anyone before.

Before Peter could gather the courage to tell his secret, his father said, "Now, I see from this weak display I need to explain magic. To command Inara's magical energies, you combine your intention with words of power. It will take some time for you to fully comprehend how magic works—with your intention, you are warping reality. Literally changing the structure of the world around you."

Peter tried to pay attention, but he couldn't get it out of his head that Red was going to come back and get him in trouble.

"See, the world is made up of energy particles you can't see—this is what we wizards can control. Watch." His father spun his staff around, which enlarged the bowl as if zooming in on it, making the brass more pixilated.

"Look, I see you're still confused." His father took the bowl in his right hand, and waving his left hand over the bowl changed it into several different shapes: a carved dragon, a locket, a book, a key, a rubber duck, and finally back to the bronze bowl.

"But you didn't use words?" Peter asked.

"Yes, well, once you command greater magical power, your intent becomes so strong, you no longer need to couple your intent with the power words. You will learn that words have great power. Always use your words wisely, even when not in a spell."

Peter's eyes widened. He wished he were that strong right now. "How long until I can do spells without words?"

"For some, never. For most—a lifetime of training. You would do well to reach my level of Grandmaster some day."

"So how long did it take you?"

"My boy, I have been practicing magic so long, my body has become a channeling device. Even so, the spells are more powerful with my staff."

Peter thought this odd, because his father only seemed to be in his thirties.

"Why don't you try again?" His father tapped the bowl. "Keep in mind what I've told you here."

Get it right! Peter closed his eyes and imagined a fire like the one on Judge Talbert's house, and waved the wand again. *"Chal'Esh."*

Flames shot out of the bowl, and grew so large his father jumped back, but not before his eyebrows were singed. He waved his pointed staff and the flame dissipated. "Okay, that was a *bit* much." He tapped his forehead with his staff, and black eyebrows re-grew on his sharp brow.

Peter looked down. He had failed.

"Don't feel bad, son. You did well for your first time— even better than I could have expected." His smile lit up with surprising joy, and he put his arms around Peter's shoulders. "I think in our next lesson, we can experiment with more Zenmage spells. You will study the book, won't you?"

Peter nodded exuberantly. The Researcher was so tall and slender, it made Peter feel small, seeing as his head only came up to the middle of his father's chest.

"We *have* to get your sister here with us."

"Do you know where she is?"

"I'm not sure . . . she seems to have fallen off the radar from my devices. But I know she made it to Inara." His father scowled, obviously aggravated by more than their conversation. "I admit she slipped through my fingers. Our enemies are stronger than I expected. I've sent my people to stop Rory from getting to the dangerous city of Turopia."

All of his years of practicing being silent, and he couldn't help but ask his burning questions. "Where is Turopia? What's so dangerous about it? Why can't you just go get her? Is the trip too expensive? I can work to make money."

"Oh Peter, that is not the problem," his father said. "I got into a bit of a scuffle with their Zenmage some years back and my punishment was banishment. Turopia is a sanctuary city the Zenmages created to protect the disgusting Ayeven and their allies."

"What are Ayeven?"

His father breathed deeply, narrowing his already small eyes. "Despicable creatures. They are the descendants of the Archangels of Earth, from several millennia ago. After all the Ayeven did to bring about the downfall of humans on Earth, they had the nerve to try and re-create their original ways on Inara. With their great magic, it's a pity they choose to use their powers to undermine human society. They are incredibly dangerous. If you see a person with wings, you can only do one thing. Run."

Peter gulped. They sounded scary. "But you're going to stop Rory from falling into the Ayeven's hands?"

"I have my most loyal disciples working on it."

"Will I see many of those Ayeven?"

"With luck, no," his father said thoughtfully. "Levicus has done a great job keeping their numbers in check, so they can't overrun us."

"They sound awful," Peter said.

The Researcher grinned widely, obviously pleased with his quick understanding of adult topics.

"I'll just have to get strong enough to defeat these Ayeven monsters," Peter said.

"I hope you do." His father chuckled. "But it is unlikely, so don't feel bad if you don't."

An idea was forming in Peter's mind. "Hey, if she gets into Turopia, I could go there and bring her home. They won't know I'm related to you, so they'll let me in."

"No!" The Researcher said harshly, and then softened. "You can never go to Turopia. It's dangerous. It's full of Ayeven."

"Oh," Peter said, crestfallen.

"Enough of this. Trust me, I have a plan, and soon we will be reunited, and this will all be over. You don't worry about it—that's adult business." His father put his arm around Peter's shoulders. "Tonight, you will practice drawing the wand and holding it with the correct finger placement one hundred times."

Peter nodded. Sounded boring, but if it would make his father proud, he'd do it. He'd do *two hundred.*

CHAPTER
— 12 —

RORY MEETS A WARRIOR

When Rory awoke, she stretched out like a cat, screeching out the sleep, eyes still closed in the morning light.

What a strange dream—haunted houses, violent fathers, dark creatures in space, and magical cottages with old people who might eat her. *Phew.* She breathed out relief, letting go of the frightening images.

Rory ran her hand along her scratchy comforter. *Scratchy?* What? She sat up straight, eyes wide open. She was in the cottage bedroom. She curled back into herself.

The worst dream she'd ever had was real. She bit her lip, anxiety coursing up her spine. She wasn't used to feeling so much fear—it left her exhausted.

The two guards stood at attention. A plate was at their feet with a sandwich and fruit on it.

Rory took the food and sat along the far wall, so she could look through the living room window. A tree with bright red leaves covered in frost contrasted with the turquoise sky.

She pulled off the chunk of meat and ate only what was left. She'd never liked the idea of eating dead animals. The best part was the fruit that looked like an apple, but tasted like an orange.

Maggie and Burt bustled around the cottage, frantically cleaning the arm chairs, shelves, and rugs. Rory slipped into the bathroom, not wanting to have anything to do with their frenzied cleaning.

She felt grubby. She splashed water on her face, soaking her eye mask. She'd completely forgotten she was still wearing it. She dropped it in the sink and looked at her freckled face in the mirror. She looked dreadfully awful. Her normally bright, blue eyes looked dull and tired. Black streaks ran down her oval face. A string of cobwebs stuck to her dark brown hair.

Gross. She used some dusty toilet paper to pull out the silky strands. She ran her fingers to comb out her hair before repositioning her silver clips on either side of her forehead. She hated having hair in her eyes.

After splashing her face with more cold water, she felt refreshed and ready to face whoever was coming for her.

She caught a glimpse of herself in the full-body mirror. Without the cape, the costume felt empty, not like a superhero at all. She sighed. But if she hadn't had the cape, then she wouldn't have escaped that creature.

Rory needed to focus, to think of a way out. Ignoring the books, she went through all her patterns and kicks. She loved how the movements helped clear her mind and release tension.

That evening, a bell rang throughout the cottage.

Rory froze in the middle of her practice kick. Her heart raced with anticipation. Who had come for her? Would she be able to escape them?

"He's here. He's here!" Maggie called from the other room.

The old woman opened the front door, revealing a middle-aged man with shoulder-length tangled brown hair, and thin stubble. He wore a long, trailing leather coat. Beneath the coat, Rory caught sight of a sword, a whip, and two daggers at his waist. A quiver of arrows and a bow were strapped to his back.

Rory gulped. This man meant business. He was here for *her*? She stood a better chance back at the house with her father. At least *he* had only possessed some freezing magic.

Rory raised her fists. She wouldn't allow him to know she was afraid. First she had to get out of this lonely room—then she would make him take her home.

Maggie and Burt bowed to the warrior.

The tall man nodded respectfully back, keeping his intense blue eyes trained on Rory. *Creepy.* Even Maggie looked apprehensive, and supposedly they were on the same side.

"We called you right away, T. Veckler." Maggie said.

"You did well." T. Veckler lingered in the doorway, inspecting Rory. He seemed to shake his head of his thoughts, and stepped towards the barrier. She felt like he was seeing right through her. At first his glare was harsh and then it softened, like there might be a hidden warmth behind that hardened exterior.

The moment was gone almost before it registered.

"Welcome to Inara," T. Veckler said in a deep, nasal voice. "It is my duty to escort you safely to the sanctuary city of Turopia."

"Excuse me, where?" Rory said, frustrated, but relieved he wasn't here to torture and murder her.

T. Veckler turned to the old couple. "We caught sight of Levicus' disciples on our way here. Two Tyrskan Warriors are outside, watching for any unnatural movement. Her entry into

Inara left a significant energy trace, and I'm sure they've come to inspect the area. We'll be leaving right away."

Rory pulled at the rubber bands around her wrist. "What are you talking about? What is going on here?"

"Not now—we must hurry," T. Veckler said. "Your life is in danger. "I will give you more information later."

"No, I demand you take me home," Rory said, sounding childish even to her own ears.

T. Veckler looked around. "Where is your brother?"

"We were separated," Rory said, approaching the barrier. "I haven't seen him in seven years."

To her surprise, the warrior scoffed. "I see your mother's plans with Ipseh didn't work out as well as she'd hoped." He shook his head. "I should've known better than to trust *him*."

Any kind thoughts she'd developed for this man instantly vanished. "You shouldn't speak ill of the dead."

T. Veckler raised an eyebrow. "Your mother isn't dead. Just missing."

"Well, I found her." Rory would never forget the horrifying memory. "Her skeleton was lying next to my crib."

The man smiled without showing his teeth. Rory felt sick.

"That must've been the nursemaid who was supposed to protect you," T. Veckler said.

"So my mother's not dead?" Rory could breathe again. There was still hope.

"We don't think so."

Anticipation overwhelmed her. Maybe her mom wasn't associated with her father anymore, and that's why they'd been abandoned. "What happened to her?"

"I don't have time for this." T. Veckler nodded to the couple. "Take down the barrier."

A row of perfectly spherical stones lined the barrier. The couple knelt at opposite ends and lifted a flap built into the rocks. In unison, they tapped a pattern into the rock-face, and chanted in a foreign language that sounded like a cross between French and German, a mix of both harsh and soft sounds. The words permeated the air and seemed to linger before dying out. They flipped the rock lids back down, and the barrier dropped with a fizzling sound.

"Come out of there." The warrior extended his muscular arm. "We need to reinstate the barrier, as feeble as it is, or Levicus' disciples could find where their master is hidden."

"So that was the creature that attacked me in the space tunnel . . ." Rory said as she stepped out of the room. It felt so good to be out.

Now that she in the main room, she could see the cottage was obviously built around the room she'd entered through. At the end of the long living room was the kitchen, and a couple more doors.

"I'm sorry you had to deal with him." T. Veckler looked actually concerned. "Did he hurt you?"

Rory swallowed—he just stole her cape and her pride. She grabbed her bag and lingered. "I'm not going anywhere with you. I want you to take me back to Rutherford."

"I'm sorry, but there is no way for us to return you there."

"You lie," Rory said, turning her back and crossing her arms.

T. Veckler set his jaw. "Even if I had the power to, which I don't—if we open the portal, that being you encountered would escape." His eyes burned with anger. "Your mother gave up everything to free the world from Levicus—is that what you want—her life to be for nothing?"

"You have more than enough weapons to take him on."

"These trinkets?" The heavily armored man shook his head. "My dear, no *one* person can defeat Levicus, certainly not I. Levicus is immortal—that is why we had to entrap him in order to be free of his dominion."

She didn't want to be the person that allowed the dark creature to escape—especially if no one could stop him. She shuddered, thinking of his desperate touch.

But that didn't mean she couldn't escape these lunatics. Rory sprinted for the front door.

T. Veckler held out his left arm, caught her, and pulled her in tight. "You should watch your telegraphing. Your eyes told me exactly what you were planning." He turned to the old couple and nodded.

The old couple knelt down and reinstated the barrier with a fizzle.

T. Veckler let Rory out of his grasp.

She spun back, fists raised.

"I know you don't believe me, but I'm not going to hurt you," T. Veckler said with a stoic expression. "It is my duty to *protect* you."

Then why was it that all his weapons made her feel *less* safe?

Maggie put a gentle hand on her shoulder. "It would be wise for you to leave with T. Veckler."

"But—"

"He once saved my life." Maggie looked off into the distance, as if recalling a painful memory. "He will protect you, too."

There didn't seem to be any other way out of this—be locked in the room, or go with him. Still, the warrior unsettled her. All her six years of martial arts study and she'd never seen one man carry around so many weapons. Even the ex-army ranger she'd lived with only carried around one gun and a knife.

"Who are you, and why should I follow you?" Rory asked.

The warrior's rough face hardened. "Just like children to waste time with questions. It doesn't matter who I am, it is my duty to guide you to safety."

Maggie reached out to touch T. Veckler's arm, then pulled back. "My lord, I know you are hardened to this way of life, but the girl is not. She deserves to know a little."

T. Veckler's face twisted in a frightening scowl. If a glare could kill, this would be the one. "You know I'm not a lord anymore. Watch your tongue."

Maggie bowed so low, her grey braid flipped over her head, touching the ground. "I'm sorry, T. Veckler. I'm sorry."

"It is understandable," T. Veckler said with a softer expression. "Old habits. But times change."

Rory glared at the warrior.

The front door swung open to reveal a teenage boy with long jet-black hair tied back in a ponytail. He wore a striking uniform. With his knee-length blue robe sporting a thick black V-neck border, and white designs, he was the opposite of T. Veckler's brown attire. The two swords across his back looked formidable.

Now *he* looked like a warrior she could handle traveling with. His face reminded her of Sun-hi's. Rory's heart ached, thinking of her distant friend she'd never see again.

"T. Veckler, come quick," the boy said. He appeared only a year older than her.

T. Veckler instantly followed the boy. "What is it, Agi?" His name sounded soft, like in *George*, the opposite of Maggie's more country-sounding name.

Before the old couple could stop her, Rory shot out the front door to see what was happening. She was in the middle of nowhere—forest off in the distance, but no other houses in sight. Three horses were tied to trees out front, and there was a massive garden beside the house.

"Look!" The boy pointed to the sky.

Rory squinted in the dual moonlight to see a black raven fly out of the trees. It had glowing red eyes.

"Good eye, Agi," T. Veckler said.

"A spy bird," Agi said. "What are we going to do?"

T. Veckler scowled and pulled a thin knife from his belt.

What was he going to do with that? The bird was too far away.

T. Veckler narrowed his brow and held the knife at his side, pointer finger over the blade.

What was he waiting for?

Then all of the sudden, T. Veckler burst into motion—he cocked his arm and threw the knife up at the raven.

The mass of black feathers plummeted to the ground.

Rory stood, mouth gaping.

Agi ran over to where the raven had fallen and brought it back. "It's carrying a coded note. I can't interpret it."

"Thanks." T. Veckler took the note and read it. He scowled. "Looks like the disciples are going to inspect an energy disturbance up north as well. We need to leave now."

It all seemed to happen at once. Agi climbed on the brown horse. T. Veckler swooped her up before she could protest, and lifted her up behind Agi.

"Get her out of here quickly," T. Veckler said. "I'll get Leopold and catch up with you."

At that moment, another man dressed in the same sky-blue, black, and white uniform as Agi ran out from the trees. He waved wildly at them. "They're coming!"

"What?" T. Veckler said harshly, but quietly at the same time.

"Leopold, how many?" Agi asked.

"Eleven disciples," Leopold said. "They're headed this way."

"Have they turned off the road?" T. Veckler said.

Leopold nodded. The older man had rich dark skin, with a wide flat nose and a dignified air about him.

T. Veckler stroked his stubbled-chin and looked off into the distance for a moment. "Agi, get down from there. We don't have time."

Agi jumped off gracefully, then lifted Rory off the horse.

"Leopold, take the horses to the stable and stay outside as back-up," T. Veckler said.

Rory's heart raced. She could run. Get away from these crazy people. Rolling hills and a small forest surrounded the cottage—other than the small barn—not the best hiding options. And what did she know about forests? No way she was going in one at night. She'd seen enough horror movies to know that wasn't a good idea.

"Inside. Now," T. Veckler said in a tone she did not want to argue with. Once inside, he leaned over and held her shoulders.

She was too startled to shake him off.

"Look, you may not trust me, but at least believe the people coming will be worse. You have to pretend you are Maggie and Burt's granddaughter. Can you do this?"

Rory nodded. The tension in T. Veckler's voice was frightening. What forces could these be that would make *him* so uneasy?

"Good," T. Veckler said. "Do not say a word. We are all at risk." T. Veckler looked up at Maggie. "Don't you have some old thing she can throw on? She looks like some warrior kid. We can't have that."

Rory hid a smile. *He said I looked like a warrior.*

Maggie held out a faded green dress and an old apron. "Here, this was my granddaughter's, before she, uh—here, we'll just put this on you."

Slipping into the back bedroom, Rory changed into the dress that smelled of mothballs, and the flowery apron.

Maggie raced to the kitchen where she turned on a wood-burning stove with the flick of her wrist. "Come here, Rory."

Rory's eyes widened. It was hard not to believe magic was real when she saw things like that.

The old woman wore a jeweled bracelet much like the one her father had worn, but with assorted gems instead of all silver. She mumbled more foreign words, and food flew out from the pantry so fast, Rory was sure it would make a mess.

Faster than Rory imagined possible, Maggie was mixing ingredients together. "Wow," Rory said aloud, not meaning to.

"We've practiced this cover-up hundreds of times." Maggie smiled as she stirred the batter. "No one suspects evil of people baking cookies. Now start rolling."

After she'd rolled a few balls, Maggie stopped her. "We don't want to be finished by the time they arrive—we have to be in the middle of baking for them to believe our ruse."

T. Veckler led Agi to the back bedroom beside the kitchen. "You'll have to hide—they'll recognize your Tyrskan Warrior uniform." He sure wouldn't stand out. His all brown outfit made him look as if he intended to fade into the background. He returned to staring out the front bay window.

Rory stood next to Maggie in the open kitchen that faced the living room. The old woman was so focused that even Rory dared not say anything. Tired of standing still, Rory tiptoed behind the old woman to peek out the kitchen window.

A V-formation of eleven white-robed figures marched steadily their way. Hoods hung over their faces. Their hands were clasped across their waists inside their oversized sleeves. Under the light of the two moons, their robes had a glow-in-the-dark effect. Rory shuddered.

Two moons. This place was weird. Her heart raced. She wished she were home.

In the middle of the V-formation, two people with folded wings were being led by ropes. "What are those creatures?"

Maggie took a quick peek out the window. "Those are Ayeven, my dear."

"They're what?"

"The Ayeven are the descendants of Earth's Archangel's offspring. Very powerful magic. They have spectacular wings like eagles." She looked away. "Unfortunately, they keep their wings hidden now because they'll be killed, or taken to labor camps for their rejuvenating blood—like the two you see there, or worse—have their wings torn off." Maggie scrunched her face. "Though that usually kills them."

Rory shuddered. How awful. "And these Archangels, what are they?"

Maggie looked out the window as if to see how close the disciples were. "That creature you met in the portal—legends say Levicus is one of the twelve Archangels the Pleadines created to guide the Humans on Earth."

She looked around anxiously. "But he went bad trying to separate himself from the other Archangels, and fostered wars among the Humans. When he was moved to Inara with the rest of the magical population, he lost his archangel power, but somehow was still able to keep his powerful magic." Maggie stood straight again. "I'm awfully glad you didn't let him out. So you can see why it was critical we were absolutely sure who you are."

"But who am I?" If this was where she was truly from, then maybe they'd have the answers she'd been searching for her whole life.

"That will be up to you," Maggie said. "It's too soon to know for sure."

Perplexed, all Rory could do was nod.

"Positions," T. Veckler whispered. He left his spot by the front window and went into the back bedroom. *Why was he leaving them?*

Burt came out of the bedroom and went to the living room to read a book. *Hardly the time for reading!*

"Roll the batter into balls and place them on the pan." Maggie pulled a glop of dough out of the bowl. "Don't say a word. Burt and I have practiced this many times—and now we have the added benefit of T. Veckler's presence. If everything goes right, we should be safe."

"And if not?"

Maggie stared forward, averting Rory's gaze. "Then they'll either kill us quickly, or take us to a work camp. It doesn't matter what happens to us—above all, we can't let them know the portal is connected to this location. Or The Researcher could free Levicus."

CHAPTER
— 13 —

RORY BAKES COOKIES

Adisciple pounded on the front door. Rory didn't mean to tap her foot under the counter, but she couldn't help it.

"It's okay to be nervous," Maggie said softly. "Anybody would be uneasy around Levicus' disciples."

Burt put his book upside down over the side of his chair, as if he were holding his page. A cup of hot steaming liquid sat beside the armchair. They really were giving off the air that the disciples had interrupted an innocent evening at home.

The old man opened the door and hunched over, making his figure look decrepit. "Can I help you?"

"Good evening, kind sir," the lead disciple said in a rough but polite voice. A thin sword scabbard hung from his red rope belt. Rory bit her tongue to keep her mouth from falling open—his uniform looked like the white-robed skeleton she'd discovered beside her crib.

Burt didn't move from the doorway.

The ten other disciples stood back from the door, still in V-formation. "Please step aside, we're investigating reports of people in the area hiding Ayeven. We'll be taking a look around."

Rory wanted to get a better look at these Ayeven creatures, but the disciples kept them outside.

Burt hadn't even answered when the lead disciple pushed his way in, his hood still covering his face.

The disciple surveyed the living space and pointed to the double doors directly in front of him.

Burt stepped beside the disciple, as if stepping directly in front of him would draw attention to the doors. "Would you like some hot tea? My wife would be happy to brew some fresh for you."

"Not now," the disciple said. "What's behind this door?"

Their ruse wasn't working.

Maggie was still rolling cookie balls as if nothing were wrong.

Rolling! Rory was supposed to be rolling cookie balls. She scooped out the sticky batter, rolled it into a ball with the palm of her hand, and plopped the oversized blob on the tray next to Maggie's perfectly round balls.

"Just our main bedroom," Burt said. "It's very unsightly to look at the place you slumber during the day—makes you want to sleep all day."

"I see," the disciple said. "Open the doors."

Maggie tensed for a moment beside her, then relaxed.

Burt nodded. He took achingly slow, deliberate steps towards the doors. Were those magical sentries going to be there and give everything away?

T. Veckler emerged from the bedroom donning his dark brown outfit, but without the weapons. Except Rory caught sight of a holster of knives on his upper thigh as he passed. "Ah, good sir, can I help you?"

"Humbly, we encroach upon you this evening searching for Ayeven to take to the work camps," the lead disciple said, though even Rory thought he was lying.

"You won't find any Ayeven here," T. Veckler said, as if he were speaking to a close friend. "In fact, we are loyal supporters of Levicus."

"And what if I were to tell you I did not believe you?" the disciple said. Two of the disciples stood in the doorway, white hoods drooping over their bowed heads.

"Then I would tell you that perhaps you will recognize this." T. Veckler pulled a bronze disc, the size of his palm, out of his belt pouch, flashed it to the disciple leader and slipped it back out of sight.

Rory stood on tiptoes, trying to see what was on the disc, but she couldn't make it out.

The disciple leaned closer, inspecting him closely. And then his voice became jovial, "It's you, I thought you were dead." He pulled off his white hood, revealing a pale man with bleach white hair.

The disciples *knew* T. Veckler?

"Ah, Sir Nestor, I thought it might be you." T. Veckler looked around, as if to reveal a secret, "I'm on a top secret mission for Levicus. I've been undercover and I expect to keep it this way. No one shall know you saw me here tonight. This old couple was kind enough to house me for the night—I don't want to give them any trouble."

Nestor nodded his head repeatedly. "Of course, of course." When he performed a proper bow, the two other disciples in the room, and eight outside bowed low in one smooth motion.

Rory caught one of the disciples sneaking a peek from under his hood. Who was T. Veckler that the disciples would bow to him? This could not be good.

Burt sat down in an armchair.

"Good sir." Nestor turned sharply to Burt. "What is this—you sitting in front of your superiors?"

If this is how the disciples treated the elderly, she didn't like them one bit.

"Standin' hurts my back," Burt said, but stood anyway.

"So, what are you really doing here tonight?" T. Veckler said, skillfully diverting the conversation. "We haven't searched homes for Ayeven since our master walked the lands."

Nestor leaned close to T. Veckler. "It's probably safe to tell you—we have instructions to discover the source of a powerful energy reading, which originated from this region."

"On whose orders?" T. Veckler said. "Is The Researcher paying attention to us again?"

"We haven't worked with him in years—he became obsessed with something a few years back, and dropped off the map. I'm not at liberty to say who, but I think you will know soon."

T. Veckler looked thoughtfully out the front door. "Taking those Ayeven to the labor camps? Levicus will be pleased."

Rory struggled to remain calm. T. Veckler was speaking like one of them.

"Yes," Nestor said. "Vicious Ayeven. Wish I could wear their wings like Levicus did, though."

Rory couldn't hold the disgust from her face like it seemed T. Veckler could. No creature, no matter how awful, deserved to have their wings removed.

"I do apologize, duty binds me to search this domicile." Nestor nodded to the disciples behind him. "I'm sure you understand—purely routine."

Two disciples, with hoods low, approached the double-doors to the room Rory had arrived in. They flung the two doors open. The barrier flashed light blue, revealing the two translucent guards.

Nestor's eyes widened, "You—" He stumbled back. "There were rumors, but I never thought—"

T. Veckler closed his eyes and sighed.

Nestor regained his bearings, and a spark of glee crossed his face. "The power—I never thought *I'd* be the one to free Levicus and become his right-hand man."

Rory squished the cookie ball in her fist.

The two disciples stared at each other, each obviously judging the situation and their opponent. And just when T. Veckler needed his weapons, he was without them.

"I regret this is how it must be," Nestor said. "I'm sure you understand."

T. Veckler stared blankly back at him.

Nestor drew his thin rapier-like sword. In one smooth motion, the two disciples beside him and the eight outside drew theirs.

T. Veckler was now surrounded by three disciples with swords drawn. How was he going to get out of this?

Nestor held his sword at T. Veckler's neck. "What other secrets might you be keeping from us this fine evening?"

"Nothing." T. Veckler made a pointed glance towards the main bedroom by the kitchen, then quickly looked back as if he'd made a mistake.

Nestor shook his head. "Still think you can fool us?" He nodded to his two disciples.

They darted towards the back bedroom.

Oh no, Agi was back in that room all by himself. How could T. Veckler do that to the boy? "Agi!" Rory yelled.

The disciple pounded at the locked door.

Agi pulled in the first disciple and smashed his head against the wall. The second disciple charged in. From behind the cracked door, swords clanged, and fizzing noises accompanied bursts of light

"You force my hand." Nestor slashed at the weaponless T. Veckler.

The warrior stepped to the side and struck Nestor's sword arm.

Nestor swung his sword back and chanted a spell.

T. Veckler ducked and kicked him in the ribs before Nestor could finish his spell.

When Nestor doubled over, T. Veckler elbowed him in the neck. The disciple dropped to the ground. "You're lucky I don't kill you, but it's better for me if you return alive to your master." T. Veckler picked up the man's thin sword. "Thanks for this."

Rory's eyes widened. She'd never seen someone actually get knocked out in real life—and so quickly.

Agi emerged from the back bedroom in his blue robes, one broadsword in each hand.

Whoa—Agi had defeated two disciples by himself? But he was so young.

The eight remaining disciples created a wall with their bodies outside the house.

T. Veckler stepped outside to face them. "Get out of my way, or I will kill you all."

And with the look on his face, Rory believed it. But then why had he spared that lead disciple?

"I see you can't count," the disciple said. "There are eight of us and only two of you."

Rory distinctly noticed he'd left the old couple out of his count.

Burt activated the panel to expose the weapons rack. He took his sword and threw Maggie's spear to her. The old couple ran outside and joined the fight.

Rory wanted to help, but she had no idea what to do. She'd never faced more than one opponent before—especially ones so skilled. But she had to do something. She grabbed a blob of cookie dough and ran from around the counter. She stood by the door, waiting for an opening to help.

"You think your Ayeven captives will fight for you?" T. Veckler nodded over to Agi.

Agi waved his hand as he said a spell—the magical ropes disintegrated off the two Ayeven's wrists.

With their soiled clothes, it looked like they'd been walking a long time. After rubbing their wrists, the Ayeven stretched, revealing filthy grey, eagle-like wings attached to their backs. Even through the grime, Rory could see the feathers' natural magnificence.

The two men gave a look of apology, and flew off.

Rory scoffed. So much for returning the favor. But she couldn't really blame them—she'd fly off too if she could.

In a flash, T. Veckler pulled a dagger from his back and threw it at the center disciple. As he easily deflected it, T. Veckler slashed the disciple on the right.

The dagger had merely been a distraction! She'd have to remember that trick.

Two disciples raised their arms towards the sky, chanting loudly.

In the middle of a block, T. Veckler yelled to Agi. "Stop those two from calling the Alrakis dragons!"

Dragons?

But the two Ayeven hadn't left at all. From the air, powerful wings flapping steadily, they attacked. A burst of light shot down at the two disciples who'd been chanting feverishly. Not expecting an attack from above, the two disciples clutched their chests and doubled over.

T. Veckler waved his thanks.

The two Ayeven nodded and flew off into the night.

Rory stood by the doorway, not sure what to do.

Leopold raced from the barn and attacked a disciple.

The disciple threw a powerful spell at Leopold, who blocked it with his gauntleted forearm. The disciple slashed and Leopold slipped closer.

The disciple lunged. Leopold changed his stance, which was the weirdest technique she'd seen someone do. But it worked—the disciple slashed the wrong location.

Leopold shoved the heel of his palm at the man's chest. A blue bolt of energy shot from Leopold's wrist, pushing the man back. The disciple slid across Maggie's garden, his once perfectly-white robes now covered in black soil.

"My carrots!" Maggie said. "I've had enough of this."

The old couple charged a disciple, quickly overtaking him.

The disciple threw a spell at them, but they ducked together. They seemed so practiced in their movements, almost graceful. Maggie thrust her spear at the disciple while Burt came from the side slashing, blocking the disciple's thinner blade.

Maggie repeatedly jabbed the disciple with her spear.

The disciple dodged.

Burt swept the disciples spell-casting hand aside over and over.

Burt winked at Maggie.

She dropped to the ground and rolled behind the disciple. He was so busy deflecting Burt's feverous attacks, he didn't sense Maggie's presence behind him.

With the disciple off-balance, Maggie swept her spear under his feet.

He fell forward.

Rory gasped. The disciple was going to be impaled on Burt's blade!

But Burt lowered his sword and stepped out of the way at the last second. He kicked the white-robed man to the ground. Burt held his sword at the back of the disciple's neck. "Don't bother getting up."

It looked like they didn't even need her help. Then something moved beside her.

Nestor clambered to his feet and faced her.

Rory stepped back. The battle raged on outside. It was just the two of them, in a world of their own. "But how? You were unconscious."

Nestor grinned, circling her. "Ayeven blood—does wonders for rejuvenation." He stumbled to the left.

So he wasn't quite grounded. That gave Rory an idea.

"Stay away from me," Rory said in her most weak and innocent voice possible.

Rory knew she couldn't last more than one exchange with this man. Not only was he much larger than her, he had magic and she didn't. She had to focus. Had to get this right the first time.

Rory threw the blob of dough at his face.

The moment he moved his arm to swat the dough away, she tucked her left leg, and kicked out to the side as hard as if she were breaking two boards. "Ahh!" she gave a loud battle cry.

Her foot connected with his kidney and he bent over.

Rory brought her fists up, ready for a second attack.

But it wasn't needed.

Nestor stumbled back, falling into the barrier. His body dropped to the ground, convulsing from shock. Even though he was unconscious, he continued to shake from his side touching the barrier.

The two quantum guards raised their spears to finish him off.

"Wait!" Rory yelled. "Don't kill him." She didn't know why she'd decided to take T. Veckler's lead. But she did know she was in way over her head. She pulled the fallen disciple away from the barrier by his red boots. Then his body lay still.

Her heart raced. Rory took several deep breaths to slow her rapid breathing. She scanned the room. She was alone.

Rory sighed, releasing the pent-up adrenaline. She'd done it—and survived. She knew she should kick him once more to make sure he didn't rebound, but she couldn't make herself do it.

T. Veckler battled the last standing disciple. The crashing blades clanged in the still night air.

Agi and Leopold approached the duel, their swords drawn.

Rory thought T. Veckler's pride would've been hurt to have someone aid him in battle, but he didn't seem to care. His expression remained stoic.

T. Veckler, Leopold, and Agi surrounded the last disciple. He threw a spell of black lightning at them.

Agi and Leopold deflected it, and sent a convulsing blue spell back at the disciple.

He took one nervous look around and bolted.

"Catch him," T. Veckler ordered.

Leopold threw a spell at the disciple, who fell to the ground.

Rory stepped outside, surveying the scene around her. Fallen disciples lay in various positions outside the cottage. Two of them groaned, and one of the disciples in the garden was slowly attempting to get to his feet, but couldn't even get to his knees.

She pulled at the rubber bands on her wrists—taking a moment to look at each of the strangers who had protected her, and yet, she was still afraid of them. She should be able to trust them now, so how come she couldn't get herself to?

T. Veckler wiped blood off his throwing knives and replaced them in the holster on his thigh. Agi and Leopold came out of the house, carrying the two fallen disciples who looked broken and bruised. Leopold went back in to get Nestor.

Maggie leaned on her spear. "What are we going to do? They know we're hiding something. More disciples will be around to inspect."

"I had hoped this wouldn't happen." T. Veckler turned to Agi. "I need you to perform some of your mind-altering magic on these disciples. They can have no memory of finding this cottage."

"But sir—" Maggie said. "I won't have such forbidden magic on my property."

"Do you have any other options?" T. Veckler said. "If we kill them, their leaders will become suspicious. It will only serve to draw attention to the area."

"I hate this," Maggie said.

"We all do," T. Veckler said, and addressed Leopold. "Reprogram their minds to report they found nothing during their search—make them believe it was a false reading."

Leopold's dark brow furrowed before he nodded. "Yes, sir."

"Sorry I can't help—I've never learned such magic," Agi said.

"Don't worry about it." Leopold knelt beside each of the disciples, performing his spell. The already unconscious disciples seemed to slip into a peaceful sleep, wide smiles across their faces.

Rory looked at the Tyrskan Warrior curiously. He must have added something nice to the spell to make them smile like that.

No one except Leopold moved for several moments. T. Veckler seemed on-guard, as if waiting for the disciples to rise and attack.

T. Veckler, Agi, and Leopold loaded the eleven disciples into Burt's wagon.

"I'll drive 'em to the road and leave a few of these." Burt grinned and clutched a few brown-tipped arrows. "The disciples will think the Splithounds bandit clan attacked."

"Smart thinking." T. Veckler slipped the throwing knife he'd used into the sheath at his side with the other two. "We'll leave right away."

Rory shivered and slunk back into the warm house that smelled of fresh baked cookies. She plopped in the armchair and watched T. Veckler, Agi, and Leopold return to the house in somber moods.

After the quick dinner Maggie had forced upon them, Rory left Maggie's dress on the bed. If she was going to be riding a horse, there was no way she wanted to do it in a long skirt.

As Leopold and Agi went to gather the horses, it gave Rory time to try and make sense of her situation, but she couldn't. Images from the battle flashed through her mind. After all her years of training, she'd stood there, completely helpless. Her mind was numb and she couldn't think straight.

T. Veckler leaned back in the other armchair, watching at her again. *Creepy.* When she caught his eye, he looked away. "Why do you keep staring at me like that?"

"You remind me of someone."

For the life of her, she could not figure the man out. Was he on the side of the disciples, or merely pretending to save them? Sure he had attacked those creepy-robed guys, but only as a last resort. And the leader seemed to know him—that could not be good. She would have to stay vigilant.

T. Veckler raised his eyebrows, giving her an opening to speak her mind. But the seriousness behind his expression told her he was in no mood for arguing.

Rory considered asking all the questions on her mind, but decided against it and stood, crossing her arms. She was too weary to argue—she just wanted to go home.

"I want to explain why you're so important to us, but not here. The story for the two Tyrskan Warriors outside is that your family died and we are escorting you to the sanctuary city of Turopia. Only a few people know about the importance of this cottage—and it's critical we keep it that way. If you tell anyone you came from Earth or through here, Levicus' disciples will find the location and free him."

CHAPTER
— 14 —

RORY AND THE ALRAKIS DRAGONS

Rory agreed with T. Veckler, but only so she could step away. The warrior's presence was so overbearing, she felt uncomfortable just standing near him.

"Listen to him." Maggie was so earnest it was hard for Rory to ignore the old woman.

T. Veckler nodded Maggie his quiet thanks, before throwing a cloak to Rory, who caught it.

"You have done your duty well," T. Veckler said to the old couple. "You will continue your assignment as planned. That garden is a clever cover."

"It also makes for great food," Maggie said.

T. Veckler turned to Rory. "Come."

Now was her chance to stay with someone trustworthy. Rory planted her feet and stared into T. Veckler's hard blue eyes. "Maggie and Burt seem to think Peter will come the same way I came. I'm going to wait here with them."

"Not an option," T. Veckler said.

Maggie put a gentle hand on Rory's arm. "We will inform T. Veckler when your brother arrives, and you can meet him safely in Turopia."

"Fine," Rory mumbled and started towards the door. At least she could control *when* she left. "Okay, I'll go with you. But I want you to tell me all about my parents."

T. Veckler was about to say something when Maggie shot him a glance. For some reason, he backed down.

Rory attempted a smile. This might work out after all.

But then he did speak. "Coming willingly was a good choice. The alternative was handcuffing you and forcing you with us to Turopia. Trust me, it's for your own good." He slammed the front door behind him.

How rude! This world was so frustrating. How could she have lost control over everything in her life so quickly?

But it looked like she had to go with him—trust or no trust. Just like another foster home, right? She recalled her lesson with Miss Kuma—faking courage until she felt it for real. Rory grabbed her shoulder bag and took a deep breath. She could do this.

Before she got to the door, Maggie tapped her on the shoulder. "How about a bag of cookies to help you on your journey?"

Rory accepted the cloth bag, eager to eat the delicious treat she so rarely got to have. "Thanks."

"You have no idea how happy we are you came home safely," Maggie added, making a motion like she wanted to hug her.

Rory tensed, clutching the bag of cookies tighter.

Maggie stepped back awkwardly. "Do come visit us when Peter arrives?"

Rory nodded and left the cottage to where T. Veckler was waiting under the stars beside three horses.

Maggie and Burt waved together from the doorway. As Rory bit into a warm, gooey treat, she wondered if she'd ever see the nice old couple again.

The two warriors looked warm in their blue knee-length cloaks. Rory wrapped her own boring brown cloak over her shoulders, pleased not only for the warmth, but also to hide her embarrassing costume.

Surprisingly, the cloak fit well. She knew she should say thanks to T. Veckler for it, but she couldn't bring herself to speak to the man.

Leopold approached her, reaching out a strong hand to her. She shook it. He had a firm, but not crushing, handshake.

"Sorry we didn't get to formal introductions yet—that was intense." Leopold adjusted the wide black sash around his waist. It had a white tree with exposed roots and a North-facing arrow in the center of the trunk. "You may have already guessed—I'm Leopold Regensburg, senior ranking officer in the Order of the Tyrskan Warriors. It will be an honor for myself and Lukagi Süssmeyer here to protect you. Have you ridden a horse before?"

Her chest ached thinking of Linette's silly obsession with having her try out new activities other than Tae Kwon Do. "Just once."

Agi stepped forward and bowed slightly, "Nice to officially meet you. That's a magnificent pendant."

"Thank you, it was my mother's." Rory returned the bow, glad she had learned about bowing etiquette in Tae Kwon Do.

"You take the girl," T. Veckler said to Agi. "And watch her closely. I can already tell she's sneaky—just like her mother."

Rory couldn't hold back a smile. She liked hearing about her mother. And he was right—she'd been watching for an opening to get away, but every time she'd seen one, she'd found herself holding back. A sense in her gut told her to stay with these people, even if she didn't trust them. She didn't know anything about this dangerous world, and so far T. Veckler and the Tyrskan Warriors had protected her.

At least on the way to Turopia she wouldn't have to ride with that grumpy warrior. Once she was there, she hoped this whole situation would be resolved, everything put right. She ran her hand over the horse's soft brown hair. Misty, the horse, leaned in to Rory's touch.

As Agi helped her onto the padding behind the saddle, she noticed dark blue gauntlets with a silver tree like the one on his sash. She wrapped her arms around him, careful not to squeeze his slender waist too tightly.

Leopold rode ahead, scouting the route.

"We'll start slowly," Agi said. "I want to ensure Misty isn't bothered by your additional weight before we get going."

As they left the old couple's land, T. Veckler called back, "Not the road. Too many spies."

Rory was relieved they were going slowly, as it was awkward being on the back of a horse again. And it gave her a chance to know him a little more. "So, Tyrskan Warriors? What do you do?"

"The twelve of us work to guard the city and run missions outside of Turopia." He had a kind voice, one that was comforting to listen to. "Once part of the order, we're a member for life, unless we break our code, or you know . . ."

Rory filled in the blank—Agi had only earned his place because one of them had died.

After traveling out of the valley, the group sped up, racing as fast as they could in the dark. Leopold rode back to check for people following them.

She'd always dreamed of getting out of Rutherford, but never dreamed it would be to a beautiful land like Inara. It was hard to believe she wasn't on Earth. As they rode along the river, sounds of frogs and insects buzzed. She saw no semblance of a modern culture—no skyscrapers, cars, or massive amounts of people. In fact, they saw no one as they rode through small forests of trees, with leaves the color of fire.

Halfway through the night, they'd stopped in a small clearing to rest, when Leopold raced in and jumped off his horse. "Commander Veckler, one of the disciples broke from the group."

"How much time do you think we have?" T. Veckler asked.

Leopold wiped the sweat off his brow. "He's taking an odd path towards the mountains—I'm not sure what he's up to. He's on foot, so we have till morning to rest before we need to leave."

T. Veckler rested his hand at the sword on his hip, and looked around. "We need to give the horses a good rest, and you should get some sleep while you can."

"Yes, sir." Leopold led his horse to a grassy area. He proceeded to remove her saddle and the padding underneath. He brushed her down, and whispered sweet words Rory couldn't hear.

Agi helped her off Misty. Her legs felt frozen in a squatting position. She raised her arms and leaned back, stretching out the kinks.

Agi removed the saddlebags and started laying out food. She'd tried talking on the ride, but it was too hard to hear with the wind.

"Hey Agi," Rory said.

The older boy didn't seem to hear her. She bit her lip, hating to call again.

The three men continued to set up camp in complete silence. She ached for someone to talk to. It was almost worse being around people who ignored her than just being alone.

They ate a quick meal. The chill, damp night air prickled her skin, and Rory pulled her cloak around her. She wandered away from the campsite. The bare trees were thick here. The dual moons cast shadows across the fallen leaves, giving off an ominous feel. Rory shivered, pulling her cloak tighter around her.

Rory found she wasn't alone. T. Veckler sat against a large tree with his legs straight out in front of him, looking up at the stars. Now was her chance. She twisted the rubber bands on her wrist. "Look, I can see you're trying to help me, but I don't understand what I'm doing here. Are you sure I can't go home? I need to find Peter."

Without looking at her, T. Veckler said, "My dear, Inara is your true home."

It seemed like he was finally ready to talk, so Rory plopped on the ground in front of him.

"Your mother kept you two on Earth for your protection," T. Veckler said softly. "What you must understand is that Levicus was relentlessly hunting Katrine. The home planet was the only place he couldn't find her, because the Pleadines forbade Levicus from returning to Earth. Your father was supposed to bring you two back after we tricked Levicus into the portal, but the disciples attacked, forcing . . . complications."

Rory's mouth dropped. *Planet?* She laughed out of nervousness and the sheer ridiculousness of planetary travel.

"It's not a joke," T. Veckler said with a stern expression.

Her joviality instantly dissipated. "No, I suppose you have no humor."

Rory was surprised her comment caused his stoic expression to falter. He actually seemed hurt by her remark. "And after all these years, you couldn't think to come get us?" Rory stood. "Do you know what I've been through? How I've had to move from place to place—and without Peter!"

T. Veckler scrunched his face. It was the same expression Rory's social workers made whenever they came to tell her it was time to move her to another home. "I'm sorry you two were separated—that wasn't the plan."

Before Rory could protest, he added, "Asdorn, the master Zenmage, programmed a whole slew of back-up spells to aid in your return when the time was right. I told Asdorn it was a foolhardy plan, but I see I was wrong." T. Veckler scoffed. "Clever old wizard. Asdorn will be eager to hear from you all about it."

But Rory didn't want to hear about their clever plan. Without a word, she marched off. She knew it was rude, but couldn't bear to have the warrior see her cry.

She slid back against an oak tree and looked up at the sky full of stars she didn't recognize, and two full moons. Sure, she may have only gotten a passing grade in her astronomy class, but that was because she had trouble focusing on her homework, not because she couldn't pick out the constellations. Rory couldn't even find the Big Dipper, or the three evenly spaced stars of Orion's Belt. Instead, a set of three bright stars forming an isosceles triangle dominated the sky.

I'm really not on Earth anymore. It was time she pushed aside any lingering hope this was all some kind of illusion. There was no escaping—she really was on another planet, and in a dangerous situation—one she wasn't quite sure how to get out of. But it explained so much. If she was really from this planet, then no wonder the social workers could never find any history of her parents.

What she did know is she had to get to this Turopia place safely, then she could find someone who could help her find her brother. If she could be with Peter, she just might be able to call this place home.

The two moons drew her in. They were not like the bright moon of Earth. Rory marveled at how different they each were. The one on the left, which was about the same size as Earth's moon, looked like a dark, starry sky contained within a sphere. The larger moon had a blue gaseous hue about it.

They were quite striking. Rory found her worries drift away. She leaned forward to soak up the moons' radiance. In that moment, she felt this world was beautiful.

✳   ✳   ✳

By midday, Rory's legs ached from the horse ride. She wanted to talk to Agi and learn more about the place, but all three warriors were focused and silent. They rode hard, only taking a few breaks to rest their horses.

After Leopold reported he'd lost track of where the disciple had gone, they were on high alert the rest of the day.

T. Veckler raised his right hand, and they immediately halted.

Rory had been resting, leaning on Agi's back when the bouncing slowed to small bumps. She pulled back, looking around. "Why did we stop?" Rory whispered.

Agi pointed up, and Rory made out a large black silhouette against the twilight sky. Screeching filled the air. She looked around frantically for where they could hide, but they were on a stretch of dead grass, littered with massive boulders. No real cover.

As the shape neared, its bulk blocked out the light of the bright white sun. Feeling the need for protection, she clasped her arms back around Agi.

"It's an Alrakis dragon!" Agi cried out.

"We must flee!" Leopold yelled.

"We won't make it to the trees—stay and fight!" T. Veckler commanded. "Hide the brat behind the boulder, and stand your ground. Watch for Levicus' disciples controlling the dragon."

Leopold and Agi looked at each other uncomfortably and nodded. "Yes, sir!"

Agi pried Rory's fingers off his waist, jumped off the horse, then pulled her off. He didn't even bother putting her down before carrying her behind the massive boulder twice his height. She might only be ninety pounds, but he carried her like she was a small bag of flour.

Agi looked her directly in the eyes, a silent communication of danger. "Stay here. Do not be seen." He slipped around to the front of the boulder, and joined Leopold.

The two Tyrskan Warriors raised their swords at the hovering Alrakis dragon. The dragon was all black, except for red under its wings and a bright red breast. If it wasn't for the fact that the creature was descending for attack, she would've found it completely magnificent. "Look up there!" Agi pointed up. "The disciple who's been following us."

A disciple rode on the dragon, which was so large it looked like it could carry off a horse in its claws for an appetizer. The dragon's powerful black bat-like wings blew dirt all around, making vision cloudy.

The dragon let out a ferocious roar, rumbling the ground around her.

Rory covered her ears. She peered around the boulder just in time to see the disciple shoot a red bolt down.

Agi dove to the side. The strike glanced off T. Veckler's shoulder. He dropped to the ground. Agi rushed to his side, but T. Veckler was already standing.

The disciple fired more blasts. Leopold and Agi combined their energies to block the spells and return the blasts. The red bolts shot back towards the dragon like a boomerang.

So powerful—they were surely going to make it.

But the disciple pulled the dragon up to deflect the blast, and it had no effect on its red breast plates. The disciple immediately shot down several more blasts.

Leopold and Agi returned the spell, and added another attack of their own. Heart racing, Rory pressed herself up against the boulder, hoping the dragon wouldn't see her.

A fierce swooshing noise came closer.

Before she knew it, massive claws grasped her shoulders, lifting her high into the air. She looked down, seeing the warriors in battle positions below.

"Help!" Rory screamed.

She expected T. Veckler to draw a bow to shoot the creature down, but instead he slipped away from the group and stepped right into the dust cloud. He chanted in a deep and guttural language—different from Burt and Maggie's spells.

Rory remained as still as possible, afraid the dragon would let her go at any moment and she'd plummet to her death.

She dared a look down. She was so high, the warriors looked like little action figures below. Nausea welled in her belly. Rory slammed her eyes shut.

The dragon let out a great roar that caused a sharp pain in her ears. She swore she heard a voice screaming 'No!' mixed in with the dragon's vibrations. Then to her surprise, it reversed course.

She was going to be taken to a dragon's lair and be eaten. She risked a look up at the disciple riding the dragon. "Let me go!"

The dragon opened his claws, sending Rory plummeting through the sky.

"Leopold!" T. Veckler shouted so loud, Rory could sense his fear.

Wind rushed through her ears, drowning out all other sounds. Her stomach clenched, like the first drop on a roller coaster that never ended. She screamed in an effort to drown out the fear, but it still lingered. She automatically grasped the air around her, fully knowing it would make no difference. Was this how she was going to die?

The valley, with its sparkling river, grew larger below her. She closed her eyes, hoping that if she had any magical powers at all they would miraculously come into being. Right now. Maybe she could even fly off like the Ayeven she'd seen earlier.

Suddenly, Leopold jumped in the air, wings expanding at the same time. He shot towards her like a bullet.

What? He had wings? And they were huge—his wingspan had to be as wide as he was tall.

The dusty land was getting uncomfortably closer. Rory kept her eyes trained on Leopold. There was no way she was going to miss him.

As he got closer, she reached out to him.

But Leopold passed her! "Leopold!" she screamed.

Leopold shot down, matching her speed. He reached out and grabbed her in an awkward hug. They dropped several feet. Faster and faster they plummeted. He reached under her legs and picked her up, holding her close to his chest.

Rory squeezed her eyes shut. It still felt like they were falling. They were going to crash! Leopold's wings flapped powerfully in long, slow motions. Barely a few feet from the ground, he regained control, and hovered a moment before setting down.

"You—you're—" Rory said as she gasped for air.

"Yes, I'm an Ayeven," Leopold said as he stood. "But only half, so I'm not accepted by my clan."

Rory clung to his neck, still in shock. A tear of relief fell down her cheek. She was alive.

Leopold didn't seem to mind as he carried her towards Agi and T. Veckler, who were racing over to them.

Rory stared in awe at his eagle-like wings folded across his back. They were dark brown with hints of tan spots, and shimmered under the light of the sun.

T. Veckler looked pale with worry. "Are you okay?"

"Thank you," Rory said from Leopold's arms, her voice coming out as a croak.

T. Veckler stroked his stubble of a beard. "That disciple got away—everyone's going to know you're here now. This is not good."

Rory felt her heart finally slowing down, and released her grip from around Leopold's neck. He set her down gently. Rory's legs folded underneath her and Leopold caught her. "How come I couldn't see your wings before?"

"The first spell an Ayeven learns when our wings come in is how to hide them." As Leopold said it, his folded wings disappeared. "But I have to expose them in order to fly."

Rory bit her lip, remembering Maggie's words. He'd risked revealing himself to save her. Leopold escorted her back to where Agi was using a spell to call the startled horses back.

When Agi had Misty's reins in his hand, he stared at T. Veckler in disbelief. "That was amazing—I thought you couldn't do magic?"

Leopold shot Agi a look, silently communicating he should keep his mouth shut.

"But where did you learn such a spell?" Agi asked. "In all my travels, I've never heard anyone use the dead language before."

"It wasn't magic, and I don't owe you an explanation." T. Veckler walked towards his grey spotted horse.

"But how you stopped the Alrakis dragon," Agi pushed. "There's something you're not telling us."

"That's right," T. Veckler spun around. "I'm the Commander. I've been doing this longer than you've been alive. And I've learned a few tricks to keep my people safe. I'm going to let your etiquette slide—but only because you're new to the Order." He rode off, effectively ending the argument.

The tension was so tight, Rory felt uncomfortable breathing in the thick silence. She made a mental note that the two Tyrskan Warriors were far less scary than their leader, but no less to be messed with. She silently hoped that him being a 'Commander' didn't mean he'd be in charge of what happened to her once she arrived in Turopia.

They rode through a colorful forest that smelled of vanilla. Off in the distance, Rory spotted a town. They were almost there!

But instead, they stopped at a large stone gazebo on the edge of town.

Agi seemed to sense her question. "A teleport location. There's an ancient network of teleports scattered across the world."

It was a stone structure with four pillars holding up a domed-roof. In the center stood a pillar holding up a glowing marble sphere. The riders led their horses onto the covered platform. T. Veckler dismounted and turned a stone dial to a symbol Rory couldn't make out. He looked around, then laid his palm on the sphere.

Instantly, everything went black and cold washed over her, as if she'd stepped into a refrigerator. Her skin prickled, much like the last part of her passage she'd travelled to get to this planet. Just the memory of it made her shiver.

They emerged in the same positions on another teleport gazebo. But the scenery had changed to a forest of towering evergreen trees. It was surprising how much the landscape reminded her of Earth.

They rode until the stars shone bright. Rory looked up at the night sky, this time searching for any dragons that might come attack them.

The group walked through a tiny village of about a dozen homes. People didn't run back into their homes or try to hide, they actually seemed pleased to see them. A couple of people even bowed.

They rode out of the village up a steep switchback path, stopping in front of a sheer cliff face. Seemed an odd place to make camp.

Agi turned back to her, "We're here."

A colossal, ominous door materialized on the cliff face in front of her. Rory's mouth dropped.

They were going inside a cliff.

The massive door was carved into the side of the sheer rock. In the moons' light, she could make out three layers to the archway. The outside border was comprised of miniature animals, the middle carvings of an ancient language, and the inner rim of spirals that seemed to move in and out of various colors.

Rory stared up in awe at the large door that had appeared out of nowhere. As they neared it, she saw that five animals were repeated throughout the entire outer arch—a head of a dragon with long whiskers, a tiger, a fox, a salamander, and a crow.

"This is one of the eleven working entrances to Turopia," Agi turned back to her. "You can't find the hidden sanctuary city unless you've been here before and been granted permission to return. Very safe."

After all that, she'd finally made it safely to Turopia. Relief washed over her, but the apprehension of what was going to happen to her next remained.

The group passed single file through a smaller door inlaid into the massive door. Upon entering, darkness enveloped her and she became disoriented. It felt like when she'd gone through the teleport location earlier.

Rory gasped at the new surroundings. She'd thought they were going inside a cliff, but she saw the starry sky quite clearly. Before her lay an expansive area surrounded by a towering natural wall. To her left was a rock wall, and to her right was a long, two-story stone guard post with a few archers atop it behind battlements.

The four archers instantly relaxed when T. Veckler gestured to them. He dismounted and turned to Leopold and Agi. "Thank you for accompanying me on this expedition.

Remember your Tyrskan code—this mission is to be held in highest confidence."

"Yes, sir," the two warriors said, then bowed.

T. Veckler turned to Agi. "Not even a word to Thurston."

Who?

Agi nodded, then dismounted. He reached up to help Rory off her horse. But she was tired of being carried everywhere. She swung her right leg around, and jumped off. She landed solidly on both feet and instinctively raised her hands in the air, like she would've done after finishing a move in gymnastics. She immediately lowered them, feeling silly with the serious warriors staring at her.

Agi patted her back and handed Rory her bag. "Well done."

The path was glowing—a sparkly dark blue. She looked deeper into the city and could not make out a single street light. The paths were lighting the entire town.

"Come with me." T. Veckler nodded her over.

Leopold whispered in her ear, "Only my fellow Tyrskan warriors know my secret—you'll keep it, right?"

"Of course, " Rory said. She watched him walk off. She hoped she'd be as brave as him some day.

Agi faced her. "I'll see you around town?"

"I hope so," Rory replied awkwardly. Now that they were out of danger, she got a better look at him. His long black ponytail had come undone, and his fancy blue uniform was completely disheveled. He had the same monolid eyes as Sun-hi. It was so cute. Rory blushed and looked away for even thinking it.

A couple of guards came to take the horses, and Agi walked off with them.

T. Veckler walked several paces before turning back to her. "Well, are you coming or not?"

Feeling resolved to take control of her situation, Rory joined T. Veckler.

At the gate, a young guard stopped them. She bowed to T. Veckler. "I'm sorry, sir. I can't let the girl enter Turopia without seeing her refugee pass."

"Thank you, Alana, but I don't have one for her yet," T. Veckler said, a look of severe frustration across his face. "She's my niece and she's come to stay with me."

Rory gasped. What? All this time searching for her family and *he* was who she'd found?

CHAPTER

— 15 —

PETER'S TROUBLE WITH A KING

A couple days later, as Peter followed his father to the courtyard, Peter strategized how he could make his father proud. Peter would focus—show off his skills— and do anything to prove himself.

The rectangular courtyard was picture perfect on that chill morning. Orange leaves fell gingerly from oak trees at the back of the garden.

Peter wondered what was in the leather bundle his father had placed on the ground. He eyed his father's staff. Its black metallic tip was carved like someone had hollowed out a three-dimensional diamond shape and just left the sharp edges. The four sides held a glowing silver gem that wasn't like any of the rocks he'd uncovered in Talbert's tunnels. It was fluid like liquid mercury, but how was that possible?

Peter reached out to touch it.

His father grabbed Peter's wrist. "You don't go around touching other people's staves or wands."

"Sorry," Peter said, and thought to try another approach. "Can I try your staff?"

"Not yet. Too high-level for you right now—you wouldn't even have the capability to fully tap into its channeling powers. It's important to use the proper device for your skill level or there could be disastrous results."

"Like what?" Peter asked.

"Control is paramount," Father said. "So it's important to switch channeling devices when you gain more mastery. As you would expect, beginner wands require less control, whereas the advanced wands require strong self-control, something it seems, you are fairly weak in."

A slight wind blew and Peter shivered.

His father pulled off his jacket and wrapped it around Peter.

A warmth spread across Peter's chest. He didn't deserve such kindness.

The long jacket trailed to the ground. Peter's eyes widened, and he frantically lifted it. "Oh no, I've gotten it dirty."

His father knelt down, pulling the two sides together. On his father, it had laid open over his black and silver vest, but on Peter the sides completely overlapped.

"Don't worry so much. I can use a simple cleaning spell later," his father said. "Why don't we try one of the Zenmage spells?"

But before they could start, a middle-aged man stepped into the courtyard. He wore rich black clothes embroidered with gold thread, and a crown atop his thick red hair. It was a simple gold band with rubies and evenly-spaced fleur-de-lis.

The King!

His father bowed, and put his hand on Peter's back, forcing him to bow too.

Peter cringed. Looking down, he got a good look at his father's shiny black metallic boots with its silver engravings.

Peter still couldn't believe he was living in the same castle as a *king*. His heart dropped when he saw who was behind the ruler. Princess Red. How was he going to get out of this?

"Lord Kyros, The Researcher?" the king said in surprise.

"My king, it has been a long time," his father said. "Your majesty, meet my son, Peter. Son, this is King Smauton Merdis."

Son. He called me son. Peter about melted into the grass before remembering his manners. Clearing his throat, he bowed again for good measure and said, "Pleased to meet you." He had no clue what he was supposed to do. He had never expected to meet a *king* in his lifetime.

Princess Red tugged on the king's sleeve. "That's the boy, father. Make him pay."

Oh boy, he'd really messed up. And here he was in front of royalty, looking silly in his father's jacket that was too big for him.

"In a minute." King Merdis acknowledged her and turned to Father. "My guards informed me you'd returned. Honestly, I'm surprised to find you alive—after you helped me with—you know, you disappeared."

"Alas, I did. I have been traveling the world searching diligently for our master," his father said.

"In your searches have you happened to stumble upon Disangelo?" King Merdis asked. "Some rumors say he performed the ultimate betrayal, but most sources say he died. I say he got what he deserved."

Disangelo? That was the name from his room, which meant that poor little boy was really dead.

"You'd think you could trust your right-hand man," the king said.

A scowl crossed his father's face. "Why does everyone call *him* his right-hand man? I led everything for Levicus!"

King Merdis raised one eyebrow. "Do not raise your voice to your king. You know full well why everyone sees him as Levicus' second. It's only natural."

"Humph," his father said. "A weakness I am sure to remedy when I get the chance."

"Father, smite him now!" the princess ordered. She seemed more like a two-year old than a young woman.

The king glared at his daughter and she stepped back, her face set with stubbornness.

"I see we have much to discuss. Actually, I'm glad you're back—I need your help with something," King Merdis said. "For now, I am here on official business. It's been reported to me your son attacked my daughter's betrothed yesterday in this very courtyard. Tried to burn him to death."

His father looked down at Peter almost as if he were hiding joy. "I'm not sure why you are here blaming my son. He only started learning magic a couple days ago—what you say is impossible."

His father looked so proud of him, Peter couldn't help but beam.

King Merdis raised his eyebrows, obviously not buying it. "Do not take me for the fool I once was. Your son is bound to be a powerful wizard."

"And he would be—had I known about him. Unfortunately, his mother kept the boy hidden from me until her death a few weeks ago." His father lied easily.

"Prove it," King Merdis ordered. An albino boy with no hair rushed to the king's side and handed him a warm drink, which steamed in the cool air. The king didn't even acknowledge him.

"Peter, do that spell I showed you yesterday," his father said curtly.

Heart racing, Peter pointed his silver wand at the bowl. What if he accidentally made a powerful blast of fire like last time?

Intention, right? Peter imagined the light of a match and cast the spell, *"Chal'Esh."*

A small flame, like a lit match, grew in the bowl.

"Daddy, you can't believe him," Red whined. "He engulfed all of Holdon in flames!"

"Red, stop it," King Merdis said. "I will have the court mages perform a test on his skill level. Will that make you happy?"

"Not until he's hung," the girl said, crossing her arms.

Peter gulped. *Hung?*

"Red, leave us, you are acting very unladylike," the king said, leaving no room for argument.

As soon as Red was out of sight, King Merdis spoke. "Before you run off again, we need to talk. Levicus' disciples showed up at *my* front door this morning asking to inspect the castle for a powerful energy reading. And now I'm thinking *you* had something to do with it."

"Your majesty, I did not want to tell you this way, but I've been working on trying to fix the broken teleport outside the castle walls—as a gift to you. I have not succeeded, and so did not wish to speak of it."

"That is a good idea." The king rubbed his goatee, quickly changing tone. "You will fix it for me. I need a faster way to get my men to the battlefield."

"With all due respect, I do not take orders from you," his father said. "I made you."

"That was almost a decade ago. Times have changed. Levicus is gone and you are nothing now." The king ignored Father's scowl. "You forget *I* am king. And *I* hold the power of what punishment your son receives."

"You can clearly see he has little magic," his father argued.

The king waved his hand. "A mere trick. My servants will come pick him up tomorrow morning for court. I am only doing this out of honor to our past relationship. And please tell your son, if he's going to harm me or my family, then he can have the same fate as the guards who let the previous king escape—a nice beheading in the square."

His father looked like he was going to blow a gasket. "You *lost* him?"

But King Merdis had already walked away.

His father gave Peter a look of death. "Tell me now. Did you or did you not burn that boy?"

Peter swallowed.

"Speak! I will have none of this mute business!"

"It was an accident."

His father looked like he was both furious and excited all at the same time. "Look, you have to be careful with fire magic. It's a unique gift. A small flame to light a candle is fine, but anything more is dangerous. You understand? You must promise me to never use fire magic outside my presence. Ever."

Peter nodded. Even if he had some special gift with fire magic, he never wanted to use it again if it caused such pain.

"Say it."

"Never."

"That's my boy." His father put his hand on his back. It was meant to be supportive, but Peter cringed. Normally he would've put some ointment on his cuts, but he didn't have any here.

"What's wrong? You cringe every time I touch you." His father looked at him curiously. "What aren't you telling me?"

Peter stared blankly.

"Speak. Or I swear I'll—"

Peter cowered and stepped back. He instinctively pulled his father's jacket tighter around him. He knew it looked suspicious, but he couldn't help it.

"I think it's time for you to give my jacket back. You need to be more responsible about remembering your cloak when you go out. It's the season of Kutall, not Salmandria."

Peter reluctantly pulled off the jacket and his tunic rose with it. He frantically pulled it back down—perhaps a little too quickly. He felt so naked without the oversized covering.

His father studied him like he was trying to figure him out. "Lift your shirt."

Peter shook his head quickly. No. There was no way he could show him his back. He would die of shame first.

His father came and lifted it anyway. The cool air pricked the scars on his back.

"I see," his father said, taking his hand and leading him to the fountain where the leather bundle lay on the ground.

Peter couldn't help feel both disgusted and comforted at his support. He thought his father was going to say something was wrong with him, but he remained silent.

"Looks like you need this lesson more than I thought." His father laid out a row of weapons on the circle of grass. "You can't go around throwing magic spells at people unless you're defending yourself. And even then you must question the severity of your attack."

Peter looked down at the row of weapons before him. There was a dagger, a broadsword, a rapier, an axe, a sharp pole with a hook at the end, and a small whip.

He let go of his father's hand. He was getting punished for burning Holdon. Even though he'd expected it, he'd hoped it wouldn't come to this. He wanted his father to be better.

His father continued his lesson, not even noticing Peter's reaction. "Seeing as how you've grown up completely unprepared for this world, I thought now would be a good time to go over the basic uses of some essential weapons."

The weapons were all laid out like in Talbert's game, where he made Peter choose which weapon he'd be punished with.

It was a trick. Peter stepped back and looked around. His heart raced. The whip lay still, but sounds of lashings filled his mind. His father was talking to him, but he couldn't hear his words.

Peter found himself being shaken. But his vision was a dark tunnel, and he couldn't make out what was happening.

"Peter!" the voice blared several times.

He rushed back into reality, like being dumped out of a whirlpool. His father stood before him, still shaking his shoulders.

"What?" Peter blinked, trying to clear his vision.

"I don't know, you zoned out," his father said with a concerned expression. "What happened? Where'd you go?"

Peter sighed. It had happened again. Thing was, he never remembered anything from his blackout sessions. He shivered, suddenly cold.

Peter diverted his eyes from the weapons.

"Okay, so no weapons today—I see that bothers you." His father wrapped them up. "Now, would you like to learn how to control your magic a bit more?"

Peter nodded eagerly. He looked around the courtyard, half expecting Judge Talbert to jump out at him and drag him back to the tunnels—but that wasn't possible. Talbert was on Earth.

"What are you looking for now?" his father asked.

Not wanting to admit he was still being a scaredy-cat, he lied, "Nothing."

To his surprise, his father chuckled. "You don't have to be so afraid of everything—I'll protect you."

Peter relaxed. He was starting to like this 'having a father' thing.

His father launched into a detailed explanation about controlling his magic, and how the proper wand can help, but Peter stared off into space, not digesting any of it.

When his father noticed, he waved his hand in front of his face. "You seem frazzled. Why don't we return to your room. I'm going to make you a sleeping draught. You're going to need your strength to get through tomorrow."

"I don't really need one," Peter said.

"I insist," Father said. "I see now we're going to have to work on those self-control issues of yours."

Peter smiled back at him, but inside he felt like a failure.

"I will speak to the king tonight and see what we can do about tomorrow's test," Father said when they'd returned to Peter's room.

The moment his father left, Peter plopped on his bed. The king obviously held little respect for his father. It seemed unlikely he'd be able to sway the king's mind. And what had his father helped him with all those years ago?

Peter lay on his bed with one of the new books his father had given him. Reading always made him feel better. But this time he couldn't focus. What was going to happen tomorrow when he failed the king's test? Would they really behead him?

He was still lost in thought when his father returned.

"Take this—it will help you sleep," his father said, tucking Peter into bed, pulling the covers up to his chin.

Without a word, Peter took the small grey bottle and downed the contents. It tasted like dirt.

A heavy dizziness overwhelmed him and the image of his father wavered. Peter tried to focus, to keep his mind clear. Pressure rolled through his insides like a wave, and his head hit the pillow. He slipped into a dreamless sleep.

CHAPTER
— 16 —

PETER'S DAY IN COURT

*S*tupid, stupid, stupid. How could Peter have been so foolish to use magic on that boy Holdon? Now Peter was going to go to court for something he couldn't even control. He hoped the judge would be a little more fair than Talbert.

Peter paced across his room. It seemed he had two options. He could either show off the power he felt brewing inside every time he used fire magic, or he could be as weak as possible, to make his father proud of him.

He pulled out his dragon wand to practice an Apprentice-level spell, when a knock came at the door.

Peter quickly put the wand in the back of his pants. He was still afraid of getting in trouble for having it. His father had expressly forbidden him from using any of the castle wands.

His father poked his head in the room, then looked down the hall both ways before shutting the door. "Good, I see you are up and ready." He looked ready for court, his black and silver outfit neatly pressed.

"Now listen. I have to be quick before the guards come to take you to the trial. Whatever they have you do—be sure to use as little magical force as possible. I'd love more than anything for my son to be a powerful wizard, but now is not the time to prove that. You have to be clever—don't focus your intention on the spell. Every time you forget your intention, your spells falter. You can do that, right, my boy?"

Peter nodded quickly. He just had to avoid creating any pillars of flame. Shouldn't be hard.

"You have your silver wand, right?" his father said.

Peter patted his right side where the wand was holstered.

His father seemed satisfied with his answer. "If you have one of your absurd fear-attacks, then think of a gentle flowing river—that should calm you down."

A little weird, but sure, he could do that. What were they going to do to test him? Would it hurt?

"Do me proud out there. There's nothing worse than being under the control of that fool of a king." His father pulled him in for a hug.

Peter smiled at the warmth and stored the feeling away.

"I must go." His father left.

Peter looked down at his green tunic and brown pants. They were wrinkled, and definitely didn't look presentable to wear to court.

He swore he'd seen an ironing spell in the *101 Household Charms and Concoctions.* He flipped through the pages in his mind until page 110 jumped out at him.

Peter pulled off his shirt and laid it out neatly on his bed. Using his silver wand, he cast the simple spell. All the wrinkles smoothed themselves out as if a hot iron was running over it. The armpit area started steaming and burst into flame.

Peter lunged for the shirt, hitting it across his bed to put out the fire. A ring of charred green cloth lingered around the hole. He was about to go through the book to find a spell to fix it when two guards entered.

He raced to put his shirt back on, and frowned at the huge hole under his arm.

"Nice work there." The first guard laughed.

The second guard snickered. "I can see the court has been waiting for nothing."

Peter scowled, trying to ignore their remarks. He dutifully followed the two guards, who looked exactly how he imagined knights from his adventure books. They each wore chainmail shirts with a black surcoat over it, with King Merdis' coat of arms—a sword striking through a gold crown of embattlements and fleur-de-lis.

Even through his fear, Peter's mouth dropped at the grandeur of the throne room. The king and the princess sat on a raised platform at the front of a long room with a vaulted ceiling.

His father stood in the crowd at the front of the room, with people richly dressed—Peter presumed them to be members of the court.

More people than Peter would have liked gathered on both sides of the room. As he passed, they pointed at him and whispered behind their hands.

The guards led Peter to the center, where a white cube with magical engravings sat on top of a stool. What was that cube going to do to him? And if something went wrong, would all these knights gang up on him?

Luckily, he didn't have to wait long. The king stood and the crowd instantly quieted. "Ladies and gentleman, we are gathered here today to test this boy's magical abilities. A charge has been brought against him that he used fire magic against Sir Holdon Fischer—"

The crowd gasped and the king continued, "Witnesses being Lila De'Marco, and my daughter Red Merdis. It was claimed Peter Kyros does not possess such skill to perform this magical action, thus I have decided to put him through the official magical aptitude test."

Peter looked to his father. What was he supposed to be doing? Should he say something to defend himself? Or was it better to tell the truth—he had done it. Maybe the punishment would be less severe if he just told the truth.

"Penalty for attacking a royal is death," King Merdis said.

Okay, so telling the truth was out. Holdon stood smirking at the foot of the stairs leading to the throne platform.

"Do you have anything to say for yourself, boy?" the king asked.

I didn't know what I was doing. I only just learned magic, is what Peter wanted to say, but he couldn't get any sound to come out. He shook his head instead.

"Let's get on with the examination. Peter, you will find a magic detection cube in front of you. It will test your inner magical strength, and display the corresponding color to your innate ability. All you have to do is say the spell *Eh'met Ro'Keseem*, putting all your intention behind it." The king leaned forward on his wooden throne. "And don't think you can fool the device. It will show the truth."

Peter shuddered. He decided he liked the kings in his books much better than this one. He pulled out his silver wand. He was ready to fail.

The king stood. "Hold on. Where is the Court Wizard? She needs to activate the cube."

Red turned to him. "Grandmaster Lynne died last week, father. All her blood was drained, how could you forget?"

King Merdis set his face. "Hold your tongue, young lady. Her assistant, Miss Fumaris, is the new Court Wizard."

A stout woman with sharp features came from the back of the hall. She reminded him of an ancient, hunched witch in the skin of a young woman's body. She wore a black dress with the king's coat of arms sewn across it in gold, and a thick black cloak. She pointed her ebony staff with its golden orb at the cube, and cast a spell.

The cube sprung to life, glowing as if a light shone inside. "The cube is ready to test the boy, your majesty." The young woman bowed as she stepped back into the crowd.

Peter closed his eyes and allowed the words of the spell to roll off his tongue. His voice came out so quietly, he wasn't even sure the cube could have heard it. It glowed a faint grey.

"Louder!" King Merdis ordered.

Peter imagined a trickling river, like his father had said, but it quickly turned into a torrential river racing through a cavern. It was not working. His palms were sweaty and he was afraid the metallic wand would slip from his fingers. He raised his arm and let it down, saying, *"Eh'met Ro'Keseem."*

The cube still glowed a light grey. Guess it had heard him the first time. But what did grey mean? Was that good? Or was it symbolic of strong magic and he'd have to die?

"Again!" the king ordered.

Peter did the spell several more times. Each time, the cube glowed a faint grey. He had no idea what that meant.

King Merdis narrowed his brow, studying Peter intently.

Peter tried to put on his most honest face possible. He didn't want to die, but he didn't want to look like a complete fool either. It was bad enough he had a hole in his shirt for everyone to see.

"The Researcher, it looks as though you might have been telling the truth." The king laughed. "Your boy barely has enough magical essence to levitate a pillow."

His father grinned from his place in the audience.

Peter beamed with pride. He had done well. His magic was weak, and his father was proud of him.

"No, Daddy. I saw him burn Holdon with fire! Do you call me a liar?" Red whined, crossing her chubby arms and looking away.

King Merdis glared at her. "You will speak your turn. Did I ask a girl's opinion? I think not."

"But Daddy, he—"

"I will hear no more on this." But even as the king said this, he seemed to consider his daughter's words.

The young Court Wizard stepped forward, and bowed deeply. "Your majesty, do forgive me, but perhaps it would be prudent to try a different wand with the boy. His wand could have been tampered with to perform poorly." She bowed a couple more times before stepping back into the line of people.

The Researcher stepped forward and bowed. "Your majesty, it is not a wise idea to separate a wizard from his wand."

King Merdis rubbed his goatee. "I disagree. Miss Fumaris offers a respectable idea. If this minimal grey color is accurate, you should have nothing to fear. Guards, give him a standard issue wand."

"As you wish, your majesty." The Researcher bowed, stepping back, his face stoic.

The knight closest to Peter handed him her wand, bowing while holding the thick end towards him. He took the wand and did the same. He felt a tingle go up his spine when holding the wand, almost like when he first touched the dragon wand, but not as strong.

The very basic strip of wood was much lighter than his silver wand, which he'd holstered. He held out the wand and was about to perform the spell, but his arm stopped. It was like his body was trying to stop him from jumping off a cliff.

"Well, go on then," King Merdis ordered.

He had to calm his fear. His father's trick hadn't worked— perhaps that line from the Zenmage pamphlet would? Something about being willing to face his fear.

Peter told himself, *I am willing to not be afraid.*

He waited for the release of fear, but it never came. He still felt the river of fear wash over him.

"Do it!" the king yelled.

But Peter couldn't get his body to move. What if the cube burst into a pillar of flame?

"Daddy, maybe he's just stupid and *wants* to get beheaded."

I'm not stupid! Peter brought down the wand and said, "*Eh'met Ro'Keseem,*" shaking as he did it.

The cube exploded. Peter raised his arm to block his face. Shards of glass flew everywhere. People screamed. Knights lunged to protect the king, the princess, and other dignitaries.

The Researcher raised his staff and the shattered pieces froze in mid-air. He muttered a spell and the shards flew back together on top of the stool.

Some people dropped their mouths in shock, while many clapped and cheered.

The Researcher had protected them all.

Two knights surrounded Peter, like he was going to attack the king or something.

The king's nostrils flared. "Lord Kyros, you swore to me your son's magic was weak."

"My Lord, I promise you I did not know of my son's gifts," his father said. "He's only been with me a week."

"I do not want to hear your drivel," King Merdis said, dismissing him with a wave of his hand.

The Researcher stepped back into the crowd. He looked over at Peter and gave him a pointed grin.

Peter's heart leapt—his father was proud of him!

King Merdis turned to face the crowd, "I hereby find Peter Kyros guilty of attacking a royal. Guards, take the boy to the dungeon, where he will await his punishment."

CHAPTER
— 17 —

RORY MEETS A ZENMAGE

The blonde guard who blocked their path was clad in leather armor, and carried a sword and dagger on her belt. "I have orders from the Vice Chancellor to stop anyone who doesn't have proper authorization, and escort them out of the city."

Rory tapped the blue octagonal light panels beneath her feet. She was used to standing around while social workers and foster parents discussed her fate. But maybe she didn't have to play the same role she used to. She grinned, "I'd be more than happy to go—"

"Enough from you," T. Veckler interrupted.

Rory scowled.

He stepped closer to the guard. "Alana, I will not be having my niece spend the night outside these walls. It's not safe."

"I don't have authority—I'll have to get permission from my captain," Alana said.

"You do that. We'll be in Asdorn's cottage."

Alana looked like she was trying to decide who was more threatening—the Vice Chancellor or T. Veckler.

T. Veckler's hardened expression won out. The guard marched off, her blonde braid swinging behind her.

T. Veckler grabbed Rory's arm. "Come."

"But you said—"

"Not here."

Rory pulled herself free. She marched ahead of the warrior up the circular stone path to the cottage atop the hill. She wished she knew who T. Veckler was taking her to. Sure, she was used to regularly meeting new guardians when she was in foster care, but there was at least some expectation they would be caring for her. In this new world, it seemed anything was possible.

A lesson Miss Kuma had tried to instill in her students popped in her head. *Don't fear the unknown; embrace it.*

Rory decided she wouldn't let the person walk all over her, no matter who he was. She would get some answers.

From the top of the hill, Rory could see out over the city—they were inside some kind of crater. It was a place unlike anything she'd seen before. The two full moons cast a blue and white glow over the large lake near the entrance. Further into the city were rows upon rows of small houses. Cutting through the center of town was a main street lined with shops, and a town circle at its farthest end. Truly a beautiful city to be trapped in.

The white circular cottage was pressed up against the crater wall. It made her think of the kind of place a hermit would live.

T. Veckler pulled a string attached to a little bell. A cheerful note hung in the air before dying off. Her heart welled with delight at the sound, and she could have sworn she caught the slightest smile pass T. Veckler's lips before fading back to its normal stoicism.

A bald man with ancient smile lines and joyful eyes opened the door wearing a rich, dark purple night robe with black trim. "Greetings, Rory," the old man said in an accent Rory did not recognize. Kind of sounded Scottish, but not quite—like it was mixed with accents from lots of places. "I'm Wolfburt Asdorn—folks call me Asdorn. You may also hear people refer to me as 'The Zenmage,' though I expect that will change shortly. It's so nice to see you all grown up."

Rory beamed to be compared to an adult for the first time.

T. Veckler bowed slightly, and gestured towards Asdorn's long robe, his eyebrows raised. "Didn't you get my Xpress message that we were coming?"

"I was lying down for a quick rest," Asdorn said. "You're a little later than expected."

"An Alrakis dragon attacked," T. Veckler said. "The disciples are on the move. Someone is leading them again. I don't like it."

"Please come inside." Asdorn stepped back into his home and held open the door.

After all the excitement, Rory would've expected Asdorn's reaction to be a little less calm.

Rory marched into the circular cottage. She was surprised to feel a sense of peace upon entering the room. All sorts of artifacts filled the low shelves, including a set of bronze bowls, musical instruments, and lots of old books, which reminded her of Peter. Colorful landscape paintings and framed hand-written poems hung on the walls between the windows.

Beside the mini-kitchen were two doors, one normal wood, and the other a large, intricately carved door. She could sense there was something magical about it.

Rory pointed at T. Veckler before he entered the cottage. "This man here whisked me away and refused to tell me anything."

To her surprise, Asdorn chuckled. "He does have that way about him."

T. Veckler scowled, but it was obviously halfhearted. "That one, sir. She's feisty. Just like her mother."

"Thank you for guiding her safely home," Asdorn said.

The moment the front door shut behind them, Rory spun around. It was time for some answers. "What is this? All this time traveling together and you couldn't think to tell me you're my uncle?"

Asdorn raised his eyebrows.

T. Veckler held up his hand. "You'll be happy to know I'm not your uncle."

"Then why—" Rory asked.

"It is the only way to keep you safe," T. Veckler said.

Rory turned to the old man. "What is going on here?"

"Rory, it is time we impress upon you the danger of your situation," Asdorn said. "If our enemy were to find out who you are, or who your parents are, they would bring you to The Researcher. After siphoning your mind for your secrets, he would likely kill you, and even worse—free Levicus."

Rory had no clue what to say. "I think you have the wrong girl—I'm nobody."

"I could do a spell to be sure, but it is simply not necessary," Asdorn said. "Only Katrine's daughter could wear that locket."

"It's striking how much you look like your mother when she was a young girl," T. Veckler said with a softness Rory wouldn't have expected from him.

With a twinkle in his eye, Asdorn added, "You have inherited your mother's bright blue eyes. I am sorry that your parents are not here to see what a beautiful young lady you've grown into. If everything had gone according to plan, you never would've been separated from them in the first place." Asdorn sighed. "But the best laid plans of mice and men often go astray."

"What?" Rory said.

"Oh nothing. Just something wise I once read on Earth. The point is, you are here now and we have to deal with the situation at hand. And unfortunately, it is a dangerous one. I am going to have to ask you to do something I would normally never expect of anyone."

"And what is that?"

"To lie." Asdorn really did look uncomfortable saying it.

They wanted her to do what? Rory furrowed her brow. Adults had never asked her to lie before. She'd always been told that lying was wrong. But maybe things were different on this world.

"T. Veckler is going to be your guardian, taking the role of your uncle, until your parents are uncovered," Asdorn said.

"No way." Rory clenched her fists.

"He is the best person to protect you," Asdorn said. "I'm sure he's as unhappy with the arrangement as you are."

"Why can't I stay with you?" Rory said. How could they expect her to live with someone who didn't even like kids? He was the farthest thing from a father she could imagine.

"I am an official in the city, and it would not be appropriate for you to stay with me," Asdorn said. "Also, T. Veckler's mysterious background works to our advantage. Everyone knows my family has long since passed. Being his niece is believable."

The room spun around her. She would rather be in that awful group home where she had to guard her belongings constantly, than live with him. "I won't do it."

T. Veckler stood up from the wall. "I told you—she's impossible!"

Rory's mind raced to think of an alternate solution. Places she'd seen. People she'd met. "What about Maggie and Burt?"

T. Veckler shook his head. "We already went over this. Two old people suddenly caring for a young girl will draw attention."

"Then how about one of those Tyrskan Warriors—surely they are trustworthy?" Rory asked. She was desperate now. Even a stranger would be an improvement.

"Believe me," Asdorn said. "I understand the predicament we are putting you in. You've never had anyone to trust, so how could I expect you to trust two more strangers? What I'm asking you to do is be *willing* to trust T. Veckler and myself."

"I don't know . . ." Rory scowled. But inside, her heart retched. She hated being reminded her parents had abandoned her, and she'd never had anyone to rely on . . . well, except her brother, until he'd left her too.

"Stop being so soft about it." T. Veckler stepped away from the front window. "An official is going to be here shortly, and we need you to say the right things. Rory, Levicus' disciples have been searching for the children of Katrine and Darius Wysman for a long time—that's why you two were safe on Earth. And now The Researcher will have his people looking for you. I'm sorry to tell you that we suspect spies have already infiltrated Turopia—it could be anybody."

"Even you?" Rory asked.

T. Veckler glared back.

Asdorn ran his hand over his bald head. "I normally don't like using the word 'should.' However, in this case, you should never reveal who you or your parents are. Your life depends on it."

"I can't believe you're making me do this," Rory said. Her heart sunk. Here she thought she was going to be safe in Turopia, and now they were telling her she wasn't?

"A person cannot 'make' anyone do anything," Asdorn said with a hint of kindness in his eyes. "Either you will do it or you will not."

Rory sunk into a comfortable armchair, eying the two men suspiciously. T. Veckler leaned against the wall by the door and Asdorn sat in a chair across from her. It was hard to take the old wizard seriously when he was wearing a dark purple night robe.

No sooner had she sat when something wet rubbed against her ankle. She jumped to her feet, ready to defend herself. She laughed when she saw what it was—a little white ferret. It sniffed around her boots.

"Ah, I see Dexter's come out to play," Asdorn said.

Rory picked up the warm little guy and plopped back in the chair. Dexter curled up in her arms and closed his eyes.

"He really likes you," Asdorn said. "Dexter never lets anyone hold him this long."

Rory smiled. She'd always had a way with animals—they liked her and she liked them. The circular shape of Asdorn's small cottage felt homey, and his space made her feel at peace. She felt the adrenaline of her journey dissolving like snow in the sun.

What was she thinking? She couldn't get too complacent. Now was the time for answers.

Asdorn stepped over to the kitchen, tapped his staff on a ceramic plate, and a dozen white dumplings appeared with candles in them. "Although several days belated—Happy Birthday."

"What?" Rory said.

"Okay, so it's not the traditional birthday cookie, but the red bean paste mochi were your mother's favorite. I can change them to cookies if you'd like."

"I appreciate the treat, but, um, my birthday was a few months ago."

Asdorn set the tray on a low table, next to a stack of books and a cloth-wrapped present with a large blue bow. Was that for her?

"Ah, but it is. The 61st day of the season of Metixber is your birth—if memory serves me, I believe it is called October 31st on Earth." Asdorn helped himself to a red bean paste mochi.

"Are you sure?"

"Yes. In fact, both T. Veckler and I were at your birth thirteen years ago. I will never forget that fateful day."

Rory pulled back her lip. How could the gruff warrior have been there? She couldn't imagine her mother letting him anywhere near her.

Rory grabbed a mochi ball and shrunk back in her chair. She forced herself to take a bite of the glutinous treat. Her taste buds were immediately hit with a pleasant sweetness. She eyed the bald man peacefully eating a mochi ball, and the warrior leaning against the wall by the door, completely ignoring the dessert.

These people claimed to know her parents. And that meant people she would *not* want to be around—family or not. Asdorn seemed like a kind enough guy, but perhaps he was simply a good actor. If she could innocently get them talking about her father, then she would know whether to trust them or not. "So you knew my mother?"

Asdorn's mouth was full. He merely nodded.

T. Veckler stared straight ahead, his face hardening.

"And what about my father?" Rory asked, pretending as if the answer wasn't important.

"We were in the resistance together, and we knew them both quite well." Asdorn smacked his lips of the gooey treat. "So well in fact she made me your Godfather."

"You really don't know where they are?"

"We have an idea where your mother might be," Asdorn said. "But after King Merdis usurped your father's throne, we have no idea where he went."

Rory wasn't sure she heard right. "Excuse me?"

T. Veckler rolled his eyes. "Yes, your father was once the king of Nadezhda," he said in a bored voice. "Darius reclaimed his kingdom after we entrapped Levicus in the portal thirteen years ago. But his First Knight, King Merdis, usurped his throne, and let The Researcher siphon Darius' mind. Last I heard, Darius escaped several years ago. Your father is probably dead, but we've never found the body."

"There are a few other displaced royalty here," Asdorn said. "And while I will not be able to introduce you to them, please know you will not be alone."

But Rory couldn't help it. She *did* feel alone. The only thing that had been enticing about this place was that it might hold the secrets to her parents—and these two didn't even know where they were. "You're lying. I know where my father is and you don't?"

CHAPTER
— 18 —

RORY MAKES A CHOICE

Veckler straightened, eyes wide. "Excuse me?"

"Sure," Rory said, glad to finally have a one-up on the warrior. It was time to reveal the truth and see how they reacted. "He came to get me, and froze my foster parents. He said he had Peter."

Asdorn leaned forward in his chair. "That doesn't sound like Darius. Explain to me what happened."

She recounted the tale of her father arriving, freezing the Gallaghers, and being chased to a dilapidated Victorian house. She almost left out the part about the strange red and gold bird who'd saved her, but she'd already come this far, she might as well go all the way. Asdorn listened carefully, never interrupting her once.

At the end of her tale, Rory leaned back in the chair, exhausted. She wasn't used to sharing so much personal information with anyone other than Sun-hi.

"Ah, so that's why you returned so soon—your Zamsara bird came to lead you home," Asdorn said. "I wondered why the time was now."

Rory stared at him blankly. There was that Zamsara word again. "My what?"

Asdorn held up a wrinkly palm. "Each of the twelve Zenmages of Inara has their own Zamsara bird. First you have to understand every Zenmage has a Lifehouse where we've stored information and lessons from our past lives—to help us fulfill our mission in balancing the world in each life. Your Zamsara bird shares a deep connection with you, and will appear to guide you to your Lifehouse when the time is right."

Rory stared at him blankly. But when she thought about it more, the red and gold bird *did* feel like a long-lost friend.

"If you look over my shoulder, you can see the door to my own Lifehouse." He leaned back in his chair and smiled slightly, closing his eyes. He sat quietly for a few moments before speaking. "I want to tell you something I do not share lightly. You have not visited your Lifehouse yet, so it is not yet the right time for you to understand your past lives—but do know this. I recognize your spirit and know that you and your brother have reincarnated together in one way or another for thousands of years. You two share the deepest bond of any of the Zenmages."

Rory pushed the lump in her throat aside. Him talking about Peter like that had made her more emotional than she wanted to be in front of strangers. Dexter nuzzled up to her, licking her face.

"I can also tell you that the man who came for you is not your father."

"Are you sure?" Rory asked skeptically. She desperately needed to know her father wasn't actually evil—that she'd interpreted the situation wrong.

"I am sorry you have been through so much." Asdorn took a deep breath, as if gathering his thoughts. "I have my own reasons to believe he's not your real father. Though you may not like my answer. First, you have to understand that in order to get to Earth he would've had to open one of the five portals—only one of which we have found. Your father followed the Way of the Warrior—and while he was a great man, a powerful wizard he was not. So, it would've been impossible for Darius to travel to Earth to get you."

Rory felt the rush of a thousand pounds lifting off. "So he's really not my father?"

"Most definitely not," T. Veckler said.

"The man who claimed to be your father—I believe he was actually a dangerous man known as The Researcher," Asdorn said. "He's Levicus' right-hand man, and will do anything to free his master. You are lucky to have escaped."

Phew. Rory leaned over in her chair, putting her head between her knees. It was all too much. She didn't know whether to laugh, cry, or scream at her predicament. At least she knew these people weren't on The Researcher's side.

But then an awful realization struck her—The Researcher said he had Peter, and that meant he was in trouble. She knew she should say something, ask them to help, but the words failed to come out.

Asdorn thought for a minute. "You say he asked for your locket?"

"But I wouldn't give it to him." Rory's hand went to her locket, wondering what was so special about it. "It's all I have of my mother."

"It was indeed Katrine's—she left the locket with you for safekeeping in case something went wrong with our plan to entrap Levicus," Asdorn said. "She knew it would stay bound to you if the worst happened."

So that's why I never lost it though all my foster homes.

"The locket is the possession of the Keepers," T. Veckler said.

"You're right. He tried to get it from me, but I wouldn't give it to him." Memories of that horrible night filled her. "He said he'd only frozen the Gallaghers, but they looked dead to me. Are you sure they're okay?"

"They are likely quite fine," Asdorn said. "You made a good choice in not giving it to him—I'm proud of you."

Rory sighed. It didn't seem that way. "It's all my fault. They were only trying to give me a home."

"It's no one's fault," T. Veckler said. "This is war. People die. People are maimed. Many lives have been lost, and while it does not diminish their pain, we can know they suffered for a good cause."

Asdorn gave T. Veckler a disapproving look.

T. Veckler's eyes widened in realization. "Asdorn, The Researcher—he must—" His rough face drained of color. "No . . . it can't be."

"Asdorn, the intense energy reading you picked up in Nadezhda—it doesn't happen any old time a portal is opened. In the old days, when The Researcher would travel regularly to Earth for Levicus on research missions, he'd use the portal on the southern continent of Baikal. Only the standard energy tracings from powerful magic were left behind. The massive disruption has to mean—"

T. Veckler paused, pursing his lips together. He shook his head in dismay. "The Researcher must have discovered the portal on our continent and brought Peter through. How are we going to get Peter out of Nadezhda? And why does The Researcher want him? Do you think he knows?"

Asdorn raised his hand. "Do calm down, my friend. We will think of something."

"My fath—" Rory started before correcting herself. She was startled by how frazzled T. Veckler seemed. "He did say he had Peter."

T. Veckler started pacing, something Rory had never seen him do. "But I know The Researcher. He'll keep Peter close, maybe even hide him. We don't even know what the boy looks like. I don't like this one bit. I should go there myself."

"You know that's not a good idea—it's too risky." Asdorn laid a hand on T. Veckler's shoulder. The warrior instantly relaxed.

"You're right—I don't know what I was thinking." T. Veckler shook his head as if clearing his unwanted thoughts.

"We have to go rescue Peter right now," Rory said. She could barely believe she was siding with the warrior.

"Nadezhda is too heavily fortified to attack," T. Veckler said.

"I'll go get him," Rory said without thinking.

"It is kind of you to offer," Asdorn said. "But it is too dangerous. With the information you've shared with us tonight, I can be sure The Researcher is after The Book of Keys—and he needs your locket to open it."

"Asdorn's right. The Researcher has been relentless in his mission to free his master, and he could use The Book of Keys to find where we've trapped Levicus."

"We will send a couple of Tyrskan Warriors to investigate," Asdorn said. "For now, the evening is getting late, and I believe it is time—"

"Time for what?" Rory interrupted.

"Perhaps it's time we teach her manners instead," T. Veckler said.

"Time to go home," Asdorn said, obviously not bothered by the interruption.

Rory grabbed another red bean paste bun and sat back down, not sure her mind could handle much more new information.

"What's important is you are here safe," Asdorn said. "And our continued mission is to protect you and your brother. I admit I am surprised Peter did not join you."

She bit her lip as an intense fear welled inside—Peter needed their help. "I haven't seen him in over seven years, not since we were separated at the Rutherford Adoption Center."

"Troubling," Asdorn said.

"Rory, it is late, and you've had a long journey," Asdorn said calmly, but quickly. "For now, would you be willing to stay with T. Veckler?"

Frustration ached in her throat, threatening tears. Rory clenched her jaw and muttered, "Fine, but I don't understand what I'm supposed to do here."

"My dear, you have come *home*," Asdorn said. "It will be our job—me and this fine gentleman here—to take care of you until times change. You will be safe here in Turopia."

T. Veckler studied her. "As long as you don't tell anyone who you are, or who your parents are."

Asdorn raised his hand. "My friend, I think she understands the situation."

T. Veckler looked away, still aggravated. *Geesh.* Did anything make him happy? She'd gone along with their crazy plan, she would've thought he'd have been at least a little appreciative of her sacrifice.

"I do believe it is time we adjourn this conversation," Asdorn said. "I'll have one of the Tyrskan Warriors give you a tour tomorrow. Would you like that?"

Rory was taken aback. It was the first time anyone had actually asked her what *she* wanted in this strange place. She perked up. "One of the warriors I traveled with?"

Asdorn nodded with a smile.

What Rory really wanted to do was spend more time with the peculiar old man standing before her. Asdorn could tell her more about her mother and her *real* father.

She eyed T. Veckler—she'd have to watch him carefully. She would stay with him for now, but she would never trust him—she'd take care of her own needs.

Obviously these people had motives of their own. She'd have to find a way to rescue Peter herself. She'd thought getting to Turopia would make things better, not worse.

T. Veckler fidgeted and pointed at Rory. "Asdorn, do you think you could help with, uh, making her look like she's from here?"

Asdorn walked to the back of the cottage and selected a ruby-tipped staff from a rack of staves. He pointed it at her.

"Wait." Rory raised her hands in defense.

"Don't worry, I'm not going to turn you into a toad," Asdorn said. "I'm just going to give you some new clothes to wear."

"You can do that?" Rory asked.

"Yes, to change your clothes. No, to turning you into a toad."

Rory lowered her hands, unsure of what to expect. With a tip of his staff and a few magical words, her filthy once-awesome superhero costume transformed into a dress and a coat that were way too big.

In surprise, all Rory could say was, "I look like a moose."

Asdorn raised a finger. "Patience for the fitting."

She hoped it wouldn't take long—she suddenly had to pee.

"*Al'goh Hat'imio Bol'Gadiym,*" Asdorn incanted.

Rory's dress and jacket shrunk to fit her small frame. She gasped. Instant fitted clothes! Even though the outfit was unlike anything she would've selected herself, it was still pretty cute. She spun around, and the skirt of the white dress flared around her. The black jacket was the same length as the light dress and had a stiff collar. Rory fingered the five buttons that ran up the front of the jacket.

It was hard to get used to all this magic. Ever since seeing the old couple use magic, she'd wanted to know more. "How did you do that?"

"A little spell I picked up on the continent of Baikal." Asdorn said. "Maybe something you can learn to do some day."

"Me? Do magic? No way." Her heart leapt with both the excitement and the absurdity of the idea. But then the last few days hadn't been quite normal either.

"It is likely," Asdorn said. "Katrine followed the Way of the Wizard and the Warrior. The gift of magic tends to run in bloodlines."

"These garments are the Academy's uniform," Asdorn explained. "Everyone, from the children of royalty to the poorest refugee, don this same uniform. That way kids don't waste their limited credits on clothes."

She didn't want to admit it, but his explanation made sense. As a foster kid, she'd been teased not only for having ill-fitting clothes, but re-wearing the same outfits over and over. She never was fond of uniforms, but that was because they were all so boring in Rutherford—nothing like the fancy uniform she was wearing now.

Asdorn held up the small package from the coffee table. "I see we got distracted and forgot to give you your gift."

Rory accepted the present, quickly tearing off the ribbon, and peeled back the magically sealed purple cloth. Her eyes widened at the silver jewelry box. It was heavy, and she could sense magic coursing through the intricate carvings. It reminded her of dancing fire.

T. Veckler's eyes widened. "You can't—"

The two had a silent communication with only their eyes as Rory marveled at the box. It opened to reveal a black sparkling lining, that looked like she was peering into a space full of stars. Wow. She'd never received anything so magnificent in all her life.

Sure she'd received presents from some of her foster parents, and Sun-hi, but they were usually the necessities: socks, underwear, books—but nothing really interesting.

"Thank you," Rory said softly. "I don't know what to say."

"Say you'll take exceptional care of it," Asdorn said with clear joy in his eyes. "That jewelry box was a special possession of your mother's. I think she'd want you to have it."

Rory felt like she was melting. Just holding the silver box brought her closer to her mother. Rory tried to give her thanks, but no words came out.

Asdorn smiled in understanding. "It is time," he said, opening the front door. "T. Veckler, take her home."

CHAPTER
— 19 —

RORY'S UNWANTED HOME

Rory clutched the jewelry box close to her heart as she followed T. Veckler down Turopia's only through street. Other than a couple of guards walking around, it felt as hollow as a ghost town. A light autumn mist hung in the air.

She hated to think how many displaced families had come to live in these rows upon rows of small square, one-story houses. But that meant people—and options.

Instead of feeling resolved after speaking to Asdorn, she had even more questions. Like why were there spies after her and her brother? What had happened to her parents? And how was she going to free Peter from that awful Researcher guy?

The old man wasn't so bad, so just maybe Turopia would make a good home. All she needed now to really feel at peace was her brother—but she'd have to get away from T. Veckler's watchful eye to get to Peter.

Rory lingered beside the lake, which sparkled under the light of the two moons. An idea struck her—she could use a technique for getting away from bad foster parents that had worked so well in the past—being obstinate and ignoring the rules. That was it!

She marveled at how the path lit up as she walked. She grinned and stepped one foot forward. The octagonal section illuminated beneath her new black-laced boot. She danced around, lighting up the path beneath her. She giggled despite herself.

"Come quickly," T. Veckler said. "I want to go home."

Rory grinned. "But not *my* home."

When T. Veckler turned back to her, Rory put on her best pouty scowl.

They turned down a row of cottages that appeared to be cut and pasted from the same pattern, with only slight variations in the color and the small front yard. The dimmed path anticipated her direction by lighting up the sections before her.

T. Veckler approached a small, faded teal green house and pulled out a skeleton key. Before he opened the door, he turned to her softly. "I am letting you stay here because it is the best option. Do not disrespect my home, and do not touch anything."

Rory nodded. It was time to lay it on. "How do you expect me to sleep and eat if I can't touch anything?"

T. Veckler gave her a frustrated look.

And so it begins. Rory held back her smirk. Suddenly aware spies could be watching them, she thought she'd better say something useful. "Yes, uncle."

T. Veckler gave a weak smile.

Drat. That seemed to reverse the effect of her first comment.

He unlocked the door, poked his head inside, looked around, and then returned the key to the satchel on his belt.

Wow, this guy is really paranoid.

"Come here." He placed his arm around her in what she supposed was a fatherly way, and led her inside. After shutting the door, and eying each of the closed windows, he dropped his arm.

Rory had expected the place to be a disorderly bachelor's pad, but was surprised to find a neat and orderly home. In the back left was a door, where she hoped to find a bathroom. Everything was so neat—even the mini kitchen. A set of one plate, bowl, cup, and silverware lay washed beside the sink.

He must have been in the middle of something when he'd left to get her. There were neatly folded pieces of parchment, quills, and ribbon sitting atop a large table-sized map in the middle of the room, as well as measuring instruments, books, and several throwing knives.

Rory's eyes widened when they fell upon the back wall. Every weapon she could imagine, and others she'd never seen before, hung on the back wall. She'd thought he carried enough on his person, but obviously not.

T. Veckler caught her gaze. "I'm a warrior. Those are my tools. You will learn to use them someday."

Having sharp instruments like that out in the open was so foreign. Things like this were usually associated with axe murderers and serial killers, not protective guardians. "You don't know anything about me."

"I know more than you think."

Rory really did want to learn how to use a sword, but she couldn't let him know that. She crossed her arms and turned away.

"I think you'll come to learn that Inara is much different than Earth," T. Veckler said. "We are recovering from a bloody world war. Times are rough. You have to know how to protect yourself, and those you love, if you are going to survive."

Rory got the impression that he had failed to protect someone dear to him. "So who was it who died because of you?"

The look of hurt on his face told her she'd crossed a line, but she couldn't help but feel pleased her plan was working. It wouldn't be long before he'd kick her out.

She might as well dig in further with something she was actually curious about. "And what could you possibly know about my home planet?"

"Plenty. I helped your mother, Asdorn, and Ipseh set up the magical house you came through on the other end of the portal."

Wow. T. Veckler had done that? Perhaps she needed to reconsider her opinion of him.

"Look, I know you don't like this any more than I do. As you are here longer, you will come to understand why this pretense is so important."

Rory yawned.

"We should get you to bed. You have a big day tomorrow, so you'll need your sleep."

"And what possibly could I do to keep myself awake?" She bet all his books were about fighting, which would be awful for night reading. "Besides, you couldn't possibly know what a girl needs."

T. Veckler looked down at her. "I see what you're doing. I've dealt with murderers, thieves, and people more cruel then you can imagine—and you think you can unhinge *me*?" T. Veckler grinned. "My girl—you are stuck with me."

Rory glared at him and crossed her arms.

T. Veckler sighed. "Bed."

Rory looked over her shoulder at the one bed. "Where should I sleep?"

"The bed, of course. And—"

"What!?" That sounded awful. It was too small to share.

"Don't interrupt. I will sleep on my chair, and you will sleep on the bed until we get reassigned a larger home. And hopefully Peter will have joined us by then."

"Oh." That made a lot more sense. Sleeping in a bed sounded amazing after sleeping on the ground the previous night.

Her game usually worked more in her favor. Rory sat down on the crisply made bed. She reached for a framed photograph of a family. "Who's this?"

Before she was able to get a good look, T. Veckler flew across the room and grabbed it out of her hand. The warrior stuffed the framed photo backwards in his belt and returned to his chair under the front window without a word.

Rory gulped. She'd gone a little too far this time. Better not say anything else—there was a difference between getting reassigned and getting beaten—and she wouldn't put an attack past this man.

She snuck into the corner bathroom to escape his rage. She silently thanked the gods this world had plumbing and toilets. But—no shower. What was the deal with this place?

By the time she'd emerged, T. Veckler had calmed down and was reading in his armchair under the front window. He looked up at her—as if daring her to make another argument.

But there'd be no more speaking tonight—the moment he fell asleep, she'd be out of here. She could find Nadezhda on her own.

Rory slipped under the rough covers. This was awful. She flipped the pillow over and lay her head down, as if she were trying to fall asleep.

It was quite some time later when the book finally fell from T. Veckler's grasp. It was time.

She sat up on the edge of her bed, watching him closely for any sign of movement. His breathing was calm—he was asleep. She stared at him, surprised at his self-control—he seemed like a violent man, but hadn't even raised a fist at her. Which was weird because she'd found the overly-nice foster parents had been some of the worst.

Rory smirked as she grabbed her cloak and bag. This was going to be easier than she'd thought. She tiptoed the few steps to the door and slowly turned the handle. She paused, listening intently for any sign of movement.

Nothing.

She pushed the door open, and closed it as quietly as she could.

Before she could take a step, the door swung open behind her. He didn't even have to say anything. The stern look communicated his fury quite clearly. "In-side," he said, as if it were two words.

Rory looked over her shoulder. She could run. Hide. Get away. "But you were sleeping . . ."

T. Veckler raised his eyebrow. "You really think I wouldn't hear you opening the door? My girl, you must remember, I've been having to defend myself my entire life. I hear everything."

"I'm not talking to you."

"Don't think you're getting off that easy," T. Veckler said, pulling her into the house. "You will not run away from me again. What do I have to do to impress upon you the danger of your situation?"

Rory turned away, crossing her arms. "I need to find Peter."

"I can't let you leave." T. Veckler glared down at her. "It is my duty to be your guardian, until the time your parents are miraculously found, or until, well . . . you die."

"Or you die." Rory turned to scowl at him.

T. Veckler just smirked. "You wish."

"I hate this place and I hate you!" Rory stomped her foot and marched over to the bed.

"I don't care what you think about me." And T. Veckler looked like he meant it.

"I was just going to rescue my brother, but you don't care about that, do you?"

"I understand your desire to be with him—you're twins." He added in a gentler voice, "Asdorn and I are working on a plan to find your brother. So please, I ask you to be patient a little longer."

"I guess . . ." It wasn't fair, but there was nothing she could do about it now. All the things Asdorn had said weighed on her mind.

"Rory—you may not believe me, but you belong here," T. Veckler spoke in a kind voice. "Your mother was born in the capital Nadezhda."

Hearing of her mother made her heart soften and the anger started to dissipate.

"Turopia will be safe for you and Peter—as long as you keep your identity a secret. I want to protect you, but I can't do my duty if you don't allow me to."

T. Veckler's words stung, and she was afraid of speaking her mind for fear her voice would crack. She felt a strange familiarity to this place and knew she belonged here, but she still felt on edge. Who could she trust in this strange city when everything she'd believed before was wrong?

"Enough talking—bed." T. Veckler watched her as she tucked herself in.

She was so distraught, she didn't think she'd be able to fall asleep, and T. Veckler sitting beside her bed didn't help.

All the worries raced through her mind. How were they going to find Peter? Would he be okay when they found him? Was The Researcher doing horrible things to him?

She wanted her brother. More than her parents, she felt that he would make everything right. He'd always taken care of her in the various foster homes, looked out for her, made her feel special. And she wanted that feeling back.

❊   ❊   ❊

A sliver of sunlight struck Rory's face. As if by miracle, she awoke slightly hopeful. She didn't like being in a bad mood. And although her new guardian's grumpy vibe rubbed off on her, she promised herself that just for today, she wouldn't let it get to her. She would try to make the best of the situation— until she could find a way to get to Peter. She was surprised to find she was actually looking forward to her tour today—she secretly hoped it would be with Agi.

"Get up, sleepy-head. I hear you moving around over there."

Rory opened her eyes and saw an old white cloak had been nailed to the ceiling around her bed. She smiled. The little bit of privacy was nice. After stretching and making sure her new school uniform appeared decent, she stepped out from behind the makeshift curtain.

T. Veckler had laid out several weapons on the table in a neat row. He was polishing a short sword. "After our experiences over the past few days, I've decided we need to dig right into your training. I'm going to take you to the Entrix this morning."

Rory blinked, trying to wake up. "The what?"

"It's our training facility. You said you've done some fighting—I think you're going to like it."

Fighting. Kicking some air would really help get some of this frustration out of her system. "Aren't I supposed to be getting a tour this morning?"

"I can see if Agi's available earlier," T. Veckler said, but he looked insulted she had dissed his idea.

"Great. What about breakfast?" Rory asked. Her stomach grumbled as if to accentuate her comment.

"Right. Food."

He pulled out a loaf of bread and a few strips of dried meat from the cabinet, a block of cheese from a smaller chilled box. He tore the bread in half, placed it with meat and a piece of cheese on a plate, and handed it to Rory.

Rory couldn't help but make a face. *That was it?* But he was holding it out so eagerly, she took it. Looked like he was trying hard this morning too—he hadn't even brought up her failed attempt to run away. "You can take the meat. I'm a vegetarian."

T. Veckler looked at her like she just said she was an alien.

"I don't like to harm animals," Rory said.

He rolled his eyes, took the meat away from the plate, and tore off a piece with his teeth before putting it back in the cabinet.

She took a bite of the bread. It had a good flavor, but it was beyond dry. She chewed and forced a smile. Somehow she knew if the day got off to a bad start, then the rest of the day would be miserable. And she wasn't ready for another awful day just yet.

T. Veckler sighed. "I guess we can put your training off till this afternoon. I'll take you to the dining hall where you can get some real food, then you can go on that tour."

Her face lit up. "That sounds great!"

"Sorry. I'm used to eating in the wild and I don't like conditioning myself to fancy food. 'Cause then I just miss it when I return to the road."

Rory thought that was an awful idea. She would much prefer to indulge and be spoiled when she had the chance. Besides, she liked her fruits and vegetables.

She brushed off her knee-length white dress and matching black jacket, trying to make it look less wrinkly. "Can you make my dress look new like Asdorn did?"

T. Veckler shook his head. "No. I don't have magical abilities."

Obviously, Rory had hit another soft spot. "Oh. Sorry." Rory smiled. She was not going to let this get her down. But she couldn't hide her disappointment.

"Right. Girls. Sorry. It's been a long time." T. Veckler went to the back corner and rifled through a cabinet. There he pulled out a small box. He set it on the high table so that Rory couldn't see its contents.

To Rory's surprise, he pulled out a wooden hairbrush. "Here. I don't know why I saved this, but here you go."

"Thanks. Do you have a mirror?"

"No. I don't need to look at myself."

But Rory thought if he did, maybe he wouldn't have trimmed his light beard a little crooked. She slipped behind the makeshift curtain, pulled out the dark hairs that were in the brush, and brushed out her own long hair. Feeling much better, she handed the brush back.

He held up his hand to refuse, "Keep it. It's yours now. I don't think the person it belonged to is coming back."

Rory was afraid to ask who. An ex-wife maybe? "Thanks."

Before she could put the hairbrush away, her new guardian was already out the front door. Rory felt slightly underdressed compared to T. Veckler in his long coat armed with sword, two daggers, whip, and throwing knives. Was all that *really* necessary just to go to breakfast?

It was still early—the town was absolutely quiet. As they walked down the main street with all the shops, Rory only saw a handful of people.

At the end of Turopia's one street stood a large temple and government building looking over a circle with a magnificent water fountain. They turned left towards a three-story stone building with a dozen wide, short steps leading up to the entrance. "What is this place?"

"It's the old orphanage. Now we just use it for meetings and our dining hall."

Rory was afraid to ask, but couldn't help herself. "And *where* might all those orphans be now?"

"With Asdorn's pushing, we cut the orphanage program several years ago. Now orphans live with families. Since raising a child is expensive, the money that once went to fund the orphanage now goes to the families. And the caretakers have access to the dining hall for food."

"I'm not an orphan," Rory said indignantly.

"Your parents aren't here to take care of you. And don't I know it."

Once again T. Veckler had succeeded in making her feel unwanted. It wasn't like she wanted to live with him either.

But why did he have to be so mean about it? She pushed those thoughts away. Instead, she thought about what it would be like when she found Peter and they started a home of their own.

CHAPTER

— 20 —

PETER'S PUNISHMENT

Peter covered his nose from the musty stench of his dungeon cell. Once his eyes adjusted to the dark, he could see people imprisoned in the cells around him.

He plopped on the rotting cot and ran his boot through the hay on the floor. His father *would* come rescue him. Peter couldn't consider the alternative. And he couldn't die without seeing Rory again. He'd find a way out if his father didn't.

Light pooled in from around the corner. He couldn't see the stars to make his nightly wish.

A mouse poked its head out of the cot and scurried through a hole in the wall. Peter jumped up to stand in the opposite corner.

The young woman in the cell next to him looked him over. "You're a little young to be down here—what has King Merdis locked you up for?"

Peter hesitated whether he should say anything to her.

"Oh come on, you can talk to me," the woman said. "I'll start—I was on another run to free a group of captured Ayeven when I got caught. Being beheaded in the morning."

Beheaded? So that really happened here? His dad better hurry. "I, uh—accidentally set Lord Holden on fire."

The other prisoners laughed.

"That brat deserved it."

"He's the one who got me thrown down here for serving his meal too cold."

Peter squinted to see a pale-skinned boy in the cell across from him. He had no hair, like the other servants he'd seen.

"Get comfortable—you'll be in here a long time, unless you're sentenced to a beheading," a gruff man said. "King Merdis loves a good public display of death."

Peter tried to sound brave. "I don't plan to be in here long. My father's going to get me out." Or so he hoped.

The young woman laughed. "And who's your mighty father that he can so easily get you out of Stinky Merdis' dungeon?"

"Lord Kyros, The Researcher."

For a moment, no one said anything. Then the young woman spat into his cell. Peter shuffled to the back corner. "What was that for?"

"Your father is the worst," she replied. "How could anyone serve someone like Levicus?"

"Power—it's all about power," the gruff man said.

The people around him sounded their agreement, but Peter was completely lost.

"Everything fell apart with the disciples when Levicus was trapped away," the gruff man said. "The Researcher knows he's powerless without Levicus. And that's why I'm sure he'll stop at nothing to free his master."

Peter sat there frozen. What was he supposed to say to that? They were probably just mad because they were caught on the wrong side of the law.

"You guys don't even know what you're talking about," an old man in the corner said in drawl. "If you studied your history, you'd know there was an era of peace on Inara when Levicus exerted his full control—well, until he accidentally trapped himself in a portal a couple thousand years ago. Levicus only wants to return us to that time."

"And I'm sure you'd have all the Ayeven wiped out too," the gruff man said. "Is that what you want?"

Peter sat there, confused.

A scrawny man in the corner cackled. "You guys are all idiots. Idiots I tell 'ya. The Ayeven got what was comin' to them."

"How can you possibly say that?" the young woman went to the cell bars to face him directly.

"Here I was gonna marry this beautiful Ayeven woman, but her mother refused. Said she couldn't be associating with 'them Humans.' What purpose can they possibly serve when they're only lookin' out for themselves?"

The woman scoffed. "Perhaps if you'd been persecuted for generations, you'd stay away from Humans too. We still put Ayeven in work camps to drain their blood for their magical healing properties. Wouldn't you want to stay far away from Humans too?"

Blech. That sounded gross. But these criminals couldn't be right. His father said Rory was in danger. Why would he have to make plans to free her if the Ayeven in Turopia weren't dangerous?

But Peter didn't have a chance to contemplate it. As the group argued over each other, the dungeon door opened and his father stepped in. His staff glowed, casting a silvery light over the cell block and the scared prisoners' faces. The woman remained at her bars, glaring at The Researcher, while everyone else scurried to the corners of their cells, out of the light.

His father hovered over the guard as she unlocked Peter's cell. "Come."

Peter couldn't help but wonder what trickery his father had performed to free him. "But how?"

"I struck a deal with the king," his father said, leading him out of the cell block that was closest to the exit. Peter looked down the two hallways that led deeper into the dungeons, but it was so dark, he couldn't see anything.

"Let's get you washed up—then we can talk."

As Peter scurried behind his father, the woman called to him, "Remember what we said."

Peter followed close behind his father. Those people's anger was so frightening. He couldn't stop worrying as they walked up the dimly-lit stone staircase and into the hallway.

"Do you want to tell me what that was about?" his father asked.

"It's just that, well . . ." Peter hesitated. What if he got in trouble for repeating their awful words?

"You know you can tell me. Trust me. I'll set you straight."

"The prisoners said the Ayeven were being wrongly persecuted, but you told me they were dangerous."

His father stopped, and kneeled in front of him. "And they are Peter—vicious creatures who care only about themselves. They have the power to help humanity, and yet they keep all their power within their tight communities. They're the reason the opposition has grown so strong and why there continues to be so much death—they've poisoned the minds of many Humans to join their cause."

"But why?"

His father's face twitched. "Look, I can't explain the entire history of the Ayeven's treachery in the corridor. You need to not be so sensitive to everything. They're the reason your mother isn't with us. Isn't that enough for you?"

"How could they?"

His father stood and pulled him in for a hug. "I know, it's hard. But you have to understand—when Levicus returned a couple hundred years ago, the Ayeven had a chance to bring peace to the world, but instead they only desired to retain their power. They fought out of greed, and they're the reason so many Humans died—and why our family was separated for so long."

Peter stared at his father blankly. As happy as he was to be freed, his heart was heavy. They walked in silence through the cold hallways towards the bathhouse.

When Peter entered the men's side, his mouth dropped. The expansive room held not only a large rectangular pool surrounded by tall pillars, but plenty of space to walk around the bath. Beautiful paintings lined the walls.

No way he was going in a communal bath and have people see his shameful scars. He turned to race out of the changing room, but his father held out his arm and caught him.

"You're filthy," Father said. "Don't you want to be clean?"

Peter knew he couldn't argue—he'd just have to make it quick. After changing into a bathrobe, Peter stayed to the edge of the large pool, but his father forced two bald, albino servants to scrub him down with soap.

Before any more people could see his scars, Peter jumped out and threw on his robe. As he stood dripping, he caught his father's disappointed glare.

Peter's heart sunk—and here his father had been so proud of him during the court test.

After he was all cleaned with fresh clothes, his father took Peter back to his room. There were so many questions he wanted to ask. But one question refused to leave. His father had avoided the topic every time he'd brought it up. It was now or never.

When his father shut the door, Peter turned to him. "I don't understand. Even if the Ayeven attacked, why did you leave us?"

His father stared off like it was a difficult question. "What I can tell you is that your mother and I had a whole life planned when the Ayeven attacked our hiding spot on Earth." He shook his head as if remembering painful memories.

Peter's chest tightened. It had been as hard for his father as it was for him. "But you never came back for us."

"I wanted to, but I couldn't find you. Unfortunately, I had to wait until your magic developed so I could use my devices, and magic doesn't develop until you're twelve or thirteen. Sure you might have had some slight magic, but it wouldn't have been strong enough for me to detect, especially on Earth where magic has been mostly eradicated."

Peter finally knew his past. His parents hadn't abandoned them after all—it was an accident. "Is mother really missing, or is she—" He couldn't say the word.

"No, my boy, she is alive. And that's why we need to get Rory out of Turopia. She alone has access to something that holds a powerful finding spell, which will help me discover your mother's whereabouts. Those Ayeven have hidden her from us for far too many years. And it's time for that to end."

Peter smiled—soon he'd have the family he'd always wanted. But the feeling of release didn't last long. Dormant anger bubbled up. After all these years, Peter thought hearing an explanation would have made him feel better. It didn't.

Now he knew why his father hated the Ayeven so much. What despicable creatures were these Ayeven that they would separate a new mother from her infants? "Those Ayeven. They ruined everything. How could the prisoners I met help creatures like that?"

His father slowly shook his head. "My son, people come up with the strangest motivations. You don't want to be like them." The Researcher walked to the bed, and patted the down comforter beside him. "Enough of that. It's time for business."

Peter dutifully sat on the bed beside his father. He felt small and unworthy of his kindness.

"Now, I worked very hard to strike this deal for you," Father said. "So don't go and mess it up."

What was he going to be doing? Some sort of hard labor for the king? He could handle that.

"In a way, it was lucky you broke the testing cube. For then I was able to use my quick action saving the king's life in my negotiations."

Peter didn't feel so lucky.

"You will be teaching Princess Red how you did that fire magic."

"But I don't even know how I did it."

"It doesn't matter. Just show her the fire magic and watch her fail. If a wizard doesn't have the gift of elemental fire, it is not something you can teach them. Just a few lessons and I'm sure she'll give up."

"But you told me never to do fire magic."

"My boy, the secret is already out. People—at least the smart ones—are going to suspect you are a Zenmage after your attack on Holdon—and your display in court this afternoon. See, only a Zenmage can use Inara's elemental magic."

"You mean like in that little book?" Peter asked.

"Yes, and we'll be having more lessons on that—though I don't know any Zenmages personally who can teach you. There are only twelve alive at any one time, so they can be hard to track down. As for Princess Red, the first lesson is tomorrow."

Peter put on a smile. "I'll need a wand."

"You can use this wand for now. Luckily I was able to get it back from the king—it's quite special to me." His father handed him the silver wand. "I'm going to have to get you a new one . . . one more suited towards your talents. But you should use this one in your lesson with Princess Red."

"Thank you." Peter accepted the wand. He preferred his dragon wand or even that wand the guard had given him, but he'd done his fire magic both times with this wand, so there must be something special about it.

"Now, it's time you learned to control your emotions," his father said. "Giving in to your anger in court today was a sign of weakness. You have to take a deep breath before acting. Do you think I stayed at the great Levicus' side by giving in to fears on the battlefield? No—you have to keep your wits about you."

Peter stared at his father, trying to control all his confusing emotions. He would do whatever his father asked to make him proud.

He was getting everything he wanted—freedom from Talbert, a father who loved him, and a beautiful place to live. But it still felt empty without Rory. "Is it going to be long before Rory joins us? I miss her."

A look of concern passed his father's face. "I admit I am having more trouble than I would have liked getting her out of Turopia. There have been some delays, but I don't want you to worry—remember travel takes time on Inara, even with the teleport locations"

But Peter didn't want to sit back and wait. After his father left, he counted down the minutes until he could sneak out to the library. He hated not knowing what was going on, and not being able to do anything about it. He trusted his father to bring Rory home, but perhaps if he were able to figure out a way to free Rory his father would be proud of him—and Rory could be with them much faster. First chance he got, he'd go to the library and see what he could find about Turopia.

As he slowly crept through the corridors, using only the light of the moons to guide his way, another thought troubled Peter. He wanted desperately to believe his father, but the prisoners words had gotten to him. He'd just have to figure it out for himself. But what would he do if he found out his father, his only connection to this world, was on the wrong side?

CHAPTER

— 21 —

PETER'S FAILED LESSON

Peter stayed in the library until he fell asleep on a book. It had taken a long time to search through indexes, since they didn't have any computers. And even if the librarian had been there, he wouldn't have asked for her assistance.

Even with his quick reading ability, his research hadn't proved fruitful. Not one of the books mentioned the city's specific location.

He'd mostly found historical information about how the four sanctuary cities were built a couple thousand years ago, before Levicus' first entrapment. They were largely abandoned for many years, until about 150 years ago when Levicus' attacks increased. Strangely, the fifth, southernmost continent of Baikal seemed to be free from Levicus' touch.

While he'd found out plenty of information about Turopia, he hadn't found out enough to free his sister. Peter stretched, and glanced over at the library's clock to see how much time he had before his lesson with Princess Red. Peter jumped up—he was going to be late!

He raced back to his room to get the supplies for the lesson.

As Peter peeked around the archway to the courtyard, he was greeted by a very chipper Princess who seemed quite eager to learn fire magic. She was back in the flowing green dress and matching velvet cloak he'd seen her in that first day. He was surprised no one had come to watch him fail.

He barely understood magic himself, much less enough to teach someone how to perform a spell. But he had to try. It was either this or death. A chill breeze rolled through the garden and he pulled his black cloak tighter around him.

"You forgot something," Princess Red said sternly.

He had both his wands and the bronze bowl. What else was there?

"You must bow before royalty." Red looked down at him over her nose, even though she was only slightly taller than him.

Oh, right. Peter bowed, and breathed in the smell of damp, fallen leaves.

Red instantly changed her tone. "That was some impressive showmanship at the trial."

Peter shrugged. "Thanks for saying so even though I messed up."

"Nah, though that was definitely a disaster in the beginning. I've never seen anyone explode the test cube before." Miss Red looked away, and continued walking towards the back of the garden. "I would ask my teacher about it, but she died a week ago, and her assistant gives me the creeps."

"I'm sorry. Do you mean the Court Wizard?"

"Yeah, it's crazy though. Daddy's keeping it real hush-hush."

Peter's eyebrows raised. "How so?"

"He doesn't want our people to be scared." She leaned closer to him like she was sharing a secret.

Peter dared not speak a word. Besides keeping his life with Talbert a secret, and his father's bizarre hidden area, no one had ever told him a secret before—especially not someone his age.

"When the guards found her, she was sucked dry of all her blood, so there must be a monster in the castle. That's why I want to learn that fire magic you did, so I can defend my people. The basic spells Master Saipha Lynne was teaching me aren't going to cut it."

The older girl inspired a sense of honesty in him. He looked away, "I've never taught anyone before . . ."

"That's okay, just show me, I'm a quick learner." Miss Red sat on the edge of the water fountain, her long green dress pooling on the stone walkway. "Thought we should do this by the water."

"Smart thinking," Peter said, puzzled by the girl. One moment she was assertive and serious, and the next she was bubbly and curious.

"Well, get on with it then," Red said in her more regal tone. She was obviously used to ordering people around.

Peter pointed his silver wand at the bowl, imagined a pyre of flame, and cast the spell, "*Chal'esh.*"

Nothing happened.

"Let me try." Red was obviously well trained in magic, for her stance and positioning were expertly drawn the moment she pulled her dagger-wand. It was like the wand was a part of her. She spun around dramatically, pointed her wand at the bowl, and said the spell in a focused voice. She must have expected it to work the first time.

Nothing.

She tried a few more times, then peered into the bowl. Not even a wisp of smoke. "You need to do it again. I must be missing something."

Peter failed at the spell a few more times.

"Your father promised me you would teach me fire magic in exchange for your release. So far I don't see that happening. Throwing you back in the dungeon is looking like a pretty good option right now."

Geesh. She didn't have to be so snotty about it. He was trying his best. *"Chal'esh!"* He said, trying out Red's demanding tone. A minimal flame flickered in the bottom.

Red scowled. "You're either doing this to make me angry, or you're just a stupid fool who doesn't know anything about magic."

"I'm not stupid!" Peter was surprised he'd actually said it aloud. He concentrated on the bowl and yelled the spell much louder than he had intended. A pillar of flame shot into the sky.

To his surprise, Red clapped her hands with glee. "You really are a newbie wizard. You seem to only be able to perform your magic when you're angry—very rookie mistake"

Red tried a few more times, with no effect, then sat back down. "I thought it would work that time. Did I say it correctly?"

Peter nodded—she was getting the guttural K-sound in the back of her throat just fine. He really had no idea what to tell her.

"Chal'esh," Peter said, but he was no longer angry—he was just excited he'd finally done it. Nothing happened.

"That's it. You're useless." Red pushed Peter and he stumbled backwards. He tripped over the uneven path and fell to the ground.

Peter scowled up at her and got to his feet.

Red pushed him back down again.

"Stop it!" Peter stood. He hated being pushed—it reminded him of the bully Marcos back on Earth.

"Do the spell," Red ordered.

Peter set his jaw and said, *"Chal'esh."* He was about to turn to her and say, *there, are you happy?* But then a huge pillar of flame shot into the sky.

"There that's better." Red tried the spell herself a few times and failed. "Can't you show me some other fire spell?"

Peter was about to shake his head no, when he remembered his life was on the line and he had to keep her thinking he could give her magical fire lessons. He tried to imagine different types of flames, with little result.

"You're going to have to figure out how to teach me that pillar trick," Red crossed her chubby arms. "I'm bored."

What if he didn't really have a thing with fire like his father said, and it was just some kind of expression of rage? And then he remembered his father's words—he could do fire magic because he was a Zenmage. But how was he going to keep stringing Princess Red along if it was clear she couldn't do it?

The princess stomped her foot. "You *will* figure out how to teach me fire magic, or I have no problem sending you right back to the dungeons.

A sinking feeling formed in Peter's gut. He was never going to be able to teach her fire magic—his own father had told him only Zenmages could use elemental fire magic. Maybe if he told the truth, she'd be more lenient.

"I'll see you in a few days," she said, waving back to him.

"Hold on," Peter said meekly.

"Did you say something?"

"It's just that, well, um . . ."

Red put her hands on her hips. "Spit it out."

Peter sighed and gave a bow for good measure. "I, uh, don't think I'll be able to teach you fire magic—it's something only Zenmages can do."

Red scowled. "I thought that was some trick you performed, not that you're one of the reincarnated Zenmages." Red laughed. "The idea that you're one of them—a weakling like you—that's hilarious."

"Well . . . that's what my father says," Peter said, taking a step back. The girl was crazy, her mood changed like a whirling tornado.

Red's round face turned beet red and she yelled, "So you lied to me?"

Peter inched back towards the fountain.

"How dare you!" Red pointed her dagger wand at his feet. "*Cha'ziz.*"

A loud pop and a bright flash exploded at his feet like a miniature firecracker. Peter leapt back.

"*Cha'ziz,*" Red yelled.

Peter ran to the side.

Red cast the spell several times in a row, making Peter dance. "*Cha'ziz.*"

The red blast struck his foot. Peter fell to the ground. His silver wand clattered out of reach.

As Peter slid back on his butt, his mind raced to think of a way out of this. He couldn't use fire magic—that would surely earn him the death sentence.

"What's your problem?" Red said. "*Cha'ziz.*"

A crack hit near his hand.

Peter jumped to his feet and sprinted towards the entrance like he was running away.

"Coward!" Red turned to face him.

Peter pulled the dual dragon wand out of the small of his back and pointed it at her. Page 29 from *Magicology* hung on the edge of his tongue. A simple burst that distracted, but wasn't supposed to hurt the opponent.

"*Gal'Aviyr!*" Peter said, pointing his wand directly at her. He hadn't gotten the grip right. He was holding it with only two of his fingers. A small wave shot out of his wand, but sputtered out as it reached Miss Red.

To Peter's surprised, Red laughed and slapped her thigh. "Kid, you've got gumption—attacking a princess."

Boldness overtaking him, Peter cast the spell three times in quick succession.

Princess Red was pushed back by the wave. "*Cha'ziz!*"

She was one step from the fountain now.

Peter shot the spell one more time, "*Gal'Aviyr!*"

Red blocked, but the wave spread wide and she was hit. The large girl tripped back into the fountain, water splashing over the edges.

Peter raced to the fountain and held out a hand to help her up.

Princess Red put out her hand and clasped Peter's . . . and pulled him into the fountain.

CHAPTER
— 22 —

RORY'S TOUR OF TUROPIA

After a quick meal in the large dining hall, where Rory got to order food from a magical wooden tablet and have it appear before her, T. Veckler led her out of the old orphanage.

Feeling more settled with food in her belly, she found herself wondering if Asdorn was right—she did need to find someone she could trust in this city. But the need to go rescue Peter in Nadezhda was stronger.

If she was going to succeed in escaping, she was going to have to be much more clever. T. Veckler had hovered at the edge of the dining hall, watching her like a hawk.

"Agi will likely be practicing in the arena." T. Veckler led her across a wide cobblestone path. "Perhaps it will inspire you to see how a true warrior performs."

T. Veckler nodded to a four-story brick building. "That's the Academy. I'll get you enrolled in classes next week—give you some time to get settled, and catch up a little."

School. Rory had kind of hoped there wouldn't even be a structured school in this place.

Rory marched ahead into the open-air arena. It reminded her of a Roman amphitheater. She paused under the archway, soaking in the ancient feeling of the stone building. On the large, oval field, Agi faced a broad-shouldered Tyrskan warrior. They sparred with wooden swords, wearing full black silk uniforms with metal helmets. A handful of girls watched from the first rows of stone seats.

The Tyrskan Warriors bowed to each other, then to T. Veckler, who returned the bow. Rory copied. There was so much etiquette to learn in this place.

"Agi, would you be able to give my niece the tour a little earlier today?" T. Veckler asked.

"On my honor, I will take care of your niece," Agi said before turning to Rory. "Should be fun. Why don't you wait with my friend Thurston Morgan while I go change?"

"Sure." Rory said, trying to sound cool. She was really struck by Thurston—he was so handsome. He had perfect features and close-cropped blond hair. It was surprising how much skill he had when he only appeared a couple years older than her.

She watched T. Veckler and Agi walk off the field. If they both were gone, maybe she would be able to get away! She picked at her peeling nail polish, trying to make it look like she wasn't waiting for her fake uncle to disappear.

But as Agi slipped down the hall to the locker rooms, T. Veckler leaned against the wall beside the bleachers, arms crossed against his chest.

"Wow, he's really protective of you," Thurston said.

Rory shrugged, happy to not be standing in awkward silence. For once, she chose her words carefully. "Guess it's 'cause I'm the last of my family, he feels responsible for me until my parents are found."

Thurston seemed surprised. "*He* has family?"

"Kind of. He's my uncle." Guess everyone else had the same impression she did. But somehow after last night, she knew there was more to the man than he let on—something he didn't want anyone else to know. Which made her want to know what his secret was even more.

"Ah, that makes more sense. That's why he went to go pick you up himself."

"Wait—how do you know—" T. Veckler had stressed it was supposed to be a secret.

"It's okay—I was offered the mission first, but I had a prior commitment. Agi seems to have taken a liking to you, and any friend of his is a friend of mine." Thurston put a hand on her shoulder. "Agi's like my little brother—take good care of him." He winked.

Rory avoided his eye contact, studying her bootlaces.

"Hey, Thurston!" One of the girls from the stand yelled.

"Come with me, I'll introduce you," Thurston said.

Thurston put his hand on her shoulder. "Girls, this is my friend Rory Veckler. She's new to Turopia, so welcome her to our fine sanctuary city."

The girls waved back. Rory couldn't help blush at his use of the word *friend*. Her friends back home would be so jealous that someone like him wanted to be her friend.

What Rory really wanted to do was learn to sword fight. Master Kuma didn't allow them to learn weapons until they reached black belt, but she'd always wanted to.

Agi ran onto the field in his Tyrskan Warrior uniform. Clean once again, Rory could make out a black and white intricate swirl design on the uniform's sharp shoulders. A holster with two swords was strapped across his back.

Compared to Thurston, Agi was a lean boy, not quite grown into his uniform yet. "Hey Rory."

"That'd be me." Why had she said it like that? Why was she suddenly so nervous in his presence?

"I hope you don't mind running some errands with me while I help you get situated," Agi said. "As the newest initiate, I get all the odd jobs."

"Sure." She didn't want to admit she was really looking forward to the tour.

"I'm proud of you for making it." Thurston patted his friend on his back. "The youngest person to ever make the Order, at fourteen."

Agi looked at the ground, obviously uncomfortable with Thurston's praise and the stares he was getting from the bleachers.

"Why don't we get going?" Agi's hazel eyes were intense, like somehow she felt understood when he looked at her. "Commander Veckler wants me to pick up some supplies for your start at the Academy." Agi turned to Thurston. "Same time tomorrow?"

"No." Thurston shook his head. "Leaving on a mission— I'll find you when I return."

Agi led Rory out of the arena, and through the busy courtyard lined with merchants selling various goods out of their colorful caravans. A merchant held out a beautiful red dress to a young girl. Rory wanted to inspect the bright dresses hanging from his caravan, but Agi turned her down the main street. The middle was a wide cobbled path and the sidewalks were made of those blue octagonal panels.

It was so awkward walking in silence with Agi, now that there wasn't a horse or wind to prevent talking.

A large woman bowed her head slightly to Agi as she passed, and Agi nodded back. What was all this bowing about? It seemed to happen almost every time someone passed Agi on the street.

"You'll find everything you need here," Agi said. "It's the only real street in town."

The main street ran from the City Hall all the way to the main door. This two-block section was lined with shops. It reminded her of old western towns she'd seen in the movies— but with less dirt. There was a café, magic shop, bookstore, weapon supply store, and several others. It was nothing like the malls back home she frequented with her friends. Rory felt glad Agi was with her. She was so overwhelmed she had no idea even where to begin.

Their first stop was Whisked Away Books. Agi was focused on purchasing a stack of books with the shopkeeper. This was her opening to escape.

Rory cautiously backed out of the store.

Agi turned around.

Too slow.

He raised his eyebrows, but didn't say anything. It was almost worse.

"Just getting some fresh air," Rory mumbled and stepped outside. She took a deep breath, and was surprised to find the air refreshing. Definitely not city air like Rutherford.

Agi stepped out behind her empty-handed.

"So where are the books?" Rory asked.

"I sent them to your uncle's place. One less thing to carry."

Rory thought of all the books Agi had just purchased, and a heavy lump formed in her stomach. She didn't have any money. And T. Veckler sure didn't look like he had hidden riches either. "Uh, Lukagi, how am I going to pay for all this?"

"Please don't call me by my full name. Just Agi is fine. Only my aunt called me Lukagi, and she's gone now."

"Oh, sorry." Rory still couldn't get her mind wrapped around all the death. All the people who had lost loved ones to tragedy around here. But she dared not ask, even though her curiosity begged her to.

Agi started down the street. "Our city runs on a system of credits. There's really only a handful of people in our sanctuary with money and even they do their part for the city," Agi explained. "T. Veckler offered up some of his credits to help you get started. He told me to tell you not to count on his credits forever. Since you are thirteen, he expects you to start community work once he finds you something suitable."

"Wait. What?"

Agi held up his hands in defense. "Not my words—those are his. Actually, I may have softened them a little. Please don't tell him."

Rory couldn't help but think Agi was cute when he was nervous. But she'd never understand T. Veckler. "Why can't he give me a break? I just got here."

"It's not really that out of the ordinary. Most kids start community work when they turn twelve—about the same time they switch from Elementary School to the Academy."

"What do you do?"

"For me, being a member of the Tyrskan Warriors counts. You should be able to find something you are interested in, or the city will assign you a station. For example, my friend Sem has an apprenticeship here." Agi pointed at the wooden sign hanging above him, *Mrs. Greene's Herb Shop.*

"I used to help around my Tae Kwon Do Studio in exchange for free lessons—do you think I could do something like that?"

When Agi stared at her blankly, she explained, "Tae Kwon Do is a martial art I study back home for self-defense."

"So maybe helping out in the Entrix would be a good fit for you." Agi pulled open the herb shop's glass door.

Rory felt even more lost in this store. Hundreds of glass jars lined the floor-to-ceiling shelves and the three smaller shelves.

The cozy place was empty except for one person behind the counter, who was obscured by a cloud of green powder. The short person was spastically filling multiple herb containers.

When the door-bell chimed behind them, the pouring stopped. Out of the cloud of herb dust stepped a girl about her age. She had wild dark hair that popped out in all directions, and wore a sage green pleated skirt with a cute short-sleeved lavender top. The bow around her neck had come undone.

Her dark brown eyes lit up when she saw them. "Hi Agi!"

The girl adjusted her thick black-rimmed glasses on her flat nose. She bowed slightly to Agi and then looked questioningly at Rory.

"Rory Veckler, meet Sem Selvin, a good friend of mine," Agi said.

"Hi!" Sem said enthusiastically, sticking out her dark-skinned hand to shake hers. "Welcome to our store! I'm the apprentice to the master of this shop, so I can help you with anything you need."

"Rory is starting at the Academy," Agi said. "Can you add a basic survival kit to my order?"

"Of course," Sem replied, speaking rapidly. "What year are you? I'm only in my first year. How old are you? Do you need a kit for the Herblore Way?"

"No Way ceremony yet," Agi said. "Just the basics for now."

Rory didn't know where to start. "I'm only thirteen." Though now that her birthday had changed, she couldn't be sure.

"Great! We're the same age. That means you'll be in my first year class. With the last Trimester just starting, I'm all out of prepared starter kits, but give me a minute and I'll go put one together for you." She raced off before turning quickly back to Agi. "Are you in need of herbs to refill your remedy kit?"

"No, not today," Agi said.

Sem sprinted behind the counter.

Rory stood there, stunned at the girl's exuberance. Rory wondered if Sem was ever still.

Agi seconded her thoughts. "Sem's a bit spastic at times, but she grows on you." He paused for a minute and added, "If you need any help with your Herblore studies, she's the person to go to."

Rory felt relieved to have help, as most of the herbs on the shelves all looked the same to her. Sure, some of them were darker or lighter, but some of the leaves looked almost impossible to tell apart. As her eyes fell on some of the more curious items in jars—salamander eyes, toad's warts, and dragon nails—Sem came bounding from behind the counter.

"Here is your starter kit for Herblore! Uh . . ." She handed the cloth bag to the Rory. "It seems I forgot your name . . ."

"Rory."

"Right. I won't forget now, I promise."

"Charge this to T. Veckler's account, and send the purchase to his home," Agi instructed.

Sem raised her bushy eyebrows, obviously shocked. Unlike Agi, she wasn't silent about it though. "You live with that mean old man?"

Rory was surprised to find herself feeling bad when hearing T. Veckler described that way. "He's my uncle."

"Oh, sorry." Sem absently fidgeted with her leather belt lined with pouches.

"I guess he has that effect on people," Rory said.

"Yeah, try not to get into his fighting class," Sem said.

"I don't think I can escape it," Rory said. "He already tried to teach me fighting first thing this morning."

Sem bit her lip, and in what seemed an uncharacteristically slow gesture, moved Rory's new leather starter kit across the counter.

"What's going on, Sem?" Agi asked.

"Please don't be mad," Sem said looking down. "But I don't have those field kits prepared yet."

"That's not like you," Agi said, looking troubled. "Captain Orlovsky wants those for our trip tomorrow. I don't want to let him down."

"I'm really sorry—it's just that Mrs. Greene's been away from the shop a lot the past couple days. I think she's having family issues. I had to do the medical orders first—I hope you understand."

Agi nodded.

"Please don't tell anyone I said that," Sem said.

"On my honor as a Tyrskan Warrior, I will say nothing," Agi said, standing perfectly straight. "Why don't I come by tonight and help you finish?"

Sem's brown eyes widened behind her big glasses. "Really? That would be great! You tell me I'm not supposed to speak ill of others, but the other apprentice is pretty useless."

"I'll stop by after our training at the Entrix," Agi said. "We're on our way there now."

"The what?" Rory asked.

Sem chimed in before Agi could say anything. "You're going to love the Entrix. Only the four sanctuary cities have them. It's a place where we go to improve our fighting skills—but the nifty part is that you're fighting illusions, not real people."

"So what's the risk?" Rory's curiosity about this place was definitely piqued. But what made her most excited was the prospect of escape. Perhaps while Agi was busy doing his set-up, she could leave. She'd just have to watch for an opening.

Agi chuckled. "That's the thing. It's a spell, so depending on the level you're fighting at, the illusion will attack harder. It's not just something in your mind. It's there. Right in front of you. Trust me, you feel the danger, especially as you advance levels."

"How many levels are there?" Rory asked.

"50," Sem said. "But no one has ever made it past level 47 on the Warrior program, and 45 on the Wizard training program."

"So what level are you?" Rory asked.

Sem shuffled her feet and let Agi answer. "People don't usually go around asking what other's levels are, but I am at 22 warrior and 32 magic.

"Don't worry though, the beginning sets are really easy," Sem said. "That's why there's a required level 1! And it won't increase the difficulty *until* you have mastered that level."

"Since you just arrived here, that's probably why your uncle is so eager to get your training started," Agi said. "I wouldn't be surprised if he assigned you a tutor."

"What? Why would he assign me something?"

"He's the master fighting instructor, didn't you know?" Sem said.

CHAPTER

— 23 —

Rory Escapes the Entrix

Rory stared up at the towering archway below Asdorn's hill. There it was. Turopia's massive door. So close.

A few cloaked travelers were leaving through the smaller inset door. Were the archers behind the battlements there for keeping people out . . . or in?

Agi pointed to the guard building beside it, which had four turrets. "That's also our training facility, and where Thurston and I live."

Rory was torn between wanting to figure this place out, and wanting to run straight through the door. But she couldn't leave with Agi right there, even if he was weighed down by a cart with 12 freshly cleaned and oiled practice swords. She'd wait for the perfect opportunity and bolt.

They walked up the path between the lake and the guard castle. Rory marveled at the Entrix—a circular building that towered over them. A massive arch contained a wide double door and a smaller inset door. What was it with this city and large doors no single human could open?

After Agi registered her at the front desk, he handed her a wooden key. At the top of a rectangular rod was a hollow circle. It looked like a 3D stick figure without the arms or legs.

"The key is used to record your training," Agi said, leading her down the hall. "You earn skill points to move on to the next level. If you attempt to let someone else use your key, the Entrix will take a whole level away from you."

"You make the Entrix sound like a living being," Rory said.

"It seems like it sometimes, because the training system will talk back to you—especially Sal."

The hall opened into a small circular room with two doors. The plaques on the doors read: *Beginning. Advanced.*

"The advanced rooms are larger, so you can do more complex training routines. When you get to level 20, you can start training with multiple people," Agi explained. "Why don't you help me set up, and then I'll show you how it works?"

Rory's heart raced. She was so close. She let her face fall in disappointment and rolled the key around in her hands. "Okay. I was just so excited to try it out."

Agi studied her for a moment. "Sure, I don't need much help to set up for our training session anyway."

Rory could barely contain her excitement. She didn't want to say the wrong thing and have him change his mind.

Outside one of the beginning rooms, Agi put Rory's key in the slot, circle-end first. The wall panel buzzed at him.

Agi tried to pull open the door and it wouldn't budge. "See? The system has a protection system, so you can't have other people move up the levels for you."

"Why would that matter?" Rory asked. "Wouldn't you just be hurting your own capabilities?"

"Yes, but you can't count on everyone to have integrity. The cheaters are usually those who need to reach a certain level to pass a class."

Rory smiled at his use of the word, '*integrity.*' It was one of the five tenets she was supposed to follow in her Tae Kwon Do school. If she wasn't planning on leaving to rescue Peter, this boy would have made a good friend.

"Between you and me, it's not the wisest thing," Agi said. "People think they can cheat so they can wear the better armor, but they don't have the proper energy to tap into the armor's higher power. Same with the weapons."

Tentatively, she inserted the key. A bell dinged and the door cracked open. Agi followed her into the large open space. The massive warehouse-like room was covered with white octagonal plates.

Agi turned to a panel on the inside of the door. "There are three main programs to choose from: Warrior, Wizard, and Potions, but there are subcategories. So when training the Warrior part of my Way, I could train swordplay, staff, or ranging skills."

"Swordplay sounds fun."

Agi pressed two buttons on the panel beside the door. "I'm going to leave. It won't allow me to train in here with you because I'm not an instructor yet. Pick up the sword when it appears, and do as the program instructs."

Rory had never used a sword before. "Will I get hurt?"

"Don't worry, you will only be fighting illusions, so they can't hurt you. You don't even get the option to turn on the pain mode until you reach level 20." Agi opened the door. "I'll be in room 11 in the advanced section if you have any questions. Though Gigim, the voice who runs the fighting program, should be able to help you."

"Okay, thanks."

"I'll come check on you after I'm done," Agi said.

The door shut and Rory stood watching it. How long should she wait before leaving?

"Good morning, Rory Veckler, if that is your real name. It will make it easier to start if you turn and face the room," a deep voice said.

Rory jumped, not expecting someone to be talking to her. She turned around. The room was now a clearing in a lush, green forest. "Uh, hello?"

"I am Gigim, and I will be your training partner for all fighting sessions. Pick up the sword atop the tree stump, and we will begin."

It would be so fun to pick up the sword and play. But this might be her only chance for escape.

"Sorry, Gigim. Another time." Rory opened the door and ran out of the room, not even bothering to take her key. A group of kids were coming her way. Rory couldn't help but stare at a girl who had bleach white skin with bright red hair that matched her overalls. Even her eyes were red.

Realizing she was being rude, Rory turned down the hall and walked briskly out of the Entrix. Her heart pounded as she walked down the hill towards Turopia's door.

She paused outside the guard station. Was she really going to do this? Asdorn's cottage stood up the hill directly in front of her. Rory squinted across the lake at the rows of houses. No T. Veckler there either.

As she turned to the massive two-story door, she expected the archers to aim at her, but they remained still.

On the smaller inset door, she was faced with a large stone dial with twelve different symbols. Was there a passcode to get out? She turned the dial a few turns to the right, then back to the left, and to the right, settling on an image of a crow.

Nothing happened. Not even vibration that she'd entered the wrong code. Afraid the guards would stop her for taking too long, she quickly turned the dial to that of a mountain.

To her surprise, the door creaked open to reveal a black hole of darkness. Rory looked over her shoulder at Turopia's landscape.

Goodbye.

Rory stepped in. Once more she was surrounded by a strange prickling sensation, like spiders were crawling all over her body.

She stepped out onto a massive rock beside a waterfall. She jumped to the left to avoid getting wet. The cold air chilled her, and she wished she'd had a warmer coat than the black knee-length jacket that went with her dress.

Now out of the spray of the water, she looked around. In front of her was a lush, green valley with a river running through it. Where was she? Hadn't she entered through a towering cliff face?

Off in the distance, she thought she made out a mountain range, but no cliffs. *This wasn't right.*

Birds chirped. Beetles buzzed. And a great roar sounded in the distance. What was going on here?

Suddenly feeling she'd made a mistake, and at least needed to go back and get a coat, and maybe a map, Rory climbed back up onto the flat rock where she had entered. But no door appeared.

She climbed behind the waterfall. It had to be there.

Heart racing, she frantically ran her hands on the slimy rock behind the pounding water. Where had it gone? It had to be here somewhere.

Drenched, but still seeing no door, she stood on the edge of the rock, looking out over the valley. She saw a village down by the winding river. That's where she'd go. She'd find someone there who could take her to Nadezhda.

Rory jumped off the wide, flat rock. She stepped carefully down through the fallen evergreen needles and leaves, trying not to slip down the steep hill. There had to be an easier path down.

After several steps, she froze.

In the middle of a clearing, a small black and red Alrakis dragon pawed at its bat-like wing. It jumped back and forth in anger, then threw itself to the ground, writhing as if trying to reach its wing with its short legs.

She had to get out of here!

Rory took a step back. Leaves crunched.

The dragon stopped, completely alert. It sniffed the air, eyes wide, his head tilting back like a velociraptor she'd seen in the movies.

It spotted her.

The dragon only came up to her hip, but she didn't want to test it. Instinctively she held up her hands. "I'm not here to hurt you. I'm going to back up now."

The young dragon cocked its head and growled. "You speak to me?" a young boy's voice sounded.

"Who said that?" Rory spun around and tripped on a jagged rock. So caught off guard by the dragon and the surroundings, she forgot how to fall properly and skidded forward on her hands and knees. She rolled a few times down the steep hill before a large boulder stopped her fall.

Everything went black.

✳   ✳   ✳

Wetness. A prickly tongue was licking her face.

Rory slowly peeked one eye open. A huge red tongue attached to a scaly black face filled her vision. Its breath was dreadful, smelling of decay and rotten flesh.

She cringed. "Please don't eat me."

"You cute," the dragon said. "Little girl speaks to Melchior." Rory heard the cute voice in her head at the same time the dragon let out a low growl. It was quite the contrast.

"Uh, hi?" She pulled herself up to a sitting position. Her head spun. *Ow.* Such an idiot. Her white dress was filthy and torn from the fall, her knees and hands bloodied. She adjusted her leg to relieve the stinging.

The small dragon leaned over her. Images of the dragon's attack on her route to Turopia filled her mind. "Please don't hurt me."

"Melchior not hurt people anymore. Melchior stop being dragon." The dragon sat down, his sharp-tipped tail wrapping around him.

Even Rory knew that sounded ridiculous. How could someone stop being what was in their nature? "So you're *not* going to eat me?"

The dragon shook his head. "Melchior can't help it if Levicus' disciples order it. Melchior hide here with girl who speaks to dragons."

"Well, I have to go home now," Rory said and added under her breath, "Wherever that is."

"Girl stay with Melchior. Take arrow out of wing." The dragon nodded to his side.

Rory looked closer at Melchior's wings, and saw the tip of an arrowhead lodged into the thickest part of his wing.

She couldn't let the little guy suffer. Rory held up her hands, palms facing the dragon in a loose fashion, as she inched closer. She watched his feet closely for any sign of attack. The dragon remained still.

She held out her hand, and he licked it.

"Melchior's wing stings. Girl make it go away."

Holding the thick frame of the black and red wing for leverage, she pulled on the remaining inch of the arrow shaft. The arrowhead broke free, blood oozing out with it.

Melchior leapt in pain.

Rory jumped back.

He danced around the clearing, as if flapping his wing would make the pain go away.

Rory inched slowly back. She could use this distraction to get away. But if it could fly, where would she go where she wouldn't be seen?

Suddenly, the dragon stopped. "Don't go. Girl be Melchior's new family," he said.

Rory couldn't get used the scary vibration of his growl mixed with his kid voice. How was she going to get out of this? "We can't be family—we're different species."

The dragon's eyes widened and he frowned. He let out a small whimper.

This was not good. "Please don't cry. I'll be your family."

The dragon smiled wide, revealing massive teeth. He jumped up like a dog and licked her face.

Rory sighed and looked him straight in the eyes. "Even so, you should go home. Won't your parents miss you?" She knew she didn't have any parents to miss her, but he was so cute, they had to be missing him.

"Papa killed over plains. Mama only sad. Baby brother not hatched yet."

"Then she needs you more than ever." Rory looked around for an angry mother. Nothing was more dangerous than a mother protecting her young. Yet, she couldn't help feeling bad for the little thing.

"Melchior stay here with girl and not grow up. Disciples use adults."

"I wish I could help you, but I have to find a village."

"Melchior help. Village at bottom of hill. Melchior show girl path." The dragon leapt up, hovering above the ground.

"Thank you."

"Melchior good dragon. Melchior sorry he not big enough to carry girl."

"That's okay." The feeling of free-falling off that massive Alrakis dragon made her chest tighten. No. Flying was not for her.

After a couple minutes of walking, the trees grew farther apart. Clear in front of her lay a heavily trodden path. It zigzagged down the side of the foothill. She could make out a closer village beside the winding river. Things were looking up. She was on her way to seeing Peter!

"Rory!" A voice called from by the waterfall. *Agi.*

She had to hurry. "Will you come with me?"

He hung his head. "Girl is right. Melchior go home."

"I hope I see you again. I think you will be a great dragon some day."

Agi raced down the hill so gracefully it was like the jagged rocks she'd tripped over weren't even there. He stood before them, swords drawn. "Step away slowly."

Rory looked from the dragon to Agi and understood his concern. "Oh, don't worry about it—Melchior is friendly."

"Melchior—who?" Agi remained focused on the dragon, his breathing tightly controlled.

"The dragon here."

"You *spoke* to it?" Agi furrowed his brow, but didn't look at her.

"Sure, why not?" Rory asked. "He's nice. Talked him into going back to his family."

"I don't talk to dragons," Agi said.

"Well maybe if you did, there wouldn't be so much fighting."

"You don't get it," Agi looked at her suspiciously." I *can't* talk to, or even understand a dragon.

That can't be right. "Just because you can't doesn't mean others can't either."

Agi shook his head. "No one can. I've travelled the world and never met a single person who can speak to dragons, or any other animals for that matter."

"Maybe he just chose to talk to me 'cause he wants me to be his family."

Before Agi could answer, the dragon leaned forward off its haunches and growled. His red wings arched open, like a cat arching its back.

Rory put her hand on his scaly back. It felt like a snake, all prickly and smooth at the same time. "It's okay. Agi a friend." *Great.* Now she was talking like Melchior.

The black and red dragon sat back down and made a scary purring noise.

"Okay, fine, I believe you." Agi returned his sword to the dual-sword scabbard on his back and raised his hands in a surrendering gesture. "Please, come home with me."

"No. I'm going to Nadezhda to find my brother," Rory said.

"You don't have to. T. Veckler and Asdorn have a plan."

"I don't belong there." Rory looked down at the valley.

"It doesn't matter whether you belong or not—it's where you're safe." Agi reached out as if to grab her.

Instinctively, Rory pushed his arm out of the way. She lunged to his outside and aimed for the side of his neck with the edge of her hand.

He grabbed her wrist and had it up behind her back so fast, she barely realized how he'd done it.

"Let me go! I hate this place," Rory said.

Melchior looked up at her, clearly insulted.

"Not you, I like you," Rory said.

Agi had her pinned up so close to him, with her elbow behind her back, she could feel his hot breath on her neck. Her left hand flailed, unable to reach him. He had her locked somehow. And she didn't know how to get out of it.

"Stop struggling," Agi said. "Please don't make me have to put you in magical handcuffs."

"You wouldn't," Rory scowled so deeply she wished Agi could see it.

"Look, I'm too young to die," Agi said hesitantly. "T. Veckler said he'd kill me if anything happened to you."

Rory was both touched and disgusted T. Veckler would kill someone for her. She was surprised to sense the boy was actually nervous. She tightened her jaw. She had to find a way out of here that wouldn't get Agi in trouble.

Rory relaxed her stance.

Agi let go of her arm and she spun around to face him. "Don't you *ever* do that again."

"Then don't try to run away," Agi said.

Here he'd been so nice to her—and now he kind of looked pitiful, begging her to return to Turopia.

"The road to Nadezhda is dangerous," Agi said. "Please come back with me. I promised I'd help Sem today. She's counting on me and my integrity is important to me."

It was like a punch to the gut. *Integrity.* Master Kuma had been pushing her to live by the school's five tenets even outside of class. Doing something that would cause another direct harm was definitely not acting with integrity. Even if Master Kuma wasn't here to see, and it wouldn't affect Rory's ability to test for her black belt, she had to make the right choice.

Rory stared Agi in his hazel eyes for one last objection, secretly hoping he would offer to help. "But I had planned to rescue my brother."

After a lingering silence, he whispered, "Plans are but dust in the wind, they rarely settle where you want."

"What did you say?"

"Just an old proverb."

"That's what Master Kuma used to tell me all the time."

"Who?"

"Just someone I'll never see again . . ."

Agi bit his lip. "I'm not supposed to tell you this, but I think it will persuade you to return home—"

"Turopia's not my home." Rory glared at him. "I'm going to find Peter on my own, so let me go."

"As I was saying, T. Veckler and Asdorn sent Thurston and Leopold to go check on your brother. They left this morning, and should return in a few days. If you're lucky, they'll have your brother."

Peter. Rory hated it, but what the boy said makes sense. All she had to do was wait for them to return with Peter, *then* they could make plan together of where to live.

"Think you can wait a little longer? If you leave, you'll miss out on seeing him. It's up to you," Agi said, then quickly added, "You know, if you don't come with me, you'll have no way to get back in, unless you just happen to run into someone who has the security clearance to find the city. You're lucky I guessed where you'd run off to."

That's why she hadn't been able to find the door! "I guess . . ."

Agi pointed to the sky, where a dark shadow flew high amongst the clouds. "Dragon! We have to get out of here!"

CHAPTER
— 24 —

PETER SOLVES A MYSTERY

The shock of the freezing cold fountain water struck Peter's spine. It cooled the throbbing of his back scars.

Princess Red rolled over on top of him, and pushed him down as if to drown him.

Peter lurched forward, gasping for air.

"There, that should teach you to mess with a royal," Red said.

As Red let her grip loose, Peter slipped out from under her. He pushed her shoulder away from him. She toppled back into the water, and Peter leaned across her to keep her from getting up. He was tired of bullies getting the best of him.

He went to pull his wand, but spotted it floating out of reach. He clenched his fist instead.

Red stuck her head and shoulders out of the shallow water. "If you're going to punch me—do it. No one's ever dared before."

It was like she was baiting him—she leaned on her elbows looking up at him, and could've easily toppled him over. He wasn't going to fall for it. Peter unclenched his fist and climbed out of the fountain.

This time, when Peter reached out to help Red up, she accepted.

Dripping wet, lips blue, and shivering from the cold, the two glared at each other—silently daring the other to make a move.

"How 'bout you m-make t-that fire now?" Princess Red asked, teeth chattering.

Peter reached into the frigid pool, beneath the layer of fallen leaves, to retrieve his dual dragon wand. Pointing it towards the bowl with all of his intention, he cast the spell.

For the first time, flames grew in the brass bowl like those from a fireplace—not an awkward pillar.

As they warmed their hands near the fire, Princess Red said, "It's a pity you're going to be beheaded in the morning. No one's ever been brave enough to attack me before. I try to get my sparring partners to go full force, but they're obviously scared to hurt the King's only daughter."

Peter knew he should've run. He considered running now, but he had no clue how to get out of the castle. The castle's front doors were always guarded, and there were no other entrances or exits.

Red studied him curiously. "You really don't know how to fight though—it requires focus—even more than when you're using the practice bowl. You have to put all your intention behind the spell—you have to really mean your attacks."

"I'm sorry I pushed you into the water," Peter said, an idea suddenly striking him. "I know the words to a spell to dry out clothes, but I'm not sure how to do it. I read it in the household book."

"Do tell," Red said. "Try it."

The words from page 47 of *101 Household Charms and Concoctions* hovered in his mind. He pointed his wand at himself first.

"No, me first—I'm the princess."

Peter pointed his wand at Red, focused with all his might, and cast the spell, *"Ag'Moletta'Mach."*

Nothing happened.

"I don't think you're pronouncing it right," Red said. "How do you spell it?"

Peter spelled it out for her.

With the corrections, Peter tried again, *"Ya'Veshia Bol'Gadiym."*

A hot breeze of air washed over Miss Red. Her dress flared and her bright red hair spiked out—like a giant hair dryer had gone over her and frozen her hair in the splayed position.

Peter bit his lip. Perhaps that was a bit *too* much intention.

Red's eyes widened. "What. Did. You do to me?"

"Uh . . ."

Before she could attack, Peter turned the spell on himself, with just as much force. Peter felt the water sucked out of his pants and shirt.

Red laughed and clutched her belly, pointing at him. "Your hair! Looks like you're scared."

Peter wanted to laugh too, but was afraid of breaking her jovial spirit. Maybe she'd let him go now. But her enthusiastic laughter was too much. He let out one loud, "Ha!"

Red's faced dropped instantly into seriousness. "Did you just laugh at me?"

Peter shook his head.

Red slapped his shoulder. "Just kidding. It's funny. Lighten up."

And when Red started laughing again, Peter happily joined her.

Soon they were rolling on the ground by the fire in the bowl laughing, clutching their sides. After the laughter fizzled out, they sat up cross-legged on the grass and faced each other.

Peter reached over and pulled a dried leaf out of her still-spiky hair.

Before he could pull it away, Red clasped his hand. "You know you're not so bad. Smart to pretend you're all weak, and then go do this fire magic and fancy household spells—but if you want to stay in my services, never lie to me again." Red let his hand go. "You didn't have to pretend you haven't been studying long. It hurts my feelings when people think I'm a naïve king's daughter."

Peter considered keeping her thinking he was lying, so he decided on the truth. "It wasn't a lie. I didn't know I could do magic until last week."

Red narrowed her brow.

Peter cowered, expecting her to lash out.

Instead, she surprised him. "Maybe you really are one of the twelve Zenmages. There's only been ten since I've been alive. I've met Asdorn, and he's old, so I don't know."

Peter fiddled with the dead grass in his cold fingers. "I really am sorry I wasn't able to teach you fire magic. Is there anything else I can help you with?"

"There's only one thing, but I'm not sure you can help . . ."

"What's that?" Peter sat up straight, eager to get on her good side.

"To catch a monster."

"Excuse me?"

Princess Red leaned in to whisper, "I believe there's a monster in the castle, and I intend to catch it."

"You have monsters here?" Peter gulped.

"I've never seen one, but that doesn't mean they don't exist." Red looked around, but they were still alone in the sunny courtyard. "My teacher was a powerful wizard—the best on the east coast. Her blood was completely drained when they found her—doesn't that scream 'monster' to you?"

Peter didn't know what to think—but he knew he was no match for a monstrous creature.

"It's either you help me, or I send you to the dungeons."

Peter rolled his eyes, but kept his mouth shut. Did she really have to keep threatening him with that over and over again? "I'll have to go to the library to look up what kind of monster it could be."

Red nodded. "I bet we can find clues in her living quarters too."

"Why there?"

"That's where Master Saipha's body was found." Red stood. "I need to get cleaned up. I can't have people seeing me like this. Meet me back here after dinner, and we'll go check it out."

Peter nodded, grateful to be getting out of a punishment. "And don't—"

"I know . . . don't forget or you'll send me to the dungeons."

"See? I knew you were a smart kid." Red spun on her heel and walked regally out of the garden, as if her dress and hair were perfect—and not splayed out like she'd been electrocuted.

After filling himself up on hot soup and bread, Peter walked boldly down to the courtyard. It was kind of fun playing detective. And if it got him off the hook for his attack on Holdon, then all the better.

Princess Red stuffed an oversized book of monsters into his arms. "Here, read this."

Peter shifted his weight to carry the book. When they got to her teacher's living quarters, he was surprised there was nothing blocking the door.

Red slipped through the tall doors, and cast a hovering ball of light to inspect something on a large table in the center of the room.

Peter gaped at the elaborate space. It was twice as big as his own. Really, it was two rooms with the four-poster bed behind an archway.

Bookcases filled with worn books and magical instruments lined the walls. Two chairs faced the fireplace, but the embers had long since died. Peter shivered and went over to light the fire.

"No!" Red ordered. "They'll know someone was in here—besides, you might disturb the evidence."

Peter wasn't sure what kind of evidence they'd find—it's not like they had scientific equipment and testing like back on Earth.

Peter leaned back in the tall-backed armchair and set down the monster book. He copied her spell, casting his own ball of light, moving his wand to make the light dance about. He looked around for any sign of a monster—blue hair, broken razor-sharp claws, or scratches in the furniture. But from what he could tell, there was no sign of a struggle.

Peter spotted sand on the rug by the feet of his armchair. It was odd, since there wasn't a beach nearby. Nadezhda's castle sat on cliffs that overlooked the ocean, but they were made of jutting black rocks—not sand.

Suddenly curious to find out more, Peter joined Red at Master Saipha's table.

She held up a square vanilla-colored card, like the kind people were throwing into the fire the night after he arrived. "Looks like she was interrupted."

Peter read, "In memory of my dearest sister Ella, and wife Belin—"

"The monster must have attacked her before she could finish her cards for the Festival of the Dead ceremony," Red said.

Peter opened the tall door and studied it. It looked worn and old, but there were no claw marks or broken hinges.

Red joined him, and took an extra look down the hallway before closing the door. "Why would she let a monster into her room?"

"Perhaps she knew it?" Peter asked.

Red shook her head. "That's dumb. She wouldn't let a scary beast into her private space. She was even selective with the students she'd accept. Though, she would've liked you— you're weird."

Ignoring the insult, Peter went over to the bed. "You said she was found in her bed?"

Red nodded.

Peter wrinkled his brow in thought.

"What are you thinking?"

"Either she stopped in the middle of her writing to go to sleep and the monster killed her while she was sleeping—or she was interrupted, and the monster put her in bed."

"Hmmm . . . I didn't think of that," Red said. "The person would have to be strong."

"Or use magic—I saw a hovering spell in, *A Guide to Magic of the World.*"

"Have you read *all* the books in the library since you arrived?"

Peter looked at the ground. "No, only four. And *Magicology* twice, just for fun."

"You're weird."

Peter pulled back the covers and inspected the pillow. "What I do find weird is there is no blood anywhere. The monster drained her blood—but I don't see a drop of it."

A foreign look of seriousness and bewilderment overtook Red. "I don't understand why she wouldn't fight . . . She was so powerful."

"I don't know—I'm sorry." Peter put what he hoped was a comforting hand on her shoulder.

Red pulled away, leaning over to inspect the comforter.

Peter cringed—he knew she shouldn't have touched her. Who was he to touch a princess?

Red picked up something, and narrowed her gaze at him. "What?"

"A long, black hair—must have been left by the killer. I've been assuming a monster had to have done this, but maybe I was wrong, and it was a human all along."

Peter nodded, not sure where she was going with this.

"And perhaps that human was you."

Peter held up his hands in defense. "Whoa, what are you talking about? I didn't even know she existed until you told me she died."

Red confronted him, and Peter stepped back into the red wallpaper. Red pressed in closer. "Don't you think it's a little strange that my teacher dies the very night you show up here? And you turn out to be this powerful wizard?"

Red took a step back, as if berating herself. "How foolish I was to believe your ruse that you are a *Zenmage*, and really just only learned magic. You were covering up your true nature all along, weren't you?"

Peter's heart raced. He had to think of something. "I didn't kill your teacher—I'm trying to help you find out who did."

"You're only doing it cause I ordered you to."

Desperately, he asked, "Lots of people have long black hair. What color was Saipha's?"

"I see what you're doing here. It was black, but it was thick, short, and curly."

Drat. That didn't help. "Um, the king has long black hair."

"Like I'm going to believe my father killed our court wizard," Red said, crossing her arms. "I can't believe I trusted you."

Peter held out his hand, "No—"

"Don't touch me," Red turned away.

Adrenaline coursing through his system, making his mind fuzzy. Then an idea popped into his head—he didn't like the theory, but it was something. "If I find out who did it, then will you believe me?"

"Well you can't leave the castle, so I'll give you until tomorrow."

As soon as Red left the room, Peter raced over to the sitting area. He dropped to his knees and ran his fingers through the tightly-woven carpet. Little grains of sand popped up like popcorn. It couldn't really be sand from Earth, could it? He'd been to the temples so many times, and had spent hours getting the sand out of his clothes.

Peter sat back with his legs folded under him. He imagined two people sitting around the roar of the fire . . . and something going terribly wrong.

He looked into the fireplace and saw a few pieces of paper completely burned, except the very top of a letter.

From the Desk of Master Saipha Lynne, Court Wizard

Your Highness,
I have disturbing news to report. You were right. I found the secret laboratory . . .

The rest of the letter was completely burnt, but Peter knew. He didn't want to, but the ache told him it was his father. If he really had killed Saipha Lynne, would Peter really turn his father over to save his own life?

Peter crushed the letter scrap in his palm and stuffed it into his pocket. He had to find out for sure. He took one last look around, and raced out of the room.

CHAPTER

— 25 —

RORY'S LOSS

R ory looked over her shoulder at the massive black and red dragon flying into view. "But we can talk to it."

"Mellia kill girl near son," the dragon roared.

Agi covered his ears.

Okay, so maybe talking wasn't an option this time.

The dragon shot a burst of fire at them and roared—just a roar, no speech this time.

Rory ignored her stinging cuts as they scrambled up the rocks, behind the waterfall. The fire hit the falling water, dissipating into steam.

Rory sighed. *That was close.*

Inside the clearing, the mother dragon snarled and encircled a wing around her son.

Agi yelled a spell. A massive door opened beside the waterfall. "Keep holding my hand, or you can't get through."

Rory squeezed his callused hand tightly.

Once through the magical door, Agi looked her over. "You're really hurt. What happened?"

"Fell." She looked at the ground, partially to avoid his gaze, and to avoid the stares of the group of refugees huddled in the entryway.

All of the refugees looked filthy and weary from travel. A blonde woman who carried a young child on her hip smiled through her weariness. One mother in several layers of clothes leaned over, both hands to her mouth. Tears fell down her dirt-streaked face. The young children looked into the city with awe. Except for an older man, none of the refugees had bothered to set down their trunks and bags, preferring to keep their few possessions close.

"I wish I had something to give them—they look hungry and cold," Rory said.

"Don't worry. They'll be given hot food in the dining hall and shown the bathhouse once they've passed through security," Agi said. "They have to make sure someone marked as one of Levicus disciples can't sneak in."

"One more thing." Agi twisted his wrist in front of her. Instantly her clothes returned to their clean, freshly pressed form.

She *really* needed to learn that spell.

"I'm sorry if I got you in trouble." She really did feel guilty. "Anything I can do?"

Agi looked conflicted. "I should take you to the healing center, but they'll notify T. Veckler. Maybe you could let Sem patch you up? She's really good."

Rory shrugged. She just wanted to sit down.

A refugee with a ridiculous toupee approached her. "Why young lady, that's a beautiful locket you have there," he said, triggering memories in the far reaches of her mind.

Rory looked down at her locket, the blue crystals sparking in the afternoon sun. "Thanks, it was my mother's."

"You must be Rory—I know a boy who is desperate to see you," the stranger said.

Rory gasped, and her eyes widened in realization of who he was . . . the man who'd separated her from Peter at the Rutherford Adoption Center when they were six. Pure hatred surged within her. "You took Peter."

The man hid a cringe at the sound of his name, but not very well. "Indeed. But, he sent me to Turopia to bring you back to Nadezhda."

A rush of excitement filled her. Peter was looking for her too!

Before Rory could respond, Agi stepped up to the man who towered over them. "She is not going anywhere with you. I don't even know who you are."

"I am Lord Talbert, servant to her father."

A curious expression passed Agi's face, but he said nothing.

She crossed her arms. "I'm not going anywhere with you. Why couldn't you bring Peter here? This is my home now." She couldn't believe she'd used the word *home*, but it felt right.

The guard, Alana, stepped in front of the refugees. "Please line up. I'll be checking your passes and performing the scan now."

Agi looped his arm through Rory's, and led her out of the entryway.

Once they were alone by the lake, Agi asked, "You know that man?"

"I can't place him," Rory lied. She wanted to tell Agi the truth about the danger she was in, but Asdorn had harped on her to keep it a secret.

Agi led her through town, past the healing center, the library, and down Main Street into Mrs. Greene's Herb Shop.

Sem immediately ran from around the counter, her apron stuffed with various bags of herbs. "I have it all set-up so we can make the packets quickly."

It took Sem a moment to notice Rory's condition. "What happened?"

"Training acc—" Agi started.

"Really, I fell outside," Rory interrupted. "Agi saved me. But I do need some patching up."

"Oh sure." Sem led her to a leather couch in the back of the store, and inspected her wounds. After running around gathering some supplies, she applied a sticky yellow paste to Rory's hand and knees. It smelled sickly sweet. Sem wrapped strips of cloth around Rory's wounds.

A little overkill on the bandages. She felt like a mummy.

"You don't have to keep these on for long, but it will help the herbs seep in so they will heal faster." Sem bit her lip and looked up at Agi. She looked so ashamed. "I can't do the spell. It's too powerful for me."

The moment Agi sounded his agreement, Sem ran around the counter. She grabbed a heavy book and flipped it open to the right page.

Agi waved his hands in a circular motion over Rory, and read the spell. As soon as Sem returned the book to the shelf, Rory felt relief from the stinging pain.

"Agi, how are you doing that without a wand or staff?" Rory asked.

He held up his arms, and his blue sleeves fell to reveal jewel-encrusted gauntlets. "I'm at a high enough level I can use river rocks and gems as my channeling devices. Really helps add flexibility in a fight."

That sounded so fun. But so far she hadn't had a chance to learn any magic in this place. She supposed she might enjoy being here more if she did.

The two of them spent the rest of the evening helping Sem put together several orders.

Rory tried to share as little about herself as possible, for fear she'd say the wrong thing. She wanted desperately to tell Sem and Agi about her struggle, but was too afraid to give anything away. It didn't make sense that a Tyrskan Warrior would be a spy, or her new friend could manage anything mischievous, but she couldn't know for sure. And she'd promised not to say anything.

Late that night, they finally finished filling the orders. An exhausted Sem leaned on Agi, who picked her up and carried her out of the shop.

Rory had rarely seen Sem so quiet. But she still had one thing to say, "Thanks for helping tonight. I sure owe you one."

"No worries." Rory walked beside Agi as he carried Sem home. It was kinda nice being in their company. And it seemed she'd followed Asdorn's instructions—and found people she could trust in this city.

"Really, Mrs. Wallace would've been so angry," Sem said. "I'd hate to lose my apprenticeship."

Rory raised her eyebrows. "But it's not your fault Mrs. Greene isn't here."

Sem shook her head, not bothering to adjust her glasses. "It doesn't matter. Wallace has power—she's one of the few people with real money in this city—not just credits. She gets what she wants. And without you, this would have been the third order that was late."

Agi scoffed. "Or we would've been here all night. I'm going to have to have a chat with Mrs. Greene about what's going on. This is her business. She should be here."

"Oh, please don't say anything on my account," Sem pleaded. "She'll know it's me."

"Fine," Agi said, adjusting Sem in his arms. "But it still doesn't seem right."

Sem waved to Rory. "See you tomorrow?"

Rory waved back, and headed to T. Veckler's house. She paused outside the front door. She wasn't in the mood to deal with T. Veckler's anger. Perhaps waiting a little longer to go inside would be better. For once she felt like she wanted to be alone.

She walked down to the lake, enjoying the path light up beneath her feet. She sat in the gazebo beside the water, which glimmered under the dual moons' light. It brought a welcome wave of calm over her.

"Can't sleep?" A soft voice said behind her.

She turned around.

Agi.

"I'm worried about my brother. He's with a dangerous person, and I'm afraid of what will happen to him. Just sitting around waiting for someone else to do something is driving me nuts."

"I understand," Agi said, leaning back on the bench. "When my family died, I remember Captain Orlovsky—the leader of the Tyrskan Warriors—pulling me away from my burning aunt and uncle. To this day, I still feel like I could've done something if he hadn't grabbed me, but logically I know it was too late for them."

"I'm sorry."

"My point is that it's not too late for you. They sent Thurston and Leopold to Nadezhda. They're two of the best. They'll bring Peter home."

"You really think so?"

"At the very least they'll bring back information on what's going on with your brother."

Rory shuddered in the brisk autumn air.

"Are you cold?"

"No," she said through chattering teeth.

Agi pulled off his blue cloak and wrapped it around her.

His heat still left on the soft fabric, she felt instantly warmed. "Thanks."

Agi stared over the lake for a few moments before speaking again. "Sem's like my little sister. I don't have any family, and with Sem's older siblings off at war, her family has accepted me into their home. So, really, it means a lot to me when someone is kind to her."

Rory didn't know what to say, so she just smiled up at him. For all his loss, he seemed surprisingly peaceful.

The two sat in silence looking out over the calm water for some time. But inside, Rory wasn't calm. Despite what Agi said, she was still worried about Peter. They were on the same planet, but in different cities—one she didn't even know the location of. Was he safe? Was The Researcher going to hurt him? How was she ever going to get him home?

※　※　※

T. Veckler had been surprisingly kind to her last night. It was as if he knew she was working through stuff.

"I'm going to help Sem in the herb shop," Rory said the next morning.

"Let me know if plans change," T. Veckler said from his place at the tall table. He'd been hunched over his lesson plans all morning.

Rory breathed in the cool morning air. It was always so quiet in Turopia in the morning and late evenings. She couldn't believe she was starting to enjoy this place so much. If only Peter were here with her. She'd thought all night about what The Researcher could be doing with Peter, and hadn't come up with any good answers.

She was almost to Main Street when an imposing figure stepped into her path. "Well hello Rory."

"Get out of my way," Rory said to the man who'd approached her in the entryway yesterday. His all-brown tunic and pants were filthy from travel.

"I have the power to make you a great offer," Talbert said. "I know you won't refuse."

Rory stepped to the side to walk around him.

He blocked her path, towering over her. "I'll be quick— you give me your locket and I'll take you to Peter."

Rory gasped. Could it really be this easy to see Peter? But if she gave this man her locket, what would he do with it? He'd said he was working for her father, which really meant The Researcher. That could only mean one thing—The Researcher really did want her locket to help free his master. Isn't that what Asdorn had told her?

"Let me make this even easier for you," Talbert said. "I have it on great authority that my associate can take you and Peter back to Earth. But only if you come with me."

It felt as if a giant anvil were crushing her. Why would he offer such a thing? To be reunited with both her brother, and return to her home on Earth? Miss Kuma? Sun-hi? She'd never see them again if she didn't go with him.

But Maggie and Burt had told her such awful things about Levicus, and she trusted the old couple. Did she really want to be the reason that evil being escaped?

"Hurry up," Talbert said, looking around. "It can't be that hard of a choice. Don't you love your brother? Or perhaps you never did."

It felt like he punched her. Rory did love Peter. *She* wasn't the one who stopped writing letters—*Peter* was the one who'd sent her a mean letter saying he had a new family when she was seven. What should she do?

Tae Kwon Do! That was the answer. Rory thought through her tenets—courtesy, integrity, perseverance, self-control, and indomitable spirit. So far she'd failed at integrity in this world, and she vowed she wouldn't again. She had to do the right thing, even if it caused her pain.

Rory took a deep breath and spewed out the words before she lost courage. "No. You tell The Researcher I'm not falling for his little trick. I know who he is. Bring Peter to Turopia."

"Wrong answer," Talbert said coldly. He grabbed her forearm, causing shooting pain to run up her arm.

He was so much bigger than her, she'd never be able to land a punch. She struggled against him.

Talbert scoffed, pulling her towards him. "This is easier than I thought it'd be."

Rory aimed a punch at his face purely to distract him. At the same moment, she spun her hand up like she was offering him a cup of tea, and pulled her hand through his thumb and forefinger. Once her wrist was free, she stepped back and kicked him in the gut.

Talbert stumbled back.

Rory looked around the quiet rows of tiny houses. No one was around.

Talbert lunged forward to grab her.

Heart pounding, Rory blocked his outstretched arms. She shifted, giving a swift round kick to his fat side. As he stumbled, she kicked him again.

Talbert barreled back at her.

She stepped out of the way and kneed him in the groin. Hard. She leapt back. The large man dropped to the ground. While cringing in pain, he pulled a vial out of his jacket.

Rory remembered Miss Kuma's teaching of recognizing the moment the defender became the aggressor. If she attacked him while he was on the ground, *she'd* become the attacker. It was time to get away. Rory turned and ran.

She'd barely made it a few feet when a glass bottle shattered at her feet. Rory caught a whiff of the thick red smoke and collapsed to the ground. She struggled to move, but was paralyzed. The houses and sidewalk around her was a blur.

Panic struck as Talbert leaned over her.

What was he going to do to her?

Talbert yanked off the locket. "The Researcher will be pleased to have this." He kicked her in the gut. "Don't you ever forget who I am. Lord Talbert. No girl is going to defeat me."

Rory cringed and watched Talbert walk out of sight.

✻　　✻　　✻

Rory didn't know how long she lay there before she heard Agi calling her name. His voice had never sounded so sweet. He raced towards her from the direction of T. Veckler's house. He'd probably gone to pick her up for a real training session in the Entrix.

She peeled her face off of the stone sidewalk panel and winced at the pain. The rest of her body was still numb. She allowed Agi to pick her up.

In Agi's strong arms, Rory looked at a pool of blood on the ground. She gasped in shock. Was that hers?

Agi saw her reaction. "Other than some cuts from the potion bottle, you are fine. The blood is not yours—it's from a blood potion. Very powerful dark magic."

Relief washed over her. So she wasn't dying from a mortal wound.

Agi paused, thinking for a moment, before turning back the other direction towards the market. A few minutes later, Agi laid Rory down on the sofa in the back of the herb shop.

Sem came running around the corner. "What's wrong? What happened? Is she okay? What should I do?"

Agi raised a hand. "Calm down, Sem. Someone used a blood potion on her. It's paralyzed her somehow. I've never seen anything like this."

Rory struggled to move. She could sit up, but just barely.

Agi caught her and let her lean on his shoulder.

He was so warm.

"What happened?" Agi asked.

Sem was looking through the wall of books behind the counter.

Rory didn't know how much she could tell them without giving her identity away. "A man who knew me and my twin brother as kids attacked me. He took my locket. By now he's already taken it to . . ."

"To whom?" Agi asked.

But Rory couldn't continue her sentence. It was too much. What if she told them and it put them in danger? No, she couldn't do that.

Agi pulled the description of Talbert out of Rory, laid her gently down on the couch, and ran out of the shop to find out if Talbert had left Turopia.

While Agi was gone, Sem gave Rory a blue tonic that tasted just awful—like she was drinking engine fumes.

"Sorry I couldn't add my signature cookie flavoring," Sem said. "But adding anything would alter the medicine's delicate balance."

Rory gagged after drinking the bottle, using all her self-control *not* to vomit the mixture back up. "Thanks."

"If this doesn't work right away, we have to take you to the healing center. I don't have any books on blood magic—very dark sorcery—only a few people can even use it," Sem said. "So what's so special about your locket? Why would someone steal it?"

Rory studied Sem's sweet face, with her wide smile, and her thick black-rimmed glasses. The girl couldn't be a spy, could she? But Sem was a talker and Rory was afraid Sem would accidentally give away her information. No—this was something Rory had to figure out on her own.

"It was my mother's," was all Rory said.

Agi returned with a sorrowful expression. "The guards reported a man matching that description left Turopia an hour ago."

Her locket, her most precious possession.

It was gone.

And even worse, now The Researcher had what he needed to free his master. And it was all her fault.

CHAPTER
— 26 —

PETER'S DISCOVERY IN NADEZHDA

Peter tried desperately to go to sleep, but when he did, nightmares of Talbert whipping him in his office plagued his sleep. And when he awoke, fears of discovering his father was a murderer filled his mind.

Peter sat up straight in his bed, wishing for that dream with the bird. He'd gotten so used to seeing the bird in his sleep, it was strange he hadn't had that dream since coming to Inara. What had happened to the magnificent blue and gold bird? Would he ever see it again?

Even though it was still early evening, Peter got out of bed. He had to figure out the truth. But how? He couldn't ask his father directly—he'd obviously lie about it.

As Peter paced his room, he put his hands in his pockets. His fingers closed around the crumpled letter—the one that mentioned his father's laboratory. What did he have in his secret area? Peter would go find out for himself. He'd go down there, clear his father, then go back to Saipha's room to find more clues.

This late in the evening, the corridors were mostly empty, except for a few servants, and guards returning from duty.

From his wanderings, he'd gotten to know his side of the castle quite well. Very few people went down to the lower levels. They were dark and not as well maintained as the main part of the castle.

When he reached the tapestry he'd emerged from that very first night, Peter paced outside of it. Was he really going to sneak in? What was he going to find? Did he even want to know?

His heart ached. He'd dreamed of finding his father and escaping Talbert for so long. His father had been so kind to him—there had to be a better answer. Peter couldn't face living with another abusive parent.

Systematically, he touched every stone surrounding where he thought it might be. He moved the candlestick to the right of the blank space.

Nothing.

He tilted the candlestick on the left. That was it!

If he hadn't been looking for it, he might have missed the surprisingly quiet door inch open. He swallowed, checked to see no one was watching, then peeked into the dark hallway. No one was in sight, so he slipped inside. As he did, the entry sealed shut behind him.

Pausing for a moment, he let his eyes adjust to the dark. He didn't want to light the torch for fear of being seen. So far, his father hadn't seemed the type to punish like Talbert did, but Peter often caught his father holding his temper back. Peter didn't want to find out what happened when he *did* let his temper loose.

The silence told him he was alone. The air was stale and made it hard to breathe. If his father slept down here, he better hurry, or be quiet in case he was sleeping. Peter inched down the dark narrow hallway, using the cold stones as a guide.

When he reached the end, he looked around the corner where the hallway bent back on itself towards the room with the portal at the end.

All the rooms lining the hallway were dark—no one was here.

Peter tiptoed into the room straight in front of him. *"Al'Brith."* A huge ball of light hovered in front of him. He was so anxious, he'd overdone it. Peter let the spell dissipate and tried again. A small orb of light hovered in front of him as he walked.

He was in a room with a metal medical table in the center. A wide counter lined part of the walls. A couple odd contraptions stood against the opposite wall. Peter turned back to the rack of glass jars on top of the counter. He held up his dual-dragon wand and the light hovered higher, revealing labels with writing on them. Most of the jars were empty, but still had strange dates and names written on them. Peter pulled out a jar beside three unused ones and inspected it.

Kutall, 1, Lynne.

Peter's hand turned sweaty, and he almost dropped it. What was his father doing with a jar of what appeared to be blood? And if he really had killed her, why did he do it?

He slipped the jar back, careful to line up the label with all the other neatly arranged jars. He stepped back, leaning over the counter. Vomit forced its way up and Peter swallowed.

Frantically, he looked around—there had to be another answer.

He inched towards the doorframe and let his light fade. As he did, he heard the secret door inch slowly open.

His father was here!

Carefully, he imagined the layout of the room, and crept slowly back. He ran his hand lightly along the cabinets, feeling for the end. When he did, he stuffed himself between the cold wall and the counter.

Luckily he was small. But if his father came in the room, he'd be discovered. He'd have to pretend that he was looking for him. As he tried to calm his pounding heart, Peter knew he had to tell—if he didn't then it would be *his* fault if his father killed someone else.

His father's strong, guiding voice drifted down the hall. Who was he talking to? This was supposed to be a secret area.

His stomach tightened and goosebumps erupted on his arms. There was no logical reason to feel this way. He shook his head and clutched his wand tightly, trying to make the unwanted anxiety disappear.

The response came in a voice of cold superiority Peter would recognize anywhere.

He froze.

His father was talking to the last person in the world he had expected.

Peter put his hand out on the cold stone wall to steady himself, even though he was already sitting. The world spun around him.

He was not free.

Judge Talbert was on Inara.

As the voices grew nearer, Peter closed his eyes to focus on his hearing.

"I told you—" his father said with forced gentleness, pausing right outside the room Peter was hiding in. "I have allowed you to stay here for one reason, and that is to assist me. You were only helpful to me because no disciples still loyal to me can enter Turopia. If you resist, I will gladly return you to Earth where you can live your life behind bars."

"Let me at the boy—just for a minute," Talbert said, "I did as you asked—pretended to be one of those filthy refugees and snuck into Turopia for you—"

"Not until I have what I want," his father said, entering the room. "Now, did you retrieve the locket from the girl, or not?"

Peter held himself as still as possible, willing his heart to quiet.

"Yes," Talbert said, hesitating. "Maybe I keep the locket for myself. And maybe *I* free this Levicus character and take the glory for myself."

"I was hoping you weren't going to say that."

Peter heard one of them take a step back into the medical table.

"No! Please!" Talbert said. "Put that away! The glory means nothing. I just want the power."

"Like I told you, you sniveling coward, the locket only grants access to The Book of Keys. Without the magic knowledge to read it, the book will be useless to you. And I promise, when Levicus is freed, as his first in command, I will insist you get the reward you deserve."

"I will do as you ask," whispered the judge.

"Ask . . . what?"

"Master."

"There. That's better," The Researcher said.

"Here."

"It's mine. After years of searching, the locket is finally mine!" The Researcher said with cold obsession.

Peter shivered.

"There's still one more item to settle," Talbert said. "I think I've waited long enough to get back at Peter. The brat ruined me."

"I would think starting a new life where you can have true power and not that false power you cherished so dearly would be enough," The Researcher said.

"But you have only shown me a taste of magic. I want to do it myself."

"In time," his father said.

"I hate you."

"Of course you do. But do as I ask, and I will make you a very happy man. If you do well, perhaps I will let you have the best revenge of all . . ."

"Beating him to death with magic?" Talbert asked.

Only years of training acting like an invisible mouse kept Peter silent in that moment.

"I was going to offer something else—" The Researcher sounded dismissive, like he was trying to get the conversation over with. He picked something up off the counter. "I have another job for you. Come with me."

Peter listened harder than he ever had in his life. Their footsteps faded down the hall—not out of the area completely, but to the portal room.

Not daring to wait to hear the rest of their conversation, Peter crept through the dark room, grateful for the small light coming from down the hall. As a flood of ten thousand thoughts coursed through his mind, Peter tiptoed down the narrow corridor to the exit.

Hot tears blurred his vision. Peter ran his hands along the wall to find the candlestick. The wall inched open agonizingly slow. He rocked in place waiting for it to open enough. He squeezed through. The moment he turned the candleholder to close of the secret passageway, he bolted down the hallway.

Although he was normally a good runner, he could barely catch his breath. He tore into his bedroom with so much force, he was afraid the large door would fall off its hinges. He turned and quietly shut it behind him. The act of trying to hold it all in caught up with him, and he collapsed on his bed. The monster book he carried fell to the ground.

No.

That wasn't his father.

His father was supposed to be loving. To protect him, and never let anything bad happen to him.

He was not supposed to be conspiring with his abuser, his worst nightmare.

Peter tossed and turned atop his covers, trying to pull his thoughts together. *I have to come up with a plan.*

But try as he might, no plan came together. In his shock, all he could think of was fleeing, but to where? And how did one break out of a fortified castle with guards everywhere?

Could he use fire magic again?

He bit his lip. Setting fire wouldn't work. He needed something subtler. If his father found out he'd gone missing, he was sure to send the king's forces, or his own followers after him.

He flipped through *Magicology*, looking for an idea. It was full of spells he'd already memorized. Nothing there. *My First Zenmage Spells* had some good advice in it, maybe he could discover something to help.

He had trouble focusing, but one introductory passage kept staring back at him:

You won't be able to tap into the full power of your Zenmage ancestry until you have released the strongholds that fear and anger have on the human spirit. While this is a journey most would do well to undertake, it is especially important for Zenmages.

You start by being willing to face your fear and call it out for what it is – the biggest deception our minds tell us. Once you have let your fear go, then, and only then, will you find true freedom.

He surely wasn't a Zenmage—it had to be another one of his father's lies—but the words stuck with him for some reason—made him feel lighter. It didn't seem possible to live without fear. He'd only recently begun to experience fearlessness without Talbert, and now it had all come crashing back. He couldn't escape Talbert, and he couldn't escape the fear.

Where would he go? He didn't know anyone on this planet, and he'd never be able to figure out the portal to get back to Earth. Besides, even if he did know, there was no way he'd return to his father's secret area—that's where Talbert was.

Peter asked himself what he really wanted, and the answer was easy: to be with Rory.

So if his sister was in Turopia, that's where he'd go. He cringed to think she could've already been injured by those *Ayeven* people. He'd have to get her out of there, and quickly.

Peter's chest tightened. *Escape.* He needed to get out of here. Then he could make other plans. He raced to fill his backpack with items he'd need— bread, a couple orange-like apples, *Magicology,* that little Zenmage book, and his dragon wand.

He put the silver wand in his belt holster just in case. The strip of leather magically tightened around the wand so it wouldn't fall out.

Bag slung over his shoulder, he paused halfway to the door. He should check the hallway first. Quickly, he dropped his bag under the desk, and went back to the door.

Opening it slowly, he poked his head outside, looking and listening. The stars were out, and the two moons shone brightly.

No one in sight.

He returned for his bag, slipped his cloak on, and left.

The moment the door closed, he sprinted in the opposite direction of his father's hidden rooms. Peter was taking the long way, but he couldn't risk running into his father or Talbert.

He expected the library to be empty, but he heard voices. On the lower level with all the tables, two people huddled over a map. Peter crouched, and closed the door quietly behind him. He slinked behind the tall check-out counter, and poked his head out.

"Nicholas, I told you, the route's clear." A dark-skinned woman with wide hips and thick black hair tapped the map. "Warlord Crokus' forces have moved South."

"But what about the bandits in Vanderville who've hijacked the teleport?" Nicholas asked. He was a middle-aged man with a bushy red beard. "Those attacks have been nasty, Harriet. We have a good shipment for those Turopians. I don't want to return home empty-handed."

Peter hoped they'd leave soon, so he could slip into the rarely used research room. Even behind the counter he felt exposed. What if the librarian returned for something, or his father came looking for him—behind the counter would be the first place he'd check.

"We'll have to take the stretch through Dusty Hollow to Turopia," Harriet said. "It's a little longer, but at least there's a safe teleport location."

They were going to Turopia. His eyes widened with a new idea. Those two merchants were his ticket out of Nadezhda.

"Then it's settled," Nicholas said.

They rolled up the large map, and Peter slipped back into the shadows of the counter.

"Don't sleep in this time," Harriet said. "We'll have to get a head start if we want to beat the snow."

Nicholas chuckled. "It's almost midnight. You don't like me getting any sleep, do you?"

Peter heard them kiss, and cringed. *Ew.*

While the couple was distracted, Peter slipped out of the library. He sprinted down the hallway.

The main courtyard was eerily empty and quiet, save for little gusts of wind swirling leaves around the center fountain. Peter shuddered under his cloak as he hid beside the base of the stairs that led into the castle.

Peter's eyes widened as the massive front doors opened to a blond man in magnificent blue robes. As soon as he disembarked from his horse, the guards shut the door behind him.

Two guards stood around a fire can, warming their hands under the archway. Eight more guards were positioned atop the highest walls, two looking each of the four directions for possible threats. They wouldn't be expecting an attack from the inside. *No, the door would never work.* Even if he could get past this door, there was still one more exit for him to get past.

He briefly considered setting it ablaze, but that seemed a little extreme. He'd never be able to fight off his father is he were caught.

He'd have to sneak into the merchant's caravan *before* it left the city. Four wooden horse-drawn caravans, like small cabooses, lined the side of the courtyard. How was he supposed to choose?

Clouds passed over the dual moons, and he made his break for the caravan closest to him. A tag with a permit hung on the door: Jemma Gómez. Okay, not the people from the library. He checked the next two caravans with no luck.

The one in front was painted a bright red with an orange domed roof. Their permit read: Nicholas and Harriet Lithman, and the sign over the door read, 'Lithman's Supplies for the Whole Family.'

This was the right one. Reaching up to open the door, he found it firmly locked. The unlocking spell from the advanced section of *Magicology* popped into his mind. *Way* too difficult for him.

He'd have to try. He took a deep breath. He could *not* put any fire magic into the spell. Accidentally burning the merchant's entire source of income would not be good.

Please. Peter said under his breath as he brought up the page in his mind. He pulled the dragon wand out of his backpack, because he seemed to have more control with it, and muttered the spell under his breath a few times.

Imagining an unhinged combination lock, he tapped the mechanism and cast the spell, "*Lif'to-ach Man'ulim.*"

Nothing.

He tried again, this time trying to perform the motions more fluidly. Peter became engrossed in the spellwork.

Someone tapped him on the shoulder. He jumped around, dragon wand raised.

It was Nicholas—the stocky man with the thick beard from the library. But where was Harriet?

Not wanting to start a fight, he immediately lowered the wand. The merchant's brows furrowed. "And what do you think you're doing? Guards!"

CHAPTER
— 27 —

PETER'S FLIGHT TO TUROPIA

Shhh, please sir," Peter said to Nicholas. "I need help."

The huddled soldiers guarding the gate paid no attention. Voices of men from higher levels of the castle searching for someone echoed in the chill night air.

Searching for him.

His father must have found him missing from his bed.

"So you want me to help you, after I catch you trying to open my lock?" Nicholas asked.

Peter looked at the ground. He was out of options. "I'm sorry. I didn't know what else to do."

The heavily-muscled merchant lifted the lock. "You must be new here. *No one* breaks into my caravan. I have the best multi-code layer system gold can buy." He stood tall, obviously proud of his security.

"Guess that's why my unlocking spell didn't work."

"Seriously. With all the wizards running around Tilla, you really think a simple unlocking spell would keep our goods safe?"

"Tilla?" Peter asked. He thought the planet was called Inara.

"Name of this continent? Where you from boy, who are you?"

"I'm nobody. Please let me in and I'll explain."

"Not so quick. Sounds like The Researcher wants someone. I'm guessing that person is you. What makes you so special that he wants you so badly?"

Peter shrugged. "Maybe 'cause I'm his son?"

A look of pure revulsion passed over Nicholas' face. Peter recognized his own hatred in the man's expression. The merchant scoffed. "When I was a small boy, I lost my entire village because of him and his master. You're lucky my wife isn't here, because she'd kill you before you had a chance to blink."

Peter's eyes widened. "Please, sir. I'm not anything like him. I'm like you. I hate him. I—I need to escape. Please don't tell him I'm here. I just need to leave Nadezhda." He cowered back toward the caravan, afraid of the backlash from speaking out.

"Tell me one good reason why I should help you and not just turn you over? Nothing is worse than being on The Researcher's bad side. Turning you over would help me earn his good graces."

Peter's mind raced. "Um, you're a merchant, right? How about I trade you something?"

Nicholas rubbed his beard, taking more time than Peter would've liked to make a decision.

Peter tried to ignore the guards running along the outer hallways that were open to the courtyard. Maybe all his years of hiding like a mouse in school would finally pay off.

Nicholas seemed to catch his worried look. "Come inside. If you have something good to offer, and a good reason for me to help you, I'll agree to hide you. If you're trying to trick me, I'll throw you outside and you can figure it out yourself."

The moment the door opened, Peter crawled into the caravan.

Mouth gaping, Peter looked around—the caravan was at least three times as big as it appeared from the outside!

Piles of crates filled with merchandise lined the walls in neat rows. In the center sat a threadbare couch with a pile of pillows. A curtain separated the area where the merchant would drive the horses.

"Well, let's have it," Nicholas said. "I don't want to get caught with you. It could mean my head. I don't even want to think what The Researcher would do to me."

Peter dumped out the contents of his backpack onto a worn patterned rug. His battered shoebox fell to the ground, spilling its contents. He lunged for his baby shirt. "Okay, anything but this."

Nicholas grabbed the shirt first. Looking at the blood stain, he narrowed his brow and threw it back to Peter. "That's all you have?"

Peter pulled both wands from his belt and held them out. Secretly, he'd be glad to be rid of the silver wand.

The merchant picked up the wooden dragon wand and inspected it. "Beautiful craftsmanship, but I dare say . . . is that a silver wand?"

"My father gave it to me. But said I'm not powerful enough to use it properly." Peter handed it to Nicholas, not sure why he looked like a little kid on Christmas morning.

The merchant inspected it, looking down its length and tested the balance in his hand. "This is very valuable. Quite rare in fact. I could fetch a price worth food for the rest of the season of Kutall with this one item."

"Please. If you sneak me out, and get me to Turopia, I'll give it to you."

Nicholas looked at him closely, like the mention of Turopia made him suspicious. He shook his head and threw both wands down at Peter. "No, I will not fall for your little trick and get you into the sanctuary city." The merchant walked towards the door.

Peter's heart raced as he heard soldiers searching the courtyard. He couldn't let the merchant send him outside.

Peter grabbed the merchant's dirty pant leg. Desperate, he let the truth spill from his mouth, barely conscious of the words he was choosing. "Please sir, I just came here from Earth. I've only been here several days. I have no idea what's going on. I just learned The Researcher is my father. I can't let him find me. Please." Peter barely remembered the last time he'd spoken so many words in one breath.

"I don't know if you are making up the grandest lie I've ever heard, or if you're telling the truth. Earth is our legendary home planet."

"Please, sir." Peter got on his knees and begged. "My twin sister is in Turopia and I have to get to her. She's everything to me."

"I will take you to Turopia with that lovely silver wand as payment. Please know if you fail the Turopian guard's inspection, you will have to find your own way back to your father, and he will have to find another way inside our precious sanctuary city."

Peter nodded vigorously. He wanted to kiss the merchant's muddy boots. "Thank you, sir. Thank you."

Quickly, Nicholas put both wands in Peter's backpack and shoved it into his arms. "If The Researcher finds this, then we're surely caught. I trust you to return the silver wand to me when I get you to Turopia?"

Peter nodded several times.

The merchant pulled back the rug to reveal wooden floorboards. He tapped the floor with his own battered wand and a hole opened. It reminded Peter of the book, *The Diary of Anne Frank*, and he shuddered.

"Inside," the merchant instructed.

Peter hesitated, but only for a moment. "What's this for?"

"Hiding Ayeven," Nicholas responded without a beat.

Peter raised his eyebrows, not sure why someone would want to hide such despicable creatures, but didn't feel in a place to argue. Jumping down the hole, he was surprised to find a cozy room with a couch and two chairs.

If Nicholas was keeping him just to turn him over to his father, then he'd be crossed by *two* traitors. He'd have to find a spell he could use to protect himself. Even though he could look through the images in his head, he opened his magic book searching for useful spells. He didn't think he stood a chance against his father, but he'd have to try.

A knock came at the caravan's door. Nicholas must have let the person in because a moment later, boots clomped on the floorboards above.

His father's familiar voice wafted through the floorboards.

Peter dove under the four-legged couch, knowing full well when the trap door was opened, he would be found. *Please don't let him catch me. Please don't give me away.*

He listened intently, but couldn't make out any of the words in their conversation. His father's cold and gentle voice was getting more irritable as the moments passed. Nicholas kept his grumbly voice calm and even. How come the merchant didn't seem nervous at all when Peter could barely stop shaking with fear he'd be caught?

Peter crouched under the couch. Waiting. Listening. Any moment his father would reach down and pull him back into his real-life nightmare.

The trapdoor creaked open. A faint light pooled in, making the shadows even more ominous.

Peter held his breath.

"Now what are you hiding down there?" his father asked. All congeniality was now gone from his voice. "I ask if you are hiding my boy, you say no, and here I find a hidden compartment. You were one of the people harboring Ayeven, weren't you?"

"No, no sir," Nicholas said. "That was my father. This is his caravan. I didn't even know it was there."

Peter couldn't believe the merchant hadn't exposed him.

To Peter's surprise, his father laughed. "Did you think me so weak I would not sense his presence below? My powers have not diminished in my master's absence, as people seem to suspect. Perhaps my being gone has allowed you to forget who I am. Well not for long."

"Boy, get up here," his father ordered, looking into the hidden room. "I know you're down there. This merchant here is a poor excuse for a wizard if he believes his old security system could mask your energy force."

Peter didn't know if his father was bluffing, or if he'd really sensed him.

"Boy, are you deaf?"

Peter didn't budge. It wasn't only because he didn't want to—his vision went blurry, like he was looking through spots, and his skin tightened. It was all over.

Before Peter knew what was happening, The Researcher jumped down the hole and turned over all the furniture on his way to Peter's hiding spot under the couch. The room filled with dust so thick, Peter could barely see.

"There you are." His father grabbed Peter, then pulled him in and gave him a tight hug. "I'm so glad I found you. I thought you were lost to me."

Peter shook his head, not sure how to respond to his sudden warmth.

"Come, let's get you out of this filthy place." The Researcher grabbed Peter's hand and led him out of the hole.

Peter looked down into the secret compartment—he'd been so close to escaping. So close.

The Researcher turned to Nicholas. "You should know better than to lie to Levicus' second." In a quick turn, he yelled, "Guards, lock up this man for kidnapping my boy."

"But he didn't—I," Peter started.

"Quiet now," The Researcher said as he led Peter out of the caravan. "I think you've been through quite enough."

Peter pulled himself out of his father's grip long enough to see Nicholas struggling to break free of the two guards. Did they really have to be so rough? Here the merchant had been so kind to him, and now he was being locked away for something he didn't even do.

What was he going to say to his father? His father thinking the merchant had kidnapped him had saved him from certain punishment. But what would happen to Nicholas now?

Back in Peter's bedroom, his father finally spoke. "Honestly, I thought you would be safer here in the capital city than where I usually stay."

Peter took a step back. "But he didn't kidnap me, I snuck out."

His father looked surprised. "Excuse me? Now why would you do such a thing?"

Afraid telling the truth would get him into more trouble, Peter lied, "I wanted to go to Turopia to rescue Rory. You said Turopia was a dangerous place, and you couldn't enter. I thought as a kid, I might be able to gain easy access and bring her home."

"I see," his father said, then just stared at Peter.

He stared back, not sure what to do.

"Now, I think you should know I don't take well to people lying to me. Or did you ignore what I said to the merchant?"

Peter shook his head, and stepped closer to his four-poster bed. He just wanted to crawl under the covers and hide.

"Now tell me the truth, or so help me, I will kill that merchant for kidnapping my son."

"It's just that—" the words clogged in Peter's throat. But he had to say something. He couldn't let Nicholas die because of him.

"Spit it out, boy."

It was all over. It was clear his father could see right through him. Maybe if he told a partial truth—ignoring that he'd killed Saipha Lynne—his father would be lenient.

Peter put on the stoic face he'd used so often with Talbert. "I saw you working with Judge Talbert, so I ran away. There. I said it. Now let the merchant go."

Peter caught his father's expression narrow in surprise for the briefest of moments, before resetting to its normal calm.

"Now, do you really think I can let a known Ayeven-harborer get away? Even if he didn't kidnap you, he's as guilty as they come." His father stepped forward, his arm outstretched as if to comfort him.

Peter pulled away.

"Now let's sit and discuss this. I see you are confused."

Peter let his father lead him to the bed. He remained silent, afraid to betray the truth he sensed bubbling within him.

"You misunderstand me." They sat side-by-side on the down comforter. "You haven't been here long enough to appreciate the dangers of Turopia. I'm glad I was able to rescue you before you got there. Otherwise, I might never have seen you again. You are just a child, so I will explain it to you."

Peter ignored the insult, continuing to glare at his father.

"Haven't you ever had to warp the truth to get someone to do what you want? That is simply what I was doing. That old guardian of yours wants to get back at you more than anything, so I simply told him what he wanted to hear. Soon Rory will be with us, and you will trust me again. You want to be with your sister again, don't you?"

Peter wanted to trust his explanation. He had often told Talbert whatever he wanted to hear to get out of whippings.

"I see you still don't believe me. I know what he did to you. As your father, I'm insulted you'd think I'd let him near you."

"I'm sorry," Peter said automatically. Then he corrected his thoughts. No—*he* wasn't the one who was sorry. It was his father who should feel sorry for lying and keeping Talbert.

His father pulled him in closer. "I think now you understand why I've asked you to stay in your room—I wanted to keep you from running into Talbert."

Peter wanted to believe him, but there was too much hurt.

"Don't you think if I truly intended you harm, I would have let Talbert come to your room? There have been plenty of opportunities for me to tell him where you are. And yet, I chose to keep you hidden from him. I think that deserves some credit."

His explanation about the judge made sense, but it didn't reconcile what he'd learned from Nicholas. "How do you expect me to trust you when you and your master destroyed the merchant's town?"

"You don't understand this world," his father said harshly, then looked off as if accessing a memory. "If I remember correctly, their town was harboring Ayeven, and in the battle to remove the filth, their town was destroyed. Really, it was their own fault for not surrendering the Ayeven right away. And that's why I'm working to get Rory out of Turopia as soon as possible."

Peter really wanted to believe him. He wanted his vision of happy times with Rory and his mother to come true. If his father was working to free Rory, why shouldn't he trust him?

"But why Talbert?" his voice came out a whisper.

His father's face narrowed. "He is a fool—they are easy to manipulate."

Peter stared at him blankly. Talbert *was* very predictable. Peter usually knew just what to do to avoid punishment— except when his own temper was triggered. He thought back to just a week ago when he hadn't caught his tongue, and his father had shown up just in time to save him from a much longer whipping session.

"You are just a kid, so I see it's hard for you to understand that I can't get into Turopia—much less find the location, and neither can my associates." His father seemed to study him for a moment. "However, I can see this is challenging for you— more than I expected. If you want, I can send Talbert back to Earth. But if I do, we'll have no way of getting Rory out of Turopia. Is that what you want? It's up to you."

Peter was struck more by someone actually asking him his opinion, than by the situation at hand. No one ever asked him what he wanted.

"Well? Now's the time to make a choice." His father rested his hand gently on Peter's shoulder. "Unless you want to tell me everything I've worked for my entire life is wrong."

Instantly the realization of what was going on hit Peter like collapsing dirt from a tunnel. His father was trying to manipulate him just like Talbert. How could he have been so stupid not to see it? He had to lie to his father to give himself time to find a way to escape and get to Rory. And he couldn't help Rory if his father thought he was on the wrong side. "Okay. Just a little longer. When Rory's here, then you'll send Talbert back to Earth?"

"I promise," his father said with a grin. "See how easy it is to tell the truth to people you care about?" He narrowed his eyes, studying Peter, and spoke softly, "Earlier, when I asked you what you were doing, you lied to me."

As Peter sensed his father's hidden fury, Peter's heart quickened.

"All of this could have been avoided if you had just told me the truth. Now you know I don't like people lying to me."

"I'm sorry, I was scared of Talbert," Peter croaked.

His father softened, wrapping his long arm around Peter's shoulders, and said in his gentle tone. "Just this once, I am going to forgive you. I'm sure you won't let it happen again, right?"

Peter shook his head.

His father pulled him in for a tight embrace. "There there my sweet boy, I won't let Judge Talbert anywhere near you."

CHAPTER

— 28 —

PETER AND THE BOOK OF KEYS

Peter couldn't believe his luck. Not only had he gotten away without a punishment, his father had actually left him alone all night. He was sure his father would've put guards on his door or locked him in, but when Peter checked, the hallway was clear.

But it still seemed he was in a precarious position. Either his father trusted Peter was telling the truth, or was just making it seem that way so he could discipline him later. He would have to be on his best behavior.

He hadn't been able to sleep all night, tossing and turning trying to figure out what was going on. There was what his father told him, the few things the merchant had said, and the stories he'd heard in the dungeon. So what was the truth?

Asking his father was out of the question. Perhaps Princess Red?

But he didn't want to do anything that would upset their already precarious relationship—especially now that he knew who'd killed her beloved teacher. Besides, she seemed to believe what her father said, and King Merdis and his father were on the same side. The only person left was the merchant, but Peter couldn't get to him—Nicholas was in the dungeon.

Peter shook his head. No way he was going down there again.

It seemed the only answer was going to research in the library—find out the hard facts. So after his father's morning visit, Peter carefully snuck down to the library—this time keeping an extra eye out for Princess Red.

But when Peter got there, he realized there was something more important to research—what his father was up to. He'd mentioned a Book of Keys to Judge Talbert. He'd figure it out, then create a plan.

The library was completely empty—something he once would have thought fun, but now only found creepy. And a little lonely.

It wasn't until the sun had set and the moons rose high in the sky, that Peter stumbled upon an explorer who had a whole row of matching books. He ran his fingers along the maroon spines. One snagged his finger—a thick book with a particularly damaged spine.

He set the large, old book atop the wooden table: *Devarious' Book of Ancient Artifacts*. He went straight for the index in the back. His eyes widened when he found The Book of Keys listed. With bated breath, he slowly turned to page 263. He almost missed it because a few pages before it had been torn out.

Legends say The Book of Keys is the oldest artifact on Inara. For many years, even I believed it was a myth, but like all great explorers, we search until we find the truth.

It is one of the great treasures the ancient lineage of Keepers protect, with the help of a great dragon. The Keeper with whom I spoke, who I dare not name, reported that the book is said to contain the long-forgotten spells of the disgraced Archangel Ipseh, before he forgot the knowledge connected to his archangel power, which was stolen by Levicus.

No one alive—that I have come across in my lifetime of travels—has ever seen the book, and my contact rightly refused to use her magnificent locket to open the chest for me.

All she would tell me is of the legends passed through the ages, which claim the book contains powerful spells of binding, finding, and minding. But one thing's for sure, I'd love to read it when it is finally opened.

Peter looked up slowly from the page. His father was searching for some ancient, legendary book, but why?

As Peter groggily snuck back to his room, he contemplated what the passage could mean.

The next day, Peter watched the white sun rise, waiting for his magic lesson, but his father never came. After it seemed certain his father wouldn't visit, Peter snuck back to the library. He had to find more information about this book his father was after.

But he had no further luck.

That evening, as he lay in the back of the garden, looking up at all the constellations, a comet streaked across the sky. The collection of ice, dust, and rocky particles were even better to wish on than stars. After he made his nightly wish to be reunited with his sister, a thought struck him. He sat up.

His father had told the king he was trying to *find* his master. What if his father planned to use this book to *find* where his master was so he could free him?

As Peter snuck back to his room, he thought of what he'd read in the library. The entry had mentioned The Book of

Keys required a locket—Talbert had given his father that very item. And his sister had a beautiful locket. Could it be possible that Rory's was the one mentioned in the book *and* the one Talbert had stolen? It seemed too ridiculous to consider that his sister had an important treasure, but Talbert had mentioned taking it from a girl *in Turopia*.

Peter hated the thought of Talbert being anywhere near his sister.

His father often told him he was thinking wrong, so it was hard to tell if he was making it up or not.

Leaning over the stone ledge outside his bedroom that overlooked the main courtyard, a horrific thought struck Peter. He swallowed, not really wanting to explore the idea. But it felt true—his father wasn't really looking for Rory at all. He just wanted her locket! If Talbert had gotten into Turopia, how come he hadn't rescued Rory? And now that he had it, would he even bother to return to Turopia?

In his gut, Peter knew his father was up to something wicked. Stealing an ancient book. Having someone lie to get into Turopia and steal a girl's locket. Freeing his master.

Peter dragged himself to bed, sensing everything his father told him *had* to be a lie. So did that mean the opposite was true? What if his father had only lied about *some* things?

Nicholas popped into his head as the answer—he seemed like a genuinely caring man. But he was still in the dungeon and Peter couldn't reach him. And it was his fault Nicholas was down there.

Peter sat up in bed.

He *had* to free Nicholas.

What was he thinking? He couldn't attempt a daring rescue. He'd surely fail. What if his father caught him? Or the king? He'd be beheaded for sure.

Feeling like an utter failure, Peter sunk under his covers, pulling the down comforter over his head.

*   *   *

Peter woke to someone shaking him.

"What are you still doing in bed?" his father asked. "We need to talk."

Peter rubbed his eyes. He didn't like the sound of his father's tone.

"Sit with me." His father patted the bed beside him. He wore a beautiful locket around his neck—Rory's necklace.

Peter blinked several times to hide his surprise. It was unmistakable with its interlocking loops covering a bed of blue crystals. Inside, Peter knew he'd find a picture of his mother. Proof that his father really had used Talbert to steal Rory's locket. But how could his father have been so cruel to take her favorite possession, and not free her?

Peter crawled out from under the warm blankets, and shivered next to his father.

"Look, I have to go on a trip for a few days," his father said. "I'm leaving tomorrow morning."

This was Peter's chance to get out of Nadezhda! "I'll pack quickly."

His father shook his head. "It's too dangerous. I have to travel to a dragon's cave. Now, if you had worked harder on your studies and controlling your magic, perhaps. But as of now, you are not ready."

Peter stood up and faced his father. "But I can help you. I'll carry things. Set up camp."

"Not needed. Only a three-day journey to where I'm going. Then I'll come right back. I want you to stay in your room while I'm gone—not even any trips to the library. Do you understand?"

Peter did. He wasn't wanted. Nothing new there. Even worse, he was still stuck in Nadezhda with no way to leave, and no way to get to Rory.

"Good. I'll bring you some more books I want you to study. I think it's time we amped up your magical training, don't you?"

"Yes," Peter forced himself to say. But really his father had given him an idea—he could find a spell to get out of Nadezhda and get to Rory.

His father stood and patted him on his shoulder. "Now that's a good boy."

Peter stared blankly at his father. Even that small touch made Peter's stomach churn.

The door opened and the young albino servant with the scar across his cheek entered. He carried a silver tray laden with Peter's breakfast.

His father turned around and stepped right into the boy.

Peter watched the events unfold as if in slow motion.

The boy's colorless face widened in horror as the tray was knocked from his hands.

The drink spilled down the front of his father's black pants and vest. The tray clattered to the floor, porridge spewing on his father's boots.

"How dare you!" his father yelled. He backhanded the boy across his cheek. A pink splotch appeared where he'd been struck.

Peter gasped, the echo of the slap still ringing in his ears. Peter took a step back, afraid he'd be hit next.

"Watch where you're going, *slave*, or I can have you assigned to a less . . . comfortable post," his father said.

"Yes, sir, I'm so sorry, sir, let me clean this up," the boy said from his kneeling position at his father's feet. Peter had never heard the boy's sweet voice before, though now it was laced with fear.

"Who gave you permission to speak?" his father said.

The boy stood and bowed several times before cleaning up the mess.

"Don't bother." His father picked up his leg, kicked the boy down, and walked away. He picked up his staff, which was leaning against the wall and mumbled a spell. Instantly his clothes were cleaned and refreshed.

The door slammed behind his father.

Peter jumped up to help the boy with the mess.

The boy silently refused Peter's help, picking up as much of the mess as he could, and hurried out of the room.

Peter slunk in his desk chair, worries taking over. His father's true colors were showing.

And now, his father was going off on a trip that gave Peter an unsettling feeling. He was flipping mindlessly through his books, desperately trying to think of a plan, when a thought struck him.

Devarious had said The Book of Keys was guarded by a dragon—and his father was traveling to a dragon's cave—*with* Rory's locket.

Peter stood abruptly from his desk. His father must be leaving to get The Book of Keys in the morning!

As Peter stared out the tall window, it all came together— he had to sneak out with his father and stop him from getting The Book of Keys. Someone like his father shouldn't have such power. But first, he had to make a plan.

Even as his quill hit the parchment, an ache in his gut told him he had one last action to take before leaving—freeing Nicholas.

Fear coursed through his body. His eyes landed on the little Zenmage book on his desk and the words rose . . . *be willing to face your fear.* He didn't have to overcome it, just pretend a little.

As he started to feel a little braver, Red's teasing words popped into his head. He was *not* a scaredy-cat—he was tired of being one. He'd create a new persona on this world—one that wasn't so afraid of everything.

Feeling invigorated like never before, Peter clenched his fist—it was time to make a plan. A good plan. He'd free Nicholas tonight.

Peter ran through his checklist. Practicing the necessary spells over and over? Check. Both the silver and dragon wands? Check. A dark cloak so he could slip unrecognized through the hallways? Backpack full of supplies and his belongings? Double check.

He sighed. He had everything he needed, except it would've been better if he didn't look like himself. But spells to cloak his appearance were way beyond his skill level.

Peter's plan included a quick jailbreak, making Nicholas tell him the truth—however inconvenient it might be—then off to the stables to hide in his father's caravan.

Peter had spent the morning watching his father ordering the king's servants to pack his caravan. Apparently he liked to travel in style. There was food, comfortable bedding, and a crate of potions—Peter knew because a servant girl had dropped a case, which was far too big for her, spilling glass and thick red, iron-smelling liquid all over the stable floor. His father had struck the girl with his staff, causing Peter to run out of his hiding space and vomit in the bushes.

Peter shook his head of his memories of the awful morning. He had to focus. Getting caught was *definitely* not part of his plan. At the bottom of the stairs facing the dungeon, Peter lurked, watching the guard reading a book. Her wand sat on the table within easy reach. A small lantern warmed the area with a yellow glow, making the shadows on the guard's face appear creepy.

He was in luck—the second guard must have slipped away, maybe down one of the other underground passages. Now he only had to overcome one guard.

Peter slipped the dual dragon wand from his belt holster. He tried to keep his hand from shaking. All he was doing was putting the guard to sleep. He didn't want to hurt her.

Suddenly, the guard looked up from her page. "You there. What are you doing?"

Peter froze. He hadn't thought of practicing a lie.

"You don't belong here, go back to the castle," the guard ordered. "It's not safe for children."

Peter hated it when adults thought he didn't know anything just because he was young.

Filled with more courage, mixed with anger, Peter hid the wand behind his back, and walked towards the guard. "I was just—"

The guard cocked her head, as if trying to figure him out.

Peter took advantage of the hesitation. *"El'schtim El'shenah."*

A wave expelled from his wand.

Nothing happened.

The guard raised her bushy eyebrows. "Nice one kid. Why don't you go back upstairs and play with your toys." She raised her wand.

Anger rose in Peter and he shouted the spell, *"El'schtim El'shenah."*

The guard shot back in her chair, instantly asleep. He really needed to figure out how to do his spells without being angry, as Red had said.

Peter slipped the keys from the guard and opened the door.

The cell block was dark, lit only by the moons, which gave the cold area a bluish hue. Peter squinted, looking down the row for Nicholas.

Peter flicked his wand and said, *"Al'Yehior."* A small ball of light hung in the air. The weary faces of the prisoners looked back at him. The young albino servant girl and the gruff man were still there. The young woman who was there during his stay was no longer there. His heart sank, realizing she must've been beheaded.

Finally, he saw the familiar bushy red beard.

Nicholas looked across the bars at him. "What are you doing here?" The filthy man had propped himself up in the corner, using only hay and his knee-length jacket for warmth.

Peter fumbled with the iron skeleton keys to find the right one. "I'm here to free you. But I want you to answer some questions first."

"Let me out of here, then when we're somewhere safe, I'll tell you everything you want to know," Nicholas said.

Hatred flared in Peter, the kind he had never felt so strongly before, not even for Talbert. This man before him, he helped those filthy Ayeven. "No. Now," Peter said, surprised by his boldness. "The Ayeven attacked my mother and separated my family—how could you possibly help them?"

The merchant leaned his head back against the wall, and said calmly, "You're just a boy. I'm not going to try to explain it to you 'cause you won't believe me anyway."

That was the second time someone had said that to him. He hated being called stupid. Just because he was quiet didn't mean he was dumb. "Try me."

The merchant looked him over for some time. "I believe what you told me in my caravan—it's the only truth you know. But I also know you won't trust me. If you believe Ayeven attacked your mother and separated you from your family, how would you ever believe what I have to say?"

Peter shrugged, his body tense with rage.

"Tell me, what do you remember of your mother?" Nicholas said.

"Nothing. My parents left us when we were infants."

"I'll tell you what I remember of mine. She was a beautiful woman with long, flowing red hair who smiled when I made her mud pies."

Like Peter cared about Nicholas' stupid mother.

"I was just a boy when The Researcher and his master, Levicus, rode through our town. Levicus was on a rampage to clear out all of the Ayeven and take their wings."

Peter's eyes widened. "Are you—"

"No, but you are kind to think so highly of me," Nicholas sighed. "I did have friends who were though. My father was adamant if we didn't help them, we were no better than the people who persecuted the Ayeven."

"Then you agree you should be punished for helping the Ayeven escape. You're proving my point," Peter said, looking over his shoulder at the open dungeon door. It was starting to seem like a bad idea to free him. Even if his father was working with Judge Talbert, maybe he was telling the truth about the Ayeven. And Peter was just blinded by his hatred of Talbert.

The merchant cleared his throat, "I clearly remember the day when my pops was teaching me how to string a bow. A great screeching filled the air, and everyone in my small village looked up to see The Researcher and his master fly overhead on the back of two black and red Alrakis dragons."

Dragons. Peter's eyes widened—there were real dragons on this planet. Nicholas' story almost made him forget about his own predicament—almost.

"When The Researcher found the hidden room full of Ayeven under our farmhouse, he sent a slash of red light to slice my father's throat. My mother—she ran with my infant brother in her arms—but he struck her in the back. I stayed hidden behind the pile of logs. I never tried to save my mother. That is the regret I live with—" The words caught in his throat.

Peter waited patiently for Nicholas to collect himself.

Nicholas wiped his eyes before continuing. "So when you accuse me of doing something wrong, I ask you, what is so wrong when your father killed *my* parents and baby brother right in front of me?"

CHAPTER

— 29 —

PETER'S DARING CHOICE

Peter didn't know what to think of the story he'd just heard. It was too horrible. Peter squinted at Nicholas in the dark, with only the light from his wand, trying to decide if Nicholas was telling the truth.

In a spark of awareness, Peter remembered where he was. He'd let his anger get the best of him. "I'm going to free you, but then I want you to tell me more about the Ayeven."

Nicholas merely nodded.

He shoved the key into Nicholas' lock, and opened the door. Nicholas stepped out.

"Thank you, little man." Nicholas looked around. "How about we free these other wrongly imprisoned people?"

Peter handed the stocky man the silver wand. "You can help me."

Nicholas accepted the wand and went straight for the albino girl who had her hands on the bars. "Come with me and you will no longer be a slave." He pointed the wand at the bar and said the unlocking spell Peter hadn't been able to master.

Slave. Had Nicholas really said slave? Peter had thought they were servants, and his father was just being mean to the boy in his room. Did that mean the boy who brought him his meals was here against his will? How awful. He couldn't wait to get out of King Merdis' awful castle.

Peter and Nicholas opened several cages. Peter pulled the key for cell number five that held a particularly wily looking woman, when Nicholas stopped him, putting his hand on Peter's wrist. "Not her. She killed a family in Dusty Hollow."

Peter left the woman in her cell.

They opened the heavy door to find the guard sleeping. The small group hovered behind them, waiting for direction. Levicus' old fortress was the most secure castle in the land—no one got in or out who wasn't supposed to be there. Well, except for his entry through the secret portal. He'd thought it was so wonderful to be here, and now he couldn't wait to leave.

Nicholas turned to Peter. "Can I use your other wand—this one is hard to control. Silver wands are made to give people without magic the gift of magic."

So that's why Peter found the wand so cumbersome, and couldn't perform his spells properly with it—the wand stunted his magic. He reluctantly handed over the dragon wand.

Nicholas waved it in front of the guard in a practiced arch. He leaned over and whispered in the woman's ear, while holding the tip of the wand to her forehead. "The king's messenger came and ordered you to let the merchant go. The Lithmans are key suppliers to our city." Nicholas turned to Peter. "There, that should stop them from suspecting you helped me escape, and stop The Researcher from coming after me." Nicholas handed the wand back.

"Follow me," Peter said, waving his hand to the group.

"What's your plan?" Nicholas asked. "How could you know of our secret pathway through the bathhouse?"

Peter cocked his head. "In my night wanderings, I noticed the back tower above the cliffs has less guards. I have rope we can use to scale down. I was going to knock them to sleep like I did this one—with your help of course."

"A solid plan, but if I may offer another?"

With Peter's blessing, Nicholas continued, "I know secrets. My lovely wife and Katrine would enter under the waterway that leads to the bathhouse. We can all go through there. It'll be cold, but we'll be alive—as long as we get out before morning."

Good thing Peter had other plans, because he couldn't swim.

Peter nodded to Nicholas and the small group crept out of the dungeon. Once they were sure the hallway was clear, they burst towards the next corner, and continued in this pattern till the tight group reached the woman's entrance to the bathhouse.

Nicholas led them through the storage closet, and out a hidden door, to a stone landing. A small waterway entered through a dark tunnel and fed through the wall, which Peter assumed led to the large community bathing pools.

"Now that we're safe," Peter said, facing Nicholas. "Tell me why you would make up such lies."

"It's no lie," Nicholas said, looking like he hoped Peter would have dropped the subject. "If you don't want to trust me, that's your choice. You're the one confronting me for answers."

Even if what his father had done was awful, Peter still struggled with the ethics of it all. Was it right to kill someone if they were harboring dangerous creatures who also killed? "But Ayeven attacked my mother."

The merchant scoffed. "I doubt it. And if they did, it was because The Researcher and his master had been persecuting them for ages."

It was all too much. What was he supposed to believe? A nagging feeling in the back of his mind forced him to press on. He had to know more, and this was his last chance to learn the truth. He closed his eyes, afraid to hear his own words. "But why was Levicus persecuting the Ayeven? They must have done something to deserve it, right?"

"My boy, I see your ears are open now, so I will tell you what I know." Nicholas stood and faced Peter. "Levicus would have you think differently—but it all started with him. The people rightly blamed Levicus for their fate—they missed Earth," Nicholas continued. "What I've been told is that Levicus quickly turned the eye of blame off him to the Ayeven—telling the people it was the *Ayeven's* fault they were moved from Earth to Inara."

Peter couldn't help but look at the merchant wide-eyed. It was such a fantastical story. He stared hard at Nicholas' pocked face, searching to see if he was telling the truth.

"The archangels gifted many humans with magic, so they were moved, along with the two disgraced Archangels, to Inara. So tell me—is there any magic left on Earth?"

Peter shook his head.

After a few minutes, Nicholas leaned forward. "I probably should add that most people see this history as legend, but I had an uncle in the Golden Circle—they study the Pleadines and their ways."

So who were these Pleadines Peter kept hearing about? And if the merchant was the one telling the truth, then why had his father lied to him? How was Peter supposed to know which one was being honest?

"See, the Ayeven were the descendants of the Archangels, the beings the Pleadines created to guide the humans of Earth to higher consciousness. The Ayeven had considerable power—you can see why Levicus wouldn't want them to be able to build a resistance against him."

Anthropologists still had no idea who the eleven temples in Rutherford belonged to—but now Peter knew. They weren't Gods at all—they were magical beings. Ancient people just thought they were Gods because of their power. Peter couldn't believe he now knew more about Talbert's obsession than he did.

"And so Levicus used the power of the whisper to breed fear into the humans. Quite brilliant really—humans are fearful creatures."

Peter looked down—he was one of them—always afraid even if he didn't want to be.

"The Ayeven were forced to separate themselves from the rest of humanity. And that seemed enough for Levicus, until . . ."

"Until what?" Peter prompted. A part of him was starting to believe Nicholas, and he was looking for a clue—anything that would show the merchant was the one lying and not his father.

"After Levicus escaped from the void, something in him was different. After a few decades, Levicus went on a rampage to kill all the Ayeven for their wings, to combine them with his own form." The merchant closed his eyes, seeming unable to go on.

"But why?"

"With their wings, Levicus had significantly more power, and could fly again," Nicholas said. "And their blood has healing properties, which can be used in the dark art of blood magic."

Peter cringed. Blood magic? No heroes he'd read about would ever use blood in a magical spell, or kill people for their own gain. Knights *fought* people like that.

"We think Levicus was weakening. Or he wanted to use it to heal his disciples after battles. Could be many reasons. I don't claim to understand the mind of a madman."

"That's awful." Peter ran his foot along the cracks in the stone floor, all fear of getting caught replaced by a deep sadness.

"So dare I ask if you believe me?"

It hurt. His chest ached and he felt empty, but was surprised to find he *did* believe Nicholas. "So if an Ayeven attacked my mother, then was she bad too?" Peter clasped his hands to stop them from shaking.

"I don't know the truth, so I will not hypothesize."

"I have to ask you—if my father wants to free his master— this Levicus person, that's bad?" Peter closed his eyes, afraid of the answer.

"I'm sorry, but under no circumstances can Levicus escape." Nicholas paused as if gathering his thoughts. "My beautiful wife is much braver than I, and she was part of the resistance to keep Levicus from destroying the Ayeven and controlling all five continents. She even fought alongside Katrine the Warrior Queen to halt Levicus' advancements."

Emotions whirled like a tornado within him. Hate. Fear. Confusion. He looked into the merchant's eyes and saw sadness. Suddenly it all clicked. Nicholas was the one telling the truth, and his father was the liar.

"I think I owe you this," Peter handed Nicholas the silver wand. "I wish I had something better to give you to make up for what I've done. I made you lose your shipment."

"I will miss my caravan, but that can be replaced. My life can't." Nicholas looked at him like he wanted to be angry, but Peter saw the man felt sorry for him. "And you have given me something—the most precious thing of all—my freedom." Nicholas set a wide hand on his shoulder.

Peter smiled despite himself. If only the rest of his plan would go so smoothly.

Nicholas turned to the group, obviously used to giving instructions. "Look, I know it's not comfortable, but we'll swim out. There's a gate at the end, but I know the one spell that will unlock it." Nicholas ushered the group and turned to Peter, who was still standing by the door. "Do you still want to go to Turopia?"

More than anything, Peter wanted to go there and see his sister—especially now that he knew Turopia was a safe place. Perhaps even a city he could call *home*.

Nicholas walked over to Peter, and kneeled in front of him. "You can come with me and I will guide you to Turopia. I'm hoping my wife will meet me there."

What a splendid offer—to get away from Talbert *and* be reunited with his sister. But the plan Peter had mused on all day rose in his mind—stopping his father from getting The Book of Keys.

Peter looked from Nicholas' bearded face to the stone floor. The waterway flowed behind them, giving off a powerful sloshing noise before being diverted at a 90-degree angle under the wall to the bathhouse. Maybe he should go with Nicholas—he was Peter's only connection to Turopia, and if he let the merchant go he may never find a way in. But Peter was also the only person who knew about his father going after The Book of Keys.

It seemed the people in Nadezhda, including the king, were on the same side as his father. So there was no one here he could even ask for help.

But why was it his problem if his father freed Levicus? Even as he thought it through, the idea weighed heavy in his gut.

Nicholas had been so good to him, and now Peter was going to reward him by allowing Levicus to escape? It didn't seem right. And his new persona on Inara wouldn't either. Just pretending to be like the hero from his favorite books made him feel more brave.

Peter tugged on Nicholas' grime-covered shirt. "I can't go with you now."

"You must have something mighty important to do if you don't want to come with me to see your own twin."

Peter nodded, afraid of the emotions rising. "I have to stop my father from freeing Levicus." His voice cracked as he spoke.

Nicholas' eyes widened in shock. "You're a brave little man. You do what you need to. I trust you will do the right thing—because you already have."

Filled with confidence at his words, an idea struck Peter. "Are you still going to Turopia?"

Nicholas nodded.

"Do you think you could take a message to someone there for me?"

"I don't see why not."

"Please find my twin sister Rory—she won't know what our last name is. Tell her—tell her . . ." What should he say?

"Why don't you write her a note?"

What a great idea! Peter pulled *Adventures of Arthur the Great* out of his bag, and tore the title page out. "I don't have a pen."

"Use the spell, *Katava Eel'Pah'Rohn*—then repeat to stop it."

Peter tapped the paper with his wand and cast the spell. A visible light, like a lightning bolt, connected his wand to the paper. Peter closed his eyes, thinking of what to say. He inscribed the words and handed it back to Nicholas.

Nicholas used the silver wand to perform a spell on the paper. "This is a nifty little spell to keep goods from getting wet. Very important when swimming." The merchant tapped his breast pocket. He handed Peter a silver pendant. "Thank you for showing kindness—you will always find a friend with the Lithmans. If you ever need help—find a merchant's guild—this pendant will prove you are a friend of ours."

"This is too much," Peter said, but still put it in his pocket—it might help him find Rory after he stopped his father.

"Good luck, little man." Nicholas seemed to give it some thought, then turned back to Peter. "If you change your mind, the advanced spell to use at the end is, *Lif'toh-ach Sha'rar Ma'yim*. Got that?"

Peter said it a few times to make sure he got it right, then nodded before sprinting out of the bathhouse. From his many castle wanderings, he was getting quite good at knowing all the nooks and crannies to hide in.

As Peter got closer to the royal living areas, he slowed down, pausing to look around each corner. He still had to hurry—he couldn't miss getting into his father's caravan before he left.

When Peter got to the stables, he waited for the two slaves to enter a horse's stall. He dragged a large crate into the back of the caravan, then climbed into the crate. If the slaves heard, they didn't care.

As Peter listened to the slaves hook up the horses and his father drive the caravan out of the stables, he curled up into a ball, running Nicholas' words over and over in his head. But no matter how Peter looked at it, he came to the same conclusion.

His father was evil.

Peter didn't think there could be anything worse than discovering Talbert on Inara, but this was definitely it.

CHAPTER
— 30 —

RORY RECEIVES A LETTER

*O**f all the worst things.* Thurston had returned a few days ago without Peter . . . and even worse, without Leopold. Thurston had raced into the shop to tell them The Researcher had killed Leopold.

Rory stared across the table at Sem and Agi, who were squishing pickled plums into jars. Rory could tell Agi sensed something was up, because he kept glancing at her with a curious expression. Sem was completely oblivious, and chatting away about the many uses of pickled plums.

Over the last few days, Rory had tried to figure out what to do, but all she could think of was storming into Nadezhda to rescue Peter and her locket . . . but after Thurston had returned without Leopold, Rory knew it was far too dangerous. Oh poor Leopold, sweet Leopold, who'd saved her from falling to her death.

If The Researcher was so cruel to a skilled warrior, what would he do to a little boy like Peter?

She toyed with the idea of asking her new friends for help, but cringed at the thought. She should be able to figure this out on her own. Even though she wasn't a fan of studying, yesterday she'd ventured into Turopia's vast library.

The library's tablet search system had come in handy. But even then, she was able to find only two references. In *Devarious' Book of Ancient Dragons*, it spoke of an ancient dragon who guarded the most ancient of the Keeper's treasures: The Book of Keys. Apparently the golden dragon's cave was near the Temple of Bordeaux. Rory wondered if she could locate it on a map—she'd have no idea how to get there, but at least she could find it.

The other result—*Devarious' Book of Ancient Artifacts*—was useless. It was safely kept in Turopia's secure vault.

In an old book of kings, she'd discovered that the infamous treasure had a long and cursed history. King Yodul Ruthing had dedicated his entire life to possessing it. He was the first person to find where the treasure was hidden and get it away from the dragon—using a specially crafted sleeping potion with Yodul's insect. Unfortunately, since he was not the rightful owner, the treasure magically made it back to the dragon's cave. The poor man had spent the rest of his life trying to get the treasure back, but never succeeded. In fact, he wasted all of his subject's money paying adventurers to aid him, and eventually was overthrown. Died a pauper. Killed by his obsession.

She'd found out plenty, but what was she supposed to *do* with the information? All she could think of was trying to stop The Researcher from getting to The Book of Keys, but how?

When Rory had finally found the courage to tell T. Veckler her locket had been stolen, he'd ripped out of the house to Asdorn's cottage without a word. The two had left in the night, so Rory was staying at Sem's place. If *they* couldn't bring Peter and her locket back, then who could?

The bell to the herb shop chimed. A stocky man with a bushy red beard stepped in.

Sem leapt out of her chair. "I'll be right with you." She wiped her hands on a hand-sized leaf that completely cleaned off the plum goo, and left a scent of pine in the air.

The man took off his traveling hat. "The Office of New Arrivals said a Rory is doing her community work here. Do you know where she is?"

Rory wiped off her hands. Was he another person The Researcher sent to attack her?

Agi stood, looking authoritative, even though he was a foot shorter than the man. He answered for Rory. "Who wants to know?"

"I'm Nicholas, and I've travelled two days to bring a message from her brother," the man said. "I can only give it to her though."

Sem whispered to Rory, "I recognize him from the marketplace. I've bought supplies from him before."

Nicholas grinned at Sem. "Oh yeah, you're the girl who likes those spicy chocolates I get from North Ratna."

"I'm Rory," she said, walking up to the counter, but staying behind it for protection.

"It's mighty good to find you," Nicholas said. "First though, Peter said you had to tell me where you're from to prove your identity."

"Why don't you tell me how you got a message from my brother first?" Rory asked.

"That's a long story—he helped me to escape King Merdis' dungeon after The Researcher threw me in there," Nicholas said. "I think your brother has gone off to do something dangerous, which is why he wanted me to give you this." He held out a folded piece of paper.

"I'm from Rutherford," Rory said, afraid to mention she was from Earth and reveal her secret. "I arrived here a little over a week ago."

Nicholas nodded and walked up to the counter. "Your brother is quite eager to see you."

Agi intercepted and inspected the letter before Rory could take it. He waved his wrists over it, while mumbling several spells. "Just a waterproofing spell was cast on this paper— nothing dangerous."

Rory took the torn title page, and read Peter's scrawl.

My dearest Rory,

I miss you. Father has your locket, and is going to use it to open The Book of Keys in three days. He'll be able to use it to find where Levicus is hidden, and free him. I'm sorry I can't be with you now—I'm going sneak to the dragon's cave to try and stop him.

Love, Peter

At the bottom, Peter had drawn a little scribble of an elephant. *He remembered.* Rory held the letter as if it made her closer to her brother just by touching it.

She wanted to thank the man, but when she looked up, Nicholas was gone.

And Peter was in more trouble than she could handle. If ever there was a time to ask for help, this was it.

"So what did your brother write?" Sem asked.

Rory folded the small letter closed.

Agi held back, waiting patiently for Rory to share. She felt more guilty under his silence than under Sem's constant questions. Rory closed her eyes. "I want to tell you the truth, but I'm not supposed to."

Before Rory could stop Sem, she'd run to the front of the store, locked the door, flipped over the hours sign to 'closed,' and ran back beside Rory.

"Okay, no interruptions," Sem said. "Tell us, before Mrs. Greene returns."

"Why don't I tell you what I know, and you tell me if it's true?" Agi said.

Rory managed a nod. This seemed a lot harder than it should be.

Agi leaned down and whispered in her ear. "First there was how you *got* to Turopia." Agi raised his eyebrows, sharing the silent communication of what he wasn't supposed to reveal.

Rory looked away.

"Come on, what is it?" Sem asked. Rory was impressed with how serious Agi took his secret-keeping—he and Sem were supposed to be best friends, and he wouldn't even let her hear.

Agi continued whispering, "You told me your parents died, but Talbert said he was working for your father. Thurston and Leopold travelled to get your brother from Nadezhda, where The Researcher has him, but was unable to get him back. Which could only mean The Researcher is your father."

Rory swallowed. This boy had figured out more than she'd expected.

"I'm not sure why your twin brother is with your father and you aren't, but I'm going to guess there's a clue in that letter you've received," Agi continued. "And most importantly, I don't think you are from the southern continent of Baikal like you told me."

Rory ran her finger on the glass countertop. "Why would you say that? Rutherford could be in Baikal."

Agi laughed, a sweet, small laugh, but a laugh nonetheless.

Sem answered for him, "Rory—didn't you know Agi is *from* Baikal?"

And this was why she didn't like to lie. It always caused more trouble than it was worth. But Asdorn and T. Veckler had forced her into it. Well, now she was tired of lying. Maybe she could share just enough so they wouldn't think she was related to that evil man. "You're wrong—The Researcher's not my father—he's was just pretending to be to get my locket."

Agi nodded, as if it all made sense.

Handing the letter to Agi, she looked away from his careful inspection. This was it. They were surely going to turn away from being her friends now.

Sem looked over his arm at the letter, her eyes widening as she read. "The Researcher wants to free Levicus? But . . . but he destroyed my family's home," she said in a whimper. But then Sem surprised Rory. "I'm sorry such a wicked man has your brother. What can we do to help?"

A rush of relief washed over her. They hadn't rejected her—in fact they actually seemed to care. "There's so much I don't know." The words she'd wanted to speak the last few days spewed out like a fountain. "What is so special about The Book of Keys? Why is my locket important? And if The Researcher can use my locket to open The Book of Keys, how can I stop him?"

Both Agi and Sem stared at her blankly. Obviously her story was not what they'd been expecting.

Agi was the first to collect himself. "This is big—I should talk to my captain about it."

"No way," Rory said. "T. Veckler and Asdorn ordered me to keep my identity a secret—there are spies after me. You can't tell anyone."

"I can help," Sem offered.

Rory smiled. "Thank you." It was so good not to feel alone anymore.

Agi looked like he was really struggling with what to do. "I'm sorry, I want to help you, but in good conscience I can't bring you in harm's way."

"Look, I know it will be dangerous—but I can't leave my brother alone out there. And I know you're only a new friend, but I was really hoping you'd help."

"I might be your friend, but I have responsibilities," Agi said.

"Why do you talk like you're an old man? Sometimes I think you forget you're only fourteen." Rory slammed her mouth shut the moment she'd said it—now was not the right time to voice her opinions.

"And who are you to talk about acting your age?" Agi said, looking hurt. "Ever since I met you, you try to be an adult— like you have to figure everything out yourself."

"Well, now I'm asking," Rory said sheepishly. "And you obviously don't want to help, so I'll go do it on my own. I'm used to it anyway."

Rory turned to leave and Agi laid his callused hand on her shoulder. "You stay. I'll leave. It's obvious you only want to be my friend 'cause you need me. Being a Tyrskan Warrior is not a joke—our code means something to me."

"Wait. No, that's not what I meant," Rory said.

But Agi had already walked out the door.

Rory looked over at Sem, who looked slightly hurt. "Are you going to leave too?"

"Uh—I work here," Sem said.

"Oh, right." They stared at each other for a few moments, Rory expecting Sem to say something. When she didn't, Rory edged towards the door. "See you at home later?"

❋   ❋   ❋

Rory walked around mindlessly through Turopia, past the Ayeven compound, the row of mansions, and all the way to the mines. Unfortunately, she passed Agi walking with a few other Tyrskan Warriors in their black uniforms. They all looked somber. No one was talking.

Weary from walking, and mad at herself for opening her big mouth, Rory returned to Sem's house. She plopped on Sem's bed. The Selvins had offered Rory her own room—staying in Sem's brother's room, but Rory preferred to stay with Sem. The previous night had been so fun—staying up all night chatting and giggling—and here she'd gone and ruined it.

Sem had obviously tried to tidy her room for her, but it only served to make it seem more disarrayed. Books were stacked all over—on her desk, under the window, and beside the bed. Rory averted her gaze from the gross experiments simmering on her desk.

Tired of sitting alone, Rory went downstairs to find out about dinner. The Selvins always ate dinner together. To her surprise, Sem had just arrived. She dropped a stack of books on the dining room table.

The two stared at each other awkwardly for a few moments.

"I'm sorry," Rory said. "I shouldn't—"

"It's not me you have to apologize to," Sem said. "I know Agi's a little strange, but he grows on you."

It wasn't that, Rory wanted to say, but knew it wasn't the right time. An understanding passed between them. "What's with all these books?"

"I know what it's like missing your brother, so I don't want to get in the way of helping you find him. Peter's letter had me worried. I went to the library to see what I could find. Thought we could look together. What can I do?"

Rory had no clue, so she told Sem everything she'd learned about The Book of Keys.

"Yodul's insect . . . I feel like I've read about that somewhere." Sem closed her eyes, and furrowed her brow—like she did every time she was thinking hard about something. That was a clue to be super quiet and not distract her.

A few minutes later, Sem raised an herb-stained finger, and spoke slowly. "I have an inkling of an idea, but I have to look it up. There's something I'm forgetting."

But Sem didn't leave because at that moment, a young man with rich, dark skin walked through the front door. He had the muscular figure of one of the guards, and a mop of curly hair. He looked so familiar.

"Mason!" Sem shot up from her chair so fast, it fell over. She raced over to him and squeezed him tightly. She turned back to Rory proudly. "This is my brother."

"Hi." Rory smiled—that's why he looked familiar. They had the same complexion and smiling disposition. She already felt comfortable in Mason's presence, just as fast as she'd felt safe with Sem. Mason was just an older, more muscular version of his sister. Except his hair was a little more tame.

"I don't know how you see through those goggles of yours. Filthy." Mason smiled and pulled them off. He wiped the lenses on his green tunic.

"What are you doing here?" Sem asked, standing as close to her brother as was humanly possible.

"So you're not happy to see me?" Mason said with a wink.

"No I am—I just thought you were fighting out West." Sem put her black-rimmed glasses back on.

"I can always leave if you prefer." Mason playfully punched Sem's arm. "Here, I picked these for you." He grinned and tossed Sem a satchel.

Rory was surprised Sem didn't open the bag right away to sift through it. Usually she was so curious about everything. "Thanks," Sem said, looking down. "I didn't make you anything—Dad didn't tell me you were coming."

Mason pulled Sem in, tightly wrapping her in his arms for a moment, before knuckling her head. "It was supposed to be a surprise."

Sem smiled back at her brother and a knowing look passed between them. Involuntarily, it made Rory's stomach twist in knots. It brought back a strong feeling of how it used to be with her brother. She *had* to be with him. Watching Sem and Mason, she knew she wouldn't be complete without Peter.

"So is this the new girl you wrote to me about?" Mason said.

"Right. Introductions," Sem said. "Mason Selvin, meet Rory Veckler, she arrived several days ago."

Mason raised his bushy eyebrow at the mention of her name, but said nothing. "So where's that boy you always hang out with?"

"Rory scared him off," Sem said.

"Hey!" Rory said.

Sem shrugged. "You were mean. I think you hurt his feelings."

Mason raised his eyebrows. "Perhaps you should go apologize. Agi's a good kid."

"I guess . . ." Even if Mason was right, she hated someone telling her what to do. She couldn't help it if Agi was so stubborn. After all, she'd already planned to apologize.

As Sem and Mason reconnected, and chatted about their plans for winter solstice, Rory's mind drifted off to figuring out what to do. Peter had surely left Nadezhda before Asdorn and T. Veckler could get there. If Peter said it would take him three days to get to the cave and the merchant took two days to get to Turopia—that meant Peter would be showing up at the cave *tomorrow.*

"Sem, I need to leave right away."

But she didn't know how far away the cave was. Would they even be able to get there in time?

CHAPTER
— 31 —

RORY'S SECRET

Clue searching sure wore a person out.

Rory and Sem lay sprawled across the books on her bed. Rory was the first to wake, completely groggy. Sem looked so angelic in her sleep. Rory was struck with worry that Sem would get hurt.

Rory poked Sem awake.

Sem jumped out of bed and stretched, reaching towards the sky. She picked up her glasses.

"Are you sure you want to come with me?" Rory asked.

Sem was silent for a moment before spewing her mind so quickly, all Rory could pick up on was, "It's time for me to have adventures outside of Turopia," and, "my brother is off doing something meaningful with his life and I'm just an Herblore apprentice," and, "I need to show my brother I'm more than just herbs."

"Thanks, Sem," Rory said, and quickly added, "I'm glad I met you." She bit her lip, afraid how Sem would respond to her moment of weakness.

"Me too. So if I go with you, will you tell me about your Keeper secret?" Sem said mischievously.

Rory couldn't help but laugh. She was hoping Sem wouldn't notice. But the girl was so smart, Rory should've known better.

"I know you're hiding something," Sem said jumping back on the bed. "The Book of Keys is one of the Keeper's treasures and your locket can open it . . ."

"I guess I must be a Keeper, because the locket is my mother's."

"Katrine Wysman? The last Keeper?"

Rory nodded.

Sem's brown eyes widened. "Your mother is my biggest hero."

"Really?" Rory could barely believe that her mother was so important. She fiddled with the loose strands on Sem's quilt.

Sem cocked her head and quietly said, "You don't know anything about her, do you?"

"Never met her," Rory said.

"Okay, I really believe you now," Sem said, her enthusiasm returned. "Katrine was one of the leaders of the resistance. Mason told me she led armies against Levicus, and was the only one to ever win. That's how she got her nickname, Katrine the Warrior Queen. But she disappeared during the fight to entrap Levicus, and no one has heard from her since." Sem added quickly, "I do hope she returns so I can meet her one day, maybe even serve as a healer in her army . . . you know, if my magic grows stronger."

Thinking of her mother made Rory feel energized again. When they brought Peter back, they'd find where her mother was.

"Please don't tell anyone," Rory said. "If the spies find me and my brother, we'll be in big trouble." She bit her lip—she'd gone this far, she might as well tell the whole story.

As they walked to the herb shop to pack supplies, Rory quickly told Sem about growing up on Earth, and how a magical bird not only rescued her, but led her to the portal.

Sem eyed Rory suspiciously. "No way—you're trying tell me you're from the home planet?"

"I guess? I'm not sure what this 'home planet' is, since I only came to Inara a week ago."

"I'm not a fool." Sem rolled her eyes. "I thought we were friends—why are you trying to trick me? I hate it when people do that."

"I'm not lying to you." Rory thought about how she'd never believe someone was an alien from another planet. Except she really had grown up on Earth—how could she make Sem believe her?

Rory pulled a rubber band off her wrist. "What about this, have you seen one of these before?"

"No, but I've never left Turopia. It could just be something from one of the cultures I haven't experienced yet." Sem unlocked the shop.

"Haven't you ever wondered how I don't know anything about this place? And . . . how you had to tell me about my own mother?"

"I guess . . . you do seem pretty ignorant, about just about everything . . . like you're experiencing it for the first time."

"Yes—that," Rory said. "Sem, you're my only friend in this place. I need you to believe me."

Sem studied her for a moment. "Fine, I'm willing to go along with your story."

Rory was about to say about how she got to Turopia, including the fight with the disciples and the scary dragon attack, when Agi entered the shop.

Considering his comrade had just died, he looked extremely well put-together. His black uniform with the silk button-up shirt was pressed, and his long jet-black hair was tied back in a neat pony tail, leaving only a few whips of hair to frame his kind face.

Rory looked down at her own wrinkled school uniform. Even Sem had found time to iron her sage green pleated skirt and lavender top.

Sem looked nervously between Rory and Agi, as if they were going to start attacking one another.

Before Agi could say a word, Rory faced him and held up her hand. She had to get out her apology while she still had the courage. "Agi, I'm sorry for what I said. Sem helped me understand there are still a lot of things I have to learn about this place. So I hope you will forgive me."

"Thank you—your apology means a lot to me," Agi said.

"And if you still want to, you know—I'd um . . . still like you to be my friend."

"Of course," Agi said, putting his arm around her shoulder. "I couldn't give up a friendship with one of the strangest girls I've ever met. I can't put my finger on it, but there's something special about you, Rory."

Sem and Rory exchanged glances. It was nice to share a secret with someone trustworthy again.

It was Agi's turn to hold up his hand. "Look—about what you said yesterday. You're right."

Rory's mouth dropped.

"Before you say anything, I'm sorry," Agi looked her straight in the eyes. "I guess what you said got to me. I don't want to act like an old man. It's just—when you've had to be so responsible your whole life, it's hard to escape that."

"I'm sorry—I didn't mean to hurt your feelings." He really was one of her favorite people in Turopia, and didn't like seeing him sad. Why was she always putting her foot in her mouth?

"And you're right," Agi said. "I'm not a kid anymore. It hurt that you said it at first, but then I realized it was true. So why hide it? I may have responsibilities, but I can still help my friends."

"Thank you," Rory said, truly grateful for his change of heart.

"Also, I had a little chat with Mason at the café last night. He kind of convinced me to help you," Agi said. "I think mostly because he recognizes siblings should be together. I know I would do anything to get my baby sister back, but we don't raise the dead here."

Neither of them had anything to say about that.

"And you didn't tell T. Veckler?" Rory asked.

"You're lucky they're still away," Agi said. "Besides, if you actually want Peter to get into the city, I'll have to help you—neither of you have the authority to allow someone else to see Turopia's door, much less open it."

Rory couldn't believe she hadn't seen that hole in her plan. Her idea was to meet up with Peter, and bring him back to Turopia. And if there happened to be an opening to get her locket back, she'd use the element of surprise on her side. Quickly Rory told Agi all that they'd discovered. "I figured out we need to go to a cave near Bordeaux Temple, but we can't find it on the map."

Agi flipped through the book of maps and tapped one of the pages. "The temple is one of the meeting places for refugees coming to Turopia. There's a mighty fierce dragon who lives near there—that must be the cave. We Tyrskan

Warriors avoid the area within a two-league radius—always being wary when we're forced to take the road that travels by his cave."

Rory was both frightened and a little excited at the prospect of speaking with another dragon. Would he be as nice as Melchior? "So you're really going to help me?"

Agi shook his head, as if in defeat. "I know you'll just go off on your own anyway, whether I go with you or not."

Rory looked at the ground sheepishly—that much was true.

"With T. Veckler not being here, I feel it's my duty to accompany and protect you," Agi said.

Rory's eyes widened. "Really? Oh thank you, thank you very much!"

Agi held up his hand. "But let's stay as far away from that dragon as possible."

Rory nodded excitedly.

"I'll whip up a sleeping draught to use on the dragon if we go near it," Sem said.

"We?" Agi raised his eyebrows.

Sem ran her foot in the carpet. "Rory said I could come."

Agi shot Rory a glare she'd never seen from him before. His furry eyebrows came together like two caterpillars attacking each other. She didn't even know he had a harshness in him. "I really can't allow you to come—your parents will be so worried."

Sem looked up to the ceiling mischievously. "Well, I guess you don't really need that sleeping draught then. I'm sure you have the skill to defend against a dragon . . ."

"Fine. You win," Agi said with exasperation. "But do you know how many extra hours of community work I'll have to do to make up for this questionable integrity?"

Sem grinned playfully. "Why, I don't see any lack of integrity here . . . I just see you dutifully protecting your charge. I'm merely a tool to help protect Rory."

Agi chuckled. "You're so silly." Then he looked at them more seriously. "We should leave right away—based on my calculations, Peter and The Researcher could be arriving at the cave any time now."

"You're right—I wouldn't want to miss my brother," Rory said.

"And let The Researcher get The Book of Keys," Agi said.

"Yes, that too," Rory said.

"I'll go grab my traveling supplies and meet you back here in thirty minutes, okay?"

Rory and Sem nodded.

Agi looked each of them sternly in the eyes. "I think you know how important it is we keep this a secret. I'm doing this to help protect Rory, but I'm not sure Captain Orlovsky would feel the same."

Sem perked up. "We won't do anything to jeopardize your position in the Order."

"Thanks." Agi turned out of the store, and Rory watched as the boy passed the front window.

"This is exciting!" Sem pulled books of the shelves. "I can't believe I'm finally leaving the city."

"What about your parents?" Normally Rory wouldn't have cared, but the Selvins seemed pretty protective, and she didn't want to get her new friend in trouble.

"I should be back by bed time. They won't know a thing—they'll just think I was working here all day." Sem grinned as she turned to the index of a particularly large book. "I mean, I don't want to scour through all these books if I don't get to go on an adventure too."

When Rory was done packing the pre-made battle potions into a leather shoulder bag, she turned to Sem. "I'll be right back."

"Hold on. I think I got something," Sem said. "I need you to find me a spider. There's always a bunch in my garden, so you can look there."

Sem shuddered.

Rory narrowed her brow at Sem. "You're afraid of spiders . . ."

Sem shook her head. "No, I'm not! Okay, fine . . . I am."

"Let me get this straight—you can handle those disgusting herbs and slimy animal parts for your potions, but you're afraid of spiders?"

"What can I say? They creep me out."

After Rory gathered her warm traveling cloak from T. Veckler's cottage, she caught the spider that was always in his bathroom. No one seemed to care Rory was walking down the street carrying a glass with a frantic spider in it.

Rory was really glad not to be doing this alone. She knew she should've been more afraid of The Researcher, but found herself more worried about being with her brother for the first time in seven years.

Her heart leapt, envisioning living with Peter. She used to think she wanted to leave Turopia, but now she liked Agi and Sem too much to leave them.

"Shhh, little guy. It'll be okay," Rory whispered to the fuzzy brown spider. To her surprise, it did a couple slower laps, then settled down at the bottom of the glass. It was as if the spider understood her.

She balanced the paper covering the glass in one hand and she pushed open the door to the herb shop. "I got the live spider you asked for."

"Oh great," Sem said from behind the counter. "I'll get this potion whipped up in a jiffy."

With her brother at her side, Rory knew she'd be able to find her parents. And then they could be a real family again. "So, um, what did you need the spider for?"

"You know the Yodul's insect you mentioned? I *told* you I had read about it somewhere. I found it in "*Ti'Fuzang's Master Herb Compendium.*"

"So?" Rory asked.

"So . . . what? I lost my train of thought."

"Something to help us with the dragon?"

"Yes. Sorry—you know better than to interrupt me," Sem said.

Rory tapped her foot, trying to be patient while Sem mumbled to herself, as if going over the beginning of the story in her mind.

"Yodul's insect was a nickname given to spiders because King Yodul of Nadezhda was so terrified of them, he even had a royal spider killer. I read that Yodul's insect is the secret ingredient in the most powerful sleeping draught you can make."

Rory picked up where Sem was going with this. "So, if we have to encounter the dragon, we'll be prepared."

"I don't plan to go anywhere near that dragon, even if shed dragon skin is worth a fortune." Sem tapped the side of the brass bowl with her wand. The steaming mixture instantly cooled. Sem poured it into a bottle with a spray-top.

Rory put a small dagger into her boot and handed Sem one too. "I decided it's safer if we bring extra weapons. I even have my wand—just in case. Not that I can do much with it."

Sem looked at the sheathed-dagger as if she didn't know what to do with it, then tucked it in her belt. "We'll just check it out, right? And if it looks like danger, we'll leave?"

They looked at each other for a silent moment, as if really deciding whether to go through with the plan or not.

They nodded in unison. "Let's do this."

CHAPTER
— 32 —

RORY AND THE CHAINS THAT BIND US

Agi burst through the herb shop's door donned in his full sky-blue Tyrskan Warrior uniform. He'd skipped wearing his cloak and wore his dual-sword holster on his back. "Is Mrs. Greene here?"

"Do you even have to ask?" Sem rolled her eyes.

"I'm concerned The Researcher can use your Keeper's locket to open The Book of Keys." Agi's knee-length robe crossed in a V-shape at his chest meeting at a wide, black slash, which showed a white tree with exposed roots and a North-facing arrow in its trunk. "So I tried to get Captain Orlovsky to send some back-up, but he's in a strategy meeting, and the Vice Chancellor refused to let me in. So it looks like we're on our own."

Looks like adults didn't listen to kids here either—even ones part of an elite group of warriors. Wait—how could Sem have found time to tell Agi her secret? "You *told* him?"

"No!" Sem said, holding her hands up defensively. "Agi must have figured it out on his own."

Agi held up a finger. "When I first met you, I noticed the three-star symbol on the back of your locket—it's the Keeper's emblem." Agi looked away. "When I was a boy—Captain Orlovsky told his story of escorting Katrine to Miss Chatelaine's fortress—the Master Keeper of the Keys. The legends of the ancient items of power she protects stuck with me."

Rory crossed her arms. "Great, now everyone knows my secret."

"Just us," Sem said. "I won't tell anyone—promise."

"Fine." Rory sighed—it was better they knew anyway.

"We'll scout the location before going in," Agi said in a tone that didn't allow for argument. "And if it appears too dangerous—we're leaving—brother or no brother. Agreed?"

Rory didn't like the plan, but she didn't have any other options. Her brother would simply *have* to be there.

They walked a nice slow pace to the entrance, so as not to raise suspicion. Rory would've preferred to run all the way out of Turopia.

"I'll do a spell that will help the guards not see you," Agi explained. "It doesn't make you completely invisible, it just warps the air slightly around you so they don't look too closely. We will wait till the guards switch out on the hour, then make our way out."

"So you *do* have some slyness in you after all," Rory teased, a wide grin on her face. "What happened to all that integrity talk you gave me?"

"My honor lies in protecting you," Agi said seriously. "And if I can get you reunited with your brother, and help get your locket back from The Researcher, I'm hoping you'll stop trying to run away from me."

It was her turn to look sheepish. "I won't run away ever again. Promise."

"It's true the guards are more there to protect people coming in, but Rory, T. Veckler has them on high alert for you," Agi said. "I bet you two didn't think about how you would get *out* of the city."

Rory and Sem shook their heads.

Agi looked around sheepishly. "We'll do it during changing of the guard in five minutes."

While Rory and Agi sat patiently under the gazebo beside the lake, Sem paced behind them.

"Calm down Sem," Rory said. "You'll draw attention to us."

"I can't—that lake gives me the willies," Sem said.

Rory raised her eyebrows, and Agi filled in the blank. "Sem almost drowned in the lake as a toddler."

"What if I promise to dive in and save you?" Rory asked. "Then will you sit down?"

Sem gave a resigned sigh and sat down between them, nervously swinging her legs.

"So how are you getting out of your duties?" Rory asked Agi.

"Thurston is covering for me. Took my shift this afternoon." A few minutes later, Agi raised his arm, as if they were his troop.

Rory and Sem stared at him blankly.

Agi turned back to them. "Move forward with me when I start. This spell takes a lot of energy to keep up, so we'll have to walk quickly. If we linger too long, someone might sense the magic tracings left behind."

Twisting his right wrist in a figure-eight pattern, Agi cast a spell.

Rory didn't feel any different, but when she looked over at Sem, her eyes immediately refocused on the bench behind

Sem. Rory knew Sem was there, but for some reason, her mind couldn't focus on her. "Neat trick."

The three of them walked as close together as possible, between the guard castle on their left and the jutting rock wall on their right. Rory was relieved Asdorn and T. Veckler still hadn't returned from their trip to Nadezhda. She was sure Asdorn would've looked out his cottage window and seen through their ruse like it wasn't even there.

On the top of the wall, two guards were playing a game in the corner, while the other two guards switched out. Having six guards didn't seem the best time to sneak out of the city, but they were so distracted, they didn't seem to notice.

Rory didn't take a full breath until she was several steps on the other side of the door. It was the towering cliff face she had first entered through. Not too far off was a majestic mountain range.

Agi raised his finger in a shushing gesture and Rory saw what he was looking at. Two guards dressed in bulky brown monks' robes were hidden on either side of the door. Rory knew the simple robes must be covering their armor, so they'd look less suspicious to anyone passing the bottom of the cliff.

How were they going to get past them when they came back with Peter?

Agi didn't drop the distracting spell until they were out of earshot. After about half an hour, they reached a teleport gazebo. It was a smaller version of the one she'd previously gone through. Rory turned the stone dial to the symbol Agi had scribbled on her map, and put her hand to the sphere.

Submerged in darkness, a tingling sensation washed over her body.

Once out, Rory patted her body to make sure she was all there. She was. Agi scanned the area. Sem looked relieved and excited at the same time.

They were now so far away from the cliff, she couldn't even see it. Off in the distance, a towering red-hot volcano rose out of the ground. She hoped they weren't going in *that* direction.

The other way looked much nicer. It had the far-off mountain range she'd seen earlier. They were now on an open hillside covered with sizable rocks, dead grass, and trees still holding onto their few orange leaves.

Surprisingly, Sem had been quiet up to this point. "Wow. My first teleport—just like Mason described."

"It should be a two hour walk to the cave." Agi pursed his lips. "I think I found a place on the map where we can wait for your brother."

Having help was nice— why had she avoided asking for it for so long?

She'd always refused it from the Gallaghers. All they were trying to do was help her, but she couldn't see how genuine they were for some reason. But now she couldn't even go back and thank them. Rory hated to think of them being sad over her disappearance, and thinking they'd failed after trying so hard.

She cringed, realizing that was exactly what T. Veckler was doing. She still didn't like the man, but at least she finally understood. A small sense of relief overcame her, and she suddenly felt stronger, like she had let go of a hundred pounds of pressure.

Rory looked at the ground and smiled at Agi. "I'm glad you came."

"Me too," Sem said. "I can't believe I'm finally out of the city."

A great roar echoed in the distance.

All three looked at each other.

"The dragon," Sem said, trembling.

Rory looked around nervously. Maybe this hadn't been such a good idea.

They walked up a zigzagging animal path through the foothills littered with boulders and lifeless trees. Rory made out a cave on the neighboring hill—exactly where they were headed.

"Oh, I almost forgot." Sem pulled a glass vial filled with creamy liquid from her shoulder bag. "Take a drop of this. It's an antidote to the sleeping draught—just in case we have to use it, we won't be affected."

"Good thinking," Agi said.

Rory allowed Sem to put one drop on her tongue. It tasted like a chocolate chip cookie. Her eyes widened. "You didn't put the spider in this, did you?"

"No, that was for the dragon's special sleeping draught."

Rory felt a twinge of guilt for telling the spider it would be okay, only to have it killed for a potion.

The three trudged on, mostly listening to Sem chatter on about all the different plants they encountered. She kept lagging behind to pick samples, then running back to catch up with them.

Rory's feet and calves ached. She looked over her shoulder at how far they'd come. Instead of the bright blue sky from earlier, gray clouds trailed them.

When Rory felt she could walk no more and needed a break, Agi stopped and crouched behind some thorn bushes on the side of the mountain. "If we hide here, we can see when Peter arrives . . . or if anybody else does."

Rory looked over the valley. The cave opening appeared as a black, snarling mouth, set in the slanted rock side of the mountain. It looked like it was going to eat the tree in front of it.

"Looks like Peter's not here yet," Agi said.

Before the weight of what they were doing could really sink in, a great roar echoed in the valley. Rory felt the vibration in her bones, like when standing too close to bass speakers.

A woman's voice cried out. "Help!"

Rory looked over at Agi and Sem, who were doing a mighty fine job of hiding their fear—perhaps Agi was a little more composed than Sem.

The dragon's roar vibrated in Rory's bones before it was cut short.

Something was wrong.

Agi closed his eyes and cocked his head to the side, like he was listening intently. "I think someone might be in the cave with the dragon."

And Agi was right.

The Researcher climbed down a magical ladder out the front of the cave. Under his arm was a wooden treasure chest.

He had The Book of Keys.

Why wasn't the dragon going after him?

And where was Peter?

"What are we going to do?" Rory asked, watching The Researcher walk to a horse-drawn caravan hidden behind a dense thicket of bushes, a look of glee on his face.

"I don't know," Agi's voice came out as a whisper. "The Researcher is the most powerful wizard besides Levicus. We'd need an army to go up against him. And even that might not be enough."

"We can't just sit here! He has my brother," Rory said. But then the reality of the situation sunk in. How selfish was she being when The Researcher now had a power that could help him free Levicus? What did her relationship with her brother matter when so many lives were at stake?

Rory hung her head. It didn't matter anyway. There was nothing they could do.

Sem laid a silent hand on Rory's shoulder, which she found strangely comforting. She really had friends in this new world.

Agi looked off in the distance, deep in thought. "We'll have to find another way to get your brother."

"But he has The Book of Keys," Rory said. "All those Ayeven . . ."

"We have to think strategically now. We can report this to the resistance—if they know to expect The Researcher, they can add reinforcements to the area—and hopefully stop him from freeing Levicus."

"But not forever—he'll keep trying." Rory fought off tears. "He's relentless."

Agi hung his head. "You are right. But we've been fighting this war a long time, and we can endure."

"The Researcher hasn't freed Levicus yet," Sem said. "There's still hope."

An idea struck Rory, "Why don't we follow The Researcher to Nadezhda? Maybe we can sneak the chest away while he's sleeping or something."

Agi shook his head. "He's traveling in a caravan led by horses—we're on foot. We'd never catch him, even if he stopped for the night."

Rory pulled at a rubber band on her wrist. It snapped. Rory let it fall into the dirt. If only she had wings like Leopold and could fly after them.

The dragon gave a great roar that vibrated the ground beneath them. Agi's hazel eyes widened double their size, and Sem squeezed the herbs in her dark-skinned palm.

"Help! Come back and untie me, or you'll be sorry," a woman's voice yelled.

"We have to do something." Rory jumped out of her hiding space. "She needs help!"

"Who needs help?" Sem asked.

"That woman inside!" Rory said. "Can't you hear her?"

"No, we have to stay right here," Agi said. "Till it's safe to go back to Turopia."

Rory shook her head. "I know it sounds crazy—but do you think I'm hearing the dragon call for help—it sounds in my head just like when I was talking to Melchior."

"I thought that was a trick earlier," Agi said.

"Well is it?" Rory pushed.

Agi squirmed. "I guess . . . but it's insane."

Sem gave Rory a look. "What are you two talking about? Rory, you can talk to dragons and you didn't *tell* me?"

Rory shrugged. "I don't know. I spoke to one dragon, so maybe?"

Everything about this place was still weird to her. She'd always been good with animals, and she wondered if this was why—they understood her. She just didn't understand them back on Earth. "This might sound crazy, but hear me out—if I can talk to dragons, *and* I'm a Keeper, maybe I can get the dragon to go after The Researcher? We could totally win!"

The moment the words left her lips, it felt right. She marched down the side of the hill, careful to stay low so The

Researcher wouldn't see her. She felt in her gut, she had *one* chance to get this right.

"What are you doing?" Agi forcefully whispered, chasing her down the hill.

As if the dragon wouldn't hear that.

Sem looked from side to side, and ran after them.

"The Researcher tied up the dragon and I have to help." Rory stopped at the base of the cave beside a large tree. "You're a Tyrskan Warrior—isn't your code about helping people?"

"Yes, but you're going into a dragon's lair. You're no match for a dragon."

"Well, come and help me then."

"What? I'm no match for a dragon either," Agi said, still doing his yelling-whisper. "It could be a trap. I don't trust it."

"Help!" the voice cried out from deep within the cave.

Sem cowered over and whispered, "Maybe we should go back."

"I'm going in," Rory said, studying the tree. "You know, if this is the Keeper's dragon, and she's supposed to guard the treasure, she's going to *want* to go after The Researcher to get it back. The dragon's not doing it because she can't. And I'm going to help her, whether you come with me or not."

Agi raised his hand. "Don't you just find it a little strange that T. Veckler does all this work to protect you and Peter sends you a letter about going to a dragon's cave? What if it was all a lie to trap you?"

"He's my brother. He wouldn't hurt me."

"How do you know?" Agi asked. "You haven't seen him in over seven years."

Ow. "Why would you say such a thing?" Rory said. "I don't care what you do—I'm going in."

Agi shook his head. "You're impossible."

Leaping to the lowest branch, Rory pulled herself up like it was a pole bar. She climbed up to the next branch, which hung over the massive cave's entrance. Rory tightly clasped the rough tree bark. Standing on the jutting branch, she held her arms out for balance. Near the trunk, the branch was thick, solid.

She took a deep breath as if she were about to run and do a flying kick on a board. When she jumped, she did not want to fall in the gap between the tree branch and the cave's floor. She sprinted and leapt into the cave.

Rory breathed a sigh of relief as she cleared the ledge by a couple feet. She smiled at herself. If only Miss Kuma could see her now.

Agi pulled Sem up into the tree and caught her as she jumped. Sem inched forward, holding the sleeping draught out like shield.

The depth of the cave was overwhelming. Because the path sloped downward, she couldn't even see all the way into the back. What she could see was the massive bulk of a great golden dragon. Putting her back to the wall, Rory squatted and crept towards the back of the cave. The voice was still crying out for help, but was becoming more subdued, as if she'd given up on a rescue.

Agi held a magical ball of light in the room that illuminated each of the dragon's hand-sized scales, and the crystals embedded in the cave's walls.

Rory's mouth dropped in awe as the path opened up to an expansive area. Sunlight filtered through a small hole at the top of the cave, illuminating a turquoise lake—stalactites reached down to their fellow stalagmites. Cave formations grew from the lake, highlighting its depth, and a great giant nest piled with bones sat in the corner.

In the middle of the cave, the dragon gave them a low, warning growl, even though it had magical bindings wrapped around its feet and neck.

Rory put on a brave smile, hoping Agi wouldn't see how scared she really was. She waved for him to join her. Agi and Sem followed.

"Um, dragon?" Rory tentatively asked, keeping as far away from the great dragon as possible, edging against the wall. "Are you the one calling for help?"

"Yes," a deep woman's voice said. There was a low growl behind it. The mix of sounds reminded her of Melchior.

The dragon nodded at her, eyes wide. It had a head like a lizard, with spiky protrusions sticking from behind its golden cheeks. Instead of bat-like wings, hers were made of thousands of sand-colored feathers. Spikes ran across her tail like a stegosaurus.

Rory froze, her eyes shifting from side to side.

"Did the dragon answer?" Agi asked. "I'd prefer to leave with my skin intact if you don't mind."

"Can't you see the dragon's chained up?" Rory said over her shoulder to him. "We have nothing to worry about."

The dragon grinned widely, exposing a set of teeth the size of Rory's arms. She leapt back, falling on her butt. Luckily, the magical chains kept her from moving.

"Keeper?" the dragon said, tilting its massive head. "Is that really you?"

"Yes?" Rory tentatively said, getting to her feet. She wasn't quite sure about claiming it.

"You're much smaller than the last one," the dragon said, sniffing her.

Agi pressed himself against the wall even more than he already was. "Can we go now? I wasn't expecting to fight a dragon on this trip."

Rory looked up at the towering dragon. "We've come to help, but I don't know what to do."

The dragon struggled and roared. "I need you to unchain me so I can get my treasure back!" Gooey saliva dripped down the front of her white dress.

"What are you doing?" Agi yelled. "You're making him angry!"

"Tell him I'm a she," the dragon said.

Rory rolled her eyes. "The dragon says she's a she."

"Then stop making *her* angry."

"And my name is not 'the dragon.' It's Mi'elcha." The dragon made a rough gurgling noise with her throat that sounded incredibly frightening, even though she was just saying her name.

Rory attempted to repeat it back. *"Meel-Ka."*

"More flem. Mi'el-CHA." The dragon roared out her name, spit flying in Sem's face.

"Yuck." Sem wiped the slime off with her cloak.

"Please hurry," Mi'elcha said. "The treasure was stolen from me by the last person on Inara who should have it. On my honor, I must get it back."

Rory could have sworn she heard a hint of fear in the dragon's voice. Which was surprising since Mi'elcha was even bigger than the Alrakis dragons.

"I want to help you, but you have to help me too," Rory said, putting her hands on her hips to make herself appear bigger.

The dragon narrowed her eyes. "Go on . . ."

"I'll help you get The Book of Keys back, but I want you to help me rescue my brother and get my locket back."

Mi'elcha dropped her head close to Rory. "Touch my cheek and you'll have a deal. Be warned though—I'll know if you're lying."

Rory cautiously walked across the cave. Avoiding her mouth, Rory stood on tiptoes to touch Mi'elcha's scaly cheek. At first Rory cringed, then she softened when the dragon leaned into her hand. She felt power surge through her arm.

"It is good to meet you, Rory Wysman, daughter of Katrine Wysman," the dragon said in a low growl. "I've had a relationship with your family for thousands of generations. It has been my sole duty to guard this treasure for the Keepers. And so, I will do as you request."

"Thank you," Rory said, amazed at the bond she felt with the dragon. She didn't want to let go.

Mi'elcha lifted her head to a regal height and told Rory the spell. She repeated it to Agi, who immediately bent down to undo the first binding.

Rory was going to say something else when her ears perked up. Someone else was in the cave.

"Rory, hurry up," a soft voice yelled from the front of the cave. "Before the dragon breaks free."

CHAPTER
— 33 —

RORY'S LITTLE ELEPHANT

Rory turned and walked a few paces to the cave opening. There was a boy, silhouetted against the blue sky behind him. Even without seeing his face, she knew who he was.

Twins always know.

Agi followed her protectively as she ran to the front of the cave.

"No! Come back!" Mi'elcha roared, but Rory ignored her.

Peter's eyes widened with joy, then changed into concern.

Rory faced him. A warmth spread across her chest—the bond with her brother was all-encompassing. It was an incredible feeling she hadn't felt in years.

"You came," Peter said.

Rory smiled, tears full of joy. "Of course I did."

"But I left you all those years ago. I thought . . ."

"You goofball." Rory stepped forward and hugged him tightly. Peter returned the embrace, and she felt her soul fill with lightness. She stepped back and held him at arms-length.

A rush of pure energy, of joy, sadness, and of what was lost and now found overwhelmed her. She wasn't used to allowing her emotions to come so freely, and now they almost overpowered her.

Peter's eyes were wet, and he didn't even bother to wipe away the tears. They hugged again and he squeezed her like he never wanted to let go.

Knowing her brother felt the same gave her a powerful sense of completeness—as if she couldn't have known what the hole felt like until it was filled. Rory felt more complete than ever before—even more than when she was home at Red Bear Tae Kwon Do, or when she and Sun-hi would have those epic sleepovers. *Now, I am complete.*

The intense moment was broken by the dragon's roar. "Don't be a fool. Hurry and free me!"

"The dragon's really angry." Peter grabbed Rory's hand. "I see Nicholas gave you the message."

"Oh but Peter, I failed—we got here too late," Rory said.

"You mean this?" Peter held out his hand. Her locket dangled from his fingers.

Rory's heart skipped a beat. "Wait. What? How did you—"

"While The Researcher was asleep on the road last night, I used a sleeping spell and switched his locket for the one a merchant gave me." Peter looked out of the cave. "Can you take me to Turopia with you?"

"Of course!" Rory said and turned to Agi, "Quick, finish removing Mi'elcha's bonds."

Agi retreated to finish undoing Mi'elcha's bonds.

Sem was still hiding in the back.

"Quick—hide the locket in case Father finds us—I snuck in after you. He doesn't know I'm here, but he's bound to notice the locket missing any moment."

Rory stuffed the locket in her boot, beside the dagger. Her heart thudded with anticipation as if she'd run a mile.

A pained wail echoed in the valley.

Peter shuddered. "He knows."

They raced deeper into the cave, where Agi knelt beside the dragon. He still had three more chains to undo. "Hurry!"

Peter grabbed Rory's arm and whispered in her ear. "Father rescued me from Earth. But Rory—I have to tell you—our father, he's not good. You can't trust him. I had a plan to escape if we were forced to go back to Nadezhda, but now that Father knows I switched the lockets, I won't be able to fool him any longer into thinking I'm on his side."

This wasn't how she'd expected their meeting to go. He still believed The Researcher was their father. He needed to hear the truth.

"Two more." Agi knelt by the dragon's back legs.

It didn't seem likely Agi would free the dragon in time. Rory needed the battle potions. She looked around frantically, and caught Sem hiding behind some stalagmites at the back of the cave.

But before Rory could get to Sem or tell Peter the truth, a tall figure walked into the cave. He dusted off his long black and silver jacket.

"Watch out!" Rory called.

Agi spun around to see who'd appeared.

But it was too late. The Researcher aimed his staff at Agi. The boy crumpled to the ground, frozen like her foster parents.

Rory's heart leapt in her chest.

The dragon slammed her tail down.

The Researcher leapt unnaturally high out of the way. When he landed out of reach from the dragon's tail, he shot Peter a look of death. "You stole it!" He threw a metal medallion at Peter's feet. "Did you really think you could fool me?"

Peter tensed, and shook his head.

The Researcher did a double-take between Peter and Rory. "You're a clever boy giving the locket back to your sister."

The Researcher pointed his staff at Rory, and she floated a few feet in the air. She was completely under his control. She fought to strike him, but only kicked the air around her.

"Let go of me!" Rory yelled.

"You will give me the locket now."

"I- I don't have it." But Rory had never been good at lying.

Peter pulled something out of his backpack. "Get your hands off my sister! *Chal'Esh!*" Peter pointed his wand, and a pillar of flame shot towards The Researcher.

Rory's eyes widened at the scary flames. Her brother could do *that*?

The Researcher used his gauntleted wrist to block Peter's spell, while maintaining his hold on Rory with his staff. "Now listen to me—you're looking at this all wrong," he said in his cold, gentle voice. "If you help me, I can reunite you with your mother."

"Liar!" Rory yelled. She pushed aside the buzzing feeling in her chest, and the loss of what she was sacrificing.

"Such sweet words, but I may be the only person in all of Inara who has the power to return Katrine to you." The Researcher tipped his staff at Rory and all her muscles stiffened. He let go, and Rory fell to the ground—where Agi had been a few moments ago. Where had he gone?

Hate burned in her. She wanted to pull the dagger out of her boot and stab The Researcher, but she couldn't move. What had he done to her?

The Researcher bent over her. She felt his long hands on her body, searching her jacket.

"Now, you will tell me where the locket is, or I will make it so you never see your brother *ever* again," The Researcher said. "But then you never tried very hard to find him on Earth, so perhaps you never really cared for him in the first place."

Rory gasped. "That's not true!"

Peter's face fell, then instantly switched to anger. He pointed his wand at The Researcher. *"Chal'esh!"*

A pillar of fire shot towards The Researcher, who sidestepped it. "Boy, you really need to learn some other spells."

But Peter had been prepared, and two more fire pillars shot towards him in quick succession.

The Researcher escaped one, just to be struck by the second. He sent a blast at Peter, who crashed against the far wall.

The Researcher returned to searching Rory.

Peter jumped to his feet and was about to strike again when he froze, eyes widening in fear.

And then she saw an imposing figure enter the cave—the man who'd stolen her locket.

Rory writhed on the ground of the cave, trying to break free of her magical paralysis, but it was no use.

Thunder boomed. Rain pelted the outside of the cave.

"What's taking so long?" Talbert asked.

"What are you doing here? And with my treasure?" The Researcher asked, losing his tranquil demeanor. "You're supposed to be guarding the caravan."

"Why Master, I have the chest so it doesn't get stolen," Talbert said with a grin. "You really expect me to stay outside in that storm?"

Peter stood in place completely frozen, as if he'd been magically paralyzed. Rory's heart wrenched at the fear she saw in his face.

"You will give me the chest now," The Researcher sneered. "It's *mine.*"

"I think you underestimated me." Talbert smirked. "Possession is nine-tenths of the law, and the way I see it, the chest is *mine.*"

"You have it wrong, *Human*—you underestimated *me.*" The Researcher swung his staff so fast, he was holding the chest before Rory finished blinking.

Talbert looked stunned. He'd lost his only collateral. "You'll still give me magic if I help you, right?"

The Researcher ignored him, set the chest down next to Rory, and continued his search.

Her own spell was wearing off, but only enough that she could wiggle her pinky finger.

Judge Talbert grabbed Peter, who writhed and kicked, but it had no impact.

Rory wanted to yell at Peter to bite Talbert's arm—it was in the perfect place!

Talbert completely ignored her brother's thrashing. "Looks like I have the upper hand again. You wouldn't want me to hurt your precious son, now would you? Give me magic now and I'll let him go."

The Researcher was so intently focused on inspecting her pockets for the locket, he didn't even look up. "Do what you wish to him. I have what I want."

"What? Father?" Peter whimpered.

The Researcher looked up, as if Peter were merely an irritating distraction. "Silly boy, you still believe I'm your father. I learned from my master not to make the mistake of having children."

Peter stopped writhing and looked like he was going to cry. But then realization crossed his face, and was consumed with a sneer worthy of The Researcher. "Well, I have a secret for you too."

The Researcher raised his eyebrows.

"I know you killed the Court Wizard," Peter said boldly.

A look of shock crossed The Researcher's face, before it settled. "No matter. She's not the first, and she won't be the last."

"I knew you weren't his father when you came to my door." Talbert chuckled. "Peter always was the naïve one."

Rory caught Peter looking over at her, his eyes full of a thousand apologies. And in that moment, Rory knew Peter had been tricked, brainwashed. But for what?

Rory attempted to move, and found she could now feel the air entering her lungs. She tested other parts of her body, slowly wiggling toes, rolling her shoulders, and twisting her head. She stayed still, waiting for the perfect opportunity to strike.

"I'm bringing the boy," Judge Talbert said. "He owes me."

"No, you're not, I don't need him anymore," The Researcher said. "I only need the girl. She came through the other portal. If she won't tell me where the locket is, I'll siphon her mind to find my master." The Researcher furrowed his brow. "Where's the third one?"

"The Asian one?" Talbert said.

"The what?" The Researcher looked confused, but dismissed him with a wave of his hand. He leaned over Rory, and spoke sweetly. "Now here's what's going to happen. My colleague is going to get back at your brother. A little revenge, have you. If you're smart, which I think you are, you're going to give me your locket, and I'll stop him."

Talbert's face filled with glee.

Peter shook his head, still locked in Talbert's arms. "Don't do it, Rory."

Rory's mind raced. She couldn't allow The Researcher to get her locket, but she had to get away before he could steal her memories.

Before Rory could respond, Agi came flying out of the shadows of the cave. The Researcher deflected his kick, and countered with a spell.

Agi gracefully landed, and ducked. He swung one sword with his right, then quickly threw a potion bottle with his left. The Researcher stumbled back, completely startled, dropping the chest.

Agi lunged for it, but The Researcher got to it first.

Fighting with his staff in one hand and chest in the other, The Researcher attacked Agi.

Rory took advantage of The Researcher being distracted, and lunged at Talbert.

The overbearing man turned to defend himself, loosening his grip on Peter. "Run!" she told him. Peter sprinted towards the back of the cave.

Talbert barreled into Rory, knocking her to the ground with his weight.

Rory scrambled to her feet just in time to see Talbert lumbering towards the lake . . . and after Peter.

Agi fought The Researcher valiantly, but Rory instinctively knew her friend couldn't hold up much longer. Agi was working so hard, and The Researcher looked like he was merely playing games. Sem was nowhere to be seen.

Rory sprinted down the ramp, deeper into the cave.

The sound of Agi and The Researcher's fight rose to a feverous pitch, to match the crashing thunder outside.

The Researcher pounded his staff on the ground.

Agi missed his block, and flew backwards, skidding against the dragon. He lay still.

"Agi!" Rory yelled, looking over her shoulder—should she go help Agi or Peter?

Mi'elcha struggled to break free. But she was still stuck in place by the last bond around her neck. She tried to blow fire, but only a puff of smoke came out.

A small figure crawled over the back of the dragon's tail.

Sem!

The Researcher raised his staff at Rory. "I don't want to hurt you, but you will come with me whether you want to or not."

He chanted a spell that felt powerful in her bones. It was stronger than the paralysis spell. She felt her muscles tense up, and an intense sluggishness overwhelm her body. He kept his staff trained on her, as her feet involuntarily walked her towards him. She was going to trip over Peter's backpack in the middle of the ramp.

No! Stop moving!

Then he tilted his staff slightly, forcing her to sidestep the pack.

She was almost in The Researcher's reach when Sem popped up behind him. Sem raised her potion bottle and a fine mist smelling of chocolate chip cookies surrounded The Researcher's head like a group of bees.

In one moment, The Researcher raised his hands to swat the cloud away, his eyes widened, and he dropped to the ground—face first. His spell released, and Rory could move freely again. She shook away the icky feeling of having her limbs controlled.

"That's what you get for hurting my friends," Sem said. She ran to Agi and dropped to her knees. She reached into the pouches on her belt and started applying herbs to Agi's wounds.

A flash of lightning brightened the cave in an eerie glow. Rory spun to see Talbert throw Peter into the lake. A deep splash sounded.

"Peter!" Rory yelled.

Her brother's body disappeared from view, ripples washing out to the shore.

He writhed back up, gasping for air shortly before going back under.

Rory's heart tightened.

He couldn't swim.

CHAPTER

— 34 —

RORY'S WITS

Rory raced towards the water to jump in, but Talbert blocked her path. "Not so fast. He'll get what he deserves."

Sem ran to the water's edge, hovering right at the edge.

"Sem! What are you waiting for?" Rory yelled, deflecting one of Talbert's punches.

"I can't swim!" Sem ran towards the dragon's nest—away from the lake.

Peter's extended arms pushed down on the water, fighting to stay afloat. He gasped for air.

Talbert kept punching, and she kept dodging, and striking back. But his arms were too long for her to get in close.

The dragon's nest was very close behind her now. Rory looked around for a weapon that would give her longer reach. On the ground was a huge bone, perhaps from an ox or other wild animal. Rory picked it up and swung it wildly, pushing Talbert back towards the lake.

Sem raced from the dragon's nest, dragging a massive thigh bone. She hurled it in the water. Peter grabbed at the bone for a moment, catching his breath, before it sank below the surface.

Rory quickly changed her stance and jumped to strike Talbert with the bone.

Talbert recoiled and grabbed her arm, pulling her forward.

Rory kneed him in the gut. When Talbert bent over, Rory elbowed him in the back.

This time, Rory knew she had to fight harder. He would not be letting her go this time.

Sem lay on the shore, half in the water, holding a long bone out to Peter. But he was too far away, and was focusing too much on breathing to reach out for it.

Talbert stood, towering over her.

While he was still off-balance, Rory kicked him in the kidneys. Hard.

Talbert got a constipated look, clutched his side and stumbled backwards—right into a tall stalagmite.

Sem knelt at the bags Rory and Agi had packed, throwing items to the cave floor. When she found nothing useful, she ran to where Talbert had taken Peter's bag. She threw a book, a shoebox, and food to the ground before exclaiming, "Rope!"

Ignoring Talbert, Rory raced to the lake to save Peter.

Talbert lunged at her, and she nimbly stepped out of his path.

It was time she upped her game. But how?

That's when she remembered the dagger hidden in her boot. She grabbed it and struck at Talbert. Problem was, she really had no idea how to use the blade.

Talbert shifted his bulk and aimed a punch.

Rory blocked and aimed her dagger, missing. She fought to catch her breath.

Then Talbert's eyes widened, and he stared at the ground beside her.

Rory made the mistake of looking over her shoulder—the locket had fallen to the ground when she'd pulled the dagger out of her boot!

In her distraction, Talbert landed a hard punch on her cheek. She cringed as shooting pain raced through her skull.

Talbert laughed and sprinted for the locket.

She had to stop him!

Rory threw the dagger at Talbert, but it flew past him, bouncing through a pile of bones.

Sem threw the rope into the water. It missed Peter by a few feet. She pulled the rope back and threw it again. Peter grasped for the rope, Sem pulling him towards shore. He leaned his head back, pulling in air . . . and water. Peter spit up and sunk beneath the water. At the same time, Sem's feet slipped on the wet floor. As she fell, the rope slipped from her hands, sinking into the water.

Sweat ran down Rory's face. She ran and did a flying side kick at Talbert's back. He fell to the ground.

When she went for the locket, he grabbed her ankle and pulled her to the ground.

Talbert got on top of her and held her hands above her head, leaning all his weight forward.

Not good. She hadn't learned any ground defense yet. Rage surged through her.

She had to get him off balance somehow.

Rory brought her knees up and shot her right hand out at the same time.

It worked! Talbert sprawled to the right, still clasping her wrist. In one motion, Rory arched her hip up, and twisted while throwing a left punch. Talbert was thrown off her, onto his back. Rory rolled over with him.

Before he could regain his senses, Rory punched him in the jaw—right where she knew it would knock a person out.

Talbert's eyes widened in shock, and he went still.

Rory couldn't make herself kick Talbert again to ensure he was out, even though she knew she should. Instead, she sprinted towards the water and dove in.

The shock of the water hit her like someone had thrown blocks of ice at her. She surfaced. Where was Peter?

He was submerged a few feet from her, his hands floating above him. Rory dove deep, the cold water stinging her eyes. She put her arms around him and shot to the surface, gasping for air when she did. Peter remained unmoving.

Rory dragged him to the shore where Sem was waiting with herbs in one hand and a bowl of paste in the other. Peter's dragon wand washed up to shore.

Rory thought desperately back to her Red Cross lessons she'd taken. She turned his head to the side to let the water drain out of his mouth and nose, then turned his head back.

Sem stuffed a little blue ball into his mouth.

"What are you doing? You'll choke him!" Rory exclaimed.

"It will help clear the airways," Sem said. "I never leave home without one."

Oh Peter, don't leave me now—not after I've finally found you.

Rory held Peter's clammy hand in several moments of intense silence.

Peter leaned to the side and expelled the water from his lungs. He curled up, gasping.

Relief washed over Rory. He might be white from cold, but he was alive. "Thanks, Sem—that really worked!"

Peter looked around anxiously.

Rory set a hand on his shoulder to push him down. "Don't worry about him. I knocked him out."

A giant look of relief passed Peter's face. Sem applied a blue paste that stunk of algae to Peter's chest.

"Sem—he's so cold. What can we do?" Rory asked, her mind racing. "Will his fire magic help?"

Sem shrugged. "I've never seen anyone do fire magic before."

"Peter," Rory whispered, stroking his forehead. "Why don't you try doing one of your fire spells? See if it warms you up?"

Peter blinked.

Sem picked up his wand from the shore and handed it to him.

Peter pointed it towards the lake and cast the spell. It came out a weak candle-sized flame.

Then Rory clasped Peter's hand. "You can do this."

He smiled, and seemed to light up at her touch.

He flicked his wand again and a larger flame came out, hovering over the lake.

A pinkness returned to his cheeks.

"Just do that a few more times," Rory said, filling with her own warmth. "Sem and I are going to get you out of here."

Rory surveyed the scene. Talbert and The Researcher were still knocked out. All they needed to do was undo the last of the dragon's bonds and fly out of here. Rory sighed. They were going to be okay.

She whispered to Sem, "Agi's knocked out closer to the mouth of the cave—do you have something that can wake him? He needs to finish freeing Mi'elcha."

"I can do that." Sem pressed herself against the wall, and slowly crept between the dragon and the wall. A smattering of broken vials and herb bomb pouches littered the ground. *So that's how Agi was able to last so long . . .*

The dragon looked at Sem with curiosity, then returned staring at The Researcher—who was just out of reach.

As if sensing it, The Researcher sat up. He shook his head, cleaning any lingering brain fog, then jumped to his feet. He held his staff high and started chanting in a deep and guttural language. It reminded her of the disciples chanting outside Maggie's cottage.

This could not be good.

But nothing happened—so what had he done?

That's when Rory saw it—her locket lay on the ground between her and The Researcher. *Drat!*

She tried to be sneaky and avert her eyes when she walked over to grab it, but The Researcher had seen it too.

He got there first. His face grew serious and Rory could tell he was done playing games.

The Researcher pointed his staff at her. Rory ducked, but it was right where he expected her to go. The force of the spell threw her back, as if a giant hand pushed her. She slid against the thick of the dragon's nest

She jumped to her feet right as The Researcher placed her locket in the circular keyhole. The three stars on the back of the locket met with the impression in the chest. A bright glow emanated from the open chest.

The dragon let out an awful roar and tried to blow fire again, but only expelled smoke.

Rory raised her small wand, feeling like it was a useless twig in the face of The Researcher's ornate staff that appeared useful for both magic *and* stabbing.

Rory held her wand steady. She had to fool him into thinking she could actually perform powerful magic.

The Researcher grinned and circled her. He seemed to be calculating something. "You are no match for me."

Rory stared him down, feigning courage.

The Researcher went to the right.

She blocked.

But it was a feign, and he swung his staff under her feet. She sprawled forward. She felt the blood on her chin.

He leaned over, poking the heel of his staff in her back, while chanting a sweet-sounding spell. A smooth chill spread up her body, like she was being dunked in ice water. She couldn't move.

She'd failed. The researcher had The Book of Keys *and* her locket, and there was nothing she could do about it.

"Now that was fun, wasn't it?" his disgustingly gentle voice asked.

Rory shivered, not from the storm's sharp wind, but from the spell he'd performed. The orange leaves blurred, and she felt the dripping chill of poison overcome her.

CHAPTER
— 35 —

PETER'S LAST STAND

Peter groaned from the floor of the cave. He was warmer now, but the memory of the freezing lake still chilled him to his core. He slowly pulled his eyes open.

Agi hid between the wall and the neck of the dragon, working to undo the last chain. He looked only a year older than him, but seemed so confident.

All the drawings in his books didn't do the real dragon justice—she was simply beautiful. Peter wanted to touch her scaly side, but was afraid to have his hand bitten off by such sharp teeth.

Peter sat up just in time to see The Researcher stab Rory with his staff.

No! Peter wanted to scream, but no sound came out.

He got to his feet, stumbling a little. There was no way he was going to let The Researcher hurt his sister. The Researcher wanted him to use more spells? That's exactly what he'd do.

Peter looked at Rory lying on the ground. Her skin was turning blue.

The Researcher grinned, making him look like The Joker. He placed his staff in the crook of his arm, so he could hold the chest with both hands.

"No, stop!" Fury replaced logic and Peter threw a pillar of fire at him. Sometimes it was good to be angry.

The Researcher blocked, barely looking up from the chest.

Perhaps a distraction would do the trick? Peter planted his feet in front of him. "I am leaving with my sister and your stupid chest. As long as I'm alive you will never free your master." He wasn't sure where such bravery came from, but it felt good.

The Researcher pressed his palm against Peter's sternum, and held the wooden chest out with his other hand. With The Researcher's long arms, the chest was out of Peter's swinging reach.

The Researcher flung Peter back with a with a flick of his fingers.

Peter landed by the edge of the lake, wincing.

The Researcher reached in the chest and pulled out an ornate, red leather-bound book. He held it up.

Peter's heart dropped. They had failed. How could he possibly get both the book away from him, *and* get Rory to safety? He needed a plan, but there was no time to develop one.

In the stress, Peter had forgotten all he'd studied. He had to take a breath and think. He breathed deeply, allowing the image of a flowing river to enter. A powerful calm took the place of the intense fear.

All it took was that moment, and the hundreds of pages of the books he'd memorized came rushing back in—like they were filling a hole.

But he had to be smart—his energy was waning, and he wasn't efficient enough with spells yet. He figured he might have enough energy left to get just a few more spells off.

Page 263 of *Magicology* popped into Peter's mind, and he read the spell from the bottom right corner. *"Mag'nil Hat'kafah."*

An icky green goo splattered over The Researcher's black jacket. He was so surprised at the new spell and distracted by the book, he missed deflecting it.

The Researcher flicked his wrist and sent Peter flying back, crashing into a stalagmite.

The Researcher pulled open the cover. He gingerly turned the first page. It was blank. He turned another page. That was blank too. He started turning the pages faster and faster. "What is this?"

He shoved the book in front of Rory. "What do you see?"

"A blank journal," Rory said weakly.

Something in Peter snapped. "Get away from her." He stuck out his wand and waved it at The Researcher, sending the biggest fire pillar Peter had ever created.

The Researcher blocked, barely looking up from the book.

Peter barreled into him with his shoulder. The Researcher kneed Peter and he dropped to the ground. Peter clutched his throbbing side. He was used to pain—this was no worse than what Talbert dished out.

The Researcher continued to study the book, applying various spells to no effect. He looked up suddenly and shoved The Book of Keys in Peter's face, "Here—you seem to be the more magical twin—read this to me now or I'll kill your sister."

Peter squinted, but all he saw was a blank page. But he thought a lie would be better than repeating the pages were blank. He rattled off a spell from an old magic book he'd read.

"Nice try, but I know that spell—now you tell me what you really see."

Peter looked around, trying to find a way out. The girl with the wild hair was helping Agi undo the dragon's binding. Rory was turning a deeper blue . . . and wasn't moving. He had to keep Rory safe just long enough to escape on the dragon.

"I see—I see . . . blank pages," Peter said.

Not waiting for The Researcher to respond, Peter cast a spell, *"Ma'Lignova."* Instantly, the black staff was in his hand. It was cold, and he tapped into a sliver of the staff's power. He aimed the green goo at The Researcher's face.

Unable to control the power of the staff, green goo splattered in all directions. It went on the dragon, the dangling stalactites, and out the cave. The dragon grumbled at him. Even though The Researcher blocked it, rogue slime still splotched his jacket.

In one smooth motion, The Researcher waved his gauntleted wrist, pulling the staff back to him and cast a spell that sent several stalactites falling around Peter.

Even as he danced to get out of the way, a falling stalactite hit his shoulder, forcing his wand out of his hand. It bounced a few feet away. He eased himself out of the circle of stalactites that surrounded him, trying desperately to catch his breath. He had to think of something clever if they were going to get out of this alive.

"If The Book of Keys won't work, then I'll just use her mind instead." The Researcher heaved Rory over his shoulder. "Talbert!" He called, but the man didn't stir.

How was Peter going to attack The Researcher without hurting Rory? And without his wand?

In that moment, the golden dragon stretched out. Mi'elcha was free!

She looked menacingly over The Researcher's shoulder. He looked from side to side, without moving his body. The dragon lifted Rory off The Researcher with her front claw.

The Researcher burst into a strike, clutching the chest tightly, and swinging his staff. A silver beam shot forth.

The dragon blocked with a burst of fire, but it still broke her connection to him.

The Researcher slammed his staff on the ground and an iridescent bubble appeared around him.

The dragon clawed at the bubble, to no effect. The Researcher's voice rose into the air, chanting a powerful spell.

Two Alrakis dragons appeared in the entry, diverting Mi'elcha's attention. The Researcher's spell from earlier had finally been realized.

Even worse—their way out was blocked.

The Researcher continued his chant.

What if they were nice like the golden dragon here? But that hope was short lived. They roared, and Mi'elcha stood on her hind legs, protecting them.

Frantically, Peter looked for a way out.

Agi yelled, "To the dragon!"

Peter looked to Rory, who was still clutched in Mi'elcha's claws. She was safe. For now.

He followed Sem towards the golden dragon, but Talbert blocked his path. He looked drunk from Rory knocking him out.

Peter could sense the dizziness coming on. Nausea swelled in his belly. He was going to black out again. Talbert was going to capture his sister—and it was all going to be because he was too weak to do anything about it.

Revulsion at his all-encompassing fear struck him like a blow to the gut. Why *couldn't* he be stronger than his old self? Especially now that he had people on his side?

The answer rang back clear. *Nothing.*

A new wave of bravery thrust into Peter's heart.

"Peter!" Sem yelled. "Come on!"

It gave Peter just the push he needed.

Peter dove for his wand. From the ground, he aimed at Judge Talbert. *"Mag'nil Hat'kafah."* All Peter's buried rage came out in a massive pile of green gloop. It covered the large man from head to toe, like he'd been dunked in a vat of booger-colored slime.

Talbert frantically tried to wipe the stinky goo off. But the goo stuck to his hands and didn't provide enough friction to remove it from his clothes. Talbert gagged from the stench. He tried to wipe his watering eyes, but it only served to make his eyes sting from the slime.

Peter ignored the disgusting man, and raced towards the golden dragon. Just as Peter joined Agi and Sem on the dragon's back, The Researcher's bubble exploded and a massive shockwave rolled through the cave.

Mi'elcha expelled an arching fire, protecting them from his blast. But it wasn't enough. The cave behind them crumbled.

The Alrakis dragons flew through the tumbling debris and charged at them.

"How are we going to get out?" Sem yelled.

Mi'elcha leapt into the air, with Rory in her claw and Peter, Agi, and Sem clutching onto her back for dear life. The two Alrakis dragons chased after them.

The Researcher started chanting another spell.

Peter closed his eyes. He had to make this spell count. With the last of his energy, Peter sent a fire pillar at The Researcher, followed quickly by the slime spell. The fire pillar raced forward, closely chased by the slime blob. As if by a higher magic, they combined in the air to create an exploding gas bomb. The Researcher was knocked off his feet before he could finish his lengthy spell.

The chest clattered to the ground.

Peter focused on the chest with all his might, *"Ma'Lignova!"*

The chest raced towards him, and for once he caught something. "Go! Hurry!"

The Researcher stood and repeated his spell with vicious fury.

Mi'elcha climbed higher into the air. The hole in the ceiling was so small—how were they going to fit through it?

The Researcher pounded his staff on the ground and the ceiling of the cave collapsed around them. Mi'elcha dodged the falling debris. They burst through the opening. Long chunks of stalactites fell through the Alrakis dragons' wings, leaving no way for The Researcher to fly after them.

A silver spark shot through the air and struck Mi'elcha's tail. She swerved sharply before catching her balance.

Soon they were flying high in the air, out of the range of his silver sparks, and the Alrakis' fire blasts.

"Hurry!" Sem yelled. "Rory's been poisoned."

CHAPTER
— 36 —

PETER'S NEW HOME

The dragon touched down on a neighboring hill—just long enough for them to transfer Rory to Mi'elcha's back. The storm was over and the silence left behind was eerie. No animals rustled in the bushes, no birds chirped, nor insects buzzed. Mi'elcha took off, and Peter felt the wind blow through his hair, cooling the sweat on his face.

The trees blurred past as if it were an ocean of dark green. Suddenly, Peter felt a strange feeling, like he'd felt in his old attic room. He turned to see two beautiful birds flying together beside them—one red and gold and the other blue and gold. They somersaulted in the air, looking content and joyful. Golden light spilled from their feathers, leaving a trail of golden dust behind them.

Sem pointed. "Wow!"

Agi's eyes widened at the sight of the birds.

Peter shook Rory awake to see, but she didn't move. Rory was looking worse and worse. Sem stuck a long purple root into Rory's mouth.

Removing the locket from the chest, Peter gingerly placed the chain around Rory's cold neck. *Don't leave me. Not now.* He stared over the edge of the dragon, urging her to go faster.

Before him loomed a massive volcano with a trickle of lava flowing out to sea. The bubbling orange and red channels contrasting the night sky were so beautiful—until he realized they were flying straight towards it. "Where are you going?"

Agi set his hand on Peter's shoulder. "It's the façade that protects Turopia's true location. It's a safety precaution—if you don't know where it is, you can't enter in any of the eleven working doors."

"What?" Peter said.

"The mirage of the volcano keeps inquisitive people from accidentally stumbling into Turopia. Sure, there are some curious people, but there are other enchantments the Zenmages provide that help keep us safe."

Zenmage. He thought of that little book. He sat up—all his stuff was gone! *His baby shirt*—the last item he had left of his mother's.

"What is it?" Agi asked. "We'll be safe soon."

"It's not that. I just lost all my possessions in the cave. I don't think I'll be getting them back." A twinge of guilt struck him for losing a library book—but he was a little out of the district to return it now.

Agi looked at him for a minute, then looked off towards the blanket of stars. "It *is* hard to lose things. I lost everything and everyone I loved when my village was burnt to the ground—I was only four. Captain Orlovsky was kind enough to take me in, but when you grow up on a battlefield you learn to let go of attachments to things."

"I'm sorry," Peter said.

"My point is, people are what's most important," Agi said. "And you have your sister now—that's what you wanted, right?"

Peter smiled. He hoped Agi would be a good new friend. It made his heart race to think he could even have a friend.

Sem leaned against Agi's side, looking weary. The little purple flower looked pitiful, having lost all its petals except one. Agi whispered a spell and tapped the barrette. Instantly, the flower grew anew with two layers of purple petals. Sem let out a weak smile.

Agi smiled and looked down at his charges. Rory's blue form leaned against his strong body.

"She'll be okay, right?" Peter asked.

"Turopia has some of the best healers. I'll get her there right away."

A bright twinkling star caught Peter's eye, and instead of making his normal wish, he thought, *Thank you for bringing Rory to me.*

As Mi'elcha approached the volcano's edge, his apprehension grew.

Peter looked around for a hidden door they could enter through, but couldn't find one. To his horror, the dragon dove right into the center of the volcano. His stomach flipped. It felt like what he always imagined a roller coaster would feel like. Exhilarating and scary at the same time!

The hot lava mirage reminded him of pulling dinner from the oven. He instinctively pulled his arm up to protect his face—not that it would have done much good had it been a real volcano. "How'd Mi'elcha know it wasn't real?"

"Dragons are ancient beings with mystical powers," Agi said, clutching Rory tightly. "They see through the threads of reality to distinguish the truth clearly."

Mi'elcha performed a loop and landed in the center of town beside a magnificent fountain.

In an instant, like ants coming out of their tunnels, townsfolk rushed out of their houses and shops with weapons raised.

Agi stood, gently handing off the unconscious Rory to Sem. He shouted to the people, holding his right arm across his chest and looking impressive in his Tyrskan Warrior uniform, "We are friends!" His voice rang loud and clear, so he must have used magic to enhance his voice.

Hundreds of people crowded towards the town center. Peter couldn't believe how many people had gathered—and so quickly. It was quite overwhelming. He wanted to hide, but all he could manage was to lean a little behind Agi.

Upon seeing the massive dragon, the crowd gasped and stepped back. Several townsfolk raised weapons—daggers, swords, spears. A few sped away like a bullet, but most just stared with wide, gaping mouths.

Six men dressed like Agi, but much cleaner, rushed through the crowd, led by a man in brown leather and carrying several weapons. He wore an expression mixed with fury and what appeared to be concern.

What was he going to do to them?

Agi jumped to the ground. The warrior from the crowd reached the boy first. "What happened?"

"The Researcher's back—I'll explain later," Agi said. "T. Veckler, the dragon's on our side—she helped us escape."

T. Veckler nodded in understanding, and made for the opening by the dragon while the other Tyrskan Warriors huddled around Agi.

The leather-clad warrior called T. Veckler seemed to assess the situation. He approached the dragon and whispered something to it. Mi'elcha grunted in return. Whether she understood him or not, Peter did not know.

T. Veckler turned to the crowd, raising his hand. "It is safe! This dragon is friendly. She is not under Levicus' control."

All but a few skeptical townsfolk lowered their weapons.

Once the people realized the dragon was friendly, they seemed thrilled to see a real live dragon. Mi'elcha was surprised with all the attention. Peter rubbed her scaly back in what he hoped was a comforting gesture. He didn't want her to rear back like a wild horse.

T. Veckler stepped up to the dragon's side, beside its great wing. "Come to the edge and I'll help you down."

But Peter wasn't sure he could trust him. He carried so many weapons. Peter shook his head.

Sem rested her hand on his shoulder, and Peter felt surprisingly comforted. "That's T. Veckler, your uncle. I guess you've never met him before."

Peter blinked. He had family? He watched Sem jump off and T. Veckler expertly catch her, and set her on the cobbled ground. Peter was about to jump off, when he remembered the chest. He grabbed it and threw it to T. Veckler.

He lunged to the side to catch it.

"Sorry!" Peter yelled.

It really was a long way down. What if the warrior stepped aside and let him fall? "Can't you do that magic trick Agi used?"

T. Veckler shook his head. "No magic."

Peter refused to be weak anymore. He took a deep breath and jumped off. To his surprise, he landed solidly!

T. Veckler patted him on the back. "Good job."

Peter took the chest from his uncle and held it tightly. He wanted to know what was so important about this ancient book.

But seeing the whip in the warrior's belt, he closed his eyes and turned away. He wasn't sure he was going to like his new uncle.

Peter's apprehensive thoughts were quickly interrupted by comments from the crowd. People pointed at them. He picked out a few phrases:

"Came in a dragon!"

"Look, mom, a real dragon!"

"Wow, a dragon-rider!"

Peter's fears melted away at the crowd's cheers. It made him feel so triumphant, flying in on the back of a dragon! No one had ever paid him any attention before.

A few townspeople brought forward large hunks of meat. But too afraid to get close, they handed the paper-wrapped packages to T. Veckler. He stepped forward and placed the pile before Mi'elcha's nuzzle.

The dragon roared. Peter guessed it was in thanks. She dug into the meat scraps.

Sem's parents fought their way through the crowd. Peter smiled awkwardly as they hugged their daughter tightly. "Your father says I'm not supposed to be mad at you for leaving Turopia without permission, since you were off being a little warrior. We are so proud of you. Our little girl, braving dragons."

"I knew you had it in you, my daughter." Sem's father slapped her on the back.

Sem looked sheepishly at the ground. "Actually, it was really them. I just used a few herbs to help out."

Peter recognized the disappointment instantly fall on Sem's father's face. Peter's mind raced, trying to think of something to say to put Sem in a better light. "You did more than that Sem. That potion you used on The Researcher was epic. And if you hadn't come with Rory, then I, uh, wouldn't be standing here right now. And The Researcher would surely be freeing Levicus."

"That's my girl. All humble. As a warrior should be." Mr. Selvin held his daughter tightly, a proud grin on his face.

Sem winked at Peter and stood there, grinning widely. "I can't believe we did it! We defeated The Researcher, and Rory's not even awake to share in the glory."

"Let us through!" Two women in rose-colored robes pushed through the crowd, carrying a gurney.

Agi magically lowered Rory down onto the gurney. They took off.

"Bye Sem—I have to—"

"I know," Sem said, pushing him off.

Peter sprinted out of the crowd after his sister. His eyes widened upon seeing the blue path light up beneath his feet.

Once in the healing center, Peter fought to stay in her room. When they were through giving her medicine, T. Veckler entered.

Before Peter could say a word, T. Veckler leaned over him. "Look, I need you to be careful what you say to people until we have a chance to talk later, understand?"

Peter nodded, holding the chest under his arm.

"Please give me the chest. There are spies and I worry someone will take it from you while you rest."

Peter shook his head. He'd fought so hard for this he wasn't going to let it go. Besides, how did he know where this man's allegiances lay?

Agi entered the room. "Can you step outside for a moment?"

Peter shook his head. "I'm not leaving my sister."

"It will be quick—I asked the healers to set up another bed in this room," Agi said. "You almost drowned—they need to apply a treatment to you, so you don't fall ill. Sem's medicine was only a temporary fix."

Peter's heart raced as he stepped out of the room. Agi was right—he still felt a chill in his bones and felt like he was constantly gasping for air, even though he was safe.

A healer rolled a folding bed into the room.

T. Veckler looked from Peter to Agi. "Why don't you give the chest to Agi—you trust him, right?"

Peter nodded and silently handed the chest to the older boy. His once bright blue uniform with the white accents was filthy and torn. The scrapes on his tan face hadn't been dealt with yet either.

T. Veckler put his hand on Peter's shoulder. "You've made a good decision."

CHAPTER
— 37 —

PETER AND RORY

Peter awoke the following day to find T. Veckler sitting beside his bed, deep in thought. His eyes were red and he looked exhausted. Peter almost didn't want to interrupt the man.

But he noticed Peter stirring anyway. "Good, you're up—I want to talk to you before we meet with Asdorn."

Peter was relieved to see T. Veckler wasn't wearing any weapons this time. Feeling a little safer, Peter sat up. Upon seeing Rory's bed empty, he asked, "What about Rory? Is she okay?"

T. Veckler held up a hand. "She is fine. I stayed with you both all night. She's no longer blue. I spoke with her this morning—seems you two have had quite the adventure. But I would like to hear it from you."

Peter recounted how he came to Nadezhda with The Researcher, who he'd thought was his father—T. Veckler confirmed he was indeed not his father—and how he tried to escape, but was caught, how the merchant had helped him, and their battle with The Researcher and the Alrakis dragons. Tired from all the speaking, Peter hunched over.

T. Veckler thought for a few minutes. "Seems you are leaving something out. Your sister told me about a Judge Talbert. Do you want to tell me about that?"

Peter shook his head. Definitely not.

"I see." He leaned back in his chair, thinking about something.

Peter didn't bother to interrupt him.

T. Veckler sat on the bed beside Peter, and spoke in a soft voice, "You don't know me, but I want to make an offer to you. Inara is a dangerous place, especially for you two. You have fears you would like to be rid of, no?"

Peter closed his eyes. His throat tightened. He couldn't say anything for fear of crumbling.

"If you are willing, I can help you work through them, and let go of your debilitating fears. We don't have to start now—we can begin when you are ready."

It hurt, but he said the words anyway. "I am ready."

"I'm proud of you." T. Veckler put his arm around him. Peter leaned in and his uncle completed the hug. At the sudden warmth tingled his arms and chest, he sobbed deeply. T. Veckler kept his arms around him until he was completely drained.

Peter pulled away and T. Veckler handed him a neatly folded purple handkerchief from his belt pouch. He almost didn't want to wipe his eyes with the delicate cloth, but he did anyway. "You won't tell Rory?"

"No. That will be your choice to tell her what you want."

Peter tried folding the cloth back up, but it remained a scrunched ball. He held it out.

"You keep it." T. Veckler stood. "Before we go meet Asdorn, I need to tell you the rules. Rory broke the rules to go get you—so I do hope you are better at following rules."

Peter bobbed his head in agreement. Rule breaking meant punishment.

"They are very important. Do you hear me?"

Peter listened intently as T. Veckler explained briefly how Rory had arrived, and the danger they were in. Peter had to pretend to be his nephew, and he couldn't tell anyone he came from Earth.

"You're not really my uncle?"

"No."

Peter sighed. "So who am I?"

"We can discuss that later, in a more private location." T. Veckler looked around as if there could be a spy in his small healing center room.

Peter was bummed to learn that the man wasn't *really* newfound family.

There was one thing on his mind he had to be sure of. He leaned close to T. Veckler and whispered, "So you're sure The Researcher isn't my father?"

T. Veckler nodded. "He has no children that I am aware of. He has no living family."

Even though he had been devastated by The Researcher's admission, he now felt relief. How could he have such conflicting thoughts?

"The Researcher is an awfully dangerous man, and you are lucky to have escaped," T. Veckler said. "Get dressed and meet me outside. I'll go get Rory."

Peter clutched his blankets. "Talbert can't get in here, right?"

T. Veckler seemed to pick up on the fear in Peter's eyes. "No—but how's this—you describe to me what he looks like, and I'll give his picture to all the guards. That way when we start letting refugees in again, he can't just sneak in. Would you like that?"

Peter nodded, and a sense of relief washed over him. He really was safe from Talbert. Safer than he'd ever imagined he could be.

As soon as the warrior left, Peter slipped on a pair of black slacks, a vest, and white and black jacket that went down to his knees. He looked down—he'd never worn such nice clothes in all his life. He wondered what the three black stripes on the sleeve cuffs were for.

And now he felt a lot more presentable, and ready to see Rory.

A few minutes later, Peter stepped into the hallway. T. Veckler leaned against the light pink wall, a leather bundle with a sword sticking out at his feet. Rory sat in a chair beside the doorway.

"Rory!" Peter exclaimed.

She jumped up and hugged him.

So many hugs in one day!

After the longest hug Peter had ever received, Rory stepped back and looked him over. "I can't believe I'm finally seeing you . . . when we're not in grave danger."

Peter nodded. There were so many things he wanted to ask, so many things he'd planned on saying when he finally saw her, but they all caught in his throat. "I was worried. You were in such bad shape."

"Nurses said they were surprised I healed so quickly. Must have been something Sem gave me." Rory paused, looking like she was struggling over something. She looked up at T. Veckler, "The nurses also said you stayed by my bedside all night. Thank you."

"It was the right thing to do," T. Veckler said, looking around.

Rory bit her lip and pulled something out of her jacket pocket. She was wearing the same school uniform Peter was, but with a fitted white dress instead of black pants. She looked away and held out her hand. "Here."

In her little pale hand was a wire elephant—the very one he'd made for her all those years ago. Peter picked it up and smiled. "I can't believe you still have this."

"Well, you're my little elephant, I couldn't lose it." Rory grinned and punched him lightly on the shoulder.

Peter laughed and handed it back. "I want you to keep it."

T. Veckler tapped his foot. "This is endearing and all, but we need to go."

"That's just grumpy pants over there. You'll get used to him." She smiled and hooked her arm through Peter's, leading the way out of the healing center, the elephant soundly in her pocket.

T. Veckler scowled at her, but didn't say anything.

But Peter smiled—the warrior didn't seem too bad to him. Anyone was better than Judge Talbert or The Researcher. Peter couldn't believe he'd had to go through so much just to get away from them.

As they walked from the healing center, past a lake to a small cottage atop a hill, Rory chatted on about all about her adventures getting to the sanctuary city.

Rory rang the bell and a sweet melody hung in the air. Peter looked around at the beautiful city before him. There were large buildings framing the city, a massive lake sparkling under the white sun, and rows of houses. One long street connected everything from what appeared to be the entrance below Asdorn's cottage, the shopping district, to the large government building beside where the dragon had landed.

The city was so beautiful, he couldn't understand how anyone could believe evil creatures lived here. If he'd been here before, he never would've believed The Researcher's lies.

A bald man in white and black robes wearing a brimless cap opened the door. Rory walked in first and pulled Peter with her. T. Veckler looked around before stepping inside, taking one last peak before shutting the door.

The chest lay on a coffee table in the center of three armchairs. Rory took a comfy-looking chair on the far end and patted the cushion beside her. Peter was relieved she wanted to sit with him—because he wanted to sit with her too. When he joined her, she smiled widely.

T. Veckler leaned against the wall by the door with his arms crossed, and Asdorn took the seat in the corner.

"We have much to discuss, though I am sure this is the first of many conversations," Asdorn said. "To start, I would like to hear your tales from each of you."

Rory tore into her story of how she went to meet Peter and try to stop The Researcher from using The Book of Keys—and how Agi and Sem had helped. "But I don't want them to get in trouble—it was my fault."

Peter grimaced when she recounted him running away from of Judge Talbert, and being thrown in the lake. Peter looked over to T. Veckler, and the warrior nodded as if to show support. It filled Peter with a strange sense of hope, so when it was his turn, he bravely shared his story of how he got here, leaving out the Talbert parts, of course.

Asdorn served some hot fragrant tea in tiny cast-iron cups, and red bean paste mochi balls, which apparently were his mother's favorite. The old wizard leaned back in his chair. "It's truly a shame you two were separated."

Rory stood. "You sure didn't think it through abandoning us on Earth."

"It was not part of our plan." Asdorn closed his eyes, thinking. "I feared sharing this would lay too heavy a burden on you, but now I feel it is appropriate for you to know.

"Your mother Katrine was a great warrior, a leader in the resistance against Levicus. It became so dangerous, Katrine hid out on Earth while she was pregnant with you. At the same time, she was working with us Zenmages to develop the trap to ensnare Levicus in the portal we'd devised."

"That fateful night when we were luring Levicus to his trap—your mother was the bait—your father Darius was supposed to stay with you and bring you back a few days later when it was safe. But things didn't go as planned, and The Researcher attacked with several disciples from the true location of the portal on the continent of Baikal."

Darius. His real father.

"Darius was captured by Levicus' disciples and brought back to Inara during the middle of our ruse—and you were left with your nursemaid, who we now know had died during the attack."

Rory crossed her arms. "I still can't believe you didn't try other methods to find us."

T. Veckler spoke this time. "You know we had no way of getting through the portal back to Earth without freeing Levicus. And the first back-up plan was the nursemaid who was *supposed* to return you when you were older, and things had settled on Inara."

Asdorn held up his hand. "We continued to search for other portals to get to Earth, and thanks to you, Peter, we now know The Researcher has a hidden portal of his own. He must be using magic to hide it, and that's why our spells were never able to uncover the portal on this continent."

"What about the other continents?" Rory asked. "Levicus is trapped in the one on Baikal, The Researcher has one here on Tilla, and that leaves . . ."

"We've had no luck on the other three continents," Asdorn said. "However, upon my direction, we had set-up several back-up plans in case something went wrong—such as the magical pipe organ that performed the complex spell to open the portal when you touched it."

Peter would have liked to see that. If only he had gone through with his original plan, they wouldn't be in this mess.

A little white ferret nuzzled Rory's ankles and she picked him up. It took one look at Peter then curled up in Rory's arms.

Asdorn tapped the side of his tea cup. "It is curious that your Zamsara birds came to fetch you at this time—both seemingly so The Researcher could get his hands on you, and so you could stop him at the perfect moment."

Zamsara bird. So that was what that blue and gold bird was?

By the knowing smile on Rory's face, it seemed she'd seen the magical bird too.

"Yes, you two did well." Asdorn chuckled. "The Researcher will have to find another way to find where his master is hidden. And I promise you he will keep trying. He is desperate to free him."

"After hearing your stories of the battle yesterday, you have given me an idea." Asdorn stood and picked up the chest. "This book appears to be the reason your Zamsara birds felt it was time for you to come home, so humor me and let me test something. Rory please hand me your locket."

Rory looked leery, but handed her pendant to Asdorn. He stuck the locket in the chest and pulled out the thick leather-bound book with iron clasps.

He set the book on the table before the twins. "Rory, could you please open and tell me what you see?"

Rory flipped over the cover and turned a few pages, then shut it. "All blank. Just like what The Researcher saw. I don't know what you expect."

"Patience . . ." Asdorn held out his hand. "And you Peter?"

Peter ran his hand over the circular indentation in the red leather cover. The book was really quite beautiful. Intricate carvings were engraved all across the cover, including a tree that stemmed from the spine and branched across the front and back of the cover. Various planets were interspersed between the branches. He gently re-opened the heavy cover, and turned to the first page. "Also blank."

Asdorn grinned.

"What, you're happy about this?" Rory said indignantly.

"No. Just what I expected. Please humor an old man and open the book together."

Rory looked at Asdorn like he was strange, then touched the top of the book cover. Peter grabbed the bottom corner and they opened the book together.

The first page was blank.

"See, still nothing." Rory turned a few more pages as if to prove something to the bald wizard.

Suddenly, lines of letters in a language Peter didn't recognize raced across the page. It wasn't even like the language of magic from *Magicology*.

"Whoa!" Rory turned to a page with a picture of five animals: A crow, a white tiger, a salamander, a fox, and a water dragon, all around a magnificent oak tree. "Beautiful."

Peter agreed. He'd never seen anything so gorgeous in all his life.

Rory turned a few more pages, while Peter would've been happy just to stare at this one. He didn't understand it, but it felt like some kind of summoning spell.

Asdorn laughed, a light, happy release.

"What?" Rory asked.

"I see you two are our newest Keepers," Asdorn said.

"What's that?" Rory asked.

"The Keepers are the family that has guarded ancient secrets of power for thousands of generations. And that is a long story for another time," Asdorn said. "I see you two will have a lot to learn. But this will be a long journey, not a sprint. Your mother would be so proud of you."

Peter smiled at the thought of his mother. He was sad that no one knew where she was, except The Researcher, and there was no way he was going back to ask him. But maybe now that he was here, on the right planet, he could be the one to find his real parents—with the help of his sister.

He was finally home, safe and in a place there was no way Judge Talbert could reach him. He was free.

Rory leaned back in the chair, obviously tired of the book. Peter couldn't get enough of it, but felt warm and safe beside his sister. Rory held his arm tightly, as if she let go, he'd slip away again.

But he had no intention of leaving her ever again.

Ever.

GET A FREE SHORT STORY

One of the joys of being a writer is building relationships with readers. I occasionally send newsletters with details on new releases, special offers, and other bits of news relating to the *Twins of Orion* series.

If you register for my mailing list, I'll send you an exclusive free short story set in the *Twins of Orion* world.

Go to www.JRoseBooks.com to sign up.

ENJOY THIS BOOK? YOU CAN MAKE A BIG DIFFERENCE

Reviews are the most powerful tool in my arsenal when it comes to getting attention for my books. Luckily, the loyal *Twins of Orion* fans are something even the big publishers can't buy.

Honest reviews of my books help bring them to the attention of other readers.

If you've enjoyed this book, I would be very grateful if you could spend a few minutes leaving a review (even a short one) on the book's Amazon page.

Thank you very much!

ACKNOWLEDGEMENTS

It begins with an idea, a spark of the imagination.

It meanders along through numerous forms, touched by the hands of many remarkable people.

It ends with the book you have in your hands.

Thank you is such an often-used word, sometimes I think the deep meaning is lost when we genuinely need it. So what I want to say to all those who have ever supported me, I appreciate you. What you do and who you are is meaningful to me.

My deepest thanks in all the languages in the world goes to my friend, Lynn Nagel. You were with me on the twins' story from the very beginning. You read the first draft, and stayed with it—offering your brainstorming wisdom through all the incarnations this book has gone through. Simply put—this book would not be what it is today without you.

A warm hug of thanks goes to all those who helped brainstorm, beta-read, fact-check, and proof this book (including, but surely not limited to): Julie Bir, my sister, Joe Massman, Jason Evans, Jeff Seymour, Angie Penland, Laurie Will, Julie Cameron, Josh Vogt, Gary Smith, Eric Mayes, Justinn Harrison, Stephanie Padilla, Michal, Kai, Lena, my mom, Corey Taylor, Michael Beverly, and Amanda Barrentine. And a special shout out to Aaron Michael Ritchey, who advised me to split this story into two books.

It is always said, but that's because it's true: Publishing a book is a team effort, and I thank everyone who has given me advice on my writing and publishing journey. I bow to you and I give you my thanks.

Trai Cartwright, my incredible editor who helped me develop the story.

Ellie Ann, my extraordinarily talented line editor who helped transform the story and bring out its hidden magic.

If you love the cover as much as I do, you will want to thank Christine Knopp, who created the beautiful illustration in your hands. And a big thanks to the talented Steven Novak, of Novak Illustration, who transformed the art into a magnificent cover. And Mia Kleve for the internal formatting.

Thank you to the critique groups I belong to. It's a gift to be a part of such a supportive writing community in the Rocky Mountain region – that includes RMFW and PPW.

A special thanks to my friends who put up with me while I locked myself in my cave, working to bring these books to life, and remained my friends when I emerged.

I've been lucky to have great teachers in my life, including William Taylor, and my beautiful voice teacher, Dr. MeeAe Nam, who taught me the value of paying attention to the little details until you get it right. I get it now.

And a deep thanks to my Rocky Mountain Tae Kwon Do family, who helped me grow as a person, and a martial artist. Rory is a better fighter because of you. Thank you especially Caer—I hope you can read this in heaven.

And to my readers—my biggest thanks. I hope you have enjoyed the first installment of the twins' story, which will be continued in Book 2: *The Shadow Titans*. May all the wishes dearest to your heart come true.

About the Author

J. Rose writes with the Rocky Mountains outside her window and her ferrets at her feet. In her other life, she's a trained opera singer. She holds a black belt in Tae Kwon Do, and studies other martial art styles for research, including Jujitsu.

When she's not having fun on the twins' story, she can be found hiking, biking, or spending time with friends. Since finishing her first 'novel' at the age of 15, she continues to have a passion for telling stories that make a difference.

You can connect with J. Rose on Twitter and Instagram at @JRoseBooks, at facebook.com/JRoseBooks, or visit her at: JRoseBooks.com

Reading Guide

For Teachers and Librarians:
Please visit JRoseBooks.com for free discussion questions and a special reading guide on the various sensitive topics covered in this book.